A CENTURY
OF STORIES
NEW HANOVER COUNTY PUBLIC LIBRARY
1906-2006

MURDER
AT THE
OPERA

MURDER AT THE OPERA

A CAPITAL CRIMES NOVEL

Margaret Truman

Ballantine Books • New York

Copyright © 2006 by Margaret Truman

Published in the United States by Ballantine Books, an imprint of The Random House Publishing Group, a division of Random House, Inc., New York.

BALLANTINE and colophon are registered trademarks of Random House, Inc.

ISBN-10: 0-345-47821-5
ISBN-13: 978-0-345-47821-4

Printed in the United States of America on acid-free paper

www.ballantinebooks.com

9 8 7 6 5 4 3 2 1

First Edition

To Sam Vaughan, who set the editorial bar high,
and who has always been there to boost me over it.

You are, Sam, simply the best editor a writer
could ever hope for.

ACKNOWLEDGMENTS

As an honorary trustee of the Washington National Opera, I look with great pride upon the wonderful men and women who have guided it into the top tier of American opera companies. It's only fitting that Washington should join other world capitals as being home to an outstanding opera company.

I thank Maestro Plácido Domingo, Washington National Opera's general director, for allowing me to set this, my twenty-second book in the Capital Crime series, against the soaring splendor of his productions at the Kennedy Center. His remarkable talent and extraordinary artistic vision have inspired the men and women of the Washington National Opera to new heights, and the nation and its opera lovers are better for it. Bravo, Maestro!

And a special thanks to Jennifer Johnston, a delightful guide to the Washington National Opera, who opened up myriad doors, behind which few are privileged to see; to Bill Wooby, whose knowledge of the Washington arts scene has enriched more than one of my Capital Crime novels; to author and opera aficionado Charles Flowers; to my agent, Ted Chichak, whose knowledge and love of opera is extraordinary; and to opera critic John Shulson, for whom opera is no mystery.

AUTHOR'S NOTE

Fifty years ago Day Thorpe, music critic of the now defunct *Washington Star*, decided along with a few like-minded souls that Washington, D.C., needed an opera company, and founded the Opera Society of Washington, later changed to the simpler Washington Opera, and in 2000 renamed the Washington National Opera by an act of Congress. This Congressional name change was not inconsequential. Not only did America now have its own official opera company, all fifty states had a stake in it, giving those who raise necessary funds for the company a broader potential source of financial support.

The Washington National Opera (WNO) has evolved and grown over the past five decades from a regional company into one of international acclaim. Its productions rival those of the leading opera companies of America—New York, Los Angeles, Chicago, Minneapolis, San Francisco—and the world.

In the beginning, performances were staged in small, cramped, borrowed theaters. But since 1971 it has staged its performances in the magnificent 2,300-seat Kennedy Center Opera House, and has been the resident opera company of the Kennedy Center ever since.

So, in reality, this book is about the Washington National Opera specifically, rather than the world of opera in general.

My decision to have people murdered at the Washington National Opera does not reflect actual events there. Of course, many great operas that have graced the stage of the Kennedy Center Opera House present murder in its most dramatic form, death throes onstage as long and lingering as the musical score calls for. But any relationship between the murdered and the murderers in this book, and those real people who make the Washington National Opera the actual, splendid institution that it is, is happily, purely coincidental.

Finally, my hat is off to those at the Washington National Opera who made the courageous decision to ignore the protests of curmudgeonly purists, and to use English supertitles to translate operas at the Kennedy Center. English supertitles, or surtitles, came into popular use in the early 1980s and have been instrumental in widening the audience for opera. They've also tempered the temptation to present foreign operas in English, as grievous a sin as belatedly coloring classic black-and-white motion pictures. As H. L. Mencken once said, "Opera in English is, in the main, just about as sensible as baseball in Italian."

Or, as Sir Edward Appleton wrote in *The Observer* in 1955, "I do not mind what language opera is sung in so long as it is a language I don't understand."

Margaret Truman
New York
2006

PROLOGUE

She died quickly and with a modicum of suffering.

This came as no surprise. Unlike so-called crimes of passion which are invariably messy, drawn out, and painful, I'd planned her death.

She had to be eliminated because she knew something that I preferred she not know, which raised the possibility that she would pass it along to others. I couldn't allow that.

Had knowing the victim made it easier or more difficult for me? Of course, having known her cast me as a suspect, along with dozens of others. Murderers who are strangers to their victims invariably stand a better chance of getting away with it. There was a brief temptation to enlist the aid of another person, someone outside our circle of acquaintances, but I quickly ruled that out. The fewer people who know about a murder, the better.

That the murder took place onstage at the Kennedy Center Opera House would lead one to believe that I have a flair for the dramatic. But that was not the reason the area was chosen as the place to ensure her silence. I'd considered a number of settings—her apartment, on the street, or in a secluded room in the Opera company's rehearsal space at Takoma Park. She provided the answer by insisting that we meet on the stage that night, actually in the early morning hours, long after everyone was gone for the evening except perhaps for a couple of Kennedy Center security guards, who wouldn't come into the theater unless given reason to, which I certainly didn't intend to provide.

It should also be pointed out that my choice of a weapon had nothing—absolutely nothing—to do with the fact that the encounter took place on the Opera House's main stage, where the Washington National Opera would soon present the latest production of Puccini's warhorse, *Tosca*. Moments before dealing the fatal blow, I thought of the justified murder of the cruel, lecherous Scarpia in *Tosca's* Act II. The major difference was that this slaying was committed in shadows and without onlookers, while *Tosca's* stabbing of the cruel chief of the secret police would take place before thousands bearing witness to her defensible action. Of course, *Tosca's* dramatic killing of Scarpia is make-believe. This one was very real; I did not break into the aria *"Vissi D'arte"* before completing the act, as Madame Tosca has done thousand of nights on grand stages around the globe.

The victim was eventually found, of course, although it took almost a full day. I'd placed the body in such a location where few would have reason to go under ordinary circumstances. When her body was discovered, there was a flurry of media and law enforcement activity, and much was made of the fact that the homicide took place inside the revered Kennedy Center, and in that institution's Opera House, where betrayal, passion, intrigue, and murder take place on a regular basis—but only during performances on the main stage. The press had a field day with opera analogies, the weapon used, the setting, and the connection of the deceased with the Washington National Opera.

In the meantime, *Tosca*, and the larger comic opera that is Washington, D.C., itself, but that too often turns deadly—must, and did—go on.

And so must I.

MURDER
AT THE
OPERA

ONE

"**M**ac, you must do it."

"No."

"It's an honor, for you and for the school."

"I don't see anything honorable about middle-aged men dressed in loincloths strutting around carrying spears. I thought we'd progressed beyond that."

Annabel knew her husband wouldn't be an easy sell. But his flippant comment meant she was making progress. There would be an obligatory protest before caving in.

"I'm not an actor," he added.

They'd finished breakfast and had taken refilled mugs of coffee out onto the balcony of their Watergate apartment. It was a warm, muggy morning in early June, a harbinger of another sweltering summer in D.C. The sky was a milky blue. Below, the rippling waters of a cleaner Potomac River danced in the sunlight. Farther up the river, the familiar spires of Georgetown University rose proudly into the air.

"Of course you're an actor," Annabel said. "You can't be a high-powered trial lawyer without being an actor. I saw you in action when you were trying cases. You were Olivier in a gray three-piece suit."

"That was then," he said. "Today I am just a stodgy professor, and happy to be."

She considered her next argument. She'd practiced her own share of theatrics while representing clients in high-profile domestic disputes. That was *then*, too. She'd given up matrimonial law to open a pre-Colombian art gallery in Georgetown, which was doing nicely. Giving up their respective law practices had been a decision they'd come to at different times, and for different reasons.

For Annabel, attempting to mediate wrenching battles between warring spouses had become almost unbearable, especially when both sides were engaged in self-destructive behavior, domestic suicide bombers intent on injuring each other.

For him, the death of his first wife and only child at the hands of a drunken driver on the Beltway one rainy night had tipped the scales in favor of his escaping what had become one of Washington's preeminent criminal law firms, abandoning it to his three partners, and becoming Mackensie Smith, professor of law at the prestigious George Washington University.

Neither Mac nor Annabel had regretted their decisions, not even fleetingly.

"Mac," she said softly, touching his arm, "using prominent people as supernumeraries in productions has gotten the opera lots of good press, which translates into ticket sales. You'll be in good company. Last year, two spear-toting Supreme Court justices wore costumes in a production. You read about them in the *Post*. And the Secretary of State and his wife did, too, the season before. This time it's professors from the area's universities. Besides, it's *Tosca*, Mac. Puccini. You'll love it."

"You know I'm not an opera fan," he said.

"But you'll become one. I guarantee it. *Tosca* is the perfect intro for you. It has all the elements of great drama—sex, betrayal, corruption, and murder—and gorgeous music." She checked his expression. She almost had him. Time to go in for the kill. "Besides," she said,

"I've already committed you." Before he could respond, she added, "It's important to me, Mac. I'm new on the board and want to make what contributions I can as quickly as possible."

He grinned. "And your first contribution is to sacrifice me?"

"You'll do it?"

"Sure. Anything for a good cause."

"The National Opera *is* a good cause," she said.

"I was thinking of you, Annie. You're the best cause I know."

He got up from the table, kissed her on the cheek, and headed inside, saying over his shoulder, "I'm running late for a faculty meeting. Busy day."

"Leave time for your fitting," she said, following him.

He stopped, turned, and said, "Costume fitting? My loincloth?"

"Yes. And stop saying it's a loincloth. It's not."

"When?"

"This afternoon. I told Harriet you'd be free after four."

"Where?"

"Takoma Park, the company's rehearsal facility. All the costumes are done there. Oh, and there's a meeting of supers tonight at the Kennedy Center. Seven o'clock. I'll go with you."

He embraced her, kissed her again, this time meaningfully, picked up his briefcase, and stepped into the hall. She stood in the open doorway admiring his purposeful stride in the direction of the elevators. He was halfway there when he suddenly stopped, turned, pointed a finger at her, and said, "You owe me one, Annie."

"Oh? When?"

"I'll collect tonight. And it will be more than just a rehearsal."

She giggled, and said just loud enough for him to hear but not the neighbors, "I love it when you talk dirty."

TWO

ac Smith sometimes thought that if he were president of the university, he would ban all faculty meetings. Occasionally, a meeting went smoothly, accomplished something, and consumed a minimal amount of time, but that was the twice-a-year exception rather than the rule. It all depended, of course, on who chaired the meeting. This day it was the new dean of the law school, a nice enough fellow with impressive credentials—and a tendency to posture. Had there been a fireplace in the room, Mac was certain that the dean would lean an elbow on the mantel and smoke a pipe, allowing for photographs, had smoking been allowed.

The meeting lasted forty-five minutes, thirty-one minutes longer than was necessary to cover the agenda. Mac was first out the door, closely followed by John Renwick, a teaching colleague who shared Mac's abhorrence of wasted time. Renwick came into Mac's office, tossed his briefcase on a small couch, and said, "Did anything useful come out of this, or did I miss something?"

Mac laughed as he opened the drapes that covered his only window and raised the blinds. "Scuzzy day out there," he said. He turned to face Renwick. "We just learned from our new leader," he said, "that someone on Capitol Hill, obviously of the right-wing variety, is considering convening a committee to investigate whether young attorneys being turned out by esteemed institutions like ours need a better grounding in old-fashioned legal principles; translation, more conservative ones. Our leader wants to be on the record as having heeded the call and explored with his faculty this alleged problem—which, of course, isn't a problem. What's new with you?"

"Not a lot. Lois wonders whether you and Annabel are free tonight for dinner, a last-minute thing. A college buddy of mine and his wife blew into town, also last-minute. Haven't seen him in years. You'd enjoy him. He's—"

"No can do," Mac said, "but thanks anyway. Prior engagement. I'm being fitted for a loincloth."

"What?"

"Annabel has ensnared me in this opera project cooked up by Public Affairs. I'm going to be an extra in *Tosca*."

"I think that's wonderful," said Renwick, mirth in his voice. "You do have good legs."

"I suggest you leave it right there, my friend."

"I envy you," Renwick said. "I love opera. You'll be in heady company, Mac. Our leader is donning a loincloth, too, isn't he?"

"So I hear."

"Well," said Renwick, retrieving his briefcase, "good luck. By the way, you won't be an 'extra' in the cast. Extras in opera are called 'supers'—supernumeraries—*supernumerárius* in Latin."

"I know, but I prefer plain old 'extra,' for the same reason I refuse to play that pretentious game at Starbucks of calling a medium-size coffee a *grande*. I always ask for a *medium* coffee when I go there, which isn't often. I make better coffee than they do and it doesn't cost me the month's mortgage."

"We have to make our stands where we find them," Renwick said, laughing and shaking his head. "I was a spear carrier in an opera while working my way through college. *Aida*. Loved it. Sorry you can't make dinner. Another time. Give my best to Annabel." He left the office, closing the door behind him.

Mac spent the next few hours fine-tuning a lecture on habeas corpus he would deliver that afternoon, taking a break from time to time to think about less solemn subjects, namely Annabel, dear sweet Annabel, who'd entered his life a year after having lost his wife and son and giving him a reason to live again. That she was a beautiful woman was beyond debate, hair the color of Titian copper, fair unblemished skin, and a figure that was at once sleek and voluptuous. He needed only to look at her in dark moments to feel his emotional tide rise. Wrapped in that package was a vigorous, surprisingly poetic mind (for a lawyer) that was seldom swayed by trivial or self-serving manipulations. That she'd readily agreed to make him her first and only husband awed him at times. Sometimes you do, indeed, get lucky.

Although they'd structured their married life to maximize time alone together, they were wise enough to know that too much togetherness could prove to be detrimental, and so they pursued the things they loved aside from each other, she her gallery and participation in a few selected arts institutions, he his tennis matches despite an increasingly bothersome knee, consulting commitments to an occasional government agency, and a twice-a-month poker game.

☙

The Washington National Opera was Annabel's latest involvement. A couple with whom they were friendly—husband and wife both ardent opera lovers—had tried to entice Mac and Annabel into buying season tickets at the Kennedy Center. As much as Annabel would have enjoyed having her husband escort her to the productions, she knew she would be unsuccessful, and contented herself with buying a single season ticket and accompanying their friends. She hadn't been steeped in opera up until that point, and wasn't sure she would find it as enjoyable as they did. But after that first season of five lavishly staged and magnificently performed productions, she was hooked, and not only couldn't wait for the next season to arrive, she became active with WNO itself, contributing a substantial sum of money and becoming a member of the Medici Society, one of many organizations devoted to sustaining and enhancing the company's financial and artistic goals. After two years of fund-raising and softly suggesting artistic visions and practical ideas to the company, she was surprised and flattered to be offered a seat on WNO's board, which she readily accepted. At the moment, she was immersed in plans for the annual Opera Ball, one of Washington's premiere formal fundraising events.

Mac was pleased with his wife's commitment and offered his steady encouragement. Of course, Annabel continued to try to cajole him into becoming involved, too, but he remained steadfast: "You don't play poker with me," he said, "and I don't go to the opera with you." And thus it remained, although the number of CDs grew rapidly, and the apartment was frequently awash with classic recordings, which Mac found increasingly enjoyable, particularly the works of Mozart, Puccini, and Richard Strauss.

"You love the recorded music," Annabel would say after he'd commented favorably on a new recording she'd brought into their home. "Why not enjoy it in person?"

"Maybe next year," he would say.

And she would say, "You said that last year."

❦

This was this year, and he would finally be going to the opera, not in black tie but in a costume of sorts, and makeup, onstage, for the world to see, including his students, fellow faculty members, and close friends. The thought made him wince and sent him back to the more pleasant and not quite unrelated topic of habeas corpus.

THREE

As eighteen GW law students listened to Professor Smith explore the subtleties of unlawful restraint and the use of writs of habeas corpus to prevent it, a class of a different sort of confinement was in session at the rehearsal facilities of the Washington National Opera Studio in Takoma Park, a funky suburban village straddling the upper northwest boundaries of D.C., and Prince George's and Montgomery counties.

❧

WNO had leased the former industrial building in the late 90s, renovated it, and opened its doors in 2000. With three separate rehearsal rooms, each the size of the Kennedy Center's main stage, multiple productions could be in rehearsal simultaneously, a distinct advantage. The building also housed the company's vast costume design, manufacture and storage areas, wig collection, and the offices of the Washington National Opera Center for Education and Training. This was the home of the world-renowned Domingo-Cafritz Young Artist

Program that brought many of the most promising singers, pianists, and directors from around the globe to Washington for intensive one-on-one training. On this afternoon, fourteen talented young men and women were immersed in a two-hour Italian lesson. The majority were American; since 9/11, obtaining visas for future opera stars from overseas had become torturous, causing the program's administrators to concentrate on homegrown talent. But this crop did include a South Korean, two Canadians, and a Spanish baritone.

The instructor surveyed the class over half-glasses. "We're missing someone," he said. "Where is Ms. Lee?"

Shrugs all around.

Charise Lee, a promising soprano from Toronto, was not in her usual seat.

"Is she ill?" asked the instructor.

"I haven't seen her all day," another student replied, echoed by others.

The instructor wrote Lee's name on a slip of paper, which he would turn in to the office following class. Unexcused absences were not taken lightly, although they happened with considerable frequency, particularly with the singers in the group.

"She told me yesterday that she was getting a cold," a stage director offered.

The instructor smiled. Opera singers were always on the verge of getting colds, or so it seemed to them. "*The* voice," they would say, referring to themselves, never "*my* voice," as though it was an entity outside themselves. Someone should write an aria about hypochondria, he mused as he began the lesson, focusing on Italian words that were easy to sing, whose consonants didn't pop, and whose vowels could be crooned.

In another part of the building, the company's wardrobe director, Harriet McKay, who'd been with the company for fifteen years, was busy scheduling fittings for the cast, chorus, and supers who were to appear in *Tosca*. The soprano playing Tosca in the production was scheduled to fly in to Washington from Argentina the following day, her arrival preceded by a reputation for being late and especially demanding about what she was to wear onstage. And, Harriet knew, for good reason. Tosca's costumes were heavy and confining, and seemed to gain weight, and heat, as the production proceeded. Ill-fitting gowns would only add to the soprano's discomfort, which could manifest itself in a less than sterling performance. Besides, the perfect costume would help ensure her immersion into the role of Tosca. She had a right to be exacting, and Harriet McKay never resented being on the receiving end of what might seem to outsiders nothing more than the unreasonable whims of a persnickety diva.

Harriet and two of the costume department's thirty volunteers sat at a desk in a corner of the wig room and went over the day's schedule. Mackensie Smith and the president of George Washington University were slated to be fitted at four. An hour later, Christopher Warren—a pianist from Toronto—and the soprano Charise Lee, students from the Domingo-Cafritz Young Artist Program, were penciled in for fittings. They'd been pressed into service as supers for Tosca's opening night due to a scheduling conflict with two of the regular supers that evening. Because the ranks of supernumeraries included men and women from all walks of life, many of them in demanding professions, such conflicts of timing were not uncommon, much to the chagrin of the woman in charge of finding—and keeping—the right bodies for each production's run. The director of this production, Anthony Zambrano, was particularly concerned that Harriet provide all female supers with flat shoes consistent with the era, recounting for her the horror of a production he'd once seen of Tosca in which one of the female supers wore spiked heels and took a tumble down a set of stairs, disrupting the entire performance.

"They're only appearing one night," Harriet told the volunteers, referring to Warren and Charise. "We'll need two extra costumes."

"What we put on them won't do for the regulars when they perform?" a volunteer asked.

"Afraid not," Harriet said. "Better get with it. We'll need the extra costumes by tomorrow morning."

"What's new with Andrea Chénier?" a volunteer asked. The Umberto Giordano opera was next on that season's schedule.

"We're renting the costumes from the San Francisco production," Harriet replied. "They should be here in a day or two." She checked her watch and stood. "I'm late for a meeting with Anthony. He's unhappy with the designer's costume for Cavaradossi, keeps changing his mind, one day he likes it, the next he doesn't. Maybe we'll finally get a definitive decision from him. *Ciao*. Bless you both. This place would fall apart without you."

Mac Smith fielded questions during the last thirty minutes of his class. Most of them were intelligent and on-point, a few weren't, especially the final one: "Are you really going to be in the opera at the Kennedy Center, Professor Smith?"

"Where did you hear that?" Smith countered.

"People are talking about it. You and President Burns."

"Well," Smith said, "what you hear is correct. Yes, President Burns and I, along with professors from American University and Georgetown, will be supernumeraries in *Tosca*. That's *supernumerárius* in Latin, but of course you already know that, being the scholars that you are. I suggest you buy tickets and expand your cultural universe beyond video games and MTV. That's it for today."

He packed his briefcase and left the lecture hall, a satisfied smile on his face. The lesson had gone nicely, although his mind had wandered at times to what was in store for him. While he'd expressed obligatory dismay at agreeing to appear in *Tosca*, he was surprised that there were moments, interspersed with dread, in which he found himself, at once, and privately, looking forward to the experience.

He'd appeared in two plays while an undergraduate, *The Man Who Came to Dinner* and *A Streetcar Named Desire*, both directed by a favorite professor, Joseph Stockdale. Mac had never harbored any desire to become an actor. His aspiration since high school had been the law, particularly trial advocacy, fueled by countless courtroom dramas he'd watched in movie theaters and on television. Stockdale had known this when he cast Mac in the plays, and made the point with the young student that acting experience would hold him in good stead when having to capture and sway a jury. The director had been right, and Mac often thought back to those experiences onstage when crafting a summation to twelve men and women.

Besides, he reminded himself, it was all for a worthwhile cause, three, actually. It was good for the university, good for the Washington National Opera, and good for his relationship with Annabel. He packed up materials to read at home that night; wished the secretary he shared with John Renwick a pleasant evening; retrieved his car, a seven-year-old blue Ford in pristine condition, from his reserved parking slot; and took 16th Street straight up until turning off onto local roads leading to the WNO facility at Takoma Park. He was early, and after finding street parking he killed time strolling the neighborhood. He and Annabel had enjoyed leisurely weekend forays to the village for its Saturday organic farmer's market, considered the best in the D.C. area. Takoma Park was sometimes called "the Azalea City," or "the People's Republic of Takoma Park" by conservatives unhappy with its well-known leftist political culture. In the 1980s it, along with Berkeley, California, and Madison, Wisconsin, had declared itself a nuclear-free zone, bestowed legal status on nonmarital partnerships, and continued to attempt to ban gas-powered lawn mowers. Takoma Park had long provided an eclectic alternative to dark-suit D.C. to its south, and the Opera was a natural and welcome addition.

The receptionist signed him in and paged Harriet McKay, who appeared almost instantaneously, welcomed him, and led Mac back through a maze of corridors and doors.

"Quite a well-dressed setup you have here," Mac said, taking in room after room of costumes, wigs, props, and passing through one of the three rehearsal areas, where a young blond woman practiced a score on an ebony grand piano.

"It's a wonderful facility and we're fortunate to have it," McKay said pleasantly. "We're also delighted that you and President Burns have agreed to take part."

"Is he here yet?"

"His office called. He's running late. We'll get you fitted first and on your way. It's always a problem with the supers."

They entered a relatively small room with two mirrored walls. An attractive young woman and a middle-aged man sitting in yellow director's chairs stood at their entrance. Harriet introduced them as two of her fitters. She pointed to one of four doors. "You can use that room over there to get undressed."

"Just my jacket and tie?" he asked.

"You'll need to take off more than that," she said. "You can leave on your shorts and socks. We'll be fitting you for sandals, too. There's a robe in there if you'll be more comfortable."

Mac returned wearing the robe.

McKay consulted notes on a clipboard. "You'll be appearing in the first and third acts, a monk in Act I, a member of the firing squad in Act III, two different costumes. We'll start with, nicely enough, Act I."

The male fitter draped a heavy burlap robe over Mac's shoulders and pinned it to better conform to his body. A pair of sandals with thin straps that wrapped around his calves up to his knees was next. "Comfortable?" the fitter asked.

Smith said, "No. I can still feel my feet."

That outfit removed and labeled with Smith's name and the act number, the female fitter brought out the costume for Act III, decidedly more elaborate than the monk's burlap and sandals. Mac stood patiently as both male and female fitters fussed with breeches, leggings, a heavy jacket, clodhopper black shoes, and a bandoleer that crisscrossed his chest. There was much marking with a tailor's chalk and pinning until the costumers were satisfied. The final item to be fitted was a red-and-gold cocked hat.

"You look splendid," Harriet said.

Mac turned to examine himself in the large mirror. "That's me?" he asked playfully.

"You'll make a wonderful member of the firing squad," Harriet said.

"I know a few people I wouldn't mind having stand in front of a firing squad," he said. "Thanks. This was less painful than I anticipated."

As he said it, the president of the university, Wilfred Burns, was escorted into the room. "My, my," he said, taking in Mac in his costume. "I'm seeing a while new side of you, Smith. Several, in fact."

"Don't get used to it," Mac said. "But I do kind of like it." He indicated his full-length image in one of the mirrors. "I might wear this to my classes, shake my students out of their lethargy."

"Whatever works," Burns said. "I must say that you're a trouper, Mac."

"And the same might be said for you," Smith replied. "Your turn to be stuck with pins."

Smith dressed quickly and was ready to leave before his boss emerged. Accompanied by Harriet McKay, he returned to the reception area, thanked her for her courtesies, and went to his car, where he used his cell phone.

"How did it go?" Annabel asked, a hint of suppressed mirth in her voice.

"Fine. Like being in a hospital. Strip to your shorts and put on a robe. At least it didn't open in the back like hospital gowns. I'm fitted, Annie. I'm ready for my close-up."

"Good. I'll meet you at the 600 at six. We'll grab something to eat there before your meeting at the Kennedy Center."

"Okay. By the way, I was fitted by a very attractive young woman. I think she was impressed with my physique."

"Uh-huh. Six at the 600—hunk!"

Smith went home before meeting up with Annabel, to feed and walk Rufus, their blue Great Dane. As he prepared to leave for the restaurant, directly across from the Center and a popular hangout for people working at that sprawling monument to JFK, Harriet McKay was on the phone in Takoma Park trying to find out why Charise Lee hadn't shown up for her five o'clock fitting. Christopher Warren had arrived on time, but there was no sign of Ms. Lee.

"She wasn't in Italian class today," Warren told Harriet. "Yesterday, she said she was getting a cold."

"She could have at least called," Harriet said, not attempting to hide her pique.

"If our agents are in town, they might know what happened," the pianist offered.

Many in the class had already hired agents, and Charise and Warren's reps had accompanied them to Washington from Toronto. Agents accompanying young artists to the WNO program were viewed with a certain disdain, seemingly always in the way, demanding things for their young clients, hovering over their chicks like mother hens. Of course, there was no way to banish them. They came on their own and paid their own way.

Charise and Warren's agents, Philip Melincamp and Zöe Baltsa, had seen to it that their promising young stars were properly settled in a secure, two-bedroom apartment they shared, with a pullout couch for guests. When the agents weren't in D.C., they were back in Toronto at the agency bearing their names, their client roster a mixed bag of young, somewhat talented opera singers with potential fame and fortune on the horizon and second-tier veterans whose better singing days were behind them, yet who still managed to land supporting roles with companies around the globe.

Naturally, there was some resentment of Warren and Lee's situation. Most of the other students were expected to pay their own rent and buy their own food out of their $1,900 monthly stipend. It wasn't a secret that Melincamp and Baltsa were picking up their two clients' tabs, which left the young Canadians with spare cash with which to enjoy the city's abundant nightlife.

"There's no answer at the apartment," Harriet said. "Thanks for being on time," she told Warren. "If you see or hear from Ms. Lee, please urge her to call me. I'm under enough pressure without having to deal with no-shows."

Later that night, as she sat in her living room with her husband, Harriet felt a chill that had nothing to do with the air-conditioning.

"Something wrong?" he asked, noticing that she'd wrapped her arms about herself.

"No," she said. "I just have a bad feeling."

"About what?"

"I don't know."

Her husband frowned. Over the twenty-three years of their marriage, Harriet had displayed occasional moments of what she called "visions," premonitions of misfortune befalling others, family members, friends. She'd been right on at least two occasions, awaking in the middle of the night with a vision, then receiving a call the following morning confirming it.

"Like a little brandy?" he asked, touching her hair as he passed on the way to the kitchen.

She grabbed his hand, looked up, and smiled. Her husband's answer to almost everything was a little brandy.

"That would be nice," she said.

He continued into the kitchen, leaving her alone with her chilling vision.

FOUR

The 600 Restaurant, at the base of the Watergate complex, was bustling as Mac walked in. The vast, three-sided bar was lined with stagehands, electricians, carpenters, basses and baritones, cooks and painters, and sopranos and mezzos from the performing arts center across the street, and Watergate residents for whom the restaurant was a neighborhood haunt. Ulysses, the bartender, was a large, gregarious man wearing a large, gregarious green-and-white-striped shirt and a flamboyantly colored tie and suspenders. He moved with a dancer's grace as he took drink orders, mixed, stirred and shook, delivered the concoctions, and engaged in a nonstop dialogue with his customers without missing a step.

Mac spotted Annabel at the far end of the bar chatting with another woman. He joined them and was introduced to Genevieve Crier. "Genevieve is in charge of supers for the Washington Opera," Annabel told her husband.

"Aha," he said. "So you're to blame."

She feigned dismay, laughed, and said, "Guilty as charged, although I'm incapable of demonstrating remorse." Her accent was British, her easy laugh universal. "No matter, I'm absolutely delighted that you've joined the cast for *Tosca*." She took a step back and slowly, deliberately looked him up and down. "You'll make a fine monk, Mr. Smith, and we all know that monks get by on very little money, which is good because we pay our supers very little."

"I get paid, too?" he said.

"A fortune for a monk. Twenty-eight dollars a performance, eight dollars per rehearsal. There'll be eight rehearsals. Eight times eight is sixty-four dollars. Egads, you'll be the richest monk in the monastery. Of course, a whole world of college kids ate off the two bucks they were paid as supers at the Met years back." To Annabel: "The money will make up for your darling hubby's commitment to celibacy, I'm sure." She scooped an oversized purse off the bar. "Must run. See you at seven. Delighted to meet you, Mackensie Smith. Your wife is one of my favorite people in the world."

"I like your friend," Mac said, taking a stool next to Annabel.

"She's a dynamo. Used to be an actress in London and Holly-wood."

"We'd better get something to eat," Mac said. "I'd hate to make my stage debut on an empty stomach."

Genevieve Crier had instructed all supers to enter through the Opera House's stage door, just inside one of the main entrances to the Kennedy Center. Annabel gave their names to an older gentleman manning the door, who dutifully checked them off against a list on a clipboard and told them where the supers were congregating. This turned out to be a large dressing room one level below the theater itself. Genevieve was already there with two men, whom she introduced to the Smiths. The rest of the supers drifted in over the next fifteen minutes—a navy commander; an orthopedic surgeon; a Department of Agriculture auditor; two housewives from WNO's vast corps of volunteers; a nightclub bouncer; a retired botanist; Mac's college colleagues; Christopher Warren, the Canadian pianist from the Young Artists program; and someone Mac hadn't seen in a couple of years, Raymond Pawkins, a retired Washington MPD Homicide detective.

Their paths had crossed a number of times when Smith was representing criminal defendants, and Pawkins had been the lead investigator in those cases. Of all the Homicide detectives Smith had run across in his previous career, Pawkins stood out from the crowd. A tall, beanpole of a man with a prominent hooked nose beneath which a dark gray moustache was carefully trimmed, he wore khaki slacks with a razor-sharp crease, a blue button-down shirt, a white linen sport jacket, and loafers shined to a mirror finish. Smith remembered only too well those times when Pawkins testified against his criminal clients, always impeccably dressed and well spoken, terse or almost effete at times, answering Mac's cross-examinations with deliberate care, never exaggerating and always on-message. He was impossible to fluster on the stand, not only because of the impressive image he presented to juries, but because he'd gone by the book in his investigations, missing little in the way of evidence and organizing his findings with exquisite attention to detail. After shaking hands and introducing Annabel to him, snippets of Pawkins' life came back to Mac. They'd had lunches and dinners together at the conclusion of a few cases, the outcome now a matter of public record, their opposing views left back in the courtroom.

Pawkins had never married, as far as Mac knew, and was deeply interested in the arts, his erudition in stark contrast to most detectives. The last time they'd been together, Pawkins was finishing up a master's degree in 19th century art at Georgetown, and was an enthusiastic member of the National Cathedral's chorus. Unusual pursuits for a cop.

"I didn't know you were an opera buff, Mac," Pawkins said in a slightly pinched voice. He'd often complained about his sinuses, Mac recalled.

"I'm not," Mac said. "Annabel is on the board and roped me in."

"Actually," Annabel added, "it's a public relations project cooked up to get some press for the company. I take it you're no stranger to opera."

"One of my passions," Pawkins replied. "I've been going to the opera since I was a little boy, thanks to a mother who believed in exposing her only son to culture. I claimed to have hated it then, but secretly loved every minute of it. I've been a super in dozens of productions over the years, much to the amusement of my friends in law enforcement."

"I think that's wonderful," Annabel said, "seeing stereotypes debunked."

Pawkins smiled, savoring the thought. "At any rate," he said, "the counselor here and I butted heads on plenty of occasions, didn't we, Mac? How nice to see us on the same side this time around, or should I say on the same stage? Actually, it's not called a stage in opera."

"Oh?" Mac said. "What is it, then?"

"A deck. The earliest stagehands were seamen who were used to climbing ropes and riggings to high places. It seems that—"

Genevieve interrupted their conversation. "Time to meet our director," she said in her lilting voice. "Follow me." She led them from the dressing room up to the cavernous main stage, where the production's director, Anthony Zambrano, was conferring with assistants. Surrounding them was the half-finished second act set, a palatial apartment in the Farnese Palace used by Baron Scarpia, the chief of the Roman police, and one of opera's most infamous villains.

"Tony," Genevieve announced with a flourish, "your supernumeraries are here."

Zambrano, a short, wiry man with sharply defined facial features, a full head of steely gray hair, and wearing a pale yellow, light-weight cardigan over the shoulders of his navy T-shirt, turned and displayed a toothy smile.

"Ah, yes," the director said, hands on his hips and head cocked as he scrutinized these men and women who would be his monks and soldiers. Zambrano, who'd been brought in from Italy to direct this production of *Tosca*, walked past each super, frowning and making small grunting sounds, a commander inspecting his troops. Mac found himself becoming increasingly uncomfortable at having his physical attributes so brazenly evaluated. Zambrano turned abruptly

on his heel and motioned for Genevieve to accompany him to a remote area of the stage.

Annabel, who'd been watching from a distance, came to her husband and gave him a reassuring smile.

"Cocky little guy, isn't he?" Mac whispered.

"They say he's immensely talented," Annabel said, "on a par with
Menotti, Zeffirelli, and Guthrie."

"That may be, but I get the feeling he's not happy with us," said
Mac.

"You're imagining things," she said.

"Interesting," Mac said.

"What is?"

"The stage floor. The deck. It gives." He bounced up and down on
the surface, which appeared to be constructed of some sort of rubber.

"They could use better housekeeping," Annabel said casually.

"What do you mean?"

She pointed to a small, irregular, maroon stain on the floor.

He crouched to see it more closely. "Looks like somebody had a
nosebleed."

Genevieve came to them.

"Everything all right?" Annabel asked.

"Not really. Anthony is unhappy with a few of my supers."

"I don't handle rejection well," Mac said, adding a laugh.

"You passed muster," Genevieve said.

"Whew," Mac said, wiping imaginary perspiration from his brow.

Genevieve lowered her voice. "He's not happy with your boss, Dr.
Burns."

Mac looked across the stage to where Wilfred Burns, president of
George Washington University, chatted with professors from the other
schools who'd agreed to appear as supers.

"I told Anthony that he couldn't dismiss certain supers like Dr.
Burns because—well, because of who they are."

"If you need a volunteer to bail," Smith said, "I'm available."

"Not on your life," Genevieve said. "Tony described you as
ruggedly handsome."

"Isn't he though?" said Annabel.

"He may not like certain supers who are here," Genevieve said, "but I have my own problems. I'm still missing a woman."

"Oh?"

"Charise Lee, from the Young Artist Program. They pressed her into duty for one performance, but she's not here. She didn't show up for her costume fitting, either."

Zambrano clapped his hands and called everyone to form a semicircle around him. He welcomed the group and said he intended to walk everyone through the basic blocking that would be used during the performance, to give them a feel for the stage on which they'd be working, although most rehearsals would be held at Takoma Park. He'd just started arranging the supers into groups when a burly middle-aged man, coveralls over a white T-shirt, came through a gap in the scenery, a backstage worker of some sort, an electrician or grip. He stood a dozen feet back from everyone and seemed unsure of what to say, or how to say it.

Zambrano noticed him. "I'm in the middle of a run-through," he said. "I insist upon a closed stage."

The intruder looked around for someone with whom to speak. Not seeing anyone, he blurted loudly, "She's dead."

"What?" Zambrano asked.

"Who's dead?" asked someone.

"The young woman," the stagehand said. "She's dead. Upstairs."

"What young woman?" Zambrano demanded.

"Oh, good God," Genevieve said, her hand going to her bosom. "I have this feeling that . . ."

Mac and Annabel looked at each other as Genevieve went to where the stagehand had now been joined by Zambrano, the Opera House's manager, and the head of Kennedy Center Security, who'd been called by the stagehand immediately after discovering the body. He spotted Ray Pawkins and crossed the stage to him.

"Hello, Raymond."

"George," Pawkins said. "What's this about a dead girl?"

The security chief nodded. "Upstairs, above the house." He

pointed to the ornate ceiling high above the 2,300 empty seats. Mac and Annabel's eyes went to where his finger indicated.

The security chief started to say something else but stopped midsentence, aware that he and Pawkins weren't alone.

"This is Mackensie Smith and his wife," Pawkins said. To Mac and Annabel: "George Jacoby. He and I go back a long way. He was MPD, too."

Mac nodded.

"The attorney," Jacoby said.

"Right," confirmed Mac.

Jacoby lowered his voice and said to Pawkins, "Looks like a homicide. I've called First District. They're on their way. I've got one of my people up there now. It's pretty grisly. I thought . . ."

"Show me," Pawkins said.

Mac and Annabel watched as Pawkins followed Jacoby into the wings.

"A homicide?" Annabel said. "Here at the Kennedy Center?"

"Is it true?" Genevieve said, joining them. "Someone has been murdered?"

"We don't know for sure," Annabel said. "But someone is dead."

"Is it . . . ?" Genevieve's lip quivered. "Is it Ms. Lee?"

"You know as much as we do," Mac said.

"Raymond has gone with Mr. Jacoby," Genevieve said. "He was a detective."

"I know," Mac said. "Why don't we all just grab seats and wait until we know more. No sense speculating." He saw two of the supers about to leave. "You might tell your flock not to take off until the police say it's okay," he suggested.

"Good point," Genevieve said, hurrying to head off their departure.

Before going down into the house to sit and wait for further information, Mac glanced back to where the maroon spot darkened the stage—deck—floor. *So much for my nosebleed theory,* he thought as he escorted Annabel off the stage.

FIVE

As Pawkins and Jacoby waited for a small backstage elevator to take them partway up to where the body had been found, Pawkins spoke with the stagehand.

"You just discovered the body?" the former detective asked.

"Yes, sir." He shook his head in disbelief. "I never go up there, no reason to. Nobody does."

"Why did you go up this time?"

"We have some cable up there. We needed it for *Tosca*. Mickey sent me up."

"Mickey?"

"My boss."

The elevator arrived and the three men squeezed into its confined interior. After ascending two flights, the door opened and they continued their journey to the highest recesses of the house, more than a hundred feet directly above where thousands of opera lovers would sit in comfortable seats waiting to be transported by the soaring voices on-stage. It was necessary to walk carefully along the narrow steel catwalks to avoid items stored on them, and to hunch over in certain areas to avoid low-hanging wires and other backstage paraphernalia. Eventually, they emerged into a round space approximately thirty feet in diameter. Thick spools of cable and rope were neatly lined up along one arc of the circle. In the center, on the cold, bare, gray concrete floor, was the body. A uniformed Kennedy Center security officer stood a dozen feet from the deceased, his body language saying that to get any closer would infect him with a disease, or perhaps wake the girl from her nap.

Pawkins went directly to the body. He brushed away unseen dirt from a small area of the floor, tugged up his pants leg, lowered one knee to that clean spot, and examined the girl more closely. He observed that she was slight in stature and was either Asian or the product of a mixed marriage. She was on her back, her arms folded up, allowing her hands, one atop the other, to rest on her chest. She wore white pants cut off just below her knees—Were they called Capri pants? Pawkins wondered. Her top, made of some silky fabric, was shiny red with the hint of a pattern in the cloth. She wore one shoe; the other foot was bare, toenails the same red as her blouse. A black fanny pack covered her groin.

Pawkins ignored the first rule of coming upon a homicide scene; make sure that she was dead. No need to check for signs of life. Her eyes were open; the pupils were of different sizes, one of three basic signs of death, along with cessation of breathing and lack of a pulse. He gently tried to move her arm. Stiff as a rake handle. Rigor mortis was complete, although he judged that it might have begun to disappear, which would mean the time of death was at least eighteen hours earlier. Her small, thin body would have hastened the onset of stiffening. He'd seen obese bodies that never did become rigid. He tried to move her arms again and succeeded in lifting them just enough to see what was beneath her clasped hands. "Oh, my," he muttered to himself. He took a second look. "Hmmm."

With Jacoby looking over his shoulder—the Kennedy Center security chief had spent most of his MPD career in a special unit assigned to protect VIPs; murder investigations were foreign to him—

Pawkins pulled a notebook and a pen from the inside pocket of his sport jacket, and jotted notes.

"How'd she die?" Jacoby asked.

Pawkins stood and continued making notes. "It appears she was stabbed in the chest, judging from that circle of blood beneath her hands. That's for the ME to decide."

Sounds coming from outside the area caused Pawkins to turn and see a pair of uniformed MPD officers and two detectives emerge from the shadows. Pawkins recognized one of the detectives; they'd worked a number of cases together.

"Hey, Ray," the familiar one said, breathing heavily and wiping his brow with a handkerchief. "Hell of a climb to get up here."

Pawkins nodded.

"How come you're here, Ray?"

"I happened to be downstairs when this gentleman discovered the body." He indicated the stagehand, who'd joined the original cop at a respectful, safe distance from the body.

The lead detective was Carl Berry, fifteen years on the force, twelve of them in Homicide—or as it had been renamed by some highly paid consultant, Crimes Against Persons.

"Nice to see you again, Carl," Pawkins said, returning the notebook and pen to his jacket. "Stay in touch."

"Sure, Ray. I'll want to get your take on this, you having been here so soon. Any idea who she is?"

"Her fanny pack probably contains that information."

Berry opened the bag and withdrew a wallet, a set of keys, and assorted makeup items. He perused the wallet, looked up, and said, "Her name's Lee." He held the card he read from at arm's length and squinted in the dim light. "Charise Lee." Consulting another card from the wallet, he said, "Young Artist Program? What's that?"

Pawkins sighed. He was very familiar with the Domingo-Cafritz program and had attended their recitals. He'd not seen her before. "An opera singer," he said sadly. "She'll sing no more."

He followed Jacoby down the torturous route to the main stage and looked out over the house, where Mac and Annabel Smith and the others sat. Genevieve Crier was with the Smiths. Pawkins went to them and slumped into a chair between Annabel and Genevieve.

"Well?" Genevieve asked. "Was someone murdered?"

"Yes," Pawkins replied, not looking at anyone in particular.

"Who?" Genevieve asked, a lump in her throat catching the word as it came out.

"Evidently a Ms. Charise Lee," Pawkins said.

Genevieve gasped, clamped her hands over her face, and sobbed. Annabel put her arm over her shoulder and whispered comforting words.

"I knew it," Genevieve managed. "I just knew it."

"How was she killed?" Mac asked.

"Stabbed," Pawkins said, "but that's unofficial. Happened a while ago, perhaps last night. Certainly not this afternoon or tonight."

Zambrano appeared from backstage and came to the stage apron. "What *is* taking so long?" he asked loudly.

Mac stood. "There's been an unfortunate incident somewhere upstairs. The police will want to talk to everyone who was here."

"I don't have time for this," Zambrano said, and stormed back into the wings.

The laconic Pawkins chuckled softly. "I was a super here at the Kennedy Center, *Don Giovanni* directed by him a few years back," he said. "He's volatile, but he has a wonderful creative sense. I was looking forward to being in another one of his productions."

"Do you think what's happened tonight will cause *Tosca* to be postponed?" Annabel asked.

"I'm sure not," Pawkins said. "They put on a production right after September eleven, which was the right thing to do. Baseball and football teams played, and life went on, as it should."

"Much of life," Mac corrected softly.

It was an hour before Detective Berry and his partner came downstairs. The group were told they were free to go, but their names and contact information were collected: "We'll want to be in touch with you in the next few days," Berry announced.

Genevieve pulled herself together before all the supers departed.

"This changes nothing," she told them. "Rehearsals will go on as scheduled. Sorry about tonight, but the show must, and will, go on."

The Smiths and Pawkins had started up the aisle toward the doors when Mac suddenly stopped and grabbed Pawkins' arm. "There's something the police should see," he said. "Back in a minute, Annie."

He led the former detective back onto the stage—he doubted if he'd ever call it a deck—and pointed to the stain on the floor.

"Blood," Pawkins said.

"I wonder . . . ," Smith started to say.

Pawkins finished his thought. "Wondering if she was killed here and moved upstairs?"

"Yes."

"A good possibility," Pawkins said.

Mac's eyes followed a route from the stain to the nearest exit into the wings. "No blood aside from the stain," he said, "no trail."

"I might have an answer for that," Pawkins said. He waved over a uniformed officer, pointed out the stain to him, and suggested he inform Detective Berry of it.

"Drink?" Mac asked Pawkins as they rejoined Annabel and left the Kennedy Center's air-conditioned coolness. It was an oppressively humid night.

"Love it," the retired detective replied, "as long as food accompanies it. I haven't eaten since breakfast."

"I've lost any appetite I might have had," Annabel said as they agreed to meet in fifteen minutes at the bar on the lobby level of the Watergate Hotel, decidedly more quiet and conducive to serious conversation than the 600 Restaurant.

Pawkins' laugh was rueful. "The only thing that sets my stomach on edge is a bad performance of a favorite opera. I've seen and, worse, heard a few of those, and the thought of food is anathema then. A nice, clean homicide? As effective an aperitif as there ever was."

SIX

The sedate Watergate lobby bar and lounge were sparsely populated when Mac and Annabel arrived. They'd said nothing to each other during the short ride from the Kennedy Center, each immersed in thought. But once seated at a secluded table, they gave voice to those thoughts.

"What a shock," Annabel said.

"At best," Mac said. "We should have asked your friend Genevieve to join us. She looked like she needed a drink. Maybe a number of them."

"Too late now. Oh, there's Mr. Pawkins."

Pawkins slid into a chair. "You didn't have to wait for me," he said, indicating the lack of glasses on the table. That was immediately rectified when a waitress approached and took their order, a snifter of Blanton's Single Barrel Bourbon for Mac, club soda with lime for Annabel, and a Dubonnet cocktail for Pawkins, along with a request for the bar menu.

Their drinks served, Pawkins pushed back his chair, folded one long leg over the other, and sipped. "Nice," he said. He raised his glass. "Good to see you again, Mac, and to meet you, Mrs. Smith."

"Please, it's Annabel," she said, returning the toast halfheartedly.

"Did you know the young lady?" Pawkins asked, his eyes focused on the menu he'd been handed.

"Ms. Lee?" Annabel replied. "Not really. Sorry, that isn't much of an answer. I've been to events sponsored by the opera at which members of the Young Artist Program performed." Her eyes misted. "I saw her a few months ago at a recital at the Renwick Gallery. She sang Michaela from *Carmen*, the young country girl. It was—it was lovely."

"Never had the pleasure," said Pawkins. "Obviously, I never will."

Annabel managed a smile. "I remember being impressed at her size. That such a big, magnificent voice could come from such a tiny package was remarkable."

Pawkins' smile was expansive. "They say that whenever you have a tenor who is heavier than the soprano, the opera will succeed. Yes, Ms. Lee seems—*seemed*—quite small-boned for an opera singer. Then again, more and more directors are trying these days to match the visual with the role." He chuckled. "It wasn't long ago that Deborah Voight—she's probably the preeminent Ariadne in the world—had her contract to perform in *Ariadne Auf Naxos* at Covent Garden canceled because the director wanted her dressed in a skimpy black cocktail dress. Well, Deborah, being a large lady, was hardly the black cocktail dress type. She refused. The cancellation created a worldwide scandal in the opera world. I suppose it worked out for her, though. She went on a diet, lost about a hundred-and-fifty pounds, and is singing better than ever. Ms. Lee's small stature would have been to her benefit—provided, of course, that the voice matched her physical beauty."

"No question that she was murdered?" Mac asked.

"Oh, no. Stabbed in the chest. I imagine the blade went directly into her heart."

Pawkins ordered onion soup and a shrimp cocktail, to be served in that order. Sirens could be heard from outside.

"Ironic," Mac said to Pawkins, "that you happened to be there tonight."

"Yes, isn't it? Interesting that you found what appears to be a bloodstain on the deck. We call it a deck in opera because—"

"Stagehands used to be sailors," Mac said.

Pawkins smiled.

"That's the extent of my knowledge, thanks to you," Mac said. "Oh, I do know that we're supers, not extras."

"Exactly," the lanky man said, refolding his long legs. "About the stain. You wondered why there wasn't a trail of blood from that spot to where the body was found, assuming, of course, that she was, in fact, murdered on the deck."

Mac and Annabel waited for the explanation.

"Whoever killed Ms. Lee was very proficient."

"A proficient killer," Annabel said. "Professional?"

Pawkins shrugged as his soup was set before him. "That's impossible to say at this juncture. What's certain is that the murderer acted swiftly. Ms. Lee was obviously stabbed by something, a knife, scissors, any sharp instrument." He paused. "Maybe a spear. There are always plenty of those backstage at an opera. At any rate, her assailant evidently—and I hasten to say that this is based purely on a cursory look I had at the wound—plunged the weapon into her chest, immediately withdrew it, and in an instant shoved some sort of material into the wound, which stemmed the flow of blood, at least long enough to move the body elsewhere without dripping a trail behind."

"Grotesque," Annabel commented.

"It sounds as though it was well planned," Mac said. "Premeditated."

"A reasonable assumption," said Pawkins, taking a spoonful of soup between thoughts.

Annabel's cell phone rang. She quickly answered, glancing about to see whether it had disturbed anyone. The adjacent tables were empty.

"Hello?" she said. "No, I'm here at the Watergate bar with my husband. Now? A half hour? Of course. I'll be there."

She clicked the phone closed and returned it to her purse.

"What's up?" Mac asked.

"That was Camile Worthington." To Pawkins: "She's chairman of the Opera board's executive committee."

"I've met her."

"They're holding an emergency meeting in a half hour."

"They work fast," Mac said.

"I hate to run, but I have to," she said, standing and extending her hand. "It was good meeting you. Mac often talks about how good a detective you were."

Pawkins stood and accepted her hand. "Knowing I might be cross-examined by your husband kept me on my toes. Good night."

Pawkins' second course arrived and he offered Mac a shrimp.

"Thanks," Mac said, dipping it into the sauce. "So, tell me, Raymond, what you've been up to since retirement. I assume being a super in an occasional opera doesn't take up all your time."

"I wish it could," he said. "I love it. When I'm not in costume, which is most of the time, I keep quite busy. I've been collecting recordings of great opera performances for years now. I must have five hundred or so, all neatly cataloged. I've been doing some writing about opera for minor magazines. I still have my four feline friends, although I don't think one of them has much longer to go. And I haven't given up working completely. I have my PI license for D.C. and catch an occasional case, usually involving something musical—stolen instruments or valuable scores—or art. Amazing how hot the stolen art market is, Mac, and how stupid those who steal it can be." He dabbed at his mouth with a napkin, and sat back. "You now have my life story," he said. "What's yours since we last met?"

"Two major changes," Mac said. "Marrying Annabel was the big event. Scrapping my criminal law practice and becoming a law professor was another."

"I was sorry about your first wife and your son," Pawkins said. "The drunk driver got off easy, as I recall."

"That's right."

"You must have wanted to kill."

"I got over it."

Mac motioned for the check. "I'm glad we had a chance to catch up," he said, "although it would have been nice if the rehearsal hadn't ended the way it did."

Pawkins reached for his wallet, but Mac waved him off. "We'll do this again, your treat."

They paused beneath the circular canopy that covered the hotel's entrance. The humidity was now visible, enshrouding them in a low-hanging mist. Pawkins handed Mac his business card. "In case you ever need an opera-loving PI."

"You never know," Mac said. "See you at the next rehearsal—if there is one."

"Oh, there will be. Nothing will keep Tosca from singing her 'Vissi d'arte' in Act II before she stabs the wicked Scarpia to death. Nothing. Not even a real murder. Sorry your wife had to run. She's beautiful."

"In every way," Mac said, and they parted.

Annabel arrived home at eleven. Mac had already changed for bed and was listening to a recording of Mascagni's *Cavalleria Rusticana* while reading a description of what was happening in the opera, which had been included with the CD. The music was familiar to him. Portions had been used as the musical backdrop for *The Godfather, Part III*. He turned down the volume when she entered.

"It's beautiful," she said, kissing him and heading straight for the bedroom. She emerged fifteen minutes later in her pajamas and robe.

"So," he said, "tell me about the meeting."

"Well," she said, "you can imagine the turmoil. A murder at the Washington National Opera, not onstage but behind the scenes, with a real victim and killer. It's never happened before. Naturally, there's great concern for what this will do to the season."

Mac winced. "More important," he said, "what it did to that poor girl."

"Don't misunderstand," she said, settling on the couch next to him. "Naturally, everyone is devastated and feels terrible for her family. They're from Toronto. Evidently, she had a tremendous future. Of all the young people in the program, she was considered to have the best chance at stardom."

"Somebody made sure that would never happen."

"The meeting went all over the lot, one subject to another. But what occurred toward the end should interest you."

"Oh? Why is that?"

"Bill Frazier, the board chairman, suggested that while the police will be investigating the murder, he thought we, the Opera board, should take matters into our own hands and try to solve it ourselves."

"Why? The last thing you want to do is interfere with the police investigation."

"Image. We take on a tremendous responsibility bringing these talented young people here to Washington to study and prepare for their careers. Having one of them killed under our very noses doesn't do much for our image. Bill says that everyone involved with the company will be prime suspects. He wants to prove that she was killed by an outsider."

Mac laughed. "What if it wasn't an outsider?"

"I brought that up, of course. No one's looking to whitewash the company and its people. If she was killed by someone in the company, so be it. But he feels—and I agree with him—that by at least demonstrating that we care enough to examine ourselves and WNO, we'll be viewed in a more positive light."

"I suppose," Mac said.

"Bill asked me to talk to you about it."

"Me? Why? I'm not involved with the company."

"But you were a top criminal attorney. Besides, meeting your old friend Mr. Pawkins might prove to be serendipitous. Genevieve was at the meeting and mentioned him, the fact that he'd been a homicide detective and loves opera. Do you think he'd—?"

"Take this on? I have no idea." He went to the bedroom, returning with Pawkins' card, which he handed to Annabel.

"He's a private investigator," she said, confirming the obvious. "Between you and him, we could—"

"Whoa," Mac said. "If you want me to call Ray and run it past him, I'll be happy to do that. But that's the extent of my involvement."

"Fine. You'll call him?"

"Sure. Mind if I turn up the volume? I particularly like this section."

Annabel placed her fingers against her lips to mask her tiny smile. Her husband, who'd never indicated an interest in opera, lately enjoyed basking in the recorded lush, dramatic music, and remarkable voices. That was good. Unfortunately, the brutal murder of Charise Lee now promised to involve him beyond music appreciation and being a super in *Tosca*.

His posture at that moment was only to call Raymond Pawkins and see if he would be willing to investigate the murder on behalf of WNO's board. But Annabel knew him only too well. He'd never be content with simply making that call. Like it or not, Mackensie Smith was about to learn more about opera than he'd ever envisioned.

SEVEN

Pawkins drove directly home from the Watergate in his 1986 Mercedes sedan. Like himself, he kept the vehicle in pristine working condition. The slightest blemish on its silver exterior was immediately buffed out, and he treated the black seats with a leather conditioner monthly. The engine was barely audible when idling. Particular attention was paid to the windows. Pawkins admitted to being a windshield fanatic, Windexing them at least once a week, often more frequently. People who saw him with the vehicle assumed he was a car fanatic, a man who attended rallies of vintage automobiles and derived great pleasure from owning such a splendid specimen. That wasn't the case. Cars meant little to him, and he found those who doted on their well-preserved four-wheel beauties to be boring. For Pawkins, it was a matter of practicality and of pride in keeping what you owned in good condition. Like himself.

He'd crossed the Teddy Roosevelt Bridge and proceeded north on the G.W. Memorial Parkway until reaching the village of Great Falls, a wealthy D.C. suburb with palatial, colonial-style homes strung along the Potomac River, the waterway that is as much of a Washington landmark as any of its man-made monuments. Few of the houses had particular historic value, but they were impressive in their size and sweeping views of the river's swirling headwaters. Another hundred years would do it.

He ended up on a narrow dirt road lined with poplar and cedar trees. He followed its winding course until arriving at his home, formerly the gatehouse to a sizable estate with river frontage. He'd rented the small carriage house until its owner, a wealthy real estate developer, decided to sell it and a surrounding two acres. As the tenant of longstanding, Pawkins had first dibs, and he purchased the house and land. It had been a bargain. The owner had always liked having a D.C. detective on the premises and readily accepted Pawkins' lower bid.

He parked the Mercedes in a detached one-car garage thirty feet from the stone-and-clapboard house and crossed a gravel patch to the front door. The outside lights, and a few inside, were on, thanks to state-of-the-art programmable timers he'd had installed. Rather than setting times for the lights to go on and off, he'd programmed in the latitude and longitude of Great Falls, using a chart provided by the manufacturer, and the day of the month. From that point forward, the timers adjusted to changes in the time of sunset and sunrise, the lights coming on a minute or so later each day as summer approached, and earlier later in the year. They even adjusted automatically for Daylight Saving Time.

The alarm system was up-to-date, too, including special motion detectors that would not be set off by the movements of his four cats.

He entered the foyer, turned off the system, and went straight to the kitchen at the rear of the house, where he put up a kettle for tea. Using the time for the water to boil, he went upstairs to his bedroom and changed into blue running shorts, a white Washington National Opera T-shirt, and sandals, stopping briefly in the bathroom to check his hair. Time for a touch-up, he decided; gray roots were showing beneath the subtle, artificial brown coloring.

The kettle's shrill whistle brought him back downstairs. A devotee of green tea, he opted instead this night for orange spice Rooibos, a recent favorite. Because he was tall, and the ceilings were low, he moved through the old house in a perpetual slight stoop, although it actually wasn't necessary. The habit of a tall man.

But he straightened once through a door off the living room, next to a wood-burning stove that he used in winter to help heat the house. The room he now entered was large and had twelve-foot-high ceilings, multiple recessed halogen lights, a Mexican stone floor covered by multicolored area rugs, and an elaborate built-in desk, its shiny black surface stretching nine feet beneath a series of narrow shelves that held an assortment of office items and small, framed pictures.

The wall opposite the desk, and a second wall spanning the length of the room and broken only by a large window, held floor-to-ceiling bookcases, their upper shelves reached by a library ladder with wheels at the bottom, and whose top ran along a metal trolley. Every inch of the shelves was filled with books.

A computer with a twenty-six-inch monitor sat on the desk. Built into the wall of bookshelves behind was a fifty-two-inch flat-panel TV. Next to it was the control unit for a Bose surround-sound system, its multiple, tiny cube speakers discreetly nestled in the room's corners. The subwoofer sat on the floor beneath the desk.

Pawkins had personally designed this addition to the carriage house. He'd had to obtain a zoning variance, which took an inordinate amount of time as well as money for a local attorney, but once the legalities had been settled, his vision of the new space was made reality by an old-school contractor whose attention to detail and dedication to quality matched Pawkins' needs. Construction had been completed a little more than a year ago. Since then, it had become his refuge, his cave where he could enjoy his music, read his books, and conduct what business came his way.

He opened a tall cabinet in which five hundred CD recordings were stored, arranged alphabetically by artist, and retrieved the one he sought, a London recording of Richard Strauss' *Der Rosenkavalier*, with the Vienna Philharmonic conducted by George Solti, and featuring the American soprano Helen Donath, whose airy voice struck a particular chord with Pawkins, whether Donath was playing Sophie in the Strauss masterpiece or Eva in Wagner's *Die Meistersinger von Nürnberg.*

He used dimmers to lower the lights, started the CD, and settled in his office chair, one of his cats, a Chartreux who'd adopted him years ago, on his lap. As the rich, melodic music swelled to fill the room, he leaned back, hands clasped behind his head, and reviewed what had happened that evening. After a few minutes of this introspection, he gently pushed the cat, Wolfgang, to the floor and started making notes on a yellow legal pad. The phone rang. He winced and stared at the receiver. The recorded opera had reached an especially pleasing section and he was loath to stop it. The phone kept ringing; the answering machine next to it had been turned off earlier that day and he'd forgotten to activate it. A button on the remote brought the stereo volume down to background level, and he picked up the receiver.

"Ray? It's Mac Smith."

Pawkins laughed and lowered the volume even more. "Twice in one night," he said. "To what do I owe my good fortune?"

"I assume I'm not interrupting something important," Smith said, "so I won't apologize."

"Good. Actually, I'm relaxing and enjoying my music. Strauss. *Der Rosenkavalier.* A perfect bittersweet comedy opera, so different from the blood and gore of his earlier works, *Salome* and *Elektra*, although they were fine, too. Quite daring. But you didn't call for my analysis of Strauss and his operas. It was good seeing you again after all this time. Thanks again for the drink and snacks. I didn't intend to freeload."

"It was my pleasure," Smith said. "I'll tell you why I'm calling, Ray. Annabel attended her board meeting. As you can imagine, this murder of the young singer has everyone shaken."

"And I'm sure there was plenty of histrionics. Opera lovers tend that way."

"I wouldn't know about that. Look, the board has decided to take whatever steps it can to resolve this internally."

"Internally? MPD will love that, a bunch of wealthy opera aficionados playing Sherlock Holmes. Will they break into 'Di quella pira' when the killer is apprehended?"

"Raymond," Smith said, "we might get further with this if you'll stop playing the obscure reference game with me. I—"

"Hardly obscure, Mac. It's from Il Trovatore, one of the most famous arias ever written."

"Be that as it may, they—the board—asked Annabel if I—if you— would be interested in taking this on as a freelance assignment. Ms. Crier evidently told them that her super had been an MPD Homicide detective. Naturally, that piqued their interest."

"Interesting," Pawkins said. "We'll work together?"

"No. I said I'd call you. That's the extent of my involvement."

"Then the answer is no."

"As you wish. I've done my duty to Annabel and the cause of opera."

"You'll at least let me bounce things off you. I'd enjoy that, matching wits again with the brilliant Mackensie Smith. Not that I won many of those courtroom battles, but it would keep me honest."

Smith chuckled. "All right," he said. "You can bounce things off me. I don't know if they've come up with a budget to cover your fee and expenses, but I'm sure they will."

"Not necessary."

"What?"

"I wouldn't think of charging the folks at WNO. Good Lord, Mac, after all these years of them staging world-class opera at my back door, the least I can do is offer my services as a gift. Besides, there might be a book in it. I've always wanted to write a book about opera, but lack the credentials. Still, if I use my investigative skills to solve a suitable murder here, publishers will be beating down my door. Meet for breakfast?"

"I, ah—sure, that would be fine."

They nailed down a time and place to meet the next morning and ended the conversation. Pawkins boosted the volume again and reveled in the final acts, especially the trio in which the three stunning lead voices blended, a moment that brought tears to his eyes.

He returned the CD to its slot in the cabinet, resumed his seat at the desk, and logged on to his computer. He spent the next fifteen minutes reviewing a variety of investment accounts, smiling at their increase in value since last looking at them two days ago. He exited that program, unlocked one of the desk drawers, and pulled out a small black notebook. He opened it and examined the most recent page, on which a number of dollar figures were noted. Then he read off a series of digits written on the book's first page and fed them to the keyboard. Seconds later, another series of dollar amounts appeared on the screen. Nothing accompanied those figures, no account names, no addresses, no headings or other information. The final figure was larger than the preceding one, prompting another small smile. He noted that last dollar amount in the book, closed and locked it in the drawer, and returned the key to where it had been hidden beneath paper clips in a coffee mug.

He logged off the computer, extinguished the lights, and left the room, stopping in the kitchen to put his empty teacup in the dishwasher. He went upstairs, a satisfied grin wreathing his face as he slipped into bed, the four cats staking out positions at its foot.

EIGHT

Readers of the *Washington Post* and viewers of TV news shows the following morning learned that the President's poll numbers had dropped to their lowest point ever; that Iran had dispatched a team of diplomats to Iraq to help that country establish a fundamentalist government; that scientists had definitively linked the continuing increase in the number of hurricanes to global warming; and that a Canadian opera singer, enrolled in the Washington National Opera's Domingo-Cafritz Young Artist Program, had been found dead in the Kennedy Center the previous night.

The front-page article in the *Post* reported that the corpse was that of Charise Lee, a twenty-eight-year-old female voice student from Toronto. Her body was found in a secluded area of the Kennedy Center and was being treated as a possible homicide. Her family had been notified and was en route to Washington from Toronto. No further details were available, according to a police spokesman. An investigation was under way.

The article was clearly written without a great deal of hard information to go on. A paragraph, lifted from a WNO press release, described the Young Artist Program. William Frazier, chairman of WNO's board, who was reached at home, stated, "Naturally, all of us at the Washington National Opera are shocked and saddened by this terrible event. Ms. Lee was a young singer of extraordinary talent, whose star in opera was bright. Our hearts go out to her family."

It was a little before seven in Mac and Annabel's Watergate apartment. Sleep hadn't come easily. Annabel had finally given up at four and tried to take her mind off the murder by going to the library and reading a book purported to be funny but wasn't, at least not in her current mood. Mac joined her at five.

"Mr. Pawkins agreed to investigate on behalf of the company?" Annabel asked when he'd settled next to her on the couch. She knew the answer but was in need of confirmation, or starting the conversation.

"Right. And he doesn't want to be paid. He says it'll be his gift to the opera."

"That's so generous. What else did he say?"

"I don't remember. He likes tossing out opera references, maybe to test me. I failed. I'm meeting him for breakfast."

"Oh? Why?"

"He wants to bounce things off me."

"I thought . . ."

"I don't mind being a sounding board. It won't go further than that."

She sat back and closed her eyes.

"You're in your thinking mode," he said.

She came forward and faced him. "It had to be someone connected with the opera, Mac. That's the only logical explanation."

"Not necessarily."

"How many people had access to the Opera House last night?"

"More than you realize. Lots of people work at the Kennedy Center who have nothing to do with the opera company, stagehands for the other theaters, back-office people, restaurant workers. Besides, I'm sure you've noticed those gaping loading doors for each theater in the complex. They're left wide open when sets are being moved in and out. Not hard for someone to slip inside."

"I wonder if she was seeing someone romantically."

"If she was, he'll be the first to be questioned. What *I'm* wondering is how Pawkins will go about investigating. At least having been a cop will help avoid ruffling feathers at MPD."

"He won't have any official status," Annabel said.

"He will with your opera people. If you're right—that it was someone involved with the opera—he'll probably have better access to them than the cops will."

He got off the couch, turned on CNN, mounted a stationary bike, and started peddling. "What's on your agenda today?" he asked.

"Meetings. I'm on the Opera Ball committee. It'll be here before we know it."

"The murder will take some of the gloss off."

"I hope not. It's our biggest fund-raiser. I think it's shaping up beautifully. Which reminds me, it's black tie. You might want to pull out your tux and try it on."

He stopped peddling. "Are you suggesting it might not fit me as well as the last time I wore it?"

"Of course not. I just thought it might need cleaning or some minor . . . adjustments." She, too, stood. "Shower time. Put on the coffee?"

"My pleasure. I'll need the car."

"No problem. I won't need it today."

～

Annabel's first meeting of the day was at WNO's administrative offices at 2600 Virginia Avenue, NW, the Watergate office building in which the infamous Watergate break-in took place, and across from what used to be a Holiday Inn. Not exactly a holiday, it had served as a staging area for Nixon's bungling burglars. As Annabel started up the stairs leading to the main entrance, Genevieve Crier burst through the doors.

"Good morning, Annabel," the energetic supers' coordinator

chirped. "Can you believe it actually happened? I mean, right there in the Kennedy Center. I didn't sleep a wink. Poor girl. I ache for her parents."

"I know," said Annabel. "Has the meeting started? I'm a little late."

"No, but they're gathering. Did you speak with your husband about Mr. Pawkins?"

"Mac spoke with him last night. He's agreed to lend a hand. They're having breakfast as we speak."

"Splendid."

"Won't you be at the meeting?"

"Afraid not. Other fires to put out this morning. I'd better get on my horse. Later, Annabel."

As Annabel again made for the doors, she noticed a TV remote truck parked across the street. A mini-van with THE WASHINGTON TIMES on its side occupied a space a few feet from it. *They're not here to do a retrospective on the Watergate break-in,* Annabel thought as she entered the building and checked in with the first-floor receptionist.

A dozen men and women were milling about the large, second-floor conference room when Annabel entered. Chairman Frazier, a compact man who moved with the assurance of a top business leader—he'd made his millions providing state-of-the-art surveillance equipment to the Justice Department—greeted her. "Glad you could make it," he said. He lowered his voice. "Did your husband speak with the private investigator?"

"Yes," Annabel said. "He's willing to help us, at no charge."

"Does that mean he won't give us his full attention?"

"I only know that Mac called him last night, and Mr. Pawkins agreed to work with us. Mac is having breakfast with him this morning, and I'm sure he'll ascertain his degree of involvement."

"Fine," said Frazier. "We'd better get started."

He had trouble establishing order. Everyone in the room was discussing Charise Lee's death and resisted his repeated requests that they take their seats. When they finally did, he indicated a printed agenda at each place. First on the list was "Charise Lee."

"I'm not suggesting that we spend much time discussing what

happened at the Kennedy Center last night," Frazier said, "except to say that we mustn't allow it to impede progress on other fronts. Naturally, our hearts go out to Ms. Lee's family and friends and we'll do everything we can to help them cope with this tragedy. But we have the opening of *Tosca*, the marketing of future productions—there are some problems with *Andrea Chénier*—and, of course, there's the ball. Before I get to that, I know that Laurie has something to say."

Laurie Webster, WNO's public relations director, said, "The media is all over this story, and it will only get worse. That a murder occurred at all is horrible. That the victim was one of our most promising students is tragic. What is important from our point of view is that we speak with one, unified voice, and that voice will be me and my staff. I urge all of you to resist media pressure to comment on last night, and to refer any press inquiries to my office."

"Laurie is right," Frazier said. "I know it's a temptation to respond to reporters' questions, but it's in our best interest not to. Unless anyone has something to add, let's move on to the second item on the agenda, the Opera Ball."

Webster excused herself: "I'd better get back to my office. Media calls were piling up when I left."

The Opera Ball chairwoman, Nicki Frolich, was next to address the gathering. It had occurred to Annabel more than once that if it had been twenty or thirty years ago, it was unlikely she would have been asked to join the Opera Ball committee. Back then, the women who led such highly visible fundraising efforts, known as "Ladies of the Balls," were for the most part the wives of wealthy men who not only had the time, their husbands' business connections generated large donations of money and services. But as more women entered the workplace, the number of wives available, or interested in such activities, diminished, and committees for premiere events like the Opera Ball, the National Symphony Orchestra Ball, the Corcoran Ball, and dozens of smaller social events drew from a less wealthy and socially connected corps of Washington women. Not that Annabel Lee-Smith wasn't an active member of the city's social scene. She and Mac were involved in a number of artistic and professional organizations, and if not on the A-list of party invitees, they had their share of invitations to events that were covered in the *Post's* Style section.

Frolich, whose husband was one of the area's best-known plastic surgeons, was experienced at spearheading big-ticket fundraisers, despite her relatively young age (no one except those who needed to know knew for certain how old she was, although the consensus was that her fiftieth birthday was still to be celebrated). Five feet, four inches tall, she gave the appearance of being taller by the way she held herself. Her silver-blond hair was styled short, with chunky highlights and short layers to make her seem taller, and to elongate her round face. Her energy level was capable of fatiguing marathoners, her smile wide, white, and genuine. She ran the committee as though it were a Fortune 500 company, and Annabel didn't doubt that should the doctor's wife have chosen to build a business career, she would have shattered the glass ceiling into many pieces.

Frolich concluded her status report by saying, "As Bill said, we mustn't allow the tragedy of Ms. Lee's death to derail our efforts to make this year's Ball the biggest and best ever, to say nothing of the most profitable." She spoke directly to Annabel and another woman who was on her committee. "We'll be meeting with the full Ball staff at eleven. You'll excuse me. I have an appointment with the florist."

Frazier went through the remaining items on the agenda. The final notation was *Internal Investigation*. "Those of you at the emergency meeting last night are aware that we've decided to conduct our own investigation into Ms. Lee's death. One of the supers in *Tosca*, a . . ." He looked to Annabel.

"Pawkins," Annabel filled in. "Raymond Pawkins. He's a retired MPD homicide detective, as well as an opera lover."

"I know him," said the woman in charge of WNO's development program. "He has season tickets, has had them for years. He's a charming man."

"Yes, isn't he?" Annabel said.

Frazier broke into their conversation. "Camile will coordinate with Annabel on the arrangements to be made with Mr. Pawkins." He was referring to Camile Worthington, who headed up the board's executive committee, and who'd called Annabel at the Watergate to tell her about the emergency meeting. They agreed to meet privately once this meeting was concluded.

Frazier concluded by saying, "I hope what Laurie said will be heeded. We don't need the press twisting what any of us say, and that includes the use of this detective to help us investigate internally. Anything else?"

Annabel and Camile adjoined to a small office adjacent to the conference room.

"When can we get together with Mr. Perkins?" she asked.

"It's Pawkins," Annabel corrected. "I don't know, but I can call Mac on his cell. Maybe they're still together."

Mac and Pawkins were in the middle of breakfast when his cell phone rang.

"Hi, sweetheart," Annabel said. "I'm here with Camile Worthington. She's wondering when she and others can get together with Mr. Pawkins."

She heard Mac confer with Pawkins. "Ray says he's free all day."

"This afternoon at WNO headquarters? Say two?" was Annabel's suggestion.

Another confab between the men. "We'll be there," said Mac.

Annabel found it interesting that her husband would be with Pawkins at the meeting. She knew he had a break in his teaching schedule while his students studied for final exams. Still, it was an indication that he would do what she suspected, take a more active part in the investigation than his protest had promised. His tendency to warm up slowly to something new wasn't a matter of being difficult. Mackensie Smith was simply a man who didn't leap into strange waters without first testing their depth and temperature. Like any good lawyer.

Mac and Pawkins were finishing their coffee. Mac had dressed casually in response to the hot weather that was pressing down on the city. He was in chino slacks, a tangerine-colored polo shirt, and sneakers.

Pawkins, on the other hand, seemed impervious to the heat and humidity. He wore a beautifully tailored, blue poplin suit, a pale cream shirt, and a tie with a graphic of the *Mona Lisa* on its blue field. The air-conditioning in the restaurant was barely keeping up with the discomforting weather, and Mac dabbed at perspiration on his forehead from time to time. Pawkins never broke a sweat; Mac thought of the E. G. Marshall character in the film *Twelve Angry Men*.

"Where do you live, Ray?" Smith asked.

"Great Falls."

Mac's eyebrows went up. "Lovely area," he said.

"How does a retired cop live in such a high-rent district?" Pawkins said. "I fell into it. I rented a gatehouse for years owned by a wealthy real estate guy. He decided to sell and made me an offer I couldn't refuse. Actually, it's pretty modest, although I've put in some improvements. How do you like living in the Watergate?"

"We're very happy there."

"That's what counts."

"You said last night that something had been wedged into the wound to stop the bleeding. Any idea what it was?"

"A sponge."

"Oh? I had the feeling that you didn't know what it was."

"I didn't. I called Carl Berry this morning before meeting with you. He's lead on the case."

"You work fast."

"The faster the better where homicide is concerned. Carl is a good guy, a straight shooter, at least with me."

"You told him you were investigating for the opera company?"

Pawkins nodded.

"I imagine the powers-that-be there would prefer to keep it sub rosa," Smith said.

"To the extent that it can be. I'll need MPD cooperation, at least unofficially." He pushed back his chair, cocked his head, and grinned. "A sponge," he said. "Now, who would have access to a sponge on an empty stage at the Kennedy Center?"

"I have a feeling you'll answer that question."

"That's my intention." Pawkins motioned for the check.

They parted on the sidewalk in front of the restaurant and agreed to meet at the Opera's administrative offices at two. As they shook hands, Mac laughed.

"What's funny?" Pawkins asked.

"We spent an entire breakfast without any references from you to operas and opera singers."

"Deliberately," Pawkins said. "I sensed your discomfort when I fell into my habit of relating everything to opera. I promise to curb the temptation. Looking forward to working with you, Mac. It's nice to be walking on the winning side of the street."

NINE

Detective Carl Berry didn't care that his coffee had gotten cold. It was bad station-house brew, hot or cold, pure shellac. He'd been at First District headquarters since returning from the Kennedy Center and was feeling the effects of having pulled an all-nighter. With him were two detectives called in to assist in the Charise Lee investigation—William Portelain, an imposing, black, bearish, twenty-year veteran whose cynicism about almost everything in life had grown over the years until reaching a point of ongoing annoyance with bosses and colleagues; and Sylvia Johnson, another African American, who'd joined the D.C. force eleven years ago after being turned down by the police department in her native New York City—too many applicants, too few slots. A cousin from Washington had urged her to come here to seek the career in law enforcement she'd coveted since childhood. She'd been pursuing a degree in criminal justice since arriving, which struck Portelain as "pretty damn dumb."

"What are you goin' to do with that degree, lady?" he grumbled each time she spoke of her studies. "Won't do you a damn bit a good. You want to get ahead here, sleep with somebody. That's the only way a chick as black as you is goin' to get anywhere."

To which she replied, "If I do, it won't be with a gorilla like you, Willie. Nothing a loser like you can do for me." He'd laugh, a deep rumble, his feelings seemingly impervious to being hurt. Nor did her put-downs discourage him from making repeated passes at her, which were both annoying and strangely flattering. Although Willie didn't represent genuine allure to Sylvia, and his persistent negativity was potentially catching, she liked him and enjoyed working cases with him. He could be a good cop when he chose to be.

"What've we got?" Sylvia asked Carl Berry.

He slid a folder across the table to her. "Asian victim, twenty-eight, female, Canadian, stabbed in the chest at the Kennedy Center. Was an opera singer, studying with the folks over at the Washington Opera."

"They had more information than that on TV," Portelain said in a voice that resembled an idling engine on a motor boat, low and throaty.

"There's more, Willie," Berry said. Although younger than Portelain, and college educated, he knew he had the detective's respect. He opened a second folder and displayed its contents on the tabletop, which included photographs taken at the crime scene.

"She was a little thing, huh?" Portelain said. "I always thought opera singers were big and fat."

Johnson didn't say what she was thinking. If being big and fat was the only criterion to be an opera singer, Willie Portelain had a new career to look forward to.

The female detective held one of the color prints at arm's length. "What is it, a sponge?"

"Right," said Berry. "The ME's office sent this one over with the rest of the initial autopsy photos."

She studied it for a moment before saying, "This sponge was found *in* the wound?"

"Right again."

"The dude who did the deed was a pro," Portelain said.

"Or a damn talented amateur, the son-of-a-bitch," said Berry. "Either of you ever see something like this before?"

They shook their heads.

"Crocker was with me last night at the scene," Berry said, "but he's been pulled to work a drive-by in Southwest. Looks like the three of us caught this one."

"Opera, huh?" Portelain said, tossing the photos he'd been examining onto the table, like a poker player folding his hand. He yawned loudly and scratched the back of his head. "These opera types are strange, man," he said. "You ever been to one?"

Johnson was still busy looking at the photographs and didn't respond, but Berry said, "A couple of times. Not my thing. I'm a Steely Dan and Pink Floyd guy, but I kind of enjoyed it. Hey, by the way, guess who's also working the case."

Portelain looked up at Berry through thick salt-and-pepper eyebrows. "Who?"

"Ray Pawkins."

It was a duet from Portelain and Johnson: "Pawkins?"

"He's retired, man," Portelain said.

"He's coming back?" Johnson asked.

"No," Berry replied, "he's working as a PI for the Washington Opera."

"He's a fruitcake," Portelain said, chuckling.

"Ray is—was—a good detective," Berry said. "Damn good."

"Why is the Opera hiring a private eye?" Johnson asked.

"I spoke to Ray," said Berry. "According to him, the Opera board wants to resolve it themselves. I told him we'd work with him, within limits."

"Ray Pawkins, huh?" Portelain said, standing and hitching up his trousers. "He was always into opera and stuff like that."

"That's right," Berry concurred. "He was at the Kennedy Center last night when the victim was discovered. He's in the next show."

"He sings, too?" Sylvia Johnson said.

"An extra, a spear carrier," said Berry. "It doesn't matter. He'll go his way and we'll go ours. The deceased had a roommate, another student from the school." He consulted his notes. "Name's Christopher Warren, a piano player. Start with him, Willie. See where he was last night, try to get a handle on his relationship with her. Maybe they were more than roommates. Ask him about any guys she might have been involved with." He handed Portelain an address. "Carlos was there at Warren's last night with two evidence techs. They cleaned the place."

Portelain nodded.

"Sylvia, get together with somebody from that program she was in at the Washington Opera. The . . ." He consulted his notes again. "Domingo-Cafritz Young Artist Program. Get an idea of what she was like, who she hung out with, other singers who might have been jealous of her, stuff like that. Maybe somebody doesn't like Asian-Canadians who hit the high notes. Or miss them. I'll get a rundown from the ME on the sponge used to plug the wound."

"And we canvas every store that sells sponges," Portelain said. "Shouldn't take us more than a couple a years."

Berry ignored him. "I'm meeting the parents in an hour. We'll hook up back here at two—unless you get lucky."

He heard Johnson ask Portelain on their way from the room, "Can they pull prints from a sponge?"

"Hell, no. What are you doin' for dinner tonight? I found this great new ribs joint that serves . . ."

Berry smiled and shook his head. Maybe his father was right, he should have gone into investment banking, or become a lawyer. Too late for that now, he thought, which didn't dismay him. Carl Berry loved being a cop. Just that simple.

The assistant medical examiner assigned to autopsy Charise Lee's body had just completed that task and was relaxing in his office with coffee and a raspberry turnover when Ray Pawkins called his office.

"Hello, stranger," the ME said. His name was, fittingly, Les Cutter. Everyone thought it was a joke when first introduced to him. "How's retirement?"

"Wonderful," Pawkins said. "I never knew I could be so busy. Hear you got the opera singer case."

"What a wonderful town this is," Cutter said. " 'My secrets cry aloud, I have no need for tongue. My heart keeps an open house, my doors are widely flung.' "

"Nice," Pawkins said. "Who wrote it?"

"I forget. What can I do for you, my friend?"

"Tell me about the sponge you found in the deceased's chest."

"How did you know about that?"

" 'My secrets cry aloud, I have no need for'—the story's around. What kind of sponge is it?"

"It's a sponge, Ray."

"Like I have on my kitchen sink?"

Cutter paused. "As a matter of fact, the answer is no. It's different than that."

"When can I see it?"

"You can't. It's evidence."

"I never would have guessed that. I'm working the case."

"You retired."

"Not as a PI. The good folks over at the Washington Opera have hired me to look into it. I won't touch. I just want to see."

"No can do," Cutter said, taking a final bite of turnover and wiping his mouth with the back of his hand. "It's already with the evidence techs."

"You have a picture, of course," Pawkins said.

"Of course. More than one."

"Make a print for me, Les?"

Cutter exhaled loudly, which made his point better than any words could have.

"Les? I'll owe you."

"Maybe."

"That's all I can ask. Here's my address." He gave the ME a post-office box number in downtown D.C. "I know you're busy, Les, but take a minute to describe it for me. How big. Usual kitchen-sponge size?"

"Bigger, Ray. Not square like kitchen sponges. Round."

"Is that so? Color?"

"White, but discolored."

"How so?"

"A cream-colored stain. The sponge has some sort of velour on both sides."

"I definitely owe you. Looking forward to the photo. Everything good with you and the family?"

"Everything's fine. I have to go."

"You're my favorite ME, Les. *Ciao!*"

Pawkins had parked his car near the restaurant where he and Smith breakfasted. He'd made the call to Les Cutter from his cell phone in the front seat of his Mercedes. Now he paid the parking fee and headed across the Anacostia River to the District's Southeast quadrant, where he found a metered spot on Eighth Street. After taking a moment to decide whether he'd parked the car in a relatively safe place, he walked up the street and entered a shop bearing the sign BACKSTAGE INC. A woman greeted him and asked what he was looking for.

"Just a sponge," he said. "A makeup sponge."

"We have a variety of them," she said, offering him a tray on which assorted sponges were neatly arranged. "We have Ben Nye, Kryolan—"

He picked one up from the tray and examined it. "Is this the largest you have?" he asked.

"Yes. It's over three inches. It's velour, perfect for applying foundation quickly to large areas."

He nodded. "How much?"

"Seven dollars."

He paid her in cash, left, climbed into his car, and took the sponge from its paper bag, holding it at various angles. He formed a small circle with the index finger and thumb of his left hand, wadded up the sponge in his right, and wedged it into the circle. He glanced in the rearview mirror. A group of teenagers with overalls hanging low and wearing baseball hats at various angles swaggered along the cracked sidewalk in his direction, laughing loudly and punching one another. Pawkins started the engine, reached beneath his seat, and withdrew a licensed 9mm Glock, which he placed next to him on the passenger seat, his right hand resting easily on it. The group stopped abreast of the car. One of them leaned over and asked, "What's up, man? You looking for something?"

"No," Pawkins answered.

"Those are some wheels, man," another member of the gang said. He came around the back of the car and placed his hand on the open window on Pawkins' side.

"Get your hand off," Pawkins said quietly.

The youth pulled back his hand and said, "Oh, I'm sorry, mister." With that, he put his hand there again.

Pawkins lifted the Glock from the seat and held it inches from the young man's face. The teenager raised both hands and backed away. One of his friends saw the gun from the sidewalk side and said, "Man's crazy. Hey, no offense, man."

Pawkins watched them move quickly down the street and disappear around a corner. He replaced the Glock beneath the seat, raised the window, turned the AC on full blast, and pulled away, thinking as he did of John Dillinger's alleged comment, *Kindness and a gun will get you further than kindness alone.*

"How true," he said aloud, and laughed.

TEN

Willie Portelain stopped for a slice of pepperoni pizza on his way to interview Charise Lee's roommate. Although he'd eaten a big breakfast only two hours earlier—eggs over easy, well-done sausage, hash browns, and whole wheat toast—he was hungry almost as soon as he'd finished that first meal of the day. His prodigious appetite was a running joke among colleagues and friends. Some suggested he cut down on his intake and drop some weight. "Body needs fuel," he'd answer, "like a car or plane. My body tells me what it wants, I don't argue with it."

"As long as he doesn't have to chase some perp on foot," other detectives said behind his back, laughing at that visual. Willie would have agreed with them. His greatest fear when on duty was to be called upon to run after someone.

The apartment shared by Charise and Warren was on N Street, between Logan and Thomas circles. Once an elegant enclave of Richardsonian and Victorian townhouses, it had deteriorated over the years into a troubled neighborhood, until a determined gentrification was launched. Still, it was one of those D.C. areas best avoided late at night.

The apartment was on the ground floor of a four-story gray stucco building, its windows covered by heavy, black wrought-iron bars. A warning label affixed to one of the windows proclaimed that the premises were protected by an alarm company. Portelain read it and grinned. The decal was store bought, just a piece of paper, not connected with any alarm company that he'd ever heard of.

He stood at the front door and took in his immediate surroundings. Not a bad block, he thought. He'd been on worse ones. He remained standing there, not attempting to enter the building, formulating the questions he would ask. Satisfied that he'd mentally covered all the bases, he leaned close to a panel on which the building's flats were listed, pushed the buzzer next to WARREN/LEE, and heard it sound inside.

"Yes?" a tinny male voice said through the small speaker.

"Police," Portelain announced. "I'm here to talk to Mr. Christopher Warren."

"He's not here."

"Who are you?"

"Who did you say you were?"

"Detective Portelain, First District Homicide." Despite the official change of nomenclature from Homicide to Crimes Again Persons, no cop used the new term.

"Just a minute," the voice from inside said. A minute later the harsh sound of the metal lock being disengaged prompted the detective to push through the now unlocked door and go to the apartment. He knocked. No one responded. He knocked again. Someone on the other side of the door coughed. Willie's fist was raised for yet another assault on the door when it opened.

Facing him was a man of medium height with a puffy face the color of bleached flour. His hair was brown bordering on blond, with long strands hanging limply over his ears and neck. He wore a rumpled tan summer suit over a pink polo shirt, and sandals.

"Detective Portelain," Willie said, showing his badge.

The man nodded. "You're here to see Chris. He's not here. He's—"

"I'm here about what happened last night at the Kennedy Center," Portelain said. "You are?"

"I'm Chris' agent. Charise's agent, too, until this happened. God, what a shock."

"You mind if I come in?" Portelain asked.

"No, of course not." He stepped aside to allow the lumbering detective to enter the small living room, which seemed even smaller when preempted by Willie's large body. As he surveyed the room, Portelain asked, "When is Mr. Warren coming back?"

"I don't know. He's playing a rehearsal at Takoma Park."

"I didn't catch your name," Portelain said, pulling out a notebook and pen.

"Melincamp. Philip Melincamp."

"You knew the deceased pretty well," Willie said.

"Yes, of course. A good agent knows his clients. At least he'd better." He made a sound that passed for a laugh.

"You, ah, you live here in D.C.?"

"No. Toronto. My agency is in Toronto. Charise and Chris are both from there."

"You're visiting."

"Yes."

"Mr. Warren, he's a piano player."

"He's a *pianist*. A very fine one."

"I don't see a piano here."

Melincamp sighed. "I was lucky to find this apartment for them, with or without a piano. He does all his practicing at Takoma Park."

"Uh-huh." Portelain noted the agent's comment. "His roommate gets killed and he's off playing for some rehearsal?"

"He didn't want to, but I encouraged him. There was nothing to be gained by staying here. Music would be an escape from this dreadful thing that's happened."

"Mind if I sit?" Portelain asked. "My back's been acting up."

"No, of course not."

Melincamp removed a pile of sheet music from a well-worn, once-red love seat and motioned for the detective to sit. The couch's cushions looked soft and puffy. Willie hesitated. He'd have trouble getting up from them, he decided, and remained standing. "When did you arrive in D.C.?" he asked, leaning against a windowsill.

"Yesterday. My partner and I arrived yesterday."

"You have a partner?"

"Yes."

"What hotel you staying at?"

"I'm not staying at a hotel. I'm staying here."

Portelain raised his eyebrows for a sweep of the room. Melincamp grasped what the detective was thinking. "The couch," he said. "Pulls out into a bed. Charise and Chris each have a bedroom back there." He pointed to two closed doors off the living room. "Your colleagues — I suppose that's what they're called — were here last night and searched the bedrooms. They left a mess."

"That so?" Portelain said. "Evidence techs are usually pretty neat. You can lodge a complaint."

"I didn't mean it that way."

"Your partner staying here, too?"

"No. She prefers a hotel. There's only room for one of us here."

Willie's feet and back were bothering him now and he decided the couch would have to do. He sank into it, struggled to come forward, and managed a position that wasn't too uncomfortable. "What's your partner's name?" He asked.

"Zöe Baltsa."

He wrote the name in his notebook, spelling it phonetically. "So, tell me, Mr. Melincamp, when was the last time you saw the deceased?"

"She may be dead," the agent said, "but she still has a name. Ms. Lee, you mean."

"Okay. Ms. Lee."

Melincamp said, "I didn't mean to offend."

"Takes a lot to offend me," Portelain said. "Been offended by the best offenders. When you see her last?"

"A week ago."

"A week ago? You didn't see her last night? Yesterday?"

"No. Zöe and I arrived yesterday with the intention to spend time with her. Chris was worried. Charise hadn't shown up in class or for her costume fitting yesterday afternoon. I was worried, too. Looks like I had reason to be."

Portelain thought for a moment about the questions he'd intended to ask. "Did Ms. Lee and her roommate, this guy Chris, have more of a relationship than just sharing an apartment?"

"What do you mean?"

"You know, were they boyfriend and girlfriend?"

Melincamp guffawed. "Of course not. They were both focused on their careers. Chris aspires to become an accompanist for singers. He's remarkably talented. Charise had the whole world in front of her. My God, what magnificent music came from that little girl. I've never seen anything like it in all my years as a singer's agent."

"What about other guys? She must have had boyfriends."

"I wouldn't know about that," Melincamp responded.

"Sure you would," Portelain said. "Like you told me, a good agent gets to know his clients real well."

"There are limits," Melincamp said. "I don't pry into their private lives."

Portelain jotted nonsense in his notebook, not because he needed a written record of what was said, but because he was deciding where to next take the conversation. He looked up at Melincamp. "I'd like to see her bedroom," he said.

"Why? They were all over it last night."

"Indulge me," said Portelain, getting up with an audible "Oomph."

Melincamp pointed to one of the closed doors. "In there. That was her room."

Portelain opened Ms. Lee's bedroom door and observed without entering. It was a tiny space. A single twin bed took up one half. He noted that the bed was stripped, probably by the evidence techs, who would want the sheets and pillowcase for analysis. He stepped inside, and banged his shin against the bed's footboard, eliciting a burst of four-letter words under his breath. A small, white dresser was against the wall. He opened its drawers. Empty. He turned and looked at the opposite wall, on which opera posters were attached with pushpins. He recognized one name, *La Boheme.*

"Anything else?" Melincamp asked from the doorway.

"No, that's about it," Portelain said. "I'd like to talk to your partner, and Mr. Warren." He handed Melincamp his card. "Have them call me to set up an interview."

"All right," the agent said, "although I assure you, they know nothing that would be of help to you."

Portelain ignored the disclaimer, thanked Melincamp for his time, and returned to his car, parked a half block away. He squeezed behind the wheel and made further notes before turning the ignition and pulling into traffic. It was almost eleven, which posed a dilemma. He was hungry, but wanted to wait until noon—conventional lunchtime—before eating again. Stopped at a light, he opened the glove compartment, found a Snickers bar, and savored it.

ELEVEN

Sylvia Johnson extracted cash from an ATM before heading for Takoma Park. Dressed in tight, cream-colored slacks, a cinnamon T-shirt, a rust-colored button-down shirt worn loose and open, and black pumps, she garnered her usual number of turned male heads as she walked down the street and entered the bank. Her ebony coloring—face, body, and hair—was exotic, memorable, and altogether stunning. She walked with purpose, long-legged strides, head held regally, a woman to be reckoned with, a splendid specimen. She'd once been approached by a photographer who'd spotted her at a Maryland beach and wanted to feature her in a *Playboy* spread. She declined, not because of modesty or morality, but for three more pragmatic reasons: her mother would be horrified; MPD brass wouldn't be pleased; and she didn't want her cop colleagues to see her in the buff. Other than that, the offer had a certain appeal.

With a fresh hundred dollars in her purse, she returned to First District headquarters, where she checked out an unmarked blue Chevy sedan from the motor pool, headed up 16th Street to the

Opera's rehearsal space, took a right at Walter Reed Medical Center, soon to be demolished in favor of a more modern veterans' health facility, and arrived at WNO's Takoma Park building. She'd considered calling ahead but decided there might be more to gain by simply showing up. It was often more productive that way.

A marked patrol car with two uniformed officers sat near the entrance to the parking lot adjacent to the building. Johnson pulled up next to it and rolled down her window.

"Hey, Detective Johnson, you caught this case, huh?" the driver asked.

"Looks like it, with Willie Portelain. Carl Berry's the lead. Anybody inside?"

"Nah. A couple of evidence guys were here earlier, cleaning out her locker, stuff like that. They told us to sit here." He laughed. "That's it, just sit here."

Johnson knew why they were here. Department brass had recently initiated a policy of dispatching marked cars to places under investigation to create a visible police presence, more for PR purposes than anything. A TV remote truck and a couple of cars containing print reporters were parked across the street. Hopefully, video of the police vehicle on the evening news would establish that MPD was on the case.

She left her vehicle next to the squad car and entered the building, where she displayed her badge as an introduction. "I'd like to speak with whomever's in charge of the Young Artist Program."

"Is anyone expecting you?"

"No, but that's okay."

The receptionist placed a call. When she hung up, she said, "Ms. McCarthy will be out shortly." She lowered her voice. "Have you found the killer yet?"

"We're working on it," Johnson said. "Did you know the victim?"

"Sure. She was here every day. She was so nice, a really great gal. And talented, too."

"So I understand. But she must have had some enemies, someone she didn't get along with."

The receptionist's face twisted in thought. "I can't think of anybody," she said.

"Did you socialize with her?" Johnson asked.

"No. Well, we had coffee together sometimes, and I got to go to some events where she was performing."

"I've seen pictures of her," said Johnson. "She was very pretty, must have had plenty of guys hitting on her."

The receptionist started to reply, when a woman entered the area and extended her hand to Johnson. "I'm Louise McCarthy, assistant to the director of the Domingo-Cafritz Young Artist Program."

"Can we speak privately?" Johnson asked.

"Sure. We'll go to my office."

After some preliminary conversation about the program and Ms. McCarthy's role in it, Johnson got to the point. "I need to know everything there is to know about Charise Lee."

"Whew," McCarthy said. "Everything?"

Johnson nodded, a notebook on her lap, pen poised.

"Where do I begin? You must understand that any knowledge I have of Charise is from my dealings with her in the program. We weren't friends in the usual sense. My role is as an administrator."

"Let's start there," said Johnson. "What sort of a student was she?"

"In what way?"

"Serious? Not so serious? A rule breaker? In trouble? Abrasive? Get along with others?"

McCarthy's responses were uniformly positive.

"Did she have any friends? Close ones?"

"I, ah—I suppose so."

"The reason I ask is that from what I've heard about opera singers, they tend to be temperamental and high-strung."

McCarthy laughed. "I suppose some are," she said, "but our students are encouraged to get along with one another."

"But there has to be some jealousy among them," Johnson offered.

"I wouldn't know about that," McCarthy replied, not sounding as though she meant it.

Johnson decided to change the subject. "When did you last see Ms. Lee?"

"I really don't remember. I know she didn't show up for classes yesterday, because one of her instructors reported it to the office."

"Did she miss many classes?"

"No" was accompanied by a shake of the head. "Her attendance record was good, I think. I can check."

"Please do."

McCarthy opened a file drawer behind her desk, removed a folder, and looked at it. "No," she said, replacing the file and closing the door. "Her attendance record is about average."

Johnson smiled. "You make it sound as though an average attendance record means missing a lot of classes."

"I don't want to mislead you," McCarthy said. "Singers in the program—all opera singers, for that matter—are naturally concerned with their voices. They're blessed with wonderful voices and take very good care of them. Charise missed her share of classes for medical reasons. She'd been seeing one of the physicians at George Washington University's Voice Treatment Center. They're tops in their field. Many of our students have doctors there."

"I see," Johnson said, noting what McCarthy had said. "Who else can I talk to, someone who was particularly close to Ms. Lee."

"Let me think," McCarthy said. "There's Chris Warren. He and Charise are both from Toronto. They roomed together."

Johnson nodded. Warren was who Portelain had been told to interview.

"Their agent would probably have more to offer than anyone. He's from Toronto, too. His name is Melincamp. Philip Melincamp. He has a partner, who might be able to help you. Her name is Zöe Baltsa."

Johnson noted the names, closed her notebook, and stood. "I appreciate your time, Ms. McCarthy. Here's my card. Please call if you think of anything that might be of interest, if anyone else goes missing." She'd picked up the "gone missing" elocution from a British cop show.

"Of course. All I can say is that I hope you find who killed

Charise, and do it fast. Having some nut wandering around the Kennedy Center killing young women is setting everyone on edge."

"We'll do our best. Now, I'd like to see the facility."

"I'll be happy to show you anything you'd like, Detective."

After an impromptu half-hour tour, which included the costume rooms, they ended up in one of the rehearsal spaces, where a young woman practiced an aria, accompanied by a pianist.

"That's Christopher Warren," McCarthy told Johnson, referring to the pianist.

"Ms. Lee's roommate."

"Yes."

Obviously Willie wasn't questioning him. Next thought: What was he doing here playing the piano so soon after his roommate had been murdered?

"I'd like to speak with him," she told McCarthy.

"I'll go tell him."

"No," Johnson said, "I'll wait until they're finished. I wouldn't want to interrupt."

She and McCarthy took seats across the large space from the performers.

"It's beautiful," Johnson said. "I don't know that song."

"It's an aria from Donizetti's *Lucia*. 'Regnava nel silenzio,' I believe."

Like most Americans, Johnson's exposure to opera was nonexistent, aside from those occasional snippets that managed to slip into the public vocabulary. She closed her eyes and allowed the sheer power and beauty of the singer's voice to penetrate her senses. She loved music, and had enjoyed the usual teenager's dream of becoming a rock star. But she didn't like rock 'n' roll, nor did hip-hop or rap appeal. Her tastes tended to female jazz singers like Ella Fitzgerald and Sarah Vaughan, Nancy Wilson and Billie Holiday. But while listening to the opera singer she recognized that this was, indeed, something special. How could anyone, male or female, produce such sounds? Singers like this must be aberrations, physical freaks, their superior vocal apparatus a gift from above. From God? Her mother would claim that, although Matilda Johnson's daughter wasn't sure, and probably never would be. It was hard to believe in a God while working Washington, D.C.'s mean streets, on which lives were taken for a pair of sneakers, or over petty jealousies.

Her mind drifted to the reason she was there, the murder. Had Charise Lee sounded like the woman performing at that moment? Would she have become a world-famous diva? Was she better than this young woman in the rehearsal hall, and if so, who would make that judgment? How long could such magnificent voices hold up? The singer sang in Italian. Were all operas written in foreign languages? If so, how could the singers learn all those languages?

She opened her eyes and observed the singer. She was tall and heavy, which fit the stereotypical belief about female opera singers. But Charise Lee had been described in the report as small, perhaps even petite. Asian-Canadian. In Washington to further her career, ending up stabbed to death. God must have had a bad hair day.

Christopher Warren and the singer finished the piece and conferred about the sheet music.

"You said it was an aria?" Johnson asked. "That's a solo, right?"

"Right, but it's more than that. Arias give the singers an opportunity to express their inner feelings and emotions musically, like a spoken soliloquy in a play." She smiled. "A large percentage of opera audiences come just to hear the arias."

"I see," Johnson said, wondering whether what she'd just been thinking would qualify as an aria.

McCarthy led Johnson to the piano, where the two musicians were preparing to leave, and introduced the detective.

"I'm sorry about your friend," Johnson told them.

The singer's eyes misted and her fist went to her mouth. "Excuse me," she said, and ran from the room.

"I'd better go after her," Warren said.

"I will," McCarthy said. "Detective Johnson wants to ask you a few questions."

Johnson and Warren faced each other. She pegged him at six feet tall, five inches taller than her. He appeared to be in good physical shape beneath his jeans and powder-blue T-shirt with a silk screen of

Mozart on the chest. He was good-looking in a conventional sense, facial features where they were supposed to be and of the proper size. More interesting to her were his eyes, as cold as a gray winter's day, and his hands, large and strong, with long fingers. A pianist's hands, she decided.

"I have nothing to say," he said flatly.

"You don't have a choice," she said, her tone matching his.

"What kind of a person are you?" he asked. "My best friend has been murdered, and you want me to talk about it? Give me a break."

"Your 'best friend' didn't catch a break, Mr. Warren. I'd think you'd want to do everything you can to find her killer."

"That's your job," he said. "Sorry, but I have nothing to say." With that, he angrily grabbed the sheet music from the piano's music desk and started to walk away.

"Mr. Warren," Johnson called after him.

He stopped and turned. "Just leave me alone," he said.

She pointed an index finger at him. "I can detain you as a material witness," she said. "Maybe you'd prefer that."

"I told you, I don't know anything about what happened to Charise."

"Fine," she said. "Then you shouldn't mind answering a few questions."

"I'm going to call my embassy. I'm Canadian. I'm not an American citizen. I have rights."

Johnson closed the gap between them. "I'm losing patience," she said. "Either we sit down and have a nice, friendly chat, or we can have a less friendly talk at police headquarters. Your choice. And don't pull your 'I'm not an American citizen' BS with me. When it comes to a murder, all bets are off. Get it, Mr. Warren? You may be Canadian, but we do speak the same language."

His face scrunched up as though trying to locate a file or program in his brain that would provide him with an answer. She noticed that his hand not holding the music was curled into a tight fist.

"Time's up," she said.

"All right," he said glumly.

And so they talked.

TWELVE

The two o'clock meeting at the Washington National Opera's administrative offices ended at three, and Mac and Annabel Smith and Ray Pawkins spent a few minutes outside the building.

"I'm glad they gave you what you wanted, Ray," Mac said. "Unlimited access to anyone and everything."

"I wouldn't have it any other way," Pawkins said. "The minute someone throws up a roadblock, you know you're in trouble."

"Where will you start?" Annabel asked.

"The Kennedy Center," Pawkins replied. "I have some friends there who might help shed some light. I'll also make contact with Ms. Lee's family and friends. By the way, you were interested in what had been stuffed into her wound that kept her from bleeding too much. I said it was a sponge. Turns out to have been a theatrical sponge." He reached into a briefcase and withdrew the one he'd purchased that morning.

"That's it?" Annabel asked, incredulous.

"Similar," Pawkins said, laughing gently. "I'm confident this is very much like the sponge that was actually used. I'll know more after I've seen the bloody one. I'd better get going. See you tonight at rehearsal, Mac."

"There's a rehearsal tonight?"

"Afraid so," Annabel said lightly.

"I thought you might drop out now that you're investigating the murder," Mac said to Pawkins.

"To the contrary. I can't think of a better situation than to be a super at this time. Amazing what you can pick up in a dressing room. You two take care."

The Smiths watched the tall, lanky detective saunter away, very much like a tourist out for a stroll through an Italian piazza.

"Interesting guy, huh?" Mac said as he and his wife headed for their car.

"Yes, interesting—and strange."

Mac stopped. "How do you mean 'strange'?"

"I don't really know," Annabel said. "There's something about him that's—well, that's off-kilter, if you know what I mean."

Mac smiled, and they continued walking. "Have you ever known a Homicide detective who wasn't off-kilter?" he said. "You have to be a little crazy to work Homicide. Either that, or it *makes* you crazy."

"Not having known many Homicide detectives, I'll take your word for it."

They got into their car and headed without delay for their Watergate apartment. Rufus would be waiting to be walked.

"What *I* find interesting about him, Mac, is the dichotomy between having spent a career investigating grisly homicides, and loving opera and art. He said he's handled some private cases where rare musical manuscripts have been stolen, and works of visual art, too. There are two very different sides to your Mr. Raymond Pawkins."

"There are two sides to everyone, Annie."

"Including you?"

"Sure."

"What's your other side, Mac? I only know one, the one I love. Will I love your other side when it emerges?"

"Surely not. That's why I keep it securely under wraps. If it ever broke loose—well, it wouldn't be pretty."

"Show it to me."

"Is that an advance, lady?"

"Take it as you will, sir."

"I intend to."

Detectives Johnson and Portelain had their own two o'clock meeting, with their boss, Carl Berry.

"Okay," Berry said, "run it past me. Willie, what did you get from the roommate?"

"Nothing. *Nada.* He wasn't there. He was—"

"He was accompanying a singer at Takoma Park," Johnson said.

"Yeah, that's right," Portelain said.

"I interviewed him," Johnson said.

"He's playing the piano right after his roommate dies?" Berry said.

"That's what I thought," Portelain said.

"So did I," Johnson concurred. "Strange guy, Carl. Cold as ice, somber, never saw him break a smile the whole time I was with him. Told me to call his embassy, claims he has rights because he's Canadian."

"Cold? Like in cold-blooded killer?"

"Maybe."

"Alibi?"

"Nothing ironclad. He claims he was out partying the night before last. Hadn't seen the deceased all day. Claims he was worried about her, but also said she often disappeared for a day or two."

" 'Disappeared'?" Portelain said. "What did he mean by that?"

"I think he meant she sort of went underground now and then, maybe needing time alone. At least that's what I took from it."

"Other people with him when he was partying? Where was the

party? Has he got any receipts? From the way you describe him, he's not the partying type."

"He said he had too much to drink and can't remember who he was with or where they went," Johnson reported.

"The more you talk," Berry said, "the less he talks, the more I'm interested in your piano player."

"Might be he decides to go home to Canada," Portelain said. "I'd haul him in and yank his passport till he checks out."

"I'm thinking the same thing," Berry said. "What else did he tell you, Sylvia?"

"That he hadn't seen her for more than a day, that she never came home the night before last. By the way, he was at the Kennedy Center last night when they discovered her."

"Right. I have his name on the list I took. He's an extra in the opera they're rehearsing."

"He didn't sound too happy about it," Johnson said. "He told me it was humiliating for a pianist like himself to be an extra—no, he called himself a 'super,' I think—and cursed whoever arranged for him to be in the show."

"Temperamental, huh?"

"According to the woman I spoke with at the Young Artist Program, they discourage temperament."

"I'll go upstairs and see if we can get a judge to issue a hold on this guy to keep him from skipping. Where's he staying?"

Johnson responded, "He says he's at the apartment he shared with the deceased." To Portelain: "You were there, Willie?"

"Yup. Obviously, the kid wasn't around, because he was with you, but a guy who claims to be their agent was there." He consulted his notes. "Name's Philip Melincamp. He's from Toronto, Canada. Got a partner named Zöe Baltsa."

"You meet her?"

"Nope, Professor. She's staying in a hotel. Melincamp bunks at the deceased's apartment."

Berry grunted, tilted back in his chair, and ran his fingers over the short-cropped salt-and-pepper hair on his temple. Willie often called him "Professor," not because of any wisdom or advanced degrees he possessed. It was the way he dressed—chinos, button-down shirts, always blue (he owned a dozen of them), nondescript ties, and tan, thick-soled desert boots. To Willie, men who dressed that way were usually seen on college campuses.

"Bring the Warren kid in," the professor-cum-cop said. "We'll talk to him again, see if his story changes."

"Let's go," Willie told Sylvia, getting up with difficulty. "Buy you a chili dawg on the way."

Berry raised his eyebrows and didn't try to stifle his smile. "Bet you haven't had an offer as good as that in a long time, Sylvia."

"You're right—fortunately. Come on, Willie, you can have your chili dog and I'll provide the Pepto."

"I love this lady," Willie announced loudly as they left Berry's office. "Love her!"

THIRTEEN

"**B**ased upon an elevated level of intercepted terrorist 'chatter,' the alert level in Washington, D.C., has been raised from yellow-one to orange-two."

That terse announcement was delivered at five o'clock that afternoon by the Department of Homeland Security Secretary, Wilbur Murtaugh. The newest cabinet member declined to elaborate, and left the podium without taking reporters' questions, leaving them, and by extension the American public, to speculate on how, where, and when they might die.

❧

It had been a day of press conferences around Washington, each producing a news story of greater consequence than the mere murder of a promising opera singer. The president had spoken that morning in the Rose Garden about progress, or lack of it, in Iraq and Korea, contradicting military leaders who painted a less rosy picture than the Commander in Chief. The Treasury Secretary delivered a glass-half-full analysis of the economy to Congressional leaders, despite numbers that indicated considerably less in the glass. The leader of the air traffic controllers' union predicted a bleak future for airline safety unless more controllers were hired. And then there was Secretary Murtaugh's announcement that some vague, unstated threat to national security had changed the color of the threat meter.

Wearing his customary turquoise bolo tie and pointy, tooled cowboy boots—he'd recently served a lackluster one term as governor of Oklahoma—he made his announcement in the Homeland Security department's temporary headquarters at the Nebraska Avenue Complex. The complex, consisting of thirty-two buildings on thirty-eight acres, was the permanent home to the Naval Security Station. Heavily guarded, it was surrounded by residential neighborhoods.

The Department of Homeland Security's decision to become tenants of the complex did not thrill its neighbors. A citizen's committee had been formed to protest the traffic congestion and parking violations that had developed since late 2002 when DHS began moving in personnel and material. The complex's community relations staff did what it could to soothe neighbors without resorting to what it considered the ham-handed truth, that a few traffic jams was an economical price to pay for protecting the neighbors and the nation against terrorist annihilation.

It hadn't been easy finding appropriate space to house the Department of Homeland Security's headquarters and many of its almost two hundred thousand employees. The situation was one of few that could not be attributed to the current president. The major problem could be traced back . . . well, to George Washington's administration. The first president had signed into law a statute requiring that all government "offices" be located within the District of Columbia, unless exempted by legislative act. The CIA, Department of Defense, and Nuclear Regulatory Commission had received such dispensation and had located their agencies outside the District. But DHS, despite its lofty mission to protect the homeland, had not as yet, and so it was limited to finding space within D.C., settling on the Nebraska Avenue Complex, at least for the time being.

The secretary's one-sided press conference had resulted from a frantic series of meetings held since early morning in secured conference rooms throughout headquarters.

❧

The genesis of those meetings had occurred three days earlier in an alley off King Feisal Street, in Amman, Jordan, where Ghaleb Rihnai played a spirited game of tric trac, the Arab name for backgammon, with a dour young Iraqi who'd moved to the Jordanian capital soon after the Americans invaded his home country. The table on which the game board rested was an overturned crate. Rihnai sipped from a lethal cup of strong black coffee. His opponent looked up from the board only occasionally to inhale from his narghile. Whenever he exhaled, the smoke from the water pipe created a haze over the board, like morning fog on a river. It was four in the afternoon, two months to the day since the Jordanian, Rihnai, and the young Iraqi had first met, or to be more accurate, two months since Rihnai had made an effort to befriend the Iraqi.

"You're winning," the Iraqi said, not attempting to conceal his displeasure.

"Yes, I see that I am, but the game is not over. Roll the dice and pray for good fortune, my friend."

The Iraqi's prayers were answered. Twenty minutes later he emerged victorious.

The Iraqi carefully returned the board, dice, and small disks to the bag in which he kept them, and the two men left the area, where others continued their games. They walked slowly and seemingly without purpose, stopping at an occasional stall to look at goods and foods being sold, or to chat with familiar shop owners. They eventually climbed the hill leading to ancient Amman, where the Jebel Qala'at, the Citadel, an ancient fortress rebuilt by the Romans during the reign of Marcus Aurelius, provided glorious views of the surrounding valleys and of Raghdan, the Royal Palace. They sat without speaking beneath a gnarled olive tree alongside a stream known as Seil Amman, a tributary of the Zerqa River.

"You saw your brother in Baghdad?" Rihnai asked, breaking the silence. His friend had returned from the beleaguered Iraqi city only days earlier.

"Yes, I saw him."

"He is well?"

"He has been arrested twice by the Americans."

"Bastards. He is free now?"

"Yes, for the moment."

"His arrests have not changed the plans, I pray."

"The plans go forward. In fact . . ."

"Yes?"

"They are ready."

Rihnai turned to face the Iraqi, whose youthful, almost angelic olive face and black eyes beneath a wet mop of jet-black hair defined sadness. At the same time, there was fire behind the eyes, simmering coals waiting to burst into flame.

"That is good news, indeed," Rihnai said. "Tell me, what part can I play?"

"You have already been of great help, Ghaleb," the Iraqi said, "but you will be called upon to play an even greater role in the days ahead. You have many friends in America."

"There are some I consider friends," Rihnai said. "My Arab friends. The Americans I know from studying at their university are not friends. They are the enemy and always will be. My friends are here, in Jordan and Iraq. You are my friend."

"And I am grateful for that. The money you have given me is so important."

"No, no," Rihnai said, wagging his index finger, "I gave you nothing. You worked and earned it."

The Iraqi's lips parted in a semblance of a smile. "The American goods you arrange to have shipped here are much in demand. I don't ask how you avoid the government and its red tape, but you obviously have your ways."

"My years with the infidels were not wasted. My degree is in business, the American way of doing business, cheat and lie, make your fortunes on the backs of the workers, and abandon them when it is time." Rihnai laughed. "I was a good student, huh?"

"Very good, Ghaleb. Very, very good."

Rihnai looked out over the stream that ran fast and deep from recent rains. He said as though addressing the water, "You say the plan is ready to be put into action. When?"

"I do not know for certain, but soon. That is what my brother has told me."

Still without looking at his friend, Rihnai said, "It will shake the Americans to their core."

"It is time. Too much time has passed since the towers came down. It is time to strike again."

"Yes. The time is here."

They returned to Rihnai's apartment, where the Iraqi fell asleep on the couch while Rihnai answered e-mail messages on his laptop. At eight, they went to one of Amman's most expensive restaurants and feasted on *mensef,* roast lamb stuffed with rice and spiced with cinnamon, pine nuts, and almonds; *makheedh,* beaten yogurt combined with the fat of mutton; *salata bi tahini* dressed with sesame oil paste; and finished their celebratory meal with many cups of *qahwa,* bitter, thin coffee flavored with cardamom seed, and rich, sticky pastries. Sated, they returned to Rihnai's apartment, where he broke out bottles of red wine that had been included in one of his illegal shipments from the United States. Drunk and happy, they hugged, and the Iraqi eventually stumbled down the stairs and into the cool, damp night.

Rihnai placed a call as soon as the Iraqi was gone. He was on the phone for only a few seconds. He played a DVD containing episodes of *The Sopranos* on his laptop, constantly checking his watch as he did. Two hours later, he shut off the computer and carried his bicycle down the stairs. After ensuring that his Iraqi friend hadn't decided to linger in a restaurant across the street, or hadn't fallen asleep on the sidewalk, he mounted the bike and pedaled fast down the King's Highway, until reaching a small village twelve miles to the east. He pulled behind a one-story gray stone cottage. A yellow light inside slithered through a crack in the drapes covering the windows. Rihnai went to the rear door and knocked—three times, a pause, then two sets of two raps each.

"Rihnai?" a male voice asked from behind the heavy, rough-hewn door.

"Yes."

A dead bolt was activated and the door opened slowly and noisily. Facing Rihnai was a large man wearing tan cargo shorts with multiple pockets, sandals, and a T-shirt without markings. He had a round, ruddy face. His hair was blond, bordering on orange. His moustache was gray and in need of trimming. Rihnai knew him only as M.T.

Rihnai stepped inside and the door was closed behind him, the bolt slid into the locked position. The room was small and square, with little furniture. A table and two rail-back chairs stood in the middle. The only light was a faux Tiffany lamp hanging over the table. A digital tape recorder the size of a pack of cigarettes was in the center of the table; a tiny microphone with cables leading to the recorder sat in front of each chair.

"Sit down," M.T. said, indicating one of the seats. "Wine? Whiskey?"

"Whiskey. Scotch if you have it."

"I always have Scotch," M.T. said, his British accent now evident. He poured from a bottle into two tumblers, placed the glasses and bottle on the table, and took the second seat. "So, you finally have something of value, Ghaleb," he said, his elbows resting on the tabletop, his hands folded beneath his chin.

"Yes," Rihnai responded, tasting his drink. He pulled a package of four Hoyo de Monterrey cigars from his pocket and offered one to the Brit.

"Thank you, no," M.T. said. "Nasty habit. You should give it up for your health, Ghaleb."

"Cuban," Rihnai said, lighting the cigar. "The best. I get them in the Canadian shipments."

M.T. laughed. "I've always enjoyed the story about President Kennedy, who enjoyed Cuban cigars. When he knew he'd be signing into law a ban on importing all things Cuban, including cigars, he dispatched his press secretary—Salinger, I think it was—to buy every Cuban cigar he could find. Delivered five hundred or so to the president."

If Rihnai found humor in the anecdote, he didn't display it. He drew on his cigar, sending a plume of blue smoke in his handler's direction, and drank more Scotch.

"I always find it interesting," M.T. said, "that even the most devout Muslims enjoy whiskey under the right circumstances."

Rihnai ignored the comment and finished what was in his glass. He slid the empty glass in front of the Brit, who refilled it.

"So, tell me what you've heard, Ghaleb. I assume it comes from your newfound Iraqi chum."

"Yes."

"Glad to hear it. It's costing us a bloody fortune providing you with cover. The pencil-pushers have been complaining. Frankly, Ghaleb, they're close to shutting down your operation."

"That would be a mistake," Rihnai said.

"I'm afraid that's not for you, or me, to decide. So, tell me why we meet here at this ungodly hour." He pushed a button on the recorder.

Rihnai spent the next half hour telling the Englishman what he'd learned from the Iraqi. M.T. said nothing during the monologue. When Rihnai was finished, he was asked, "You have faith in your friend's account of things?"

"Of course. He met with his brother only days ago in Baghdad. His brother has worked himself up in the organization there. He now holds an important position in the insurgency. He is close to the top."

"Hmmm," M.T. said, pushing his chair back on the planked floor and crossing his legs. He smiled. "If what you tell me bears fruit, Ghaleb, I'd bloody well say the money has been well spent. Anything else?"

"I need to leave Jordan."

"Oh?"

"I believe I have exhausted my effectiveness here."

"I'd say your effectiveness, as you call it, is just beginning. Having this link to your informant's brother in Baghdad can be of continuing importance."

Rihnai shook his head. "It is over," he said. "I want to go back to the States."

M.T. sighed deeply and extended his hands in a gesture of futility. "It's not my call, Ghaleb."

"Then speak with someone who can arrange it."

"I'll see what I can do."

"I'll need extra money."

M.T. nodded.

After a final refill, Rihnai announced that he was leaving.

"Stay in touch, Ghaleb," M.T. said, walking him to the door. "Here." He handed Rihnai an envelope. "A small bonus for you. Good work."

Rihnai exited the building, got on his bike, and headed for home on the dark, lonely road. It had started to drizzle; he cursed getting wet, his shirt beginning to stick to his back. Had the road not consisted of myriad turns, many of them hairpins, he might have become aware of the small, black European sedan that had fallen in behind him, its lights off, the two men in the front seat saying nothing to each other as they maintained a respectable distance from the bike rider. Rihnai, bone-tired, remained oblivious to their presence all the way to the street on which his apartment was located. By the time he'd dismounted the bike, he was soaked to the skin, rivulets running from his hair down his cheeks and over his nose.

He'd pulled keys from his pocket and was opening the downstairs door when he first became aware of the car, which moved slowly and quietly over the rutted concrete road. It took him a few seconds to react to the vehicle's lights not being on. By the time he did, the car had pulled to within a few feet of him, and the man in the passenger seat opened fire, four shots in all, each striking their intended target, Ghaleb Rihnai—three in the abdomen and one in the right eye, taking off the side of his head and sending him spinning down, face-first, into a puddle.

FOURTEEN

Ray Pawkins watched the six o'clock news on his fifty-two-inch TV. Like most Washingtonians, the Secretary of Homeland Security's announcement that the terrorist alert level had been raised caught his attention. Not that it mattered, he knew. Nothing would change. People would go about their daily routines whether the Homeland Security popsicle was green, yellow, or orange. Sure, people would be a little more alert, eyeing dark-skinned men or women wearing winter coats in the heat of summer, or knapsacks on the floor outside a phone booth while its owner made a call. But in real terms, it would be life as usual. As far as Pawkins was concerned, the terrorists needn't bother with ever again physically attacking America to accomplish their goal of bringing it to its knees. Each time the alert level went up, millions of dollars were consumed responding to the rumor. They could bankrupt the country without lifting a finger again except to occasionally "chat" among themselves.

But one thing the secretary said had piqued Pawkins' interest. The elevated alert was restricted to Washington. This latest threat, real or imagined, had focused on D.C., which surprised Pawkins. No city in the country was more secure these days than the nation's capital. There were concrete barriers everywhere, and streets that were even remotely proximate to the White House had been closed. Fly a mile off course in a Piper Cub and on your wingtips you had two F-16s with orders to shoot you down if you didn't tune to the right radio frequency and set down pronto. Sure, you could always knock off a congressman or senator. They were everywhere. Get one to come to dinner at a marginal restaurant with faded color photos of its dishes in the window, and food poisoning would do the trick. Wait until an elected official crossed the street and gun it. Not hard to knock off a member of Congress, or thousands of other government workers who represented the country. But that would be small potatoes for any self-respecting terrorist. You had to get more yield, which meant multiple deaths, or an attack upon someone of *real* importance. The president? Fat chance. He had more security surrounding him than a hip-hop star.

Thinking of the president brought a smile to Pawkins' lips. The last president to attend a Washington National Opera performance at the Kennedy Center prior to the current one had been Ronald Reagan. Detractors claimed he went only because he enjoyed dressing up in a tuxedo, but that was only partisan conjecture.

To the surprise of many, the man occupying the White House these days, Arthur Montgomery, was a regular at performances when he was in town. Whether he, like Reagan, truly enjoyed those evenings was anyone's guess. The first lady, Pamela Montgomery, had enthusiastically supported the Lyric Opera of Chicago when her husband was mayor of that city, and later governor of the state, and she'd championed the Washington National Opera shortly after they'd settled in the White House. Did the president revel in the magnificent productions on the Kennedy Center stage, or did he have to fight to stay awake? It didn't matter. He showed up on his resplendent wife's arm, and that was good enough. They would, according to an announcement from the White House, attend the opening night of *Tosca*.

Pawkins looked at his watch. He was due for the seven o'clock rehearsal.

He'd spent part of the afternoon there chatting with an old friend, who escorted him back up to where Charise Lee's body had been found.

"Who ever comes up here?" he'd asked, examining the perimeter of the space far above where the audience would sit during a performance.

"Damn near no one" was the response.

"Which means that whoever killed her knew of this space," Pawkins murmured, "and how to get up here."

"Or maybe somebody showed him," his friend offered.

Two people involved? Unlikely. But it could be. Pawkins looked up from where the body had been. "Somebody who worked here at the Center?"

"Don't look at me, man."

Pawkins straightened. "Who else would know about this place except for someone who worked here backstage?"

His friend shrugged. "You done here?" he asked.

"Yeah, I'm done. Thanks for bringing me."

"Gives me the creeps," said his friend as they began their descent to the stage. "Pretty young kid like that, her whole life ahead of her."

"Maybe she should have picked her friends better," Pawkins said.

"You figure it was somebody she knew?"

"It usually is. But in this case? I don't know. Could have been some horny grip or lighting tech who found her too attractive."

"You really think that's what happened?"

"No, but you rule out nothing. A stranger would have strangled her, not stabbed in her chest and then have had the wherewithal to plug the wound."

"Jesus."

"*He* wouldn't have approved," Pawkins said as they reached the stage and stood near the computer where the lighting director plied her trade during performances. "I owe you."

"Anytime, Ray. Hey, you're in the show coming up, right?"

"*Tosca.* Tell me something, you work with all the shows that come in here, right?"

"Right."

"Not just the Washington Opera."

"Right again. Road shows of musicals, ballet, concerts, whatever comes along."

"What about the people from the Opera?"

"What about 'em?"

"Are they more difficult to work with than others?"

His friend laughed. "Funny you should ask that. I was telling my wife the other night that the opera people are just about the easiest to get along with, a lot easier than traveling celebrities. Some of *them* give me a royal pain in the keister."

Pawkins also laughed. "That goes for directors like Anthony Zambrano, too?"

"Well, he's another story. See you around, Ray. How's retirement?"

"Tiring."

While Pawkins readied to head out for a quick dinner and the rehearsal, theatrical agent Philip Melincamp waited impatiently for his partner, Zöe Baltsa, to show up at A.V. Ristorante Italiano on New York Avenue. Besides serving well-cooked Italian food since 1949, it was the only restaurant in the District with an all-opera jukebox. Melincamp plugged in coins and the voice of soprano Galina Vishnevskaya singing an aria from Mussorgsky's *Boris Godunov* wheezed from the old box. Listening to Vishnevskaya reminded him of when she and her husband, Rostropovitch, had left the Soviet Union and blasted the Communist government in her autobiography, naming names of snitches in high places, including the famous mezzo Obratzsova. All of opera's drama wasn't on the stage.

The music helped soothe his frazzled nerves, and his anger at his partner's lateness. She was always late, it seemed, bursting onto the scene full of flowery excuses and affected charm.

He looked at his glass of house red and checked his watch. At times like this he wished he hadn't taken Zöe as a partner. When he had put aside his qualms, it was because he didn't see any viable choice. He was low on funds, rent was due, his wardrobe had slid into shabby, and his credit cards were at their limits. Along came Zöe, fresh from a divorce from a wealthy titan of Canadian industry who'd paid whatever it took to get rid of her. This slight disagreement had made her rich, and in search of something to do with her newfound wealth and freedom.

✑

He'd been introduced to her at a Canadian Opera Company's production of Mozart's *The Marriage of Figaro* at Toronto's Four Seasons Centre for the Performing Arts. He was sipping white wine during intermission, bought for him by an opera critic for the Toronto *Globe and Mail*, when a mutual friend waltzed her over to him.

"You're an agent, I understand," she said.

"That's right."

"Representing opera singers."

"Among others. I also have musicians and—"

"I was an opera singer," she said.

Oh, God, he thought, *what does she want from me, to resurrect her career, which was probably a dismal failure because she—*

"I studied in the States and lived in Germany for three years. I studied there, too."

"You sang there?" he asked.

"A few small roles. I went there because all the good roles here were going to European singers—Gawd, talk about outsourcing—and supposedly the German companies welcomed American sopranos, but it wasn't so welcoming for me. Well, with one exception. I met my former husband there. He saved me from the trials and tribulations of being an unwanted opera singer."

His mood brightened. "What was your husband doing in Germany?" he asked, not interested in the answer but looking to keep the conversation going until the ringing of the little bells, announcing that the second act was about to start, could save him.

"He owns companies there, and elsewhere."

"Really. What sort of companies?"

"Big ones." She smiled and batted her long, fake lashes at him. Her dress was cut low, exposing an ample amount of freckled bosom, and hemmed high enough to showcase a nice set of legs.

"Big ones?" he said with a wry smile, the double entendre not going over her head.

"Yes. Have you ever considered taking on a partner?" she asked.

"No. Well, it's crossed my mind on occasion but I've never given it any serious thought."

The bells sounded. She placed a well-manicured set of fingers tipped with crimson talons on his sleeve and said, "I'm looking for an investment that will bring me back into the opera world. Call me."

"Your name is Baltsa?" he said. "Zöe Baltsa? Any relation to Agnes Baltsa, the soprano?"

"No. It's my married name. My maiden name was Nagle. I'm keeping my married name—and his money. I'm in the book. No, I'll call you. Melincamp? That's the name of your agency?"

"Right."

"You'll hear from me. Enjoy the rest of the opera. The sextet at the end of Act Three never fails to delight me."

He watched her wiggle away and thought that maybe this was his lucky night, not because he might end up in bed with her, but because her ex-husband had "big ones." He reentered the theater with renewed vigor.

The infusion of money by his new partner worked wonders to turn around the Melincamp Artists Agency's financial picture. Now the Baltsa-Melincamp Artists Agency, its run-down offices were abandoned in favor of space in a downtown high-rise more befitting a talent agency "of world renown." Zöe hadn't exaggerated about her husband's money. It seemed endless, and she spent it freely, hosting expensive fetes for her rich friends and opera patrons, draping herself in the latest designer clothing, and traveling the globe to, she claimed, find the world's most promising future opera stars. She forged alliances with arts centers in myriad countries—England, France, Italy,

Norway, and Sweden, and some in the Middle East, including Egypt, Jordan, and Saudi Arabia, where she'd befriended a sheik reputed to be worth a couple of billion dollars, give or take a million. A full-time publicist was put on the payroll to extol Zöe's exploits in the media. She was invited to opening nights in dozens of cities, invitations she gobbled up with glee, her publicist always at her side to generate local press.

For Melincamp, having taken her on as a partner proved to be both a blessing and a curse. The terms of their written contract, drawn by one of her attorneys, read like a prenuptial agreement. She named herself president and executive director of the agency in the contract, and had final say over all agency expenditures. In effect, Melincamp had been relegated to junior partner status, his role to run the office administratively, including a small division he'd started pre-Baltsa, "Reach for the Stars." Talent was invited to submit tapes for "expert evaluation and a possible contract." It was akin to literary agents charging a fee to read a manuscript, or alleged talent agents for kids collecting fees from hopeful parents in exchange for "professional photographs and possible modeling assignments."

Although he often expressed dissatisfaction to friends, he wasn't all that unhappy with the arrangement. Zöe was away most of the time burnishing her image, her absences welcome. She was, as far as Melincamp was concerned, the nastiest woman he'd ever known, and he'd known a few in his life. She was overbearing, demanding, and had a mean streak that resulted in his ducking more than one missile thrown his way. She was also one of the most prejudiced people he'd ever met, with a bad word for virtually every minority. She was anti-black and anti-Semitic, but reserved those judgments for when she and Melincamp were alone together. In public, she was amiable and all-embracing, a nonsinging diva with an outsized ego and a willingness to indulge it at every whim.

But as a practiced pragmatist, he'd put up with it. Why not? Although the terms of their agreement gave her the lion's share of any profits, and he was on salary, he still had more walking around money than when he was scraping for funds to pay the rent. His love life had picked up, too. Occasionally, they'd end up in bed together when the mood struck her, which wasn't often. There was no seduction involved. She wanted sex at that moment, and he was handy. Could be worse, he reasoned. He'd made a pact with a she-devil. So what? Sometimes you had to do what you had to do. But that didn't need to be forever. There was a clause allowing him to buy back her stake in the agency, and he dreamt of one day invoking it. It was far out of his reach financially, and he didn't know whether he'd ever have enough money to walk in one day, slap a fat envelope on her desk, and say, "*Hasta la vista,* baby. You've got until five this afternoon to be gone. Gone! Hee-haw!"

Zöe flounced into the restaurant twenty minutes later and joined him at the small bar. She pulled a cigarette from her purse and lit it, the smoke drifting and causing him to cough. It wouldn't matter if they changed seats. The smoke would come his way no matter where he sat. Of the things he disliked about Washington, D.C., its liberal smoking policy in bars was high on the list.

"So," she said after a series of rapid puffs and a determined crushing of the half-consumed cigarette in an ashtray, "tell me where you've been."

"Where I've been? I've been at the apartment. I babysat Christopher until I got him to pull himself together and go to Takoma Park to rehearse with that no-talent Italian mezzo. That's where I've been. Oh, and I spent a very unpleasant half hour with a big, black detective who grilled me like I was some drug dealer or child molester. I got out of there the minute he left."

"What did you tell him?"

"I told him I hadn't seen Charise since we arrived."

"And?"

"And what?"

"What did he say?"

"Look, Zöe, this is not the time or place for me to give you a play-by-play of what happened. He'll want to talk with you."

"Why?"

"Because he—"

"You told him I was here in D.C.?"

"Yes."

"Why?"

"Because—because he would have found out anyway. Are you hungry? I never had lunch."

"No. There's a flight from National to Toronto at nine. I suggest we be on it."

"We can't."

"Why?"

"Because it will look suspicious if we leave. You know how cops think. If we leave, they'll think we had something to do with Charise's murder. Leaving is the worst thing we can do. We stay, talk to them all they want, and *then* we leave."

She lit another cigarette. "Maybe you're right," she said.

"I know I'm right. They make a great shrimp Fra Diavolo here. It's good with pizza *bianca*. Wine? Red or white?"

"How can you think of food?" she said, disgust in her voice and on her heavily made-up face.

Melincamp stared at her. The smoke from her cigarette still stung his eyes, and he turned away. He had two urges at that moment. The first was to punch her in the face. But that wouldn't have been appreciated in a public place. The second was to announce to her that it wouldn't be long before she was past-tense, that he'd soon have enough money to buy her out. Maybe he'd punch her before laying that news on her, he thought. That contemplation made him feel better. He called for a waiter and ordered shrimp Fra Diavolo and a small pizza *bianca*.

"Oh, Gawd!" she said.

"And red wine," he said. "The house wine will be fine."

❧

Pizza was also on the menu at the Department of Homeland Security.

Immediately after his announcement, Secretary Murtaugh had

left for a meeting at the White House with President Montgomery and members of his National Security staff. Those in the Nebraska Complex who'd crunched the intelligence for their boss took a breather. Pizza was ordered in, prepared by a neighborhood shop that had been cleared to deliver food to the offices. Over pepperoni and mushroom slices and soft drinks, they discussed the information they'd received, upon which they'd based their recommendation that the color be changed on the Lifesaver, known as the threat barometer.

"I hope it's not another hoax," one said as he tried to dab away tomato sauce.

"Not this time," a colleague said. "Our guy in Amman—the Brit, M.T.—says his source is highly credible. We met the source, remember? The Arab kid who'd studied here. He went through the training, spoke really good English."

"Yeah, I remember him," said one of the men at the table. "Name was—ah, Gallop, something like that."

"Right. Martone recruited him."

Another analyst at the table laughed. "So M.T. says Gallop, or whatever the hell his name is, came up with good info from this Iraqi he turned. Why the hell is it that we put more stock in what British Intelligence says than we do in our own?"

"Because they talk better," someone said. "They sound more believable, the King's English and all." He did a poor imitation of a British accent.

"Yeah, maybe so, but this guy's been pretty good. He—"

Their banter was interrupted by a message received over a secured line. The analyst who'd expressed confidence in the British contact in Jordan read it, scowled, and angrily tossed it on the table. It landed in the almost empty pizza box, picking up a greasy red stain at its corner, like blood. The others read it, too.

"Damn," the first reader of the message said. "Looks like Mr. Gallop didn't cover his tracks good enough. Our British friend will have to get himself another source." He got up from the table, took the message from the last person to have read it, and started from the room. "I'd better run this upstairs."

FIFTEEN

Portelain and Johnson stopped at a fast-food outlet, where the portly Portelain downed a chili dog with relish (in both senses of the word) while his comely female partner sipped a Diet Pepsi and watched him enjoy his snack.

"Best in the whole damn city," he proclaimed.

"If you say so," she said. "Come on. Let's pick up the Warren kid before he decides to cool off back in Canada."

"I'll bet it is cooler up there," Portelain said, wiping perspiration from his brow as they headed for their car.

"I didn't mean the weather," she said, slipping into the passenger seat while he wedged himself behind the wheel. They drove to N Street and parked at a hydrant in front of the four-story gray building.

"This is it?" Johnson asked, her eyes automatically sweeping the scene in search of potential trouble.

"This is where the man lives," said Portelain. "Where the victim lived, too. *And* their manager when he's in town."

"The apartment's that big?"

"No. Tiny little place, but it's got two bedrooms—closets used as bedrooms is more like it—and a pullout couch in the living room."

"Cozy," she said.

"Crowded," he corrected. "Let's go. Hope the dude's home."

Portelain was about to open his door when Johnson's hand on his arm stopped him. "There he is," she said, pointing to Warren, who'd come around the corner.

"Doesn't look like a piano player to me," Portelain said.

"What's a piano player supposed to look like?" she asked.

"I don't know, little and nerdy, long hair, weird."

She didn't bother debating the stereotype as Warren reached the building's entrance, paused, and noticed the unmarked, illegally parked vehicle. He squinted to see through the tinted glass.

"Let's take him," Portelain said.

"Looks like we won't have to," Johnson said as Warren approached the car.

Johnson lowered her window. "Hello, Mr. Warren."

"What are you, following me?" Warren asked, his lip curled.

"Just need to ask you a few questions," Johnson replied.

"I've already told you, I have nothing to say."

"That may be," she said, "but we'd like to hear you say it again—for the record. Come on, get in. We'll spend a few pleasant hours at headquarters and that'll be it. Our boss is anxious to meet you."

Warren guffawed, without humor.

"This my partner, Detective Portelain," Johnson said. "He wanted to meet you, too."

Warren, who cradled a thick file folder to the Mozart on the chest of his T-shirt, looked at Portelain. The detective smiled. The young Canadian stepped back from the open window, his expression reflecting his ambivalence. Portelain opened his door and got out. Warren continued backing away.

"Hey, man, don't do somethin' silly," Portelain said as he came around the front of the car. Johnson, too, slipped out of the vehicle.

"Grab him," Johnson said as Warren turned and started walking up the street at a brisk clip.

Portelain took off after him, taking heavy steps, walking as fast as he could. Johnson ran by him. Seeing her, Warren, too, began to run. Portelain progressed from walking to a lope. He stopped to pull his gun from its shoulder holster, and to take in some air. As he did, he saw Warren disappear around the corner, with Johnson close on his heels. "Oh, man," Portelain said as he started moving again, hoping his partner could corral Warren. "Get him, baby," he muttered as he reached the corner and peered down the cross street. Johnson stood on the sidewalk a hundred feet away. "He's down there," she yelled at her partner, pointing to a narrow alley that ran between buildings.

Portelain reached her, his breathing labored.

"In the alley," she said, pointing again. "No way out."

Portelain peered down the alley. It ended thirty feet away, at the rear wall of an apartment or commercial building. Both sides were lined with walls high enough to make scaling them virtually impossible unless the Canadian was Spider-Man.

People on the street became aware of the commotion and surrounded the two detectives. Portelain still held his revolver.

"Put it away, Willie," Johnson said.

He followed her suggestion.

"He's not armed," she said.

"Hope not. We call for backup?"

"No."

She stepped into the alley, with Portelain close behind.

"I made a collar in here once," she said. "There's that Dumpster and some garbage cans."

"I see 'em," Portelain confirmed, still breathing heavily, and wincing at a stitch in his side and a dull ache in his left arm.

"You okay?" she asked.

"Me? Hell, yes. Let's go. We got a crowd."

They took slow, tentative steps into the alley, each staying close to a wall and twelve feet from each other, eyes and ears on alert.

"Hey, dude," Portelain barked. "Let's not have anybody get hurt here. Let's wise up and play it cool."

There was no response.

They reached a point only a few feet from the Dumpster, overflowing with fragrant garbage, and glanced at each other. The sound of something hitting the Dumpster's metal side caused them to stiffen.

"Look out!" Portelain yelled as Warren burst from behind the trash container and attempted to run between them. His sudden move caught Johnson by surprise, but Portelain reacted quickly, extending his sizable arm and catching Warren in the face, on the nose, sending the young man tumbling backwards, his head making hard contact with the Dumpster. Johnson immediately pulled cuffs from her belt and jumped on him, her knees pinning his arms to the concrete alley floor. Portelain stood over the fallen man's head and said, "See what you done now, you dumb bastard? See the trouble you put us to?"

Warren's response was an anguished cry, a combination of sob and fury. Portelain helped Johnson turn Warren over and she secured his wrists with the cuffs.

"Don't hurt my hands," he blubbered as they yanked him to his feet. Blood ran from his nose down over his mouth and chin and bloodied Mozart. They propelled him out of the alley, to where dozens of people watched.

"What did he do?" someone yelled.

"Who is he?"

Johnson and Portelain ignored the onlookers and pushed Warren down the street in the direction of their car.

Warren balked, and shouted, "Police brutality!"

A tall, heavyset man with a white beard and ponytail yelled to someone else in the crowd, "They beat the crap out of the guy."

The detectives urged Warren forward. They turned the corner and were almost to the car when Portelain suddenly stopped.

"What's the matter, Willie?" Johnson asked, her right hand gripping Warren's cuffed wrist.

Portelain released his grasp of the manacles and sat heavily on a low stone wall. "Don't feel good," he rasped.

He's having a heart attack, Johnson thought. "Wait here." She pushed Warren to the car, where she opened a rear door and shoved him inside, facedown. She slammed the door shut and came around to the driver's side, stopping only to glare at people who'd followed them. "Get away!" she commanded. With one eye on Warren, who struggled to right himself, she called Dispatch and asked for backup and an ambulance. Her request confirmed, she looked to where Porte-lain was still on the wall, head lowered, hands pressed against the top of the wall to support himself.

"I want a lawyer," Warren said from the backseat. He now sat up-right, his hands behind him. "I want somebody from the embassy. You can't do this to me."

"Shut up!" Johnson snapped. She was torn between staying with him and going to where Portelain sat.

She didn't have to ponder that decision long because two squad cars and a city ambulance roared down the street, lights flashing, horns wailing, and came to a haphazard stop, blocking all traffic. Johnson grabbed the first uniformed officer she could and told him to watch Warren while she went to where two EMTs were talking with Portelain.

"You all right, Willie?" she asked.

"Yeah, I'm all right," he said. "Just got a pain, that's all. Damned arthritis."

Johnson took one of the EMTs aside and said, "Don't listen to him. I think he's having a coronary."

"Why do you say that?" the EMT asked.

"Because—damn, just get him to a hospital."

A few minutes later, Portelain, despite a series of vocal protests, was being slid on a gurney into the recesses of the ambulance. By now, the crowd had grown considerably and included a reporter from the *Post* and a TV crew. Johnson heard the female TV reporter ask no one in particular, "What happened here? What did you see?"

The big man with the white beard pushed his way to the front of the crowd and said, "This white guy was just minding his business when these two cops jump him and beat the living crap out of him."

Someone else confirmed it.

The reporter spotted Johnson and started toward her. The detective waved her away and said to the uniformed cop standing guard over Warren, "Take him in and book him for resisting arrest and assaulting an officer. I'm going to the hospital with Willie." She stopped the ambulance driver who was about to leave and said, "I'm his partner. I'm going with him." She ran around to the rear, opened the door, and joined Portelain and the second EMT inside. "You'll be okay, Willie," she said, touching his hand. "You'll be just fine."

The crowd dispersed. The big man with the white beard insisted that an officer take down his name as a witness to police brutality. As the cop dutifully recorded it in a notebook, thinking all the while that he'd like to practice some brutality on this guy, a homeless man with urine-stained chino pants and carrying a bulging knapsack entered the alley where Chris Warren had been apprehended. The sheaf of sheet music Warren had been carrying with him had ended up strewn over the alley floor. The homeless citizen picked up the loose sheets, examined each of them like a pawn-shop owner evaluating a ring someone was looking to hock, and tossed them one by one on top of the refuse already in the Dumpster. *Sometimes you get lucky,* he thought. *This isn't one of those days.*

SIXTEEN

There was a time in Mackensie Smith's life that taking an afternoon off was anathema. Catching a movie matinee was out of the question, even when there was little to do in his law office on a given day. And to enjoy a sexual episode while the sun still shone was—well, the guilt associated with it wasn't worth the pleasure. Not guilt for engaging in sex, but for doing it during working hours.

But he'd changed.

He and Annabel had returned to their Watergate apartment after the meeting at WNO's administrative offices and thoroughly mangled the king-size bed they'd so carefully made up that morning. Sated, they made the bed again—both were committed neatniks—and enjoyed a postcoital glass of mango juice on the terrace.

"Do you know what I thought about while we were in bed?" she asked.

"Not me?"

"Of course you. But for a moment, I pictured myself as Delila in *Samson and Delila.*"

He grinned. "And I was Samson?"

"Yes."

He placed his fingers on his receding hairline. "Is that what happened to my hair?" he asked. "You cut it off to rob me of my strength?"

"I had a little help from Mother Nature. By the way, Delila in the opera is pronounced *Dah-lee-la,* with the emphasis on the final 'la.' At least that's how Saint-Saëns pronounced it."

"I wouldn't doubt it for a minute. So, what's on our agenda for the rest of the day?"

"There's the rehearsal at seven."

"I almost succeeded in forgetting about that."

"Which I would never let you do. I thought I might go up to Takoma Park and ask around about Charise Lee."

"Why?"

"Oh, I don't know, to get a feel for how and why her murder might have happened."

"Now, hold on a second," he said, sitting taller and facing her directly. "Solving the young lady's murder isn't your business."

"How can you say that?" she countered. "I think it's everyone's business. After all, I am on WNO's board. We all have an obligation to do whatever we can to help find her killer."

"Wrong," he said, his finger stabbing the air for emphasis. "The police are responsible for that and—"

"And your Detective Pawkins."

"Right. They're pros, Annie. I'm sure that between them they'll talk to anyone and everyone who might have something to offer. As for us, we've already done our duty. Pawkins is on the case because of you and me. Leave it at that."

"And you?" she asked.

"What about me?"

"You'll be content to simply sit back and let the so-called pros do the job? What if we can come up with something that would be helpful to them?"

"If that happens by accident, fine. Aside from that, we have other things to worry about, like my classes and your gallery. And, of course, my debut as an opera star."

"That's right," she said brightly, as though he'd made a revelatory statement. "Your debut. A star is born. I hope the paparazzi aren't lurking downstairs."

They left the terrace and went their separate ways, agreeing to meet up at the Kennedy Center at seven. He headed for his office at GW to catch up on paperwork, and she said she was going to her Georgetown gallery to do the same.

"You take the car," he said. "I'll walk."

"Sure you can?" she asked wickedly.

As he headed off at a pace health fanatics would term a "power walk," she climbed in their car in the parking garage beneath the Watergate and pulled out onto the street. But instead of going to Georgetown, she went up 16th Street toward Takoma Park and the Washington National Opera's satellite facility. Although she knew that Mac was right—that they were not in the business of solving murders—there was a compelling need to touch base with those who'd been affected by the crime. Since joining the board, she felt very much a part of the Washington opera community. *Besides,* she silently admitted to herself, *I'm as curious as the next person when it comes to the murder of an opera singer inside one of the nation's cultural icons, the John F. Kennedy Center for the Performing Arts.*

As she drove, she found herself hoping for one thing, that the person who killed Charise Lee wasn't one of the young singer's colleagues in the Domingo-Cafritz Young Artist Program. Let it not be someone who would sully the sterling reputation of that program, and of the Washington National Opera itself. But hoping, she knew, was one thing. Reality so often turned out to be damningly different.

Chris Warren was delivered to the First Precinct, processed at the front desk, and placed in a holding cell until Detective Carl Berry was ready to question him. The young musician had become silent and sullen during the ride in the patrol car and refused to answer questions posed by the desk sergeant, including giving his name. The only thing he would say was "I'm a Canadian citizen. I want a lawyer."

"Sure, son," the dour sergeant said. "The Mounties will be here any minute to rescue you."

As the processing took place, Berry was on the phone in his office talking with Sylvia Johnson, who'd called from the hospital.

"How's Willie?" Berry asked.

"Okay, I guess. He's in the emergency room. They're running tests."

"Looks like a heart attack?"

"That's what I thought, but I'm no doctor. I'll get back to you once I know more. Look, Carl, about the Warren kid. He gave us a hard time, ran off, tried to hide in an alley behind a Dumpster. He made another run for it but ran into Willie's fist."

"Ran into it?" Berry said, his tone mirroring his amusement at the description.

"Exactly. Willie stuck out his arm and the kid ran into it."

"Okay," Berry said. "Did he say anything before making contact with Willie's arm?"

"Nothing incriminating. He just kept harping on the fact that he's Canadian."

"I know. Kowalski at the desk told me that. He's asked for a lawyer."

"He's not dumb."

"We'll see. You read him his rights?"

"No. It was too chaotic with Willie down."

"Okay, I'll do it. Maybe he'll want to talk without counsel. We've got his passport. We'll notify his embassy, like the law says. Are you going to hang in there with Willie?"

"Yes."

"Stay in touch."

His next call was to have Warren brought to an interrogation room—"interview room," as they preferred to term it. Warren had been allowed to clean up a bit, but his swollen nose and purple cheek couldn't be washed away, any more than the rust-colored stains on Mozart's face could be.

Berry stood outside the room with another detective and observed Warren through the one-way glass. The Canadian sat slouched in a straight-back wooden chair. He was alone in the room. His eyes darted from wall to wall, frequently coming to rest on the mirror. Berry held four pieces of paper in his hand, one the standard Miranda warning; the second a statement to be read to any foreign national being detained or arrested in the United States; the third a series of notes he'd taken during his earlier meeting with Portelain and Johnson; and a standard form, already filled out, to be faxed to the Canadian Embassy alerting it that one of its citizens was in police custody.

"He looks guilty as hell," the other detective commented.

"He sure acted it," said Berry. "What'd he run for if he had nothing to hide?"

"You'll find out," the second detective said, slapping Berry on the back. "Want me in there with you, play good cop, bad cop?"

"No. Too early for that, but hang around. Let's see how it goes."

Berry's entrance into the room caused Warren to straighten in his chair.

"Mr. Warren, I'm Detective Carl Berry," Berry said, taking the only other chair in the room.

"I want a lawyer, and I want to talk to somebody from my embassy. I'm a Canadian citizen."

"I know that," Berry said. He slid a printed copy of the Miranda warning across the table and asked Warren to silently read it while the detective read it aloud. When he was finished, he pushed a pen at Warren and asked him to sign it. Warren angrily swept the paper and pen off the table.

"Have it your way," Berry said. He consulted the second sheet of paper he'd carried in with him. "As a non-U.S. citizen," he read, "who is being arrested or detained, you are entitled to have us notify your country's consular representative here in the United States. A consular official from your country may be able to help you obtain legal counsel, and may contact your family and visit you in detention, among other things. If you want us to notify your country's consular officials, you can request this notification now, or at any time in the future. After your consular officials are notified, they may call or visit you. Do you want us to notify your country's consular officials?"

"What do you think I've been saying all along?" Warren replied.

"Had to read it to you," Berry said, smiling. "For the record." He showed Warren the fax. "Everything correct on it?" he asked. "We'll fax it over to your embassy right away. You can see I've indicated that you want an attorney assigned to you. I'm sure the folks at the embassy will arrange that."

"It looks okay," Warren said, the defiance in his voice fading.

Berry let silence dominate for a few seconds.

"I don't know why you arrested me," Warren said softly. "I didn't do anything."

You've been warned you don't have to say anything without a lawyer, Berry thought. *Anything you say can, and will, be used against you in a court of law.*

"You haven't been arrested," Berry said. "We just wanted to ask you a few questions."

"Then why did you send cops to bring me here?"

"I'll tell you why, sir. Detective Johnson asked you questions at that place where you were playing the piano—Takoma Park, right?"

Warren nodded.

"And she told me that you weren't very cooperative."

"I had nothing to tell her. I didn't have anything to do with Charise being murdered."

"Maybe, maybe not. But you were her roommate, which means you were close to her. We tend to look first at people who were close to a murder victim."

"Close? You mean like husbands or wives, or boyfriends and girl-friends?"

"Uh-huh."

"I wasn't anything like that with Charise. We roomed together, that's all."

"You're both from Toronto."

"That's right."

"You knew each other there? I mean, before coming here to Washington?"

"Yes," he mumbled. Then he said with more animation, "But not well."

"She was a pretty girl, as I understand it," Berry said.

"She was. Yes, she was."

"And talented." He grinned and spread open hands in a helpless gesture. "I don't know anything about opera, but I'm told she had a great future as an opera singer."

Warren shrugged. "She was okay," he said.

"Just okay?" Berry asked, his interest heightened.

"Yeah. I've worked with better singers."

"As I said, I wouldn't know about that."

"Where's my music?" Warren asked.

"What music?"

"I had music with me when they arrested me."

"I wouldn't know about that, either."

The door opened and a detective handed Berry a note.

"Looks like your embassy is on the ball," Berry said. "Someone from there wants to speak with you. You can use that phone over there in the corner. I'll leave you alone."

Berry left the room as Warren went to where the phone rested on a low, empty bookcase and picked up the receiver.

"They're sending a lawyer," the second detective said.

"Yeah, I'm sure they are," Berry said. "I wanted to get into that so-called alibi he said he had before a lawyer got involved."

"What'd he claim?"

"He claims he was out drinking and got drunk, too drunk to remember who he was with or where he was."

The other detective laughed. "Maybe he went out to celebrate offing the kid."

"Maybe he didn't go out at all," Berry said. "He's no big drinker. I'm sure of that."

"Looks like he might have gotten in a fight wherever he was. That's a mean-looking face."

"Willie."

"Portelain?"

Berry smiled. "Sylvia says the kid made a run for it and Willie's arm happened to get in the way."

"Plays for me," said the second detective.

"We'll see how it plays for his lawyer. I can smell a brutality charge on the horizon."

Berry looked through the glass. Warren had concluded his phone conversation and retaken his chair.

"Let him sit there until his mouthpiece arrives," Berry said.

Berry had no sooner returned to his office than a clerk delivered the news that a judge had approved the surrender of Warren's passport, pending any legal challenge that would cause the decision to be overturned.

"Great," Berry said, thinking that every once in a while judges do the right thing.

He took a call announcing the arrival of Warren's attorney, and met him in the interrogation room.

"Harlan Kendall," the attorney said, handing Berry his card. "Our firm is on retainer with the Canadian Embassy. What are you charging Mr. Warren with?"

"Nothing at the moment," Berry replied. "He's a person of interest in the murder of his roommate, Charise Lee."

"The opera singer," Kendall said. He was a sausage of a man wearing a tailored blue suit, white shirt, and regimental tie, which would have draped better on a taller, thinner man. "Looks like you caught yourself a big one."

"We've caught bigger," Berry said.

"Is my client a target of the investigation?" Kendall asked while ruffling through papers from his attaché case.

"I told you, he's a person of interest in the case. I should also tell you that he's been booked for resisting arrest and assault on an officer."

"That's a lie," Warren said, rising a few inches from his chair. "They beat me up."

Kendall dropped the papers on the desk. "Judging from his face," he said, "I'd say he *was* beaten."

"File a charge," Berry said.

"Who was the arresting officer?" The attorney asked.

"William Portelain. He's in intensive care at the hospital as we speak. He had a heart attack trying to subdue your client."

Kendall looked at Warren.

"He hit me in the face," Warren said, "and knocked me on the ground."

"I'd like to speak with my client privately," Kendall said.

"Sure," Berry said, and left, instructing the uniformed officer on duty outside the room to shut off the concealed microphone.

After ten minutes, Kendall opened the door and asked Berry to rejoin them. "My client," the attorney said, "is willing to drop any charges of police brutality in return for you dropping all charges of resisting arrest and assault on a cop."

"I've got a veteran detective in the hospital clinging to life because of your client's dumb behavior. All we wanted to do was question him, and he takes off like a three-strikes-and-you're-out felon. Consciousness of guilt?"

"Can we talk privately?" Kendall asked Berry.

"Sure."

Again outside the room, the attorney said, "Look, this is no killer, and he's no tough guy who assaults cops. I spoke with the people at the program he's in with the Washington Opera. He's a sensitive, brilliant pianist, maybe a little high-strung, like most artists, but an okay kid. No record back in Canada. I checked. He's minding his own business on a sunny afternoon and two detectives confront him on the street, scare the hell out of him. He bolts. Come on, Detective, let's be reasonable here."

Berry's response was to hand Kendall the court order concerning Warren's passport.

"This'll never stand up," Kendall said.

"I think it will," Berry said. "We drop the charges on the condition that he reconsiders charging my detectives with brutality *and* he answers questions concerning the murder. Deal?"

"He doesn't legally have to. Answer questions."

"Right. He also doesn't have to leave here as long as the charges are pending against him. A couple of nights in our five-star hotel until a judge gets around to arraigning him might help clear his high-strung head. Of course, we don't have a baby grand for him to practice on, but . . ."

"I'll encourage him to answer your questions."

"Do more than just encourage him, Counselor. If he acts like the innocent person he claims to be, and if he makes sense, we have a deal."

Kendall and Warren conferred again in the interrogation room. Kendall emerged and nodded at Berry, who rejoined them around the table.

"Okay," Berry said, "let's start over, Mr. Warren. Tell me where you were the night your roommate, Ms. Lee, was killed."

Warren looked at Kendall, who nodded.

Warren avoided Berry's inquisitive eyes. "I was—I was at a piano recital that night."

"Where?"

"The Kennedy Center."

"You were at the Kennedy Center that night?"

"Yes."

"You told Detective Johnson that you'd been out drinking with friends."

"I know, I . . ."

"Why did you tell her that if it wasn't true?"

"I don't know. I guess I thought it would sound better."

Kendall's eyebrows went up.

"Okay," Berry said, "let's get this straight. You weren't out drinking that night but you were at a recital at the Kennedy Center. Sure *that's* the truth?"

Warren nodded.

"What time was the recital?"

"Six, I think."

"Where in the Kennedy Center?"

"The Millennium Stage."

"What theater is that?"

"It's not a theater. It's a stage they set up in the lobby. They have performances just about every night there. It's free."

"Who was the pianist?"

"Boris Larkin."

"What did he play?"

"I don't know, different things, pieces from well-known operas."

"Did you speak with him after the performance?"

"No."

"What time did it end?"

"About seven thirty."

"That's pretty early. Did you see Ms. Lee at the Kennedy Center while you were there?"

"No."

"What did you do after?"

"I had dinner."

"Where?"

"A little Indian restaurant downtown."

"Which one?"

"I don't remember. I felt like Indian food and walked into the place. I never did catch the name."

"You were alone?"

"Yes."

"How did you pay?"

"Cash. I gave them cash."

"They give you a receipt?"

"Maybe. I don't remember."

"And then?"

"Then I . . . then I went back to the apartment and watched TV."

"Alone?"

"Yes."

"I understand your agent is in town and staying at the apartment. Was he there?"

"No. I never saw him that night."

The questioning lasted another fifteen minutes. Berry ended the session by saying, "We'll be keeping your passport, Mr. Warren."

"You can't do that," Warren almost shouted. "I'm a Canadian citizen!"

Kendall calmed his client and explained that he and the Canadian Consulate would work on his behalf to get the passport back. The attorney reminded Berry that he and his detectives were not to question his client again without his being present.

"Wouldn't think of it," Berry assured. "You're free to go, Mr. Warren, for the moment."

After Kendall and Warren had left the building, Berry went to his office, where Sylvia Johnson had just arrived.

"What's with Willie?" Berry asked.

"They're keeping him overnight, but they ruled out a heart attack. The doctor read the riot act to Willie. His blood pressure is off the chart, and a test showed an enlarged heart." She laughed. "They told him he has to eat a healthier diet, lose weight, exercise, the works. No more chili dogs, or pizza for breakfast."

"He's lucky. It's a good warning."

She asked about Warren, and Berry filled her in on how the questioning had gone.

"What do you think?" she asked.

"I think we should keep close tabs on Mr. Warren. In the meantime, let's call it a day. You up for dinner?"

"Sure. And a drink. I'm off duty."

"So am I. Come on, let's hoist one for Willie."

SEVENTEEN

When the rehearsal at the Kennedy Center was over, the director, Anthony Zambrano, assembled the supers for some last-minute comments, which quickly shifted into a discussion of *Tosca* and Zambrano's vision of this particular production. Annabel had joined Mac on the stage, where he was sitting with his boss, GW's president, Wilfred Burns, the other academicians-cum-supers, and Ray Pawkins in a semicircle around the director. It struck Mac that aside from him and his professorial colleagues, everyone else was well versed in *Tosca* and opera in general, and eager to display their knowledge. He felt a little out of it as Zambrano spoke in baroque terms about how he intended to break new ground and set a higher standard for future directors of the Puccini masterpiece.

"Is *Tosca* considered his best work?" Mac asked, wanting to have something to offer.

Zambrano's face lit up. "An excellent question. But who is to judge which work by a genius is his best? For me, I find the raw emotional power and dramatic foundation of *Tosca* to be compelling. But he also wrote *Madame Butterfly* and *La Boheme*, among other magisterial works. Who can say?"

"Is *Tosca* the most widely produced opera?" another super asked.

"Strangely not," Zambrano replied, chewing his cheek as he sought a basis for his response. "I believe—and correct me if you know better—that *Madame Butterfly* has been the most produced opera in the past ten years, at least in the United States. *La Boheme*? They are one and two, if I'm not mistaken. But *Tosca* is Puccini's strongest work. Sarooodledum, as George Bernard Shaw termed it—he was fond of playing on the name of the playwright Victorien Sardou, whose play, *La Tosca*, was the basis for Puccini's operatic version."

It was enough of an answer for Mac, but Zambrano segued into his analysis of how Puccini's operas stacked up against the operas of Mozart, Verdi, Bartók, and other familiar names, as well as some that weren't. Mac's mind wandered, his eyes going to that portion of the main stage where Charise Lee's blood had been spilled. Someone had attempted to clean it, leaving a milky circle around where the stain had been.

Zambrano finished his dissertation, thanked everyone for coming, and announced that future rehearsals would be at Takoma Park, until the technical and dress rehearsals, which would be held at the Kennedy Center.

Genevieve Crier, who'd been there at the beginning of the rehearsal and quickly disappeared, returned as Mac and Annabel were about to leave with Pawkins.

"So glad I caught you," Genevieve said in her lilting British accent. "Did it go well?"

"Sure," Pawkins said. "How can a supers rehearsal go bad?"

"I can think of a way," said Annabel as they walked through the Hall of Nations, the flags of every nation with which the United States has diplomatic relations lining the spacious public area.

"Gracious, yes," said Genevieve. "Having a super murdered certainly ranks as . . . well, I don't know, something going bad."

"It didn't happen at a rehearsal," Pawkins said, sounding annoyed at having been challenged.

In her relentless cheerfulness, Genevieve didn't seem to have picked up on the former detective's shift in mood. As they stopped at one of the exit doors, she reached into her bulging shoulder bag and pulled out a magazine.

"May we have a drum roll, please," she said, handing it to Pawkins. "Page one thirteen. You're now famous, Mr. Pawkins."

"What's this?" Annabel asked.

"An advance copy of the latest *Washingtonian*. Our Raymond Pawkins, former Homicide detective on the city's mean streets, more recently art and music connoisseur, is all over the place."

Pawkins opened to the page Genevieve had cited and held it up for Mac and Annabel to see. Looking back at them was a large color photograph of Pawkins leaning casually against the set from Washington National Opera's previous production, Mozart's *Die Zauberflöte*, more popularly known as *The Magic Flute*.

"Grrrr," Genevieve growled. "I had to positively break his arm to get him to agree to the interview and photo shoot. The editor loved the idea, a profile of a hard-nosed Homicide detective pursuing the arts, including performing as a super in our productions. It's such good press."

"You didn't tell us about the article," Annabel said to Pawkins.

"My natural modesty wouldn't allow it," he said, hand to his heart.

"I can't wait to read it," Annabel said.

"Here," Pawkins said, giving it to her. "I already know what I said. Anyone up for a drink?"

"Not us," Mac said. "We need an early night."

"Genevieve?" Pawkins asked.

"I thought you'd never ask—or forgive me."

As Mac and Annabel started to walk away, Genevieve said, "Annabel, don't forget the Opera Ball meeting tomorrow."

"I won't," Annabel said over her shoulder. "It's on the calendar."

❧

Mac walked Rufus, and mixed his own blend of coffee for the morning, before changing into pajamas and joining Annabel in bed.

"A nice early night," she said. "Good book?" He'd picked up where he'd left off in E. L. Doctorow's *The March*.

"Excellent," he replied, glancing at what she was reading, the magazine Pawkins had given her. "Any startling revelations about our gadfly detective?"

"Is that how you view him?"

"Well, he seems to enjoy a little bit of this, a little bit of that. A dabbler."

"Listen to this," she said, rearranging herself so that she knelt beside him. "It says that although he spent his law enforcement career in Homicide, he became involved in a couple of cases handled by MPD's art squad."

"Doesn't surprise me," Mac said. "He told me he does PI work in cases involving musical manuscripts and works of art."

"The writer cites this one case that I certainly recall. I'm sure you do, too. Remember when that musicologist from Georgetown University was murdered? Aaron Musinski?"

"Sure. It was big news."

"Pawkins was the lead detective on it, according to this article."

"As I recall, there was controversy about some missing music. Do they mention that in the article?"

"No. It's just a few lines summing up some of the big cases he'd handled while a cop."

She hopped out of bed. "I'm going to Google it," she said on her way to the study, where one of their two computers was located. He followed and stood behind her as she typed in "Aaron Musinski." A full page of sites in which the subject was mentioned came up on the screen, with dozens of additional possibilities listed on subsequent pages. She clicked on the first site, and one of the *Washington Post* articles about the murder appeared. They read in silence. She pulled up other sites, too. When they were finished reading, she spun around in her chair. "Fascinating," she said, but without much animation.

෮

The Aaron Musinski murder had occurred six years earlier. Musinski, a professor at Georgetown University, was considered one of the world's leading experts on the music of Wolfgang Amadeus Mozart. He'd written extensively about Mozart, and his most recent book, published the year in which he was murdered, was considered the seminal work on the subject.

Musinski was no genteel academician. Short and built like a wrestler, his head shaved, he was a pugnacious, intensely private man in his personal life who scorned the views of fellow Mozart scholars and wasn't reticent about attacking them in magazine and journal articles and other venues. *Washingtonian* magazine, in one of its yearly "Best and Worst" features, listed him among the most disliked professors in the D.C. area. His sour relationship with colleagues at the university was openly known and discussed; his tenure was assured, however, because of his stature in his field and his ability to generate large donations to Georgetown's Department of Music. His frequent absences—he spent considerable time in Europe—were overlooked for the same reasons. One wealthy donor, who requested anonymity, told a magazine writer, "Every time Professor Musinski asks for a contribution, I'm afraid that if I decline he'll grab me in a headlock and throw me to the ground. I don't mean that literally, of course, but it sometimes seems that way."

On the day of his death, Musinski had taught a graduate seminar at the school. According to his students, he'd seemed especially distracted and short-tempered, although as one of them said, it was hard to make such distinctions with the professor. His fuse was always short, and he wore his disdain for his students on the sleeve of the black cardigan sweater and black T-shirt he seemed to never be without.

Others told the police that they'd seen him hurry from the building immediately following the seminar, get into his vintage red MG sports car, and race from the parking lot.

That was the last time Aaron Musinski was seen alive. His only known family member in the Washington area, a niece named Felicia James, called 911 at ten-thirty that night to report a break-in and murder at her uncle's home, a quaint, albeit poorly maintained Victorian town house on Georgetown's Q Street. When the police arrived, led by Detective Raymond Pawkins, Ms. James was sitting on a weathered white wrought-iron love seat in the small garden at the rear of the house, a jumbled jungle of vines, heavily laden trees, and tall grass. She was in shock, and it took gentle prodding by Pawkins to convince her to lead them to her uncle's body.

They followed her inside through a back door off a moss-covered brick patio, which led to a small kitchen. The rest of the house's first floor had been converted into an office and study, except for a small card table off the kitchen at which he'd obviously taken his meals. Floor-to-ceiling bookcases covered each wall. A series of crude folding tables overflowed with books and papers, which were also strewn on threadbare Oriental rugs with frayed edges. Briefcases and shoulder bags of various sizes and shapes were piled in a corner.

His body rested on a pile of newspapers. His blood had soaked into the papers, prompting Pawkins to think of the old riddle: What's black and white and red (read) all over? *Newspapers.* Musinski had been bludgeoned to death. The weapon, a bloodied fireplace poker, lay next to him.

"Do you live here, too?" Pawkins asked the niece.

"No, but I visit my uncle often. He lives alone and I worry about him." She cried.

Other detectives searched upstairs, where the bedrooms were in equal disarray.

"When did you last speak with your uncle?" Pawkins asked.

"This morning. I usually call him before he leaves for school."

"Anything unusual about him this morning?"

"No. He sounded tired. He'd come back from London two days earlier and was still suffering jet lag. But no, he was his usual self."

The detective was aware of Musinski's reputation from having read stories, and hesitated to ask his next question: "Did your uncle have any enemies that you're aware of?"

"He was—my uncle was a controversial figure," she replied, "but I can't imagine anyone disliking him enough to want to kill him. He was actually a very sweet man."

As only a favorite niece could view him, Pawkins thought.

Evidence technicians and someone from the ME's office arrived and went through their required tasks. While they did—and while Ms. James retreated to the garden—Pawkins went through the contents of the large space Musinski had devoted to his life's work. *How could the man find anything in this mess?* was what he thought as he picked up, read, and dropped materials back where they'd been on the tables. Two hours later, he fetched Musinski's niece from the garden.

"You all right to drive home?" he asked.

"Yes, I'll be fine. The shock is wearing off. All I care about now is that whoever did this pay the price."

"We'll do our best to make that happen," Pawkins said. "By the way, did your uncle have a will?"

"Yes."

"Who's the beneficiary?"

"I am."

"I see. We'll be wanting to talk to you again, Ms. James."

"Of course. I want you to know that I loved my uncle very much."

"I don't doubt that for a minute," Pawkins said.

As he walked her to her car, patrolmen were stringing yellow crime-scene tape around the house, while neighbors peered anxiously from their front steps and through windows. "The house will be off-limits for a day or two," Pawkins advised. "But if you want to come back, call me and I'll arrange for someone to accompany you."

"Thank you. I appreciate that. Good night."

Pawkins spent the better part of the following day at the house, and after a dinner break, he returned and continued to search for clues as to who might have murdered Aaron Musinski. At the same time, he methodically examined some of the contents of the professor's working space. It was a treasure trove of scholarly works on music, with much of it devoted to his favorite subject. Pawkins pulled down one of the books Musinski had written on the musical genius Mozart's life and read a few chapters. The man certainly knew his stuff, Pawkins recognized, and Musinski didn't hesitate to harshly condemn the conclusions of others.

Three days later, Pawkins received a call from an obviously distraught Felicia James.

"What can I do for you?" the detective asked.

"I'm at my uncle's house. You must come right away."

"Whoa, slow down. You sound upset. What's going on there?"

"Please, Detective, it's very important."

Ms. James met him at the door. Her face mirrored the distress in her voice. They went to the main room that had served as Musinski's study and office. Ms. James handed Pawkins an opened envelope. The address indicated that it had been sent to her home, and was marked REGISTERED, RETURN RECEIPT REQUESTED.

"What's this?" Pawkins asked.

"Read it. It's been at the post office. I have a box there. I didn't have the energy to pick up my mail before today."

The return address was Aaron Musinski's. Pawkins opened the envelope and read the one-page letter it contained.

"Wow!" he said, handing it back to her.

"It's not here," she said flatly, indicating the room with a sweep of her hand.

"Are you sure?"

"I've looked everywhere. I picked up Uncle Aaron at the airport when he returned from London. He'd gone there to meet with a friend, another Mozart expert. My uncle and this friend had worked together for years searching for missing Mozart scores. Uncle Aaron was an expert on all of Mozart's works—operas, symphonies, string quartets, even the one ballet he wrote. But his special interest was in a series of string quartets supposedly written by Mozart with his idol, Franz Joseph Haydn. Those scores have never been seen by anyone, at least as far as the world knew. But as you can see by the letter, Uncle Aaron and his colleague in London found them." She leaped up from her chair and exclaimed, "They actually found them! Do you know how monumentally important that is?"

"I can imagine," Pawkins said. "You said whatever he found isn't here. How do you know?"

"Because I've searched everywhere." She went to the corner

where the briefcases were stacked and held one up. It was a battered, supple leather case. Judging from the way it hung from her fingers, it was empty.

"Uncle Aaron had this with him when he returned from London. It was bulging when he came through Customs. I even asked him what was in it; he said it was just a lot of junk. That's what he called it, 'junk'! Now it's empty. Don't you see? He had the Mozart-Haydn scores in it, and now they're gone. Whoever killed him knew about those scores and murdered my uncle in order to have them."

"That could be," said Pawkins. "Any idea who might have known what your uncle found and would kill to get it?"

"Some of his jealous detractors," she answered. "I can give you a list."

"That will be helpful. I'll follow up on it."

The murder was never solved, nor were the Mozart-Haydn scores ever recovered.

∞

Annabel read a final line from one of the websites devoted to the Aaron Musinski murder and the disappearance of the scores.

> When asked about the possible whereabouts of the scores that allegedly were behind the murder of Aaron Musinski, the lead detective, Raymond Pawkins, said, "Lord knows. There's a large, black hole out there into which priceless works of art disappear, with wealthy men in it who'll pay anything, and even kill, to possess them. I doubt if we'll ever know."

EIGHTEEN

The white Chevrolet Suburban had been sitting at the Al-Karama-Trebil border checkpoint between Iraq and Jordan for the better part of an hour. Finally, the driver, an Iraqi dressed in a flowing white dishdasha, was allowed to pull up to where Jordanian troops checked the steady flow of vehicles heading for Amman on the heavily traveled Baghdad-Amman highway, the infamous and dangerous Route 10. The driver rolled down his window and handed the security guard the necessary papers. The guard frowned as he examined them, handed the papers back, and poked his head through the window to see the passenger in the rear seat.

"Hello," the passenger said with a wan smile. He extended a hand that held his British passport. The guard went to where another uniformed soldier leaned against the gate smoking a cigarette. They both looked at the document. One said something that made the other laugh. The passport was returned, the gate opened, and the vehicle was allowed to enter Jordan.

The passenger settled back and closed his eyes. He'd dreaded the six-hundred-mile trip since being told to go to Amman by his superior in the Baghdad office. He might have opted out of the assignment, using his senior status and age in the British Foreign Service—he was within a year of retirement—but decided to make the journey. This was important, he knew. Sending a younger, less experienced case officer would not be prudent. The man was Milton Crowley, the only son of a British father and Jewish mother. The Jewish side of his heritage was seldom acknowledged, especially since being posted to Iraq. The flames were high enough there without fanning them further.

His driver had said little during the leg from Baghdad to the Jordanian border, for which Crowley was grateful. Both he and the driver had been on the alert for any sign of "The Group of Death," an Iraqi insurgency group that had recently been attacking vehicles on Route 10. Twice they'd had to pull far off to the side of the road to allow U.S. military convoys to pass, their soldiers' weapons trained on the white Suburban. But now that they were in Jordan, the driver visibly relaxed and became verbose, looking in his rearview mirror while talking although somehow keeping his eyes on the road. Crowley could have done without the chatter. He wanted to nap but knew that was impossible. The endless, singsong flow of words from the driver, coupled with an inborn inability to sleep in vehicles or on planes, kept the slight British diplomat awake the entire trip.

They eventually reached downtown Amman and pulled up in front of the Le Royal Hotel in Jebal Amman, on Zahran Street, the Third Circle. The city's newest luxury hotel, thirty-one stories high, was the tallest building in Amman. Crowley had stayed there before on a previous trip and suffered the same reaction he always had when in hotels, a profound yearning for his quaint, peaceful cottage on a river in Wareham, Dorset, England. One year to go before returning there permanently. It could not come fast enough.

His senior status would have allowed him to choose one of the suites on a high floor, with sweeping views of the city. But views no longer meant anything to Crowley. You've seen one view from a hotel window, you've seen them all. Besides, he was uncomfortable being surrounded by windows. A lesser room, on a lower floor, with but a single window was more to his liking.

He napped in the darkened room. Somewhat rested, he showered and shaved. His image in the mirror was not what he wished to see. He showed his age—the chicken neck, the sparse, unruly gray hair, and the gray stubble on his chin and cheeks. A discernible weariness in his eyes testified to there being far fewer days ahead for him than behind.

He dressed in the same wrinkled blue suit and the same shirt and tie he'd worn during the drive and went to one of the hotel complex's thirteen restaurants, where he had a lager, a pasta dish, and a salad. His watch said he had another hour before he had to leave. He sat in the lobby for a few minutes but found it too busy. Two thousand people attending an affair in the Ishtar Ballroom kept spilling out into the lobby; nostalgia for his idyllic English countryside cottage was almost painful.

He returned to his room and passed the rest of the hour there before taking a cab from the hotel to the town of Debbin, approximately fifty miles to the north of Amman. After consulting a slip of paper, he instructed the driver to let him off at an entrance to the Debbin National Park, thirty miles of pine forest stretching from Debbin to Ajlun. The driver expressed his concern at letting the little Englishman off in such a dark and secluded spot, but Crowley assured him he would be fine. "Someone is picking me up any minute," he said. The moment the taxi pulled away, a silver Mercedes that had been parked a few hundred feet away, its lights extinguished, came to life and approached. M.T., the burly Brit who'd been Ghaleb Rihnai's handler, rolled down the window. "Evening, mate," he said.

"Good evening," Crowley replied, coming around to the passenger side and getting in.

"Not an especially cheery place to meet up," M.T. said, "but safer than in town."

Crowley said nothing as M.T. pulled away and drove into the park till they reached a secluded picnic area covered by a canopy of pines and oaks; a little, colorful field of wildflowers looked like a painting in the car's halogen headlights.

M.T. turned off the lights and ignition and cracked windows on both sides. "Good trip?" he asked.

"Horrid. Tell me about Rihnai."

"Not much to tell, really. Poor bugger had half his head blown off. We'd just had a meeting at one of the safe houses. Can't use that place again. It's been compromised. Not quite sure how that happened, or how Rihnai was found out, but working on it."

"The young Iraqi he befriended as a source. Do you know him?"

"Afraid not. Never did meet him or know his name. Clever chap, the former Mr. Ghaleb Rihnai was. He evidently knew that as long as he kept his Iraqi source to himself, he held the trump card. Didn't get him very far, though. A bloody shame what happened to him. He wanted out, wanted to go back to the States. Maybe he knew someone was on to him."

"And to you," Crowley said. "Look, I've been sent here to make sure that there's a sense of urgency on your part. The Americans are damned edgy about what your Mr. Rihnai came up with. You said in your communiqués that the attack was being choreographed out of Cairo. Explain. How did this Iraqi patsy know that?"

"Through a brother in Iraq, according to Ghaleb. This brother, another name he wouldn't share with me, is connected there. At least that's what he claimed."

"This concerns me," said Crowley, lowering his window farther to allow more night air into the Mercedes. "All I hear from you is 'he claimed' and 'as far as I know.' If al-Qaeda successfully pulls off this attack, the fallout will be significant. We've got to have more specifics."

"Back off, Crowley," M.T. said. "I'm doing all I can here, with bloody little support. If Ghaleb hadn't been taken out, I've no doubt that those 'specifics' you want would be forthcoming. But damn it, man, I've given you all I can. Ghaleb said that bin Laden has personally ordered the attack, and that it's being activated through an al-Qaeda cell in Cairo. Oh, yes, and there's some vague Canadian connection. Sorry, mate, but that's all Ghaleb had to say about that. His Iraqi source was intending to go back to Baghdad and confer there with his brother. We would have learned more *specifics* if Ghaleb hadn't gotten it."

Crowley said nothing.

"You'd think the bloody Americans would do their own snooping," M.T. said. "Hell, it's them at the receiving end of the attack. Doesn't make sense to me why we're digging up dirt for them, sticking out our necks. I've got a contracting business to run here in Jordan, plenty of work to keep me busy without playing spy games for the Yanks."

"When can you find out more?" Crowley asked, ignoring the diatribe.

"Probably not fast enough for you, Crowley. Not without Ghaleb and his Iraqi chum."

"Keep trying."

"Easy for you to say, mate. Staying in Amman long?"

"No."

"Back to Baghdad?"

"No. Washington. Tomorrow morning."

"I'm due for some R-and-R myself," M.T. said.

"Take me back to the city," Crowley said.

"Right you are, mate. I'm a full-service provider, handler, and chauffeur. On the side, I fix boilers in this bloody place." He started the car, turned on the lights, and drove away, the angry sound of the engine mirroring his mood. He dropped Crowley off at a taxi stand on the outskirts of the city.

"Always a pleasure," M.T. said as Crowley exited the car without saying a word and climbed into a waiting cab. "And your mother, too," M.T. muttered as he watched the taxi disappear into a dense fog that had descended upon the city.

NINETEEN

Sylvia Johnson and Carl Berry were going over the day's schedule when Willie Portelain came through the door.

"What are you doing here?" Berry asked. "You're supposed
to be in the hospital."

"Got sprung, man. I told them I was feeling topnotch and had important work to do, said the city needed me."

He eyed the half-eaten jelly donut sitting on a napkin on the desk,
which Sylvia moved behind a pile of file folders.

"So, Willie," Berry said, "I understand you're going on a diet."

"Supposed to be," he chortled, "only I don't know what good it'll
do. These docs—man, they don't know a hell of a lot. They poke
around and stick you with all sorts a needles and then tell you to go on
a diet and exercise. I've got pills, little white ones and little blue ones.
You'd think they'd learn more than that in medical school, huh? Exercise? Get nothin' but on this job. Right? The way I figure it, the man
upstairs has everybody's name on a list. He checks you off as you
croak. When it's your name that comes up, good-bye baby, *hasta la*

vista, cash in your potato chips. All the diets in the world ain't going to change that."

"That's one of the dumbest things I've ever heard from you, Willie," Sylvia said.

"Watch your mouth, girl. Just 'cause you were born with good genes don't mean everybody was. Our number comes up, that's it. In the meantime, here I am, ready to save Washington from the bad guys." Then, quietly, to Sylvia: "Thanks, baby, for taking care of ol' Willie yesterday."

"You'd do the same for me," she said.

"I'd do more than that," he said, giving her what passed for a leer. "So, what's up for today?"

"The Lee case," Berry said.

"How about that punk piano player?" Portelain asked.

"The one you coldcocked?" Berry said.

"That's him," Willie said. "Hey, I didn't hit the punk. He ran right into my arm."

"So I heard," said Berry. "Look, in the first place, he's no punk. He's maybe a little stupid when it comes to self-preservation, but from what we know, he's a first-rate pianist. He's not bringing charges."

Portelain guffawed. "Him? Bring charges? For what?"

"Police brutality."

"Screw him," Portelain said. "I—"

"Forget about that," Berry said. "Our friend doesn't have an alibi that can be corroborated. He stays bright on the radar screen. I figure we let him stew for a day or two, lick his wounds, and do some thinking. In the meantime, I want you two—I assumed it would only be Sylvia, but now that you're here, Willie, I want both of you to question those agents, Melincamp and his partner . . ." He checked his notes. "Ms. Baltsa."

"I already talked to Melincamp," Portelain said. "He's a strange-o."

"Talk to him again. Public Affairs is swamped with media inquiries. We need something to feed them. PA is holding a press conference at five. It would be nice if I could tell them we're making progress. Get back over to the Kennedy Center in your spare time and pump anyone who was there the night she was killed. Let's not limit things to the victim's inner circle."

"In our spare time?" Willie snorted.

"PA will say we're making progress whether we are or not," Johnson said. " 'No specifics,' " she said, mimicking a department spokesman. " 'We aren't able to comment on an ongoing investigation.' The usual."

Berry stood and stretched. "Let's move," he said. "Oh, did you two see this?" He held up a copy of *Washingtonian*.

"No," Johnson said, taking the magazine.

"Page one thirteen," Berry said.

Johnson opened it.

"Man, what's he got his picture in there for?" Willie asked.

"The Washington Opera," Berry replied. "Remember? He used to hang out with those people."

"He was in some of the shows," Johnson said.

"Right," said Berry. "Take it. I've read it. Talk to those two agents, and check in with me later. Good to see you back, Willie. Do what the doctors told you."

As Portelain and Johnson headed out to interview Philip Melincamp and Zöe Baltsa, Berry met with his superior, Cole Morris.

"Anything new on the Kennedy Center case?" Morris asked.

"No," Berry said. "Her roommate, the piano player from Toronto, Christopher Warren, isn't off the hook. Johnson brought him in yesterday."

"So I heard. He got banged up?"

"Yeah, but not to worry. He's not bringing charges."

"What's with Willie Portelain?"

"He's okay, out of the hospital. He and Johnson are interviewing two talent agents from Toronto, the ones who represented the victim and Warren. I've got the victim's parents in town." He checked his watch. "I'd better get over to their hotel. They didn't want to come here."

"Did you see the article on Ray Pawkins in *Washingtonian*?" Morris asked.

Berry laughed. "Yeah, I did. He always had a knack for self-promotion. I could never figure the guy. He was there the night they discovered the singer's body at the Kennedy Center."

"Was he? Why?"

"He's an extra in the next opera they're doing. He always loved that sort of thing. Oh, by the way, Pawkins is working for them."

"Working for them?"

"He's signed on as their PI."

"To do what?"

"Catch the singer's killer before we do."

"I'll be damned. That's all we need, somebody working private and getting in the way."

"I'm supposed to meet with him."

"To do what?"

"Discuss the case."

"The hell you are."

"It can't hurt."

"We don't discuss ongoing investigations, remember?"

"I know, Cole, I know, but maybe he'll come up with something that will help us."

"Or get something from us that'll help him."

"Let's see how it plays out."

"Suit yourself. Hey, Carl, speaking of Pawkins, there might be a break in the Musinski murder."

"Musinski? The college professor at Georgetown U? How far back does that one go, five, six years?"

"Six. There was that graduate assistant at Georgetown who looked good, only we could never put enough together to charge him. Forensics might have linked him to the scene."

"Took them long enough. They mention that case in the article on Ray."

"We'll want to talk to Pawkins at some point. He was lead on it."

"I'll mention it to him."

"Yeah, do that. Be straight with me. Is Willie fit for duty?"

Berry nodded. "He says he is."

"And you say?"

"I say that if he says he is, he is. He's supposed to go on a diet."

It got a fat laugh from Morris. "And the President's press secretary will be candid at news conferences. Keep in touch."

Charise Lee's parents were staying at a downtown Holiday Inn on New Jersey Avenue. Berry went to the desk and asked for Mr. and Mrs. Lee's room.

"I'm sorry, sir, but we don't have anyone named Lee registered."

"They're from Toronto," Berry said.

"I can't check names on that basis," the young male clerk said. "Sorry."

Berry considered pulling out his badge and encouraging the clerk to do better, but decided he'd wait before pulling rank. He took a seat in the functionally furnished lobby and took in the comings and go-ings of hotel guests. Across the room he saw an older Caucasian man and much younger Asian woman sitting close together on an orange vinyl love seat. *Could be*, he said to himself as he crossed the lobby and stood over them. "Mr. and Mrs. Lee?" he asked.

His sudden appearance startled them. The woman, slender and wearing a simple dress made of a shiny black material, as black as her hair, quickly stood; the man remained seated.

"I'm sorry," Berry said. "I'm looking for the parents of a Ms. Charise Lee and—"

"Yes, yes," the woman said. "I am her mother."

"Oh," Berry said, introducing himself. "I checked with the desk and—"

The man stood. Berry pegged him to be in his early seventies. Bald on top, spigots of unruly black-and-gray hair poking out on the sides of his head, and tufts of hair protruding from surprisingly large ears. He needed a shave, and was slightly hunched, the posture of a man who'd stood bent over for too much of his life. He wore a wrin-kled gray suit and a plain black tie whose knot did not meet his throat.

"I'm Charise's father," he said in a raspy voice.

He and Berry shook hands. Berry surveyed the lobby. "Maybe you'd rather we went to your room," he suggested.

"Yeah, that'd be better," the man said.

His wife looked at a sign pointing to the hotel's lobby-level restaurant.

"Would you like to go in for something to eat?" Berry asked. "Coffee or tea, maybe?"

"We don't have to eat," the man said. "Maybe a cold drink."

Berry saw that the restaurant was virtually empty. He motioned for them to follow as he went inside and told the hostess he needed a table for three, preferably in a corner where they could talk. She took them to just such a table, placed menus on it, and left. Seated, Berry said, "I'm a little confused. The hotel doesn't have any record of you having checked in."

"The name's not Lee," the man said. "That's Betty's name." He indicated his wife.

"But—"

"Yeah, I know," the father said. "It's confusing. My name's Seymour Goldberg. Charise decided Goldberg wasn't a good name for an opera singer, so she took Betty's name. I told her names don't matter and that she should be proud of her real name, but you know how women can be."

Berry glanced at Betty for a reaction and received a blank look. "It was a better name to use," she said in a soft, flat voice.

"See what I mean?" Seymour said.

"Yeah, well, I am really sorry to be meeting you under these circumstances," Berry said, "and I am very sorry about the death of your daughter."

"Thank you," Mrs. Lee-Goldberg said.

It was tea for her, coffees for the men, and Berry insisted upon a double order of English muffins to be shared.

"Have they asked you to identify the body yet?" the detective asked, wanting to get that question out of the way.

"We're going later today," Charise's father replied. "Who did this to her?"

"We don't know yet," Berry said, "but we're working hard to find out. I'm hoping you might have some information that will help us."

"What could we know?" Goldberg said. "We live in Canada. Charise decided to come to Washington to study opera with the big names here. I didn't want her to go, but—"

"It was her choice," the mother said. "She said she would learn so much and become a better singer."

"I admit I don't know much about opera," Berry said, "but I understand your daughter was a very talented young lady."

"Yes, she was," the mother agreed.

"She had the voice of an angel," the father said. He placed his hand on top of his wife's, and tears formed. Embarrassed, he wiped them away with the back of his other hand. "She got involved with the wrong people," he declared.

"I'd be interested in hearing more about that," Berry said, their drinks and muffins on the table.

"Maybe we shouldn't talk about it," the mother said.

"Why not?" Goldberg said. "It's true. I warned her about the sort of people who take advantage of talented young women like her. Those two agents got ahold of her and—"

"Mr. Melincamp?" Berry said.

"That's right. Melincamp and that woman he works with."

"Zöe something," Berry said.

"That's her," Mr. Goldberg said.

"What about a piano player named Warren?" Berry asked.

"Christopher," Betty Lee-Goldberg said. "He's a nice young man."

"I don't agree," her husband said, taking a bite of muffin and a sip of coffee heavily doctored with sugar and half-and-half.

"Oh?"

"He used her, Mr. . . . you said your name was?"

"Berry, Detective Carl Berry."

"I'm sorry, Mr. Berry—Detective Berry—I don't remember names that good anymore. Christopher Warren used Charise's talent to make his own career better. I saw through him the minute I met him."

"He accompanied Charise when she sang," the mother said. "He's a very good pianist."

"Were they more than just friends and professional colleagues?" Berry asked.

"Meaning, did they sleep together?" Goldberg asked.

Berry nodded.

"I suppose they did," the older man said. "I warned Charise about that. She was such a naïve young girl." Tears again formed and he angrily rubbed them away. "I'm sorry," he said. "I just can't believe this has happened. It wouldn't have happened if she'd stayed home and not come here. She had a wonderful voice teacher in Toronto, but Warren and those agents convinced her to audition for the opera school here." He hit the table with his fist. "And all that talk about saving the world. Her friends were full of that stupid talk. They sounded like Communists!"

"Communists?" Berry said.

"Radicals. Believe me, I know about such things. I lost people in the Holocaust. Family. Radicals! Like Hitler. I told her that if she wanted to save the world, she should become successful and be a good citizen, make money and give some to the poor. That's the way to save the world, not the way her friends with the long hair and tattoos said. The wrong people. That's why she's dead. Always the wrong people."

His wife touched his hand and said, "Please, Seymour, it doesn't help."

"Excuse me," Mr. Goldberg said, using the tabletop for leverage as he stood unsteadily and shuffled off in the direction of the restrooms.

"I know how difficult this is for both of you," Berry said.

"You must forgive Seymour," his wife said. "He had such hopes for Charise. We both did. It has not been easy for him to support her career. He has worked as a tailor all his life, worked hard, and always found the money for her university and the private lessons."

"Was Charise your only child?" Berry asked.

"Yes."

Berry was pleased that the conversation, in Seymour's absence, had turned to something less grim for the moment than the murder of their daughter. He'd graduated with a degree in Sociology and had always been fascinated with the way people lived their lives, the decisions they made, and the paths and many detours their journeys took through this temporary life. That was one of the reasons he'd become a cop. It offered a unique and rich vantage point from which to indulge his interest in the human condition.

"You say he's a tailor. Does he still do that for a living?"

"No, I'm afraid not. You noticed his hands. Arthritis. He can no longer work with needle and thread. We have a small launderette in Toronto." She smiled. "I was working in a laundry when we met. I think Seymour thought it was appropriate for a Chinese woman to be doing laundry."

Berry joined her gentle laugh. "A little typecasting, huh?"

She nodded.

Goldberg returned and resumed his place at the table.

"Tell me more about Christopher Warren and the two agents," Berry said.

Charise's mother supplied, "Charise said it was important for an opera singer to have an agent. She said it would open doors for her, doors she herself could not open."

Her husband started to speak, but his wife added, "Besides, Mr. Melincamp made it possible for Charise to come here to study. He has been paying for where she stayed with Christopher."

"How did she get along with them," Berry asked, "the agents and Christopher Warren?"

"We don't know," Seymour said.

Berry's eyebrows went up. "She never confided in you about them and her relationship with them?"

Husband and wife exchanged a nervous glance before she said, "Charise has been estranged from us for some time."

"Over what?" Berry asked.

"She wouldn't listen to us," Seymour said, his voice taking on sudden strength. "She was headstrong."

"Like young women these days," his wife defended.

"I know what it's like out there in the world," Seymour said, the weary tone having returned. "I didn't want her ending up taking in other people's dirty laundry, their soiled underwear and smelly socks. I told her what it takes to succeed, but she had her own notions."

Berry sympathized with the older man, but wondered whether he'd been too heavy-handed with his only child and pushed her away. It happened, he knew. His own father, a college professor, had been furious when his son announced he intended to go into law enforcement after four successful years in college, and had basically shut down communication between them for the two years before his father died one afternoon of a massive heart attack while lecturing a classroom full of students. Their rift should have been healed, but it was too late for that now. His relationship with his aging mother, while long distance, was good, and he worked hard at keeping it that way.

He checked his watch. It had been an interesting meeting, but nothing tangible had resulted that would aid in the murder investigation.

"Are you sure there's nothing you can tell me about people in your daughter's life that might shed light on her death?" he asked.

"Something like whether Warren or the agents might have had a reason to kill her?" Goldberg asked.

"Yes," Berry said.

Husband and wife looked at each other.

"That couldn't be," the mother said.

"Couldn't be?" Berry said.

"They would not have hurt my daughter," she said. "Everyone loved Charise."

Somebody didn't, Berry thought.

He gave them his card and urged them to call if they thought of anything. After paying the bill, and again offering his condolences, he left them at the table, one half of a cold English muffin the remnants of their having met.

TWENTY

The meeting of the Opera Ball committee was spirited, and at times contentious.

The pressure was on, the date of the gala rapidly approaching. Adding to the sense of urgency was the murder, the tragic nature of Ms. Lee's death, and rampant speculation about who'd killed her. Since Mac Smith had arranged for the private detective to investigate the crime, Annabel was a target of probes into what progress her husband was aware of.

"I really don't know any more than you do," Annabel replied. "I just know that Raymond Pawkins, who used to be a Homicide detective, has agreed to work with us, and that the police are vigorously pursuing it, too."

"Oh, come on, Annabel," one woman said, "I just know that you and that handsome husband of yours already know who the murderer is and are just waiting for the right time to announce it."

Annabel was tempted to educate her questioner about why that scenario was unlikely, at best, but instead simply denied it. Another member of the committee who'd overheard the exchange said, seriously, "It would be wonderful if it could be announced prior to the ball. That would make the evening especially meaningful."

Another woman disagreed: "I don't think it would be wonderful at all. It would only deflect attention from the ball."

As with any undertaking of the scope of the Opera Ball, there were bound to be mishaps, and thorny issues to be resolved. On this day, the ongoing and nettlesome chore of seating arrangements topped the agenda.

The festive evening would begin with sit-down dinners at more than thirty foreign embassies, hosted by their ambassadors. Five hundred leaders of Washington's diplomatic, corporate, government, and arts communities would pay handsomely for the privilege of attending these relatively intimate, pre-ball dinners featuring food indigenous to each embassy's home country. Some couples lobbied for seats at the British, French, and Spanish embassies as hard as professional lobbyists fought for pet bills in Congress. Others, who prided themselves on an appreciation of ethnic food, happily signed up for dinners at less popular venues. But no matter where you ended up sitting, the Opera Ball was a yearly social event not to be missed. As Thorstein Veblen's seminal work on status in America, *The Theory of the Leisure Class*, had proffered, we'd gone from hunting and fishing skills as signs of social standing to what he termed the "modern-peaceable barbarian" stage, in which social status now involved signs of affluence, tuxedoed men arriving at galas in large, expensive cars with ladies in designer fashions on their arms. See and be seen. It was a lot better than being skilled with a crossbow, Annabel thought when first reading it.

Following those private dinners, everyone would head for the main event, the ball itself, hosted this year by the Brazilian Embassy on Massachusetts Avenue, where Brazilian desserts—*Manjar Branco*, a coconut flan with prune sauce; Cream Sago, tapioca pudding with red wine; and Peach Mousse—would be savored, and couples would dance the night away beneath a massive tent to the music of one of

D.C.'s favorite society orchestras. Later, as whiskey and wine and heat and humidity loosened lips and lacquered hair, two Brazilian samba bands would send the revelers home filled with fond memories, and with the Washington National Opera's coffers fatter as well.

The seating charts for the various embassy dinners were displayed on a large easel, with problem ones circled in red on the master layout.

"The Zieglers insist upon being seated next to the Carlsons at the Colombian Embassy," the woman in charge of seating said. "Ken Ziegler has a deal pending with the bank where Carlson is CEO." She threw up her hands. "I simply can't juggle this anymore."

"You have to accommodate the Zieglers," ball chairwoman Nicki Frolich said. "He's funding the Mexico vacation door prize."

"Fine. *You* call Dr. Federman and tell him we've changed his seats. I'm tired of being growled at."

"All right, I will," Frolich said.

Another board, on which personal likes and dislikes were listed, was placed on the easel as a reminder of how such details must be honored—nothing with peanuts on a certain senator's meal, keep a certain journalist far away from a member of the administration who'd been savaged in a piece written by the journalist, and other admonitions that, if ignored, could result in unhappiness for those involved.

The woman in charge of party favors reported that the manufacturer of the custom-designed velvet bags in which an assortment of donated goodies would be placed had suffered a wildcat strike and might not be able to fulfill the order in time. A subcommittee, one of many, was formed on the spot to come up with a contingency plan, including driving to New York to pick up substitutes.

As the meeting wound down, Annabel, who'd agreed to be on the subcommittee exploring other sources of favor bags, sat back and reflected on this ambitious undertaking of which she'd chosen to take part.

There were those who viewed the Ladies of the Balls as dilettantes, wives of wealthy men, who clamored to serve on fundraising committees to advance their social status within the community. But

Annabel knew that was flippant and often inaccurate. Yes, there were such women, but Annabel had observed that they were generally shunned by those in charge. It was serious business, this mounting of a major social event in the nation's capital, with a lot at stake, and the women with whom she'd been working closely were anything but dilettantes. They put in twenty-hour days, and their painstaking planning would make any military commander about to launch a major invasion proud. Huge society events like the Opera Ball, and others, didn't just happen. They resulted from the hard work and creativity of countless volunteers, and Annabel was proud to play a role, no matter how inconsequential.

☙

Detective Carl Berry also had more meetings on his agenda.

He left the Holiday Inn after his introduction to Charise Lee's parents and went directly to the Round Robin Bar at the Willard Inter-Continental Hotel, where Ray Pawkins sat nursing a mug of Irish coffee minus the Irish. The Round Robin was Pawkins' favorite D.C. bar, which put him in good company. Looking down upon him were the photographs of former distinguished guests—Abraham Lincoln, whose first presidential paycheck went to pay his bill there; Mark Twain, whose white-suited forays from the bar into the hotel were, as his biographer Albert Bigelow Paine put it, ". . . like descending the steps of a throne room, or some royal landing place, where Cleopatra's barge might lie"; Charles Dickens; Buffalo Bill Cody; John Philip Sousa; and Carrie Nation, the hatchet-wielding prohibitionist who prompted management to place a sign above the bar: ALL NATIONS WELCOME EXCEPT CARRIE."

Berry slid onto a stool.

"Drink?" Pawkins asked.

"Too early for me," Berry said. He ordered a tomato juice. "You're buying, of course," he said with a playful tap on Pawkins' shoulder. "This place is too rich for my blood."

"True," Pawkins agreed, "but the drinks are large and the ambience agreeable. Besides, we're surrounded by the ghosts of Washington history. So, tell me what's going on at the great law enforcement agency in the sky."

"There's never anything new over there," Berry replied, "but you know that."

"Still working the Lee case?"

"Uh-huh."

"Nothing new on that, either?"

"I just spent an hour with her parents. They're in from Toronto."

"And?"

"They had nothing to offer, except that the father—he's a lot older than his wife—he's not a fan of the pianist who roomed with the victim, or the two talent agents she hooked up with."

"The Melincamp-Baltsa Artists Agency," Pawkins said.

"You know them?"

"I did some research. She could have done better. They're third-tier agents. Melincamp has been accused of pocketing client money. He was down-and-out when the moneyed Ms. Baltsa bought her way into the agency."

"Tell me more," Berry said.

"Not a lot more to tell, Carl."

"He can't be all take, no give," Berry said. "He's paying for the apartment here in D.C. that Lee and Warren were staying in."

"I'm not surprised. From what my opera friends tell me, Charise Lee had one hell of a future as a soprano. Of course, she's from the new school of soprano-lite singers, smaller voices in smaller bodies, that seem to have displaced singers with traditionally big voices, the kind that can fill a vast opera house without miking. They're certainly pleasant to listen to, and to look at, but they lack that palpitating, bigger-than-life presence that the truly great opera singers possess. Still, if what I hear is true, this now very dead soprano-lite might have become the darling of the opera world in a few years, which could pay off in spades for Melincamp down the road. Laying out some rent money early on in her career might have been a smart move."

Berry sipped his juice and thought before offering, "If she

promised to be a meal ticket for him, that would pretty much rule him out as her killer. No motivation to have her dead."

"On the surface. But Melincamp's a whore. Maybe he was stealing from her and she got wind of it, threatened to blow the whistle."

"Doesn't play," Berry said. "She was a young singer getting started. How much money could she have been making? Hell, she was just a student here."

"Wrong, my friend. Anyone accepted into the Young Artist Program here at the Washington National Opera is more than 'just a student.' They're very special talents who had to prove their mettle to none other than the maestro of maestros, Plácido Domingo. No, Carl, anyone accepted here has a bright future, indeed."

"I'll take your word for it," Berry said. "Tell me more about Melincamp and his partner."

"Melincamp's a low-life. He talks a good story but is always looking for a buck. He and Baltsa aren't exactly copacetic partners, like Rogers and Hart, or Ben and Jerry. The way I hear it, he'd kill his mother for a lot less than you or I would."

"I wouldn't for any money," Berry said.

"You always were too serious, Carl. I was joking."

Pawkins reached into his small, leather shoulder bag and handed Berry the sponge he'd purchased at the theatrical supply shop. "Like this one?"

Berry's fingers made indentations in the sponge. "Where did you get this?"

"A store. I offer it to dissuade you from jumping to the conclusion that the killer had to have been someone involved with theater, specifically the opera. Anyone could have bought it the way I did." He laughed and checked his watch. "Almost time for a real drink. Here I've been telling you everything you need to know about the Lee case, as well as what's wrong with opera singers today, and nothing from you. Where does *your* investigation stand?"

"I've got people questioning the agents. We brought in Warren. Dumb kid bolted and got a faceful of Willie Portelain's fist."

"And he has an airtight alibi, I assume."

"Anything but. We'll start interviewing everyone in that Young Artist Program. Maybe we'll get lucky and come up with somebody who had it in for the victim, a guy she jilted, another singer who was jealous. I understand that opera singers can get pretty jealous of one another. In the meantime, we're still at square one. Hey, Ray, I saw the article about you. Pretty nice."

"My fifteen minutes of fame. I wasn't pleased with the photograph. I'm a lot younger and better-looking than the picture shows."

Berry cocked his head and exaggerated his scrutiny of Pawkins' face. "Yeah, you're right. Look, Cole wasn't happy when I told him we'd be getting together on the Lee case, but he didn't say no. I can use your help."

"And you'll have it."

Pawkins paid with a credit card.

"Let's stay in touch," Berry said as they stood on the sidewalk.

"Absolutely. I may have to run out of town for a day or two, but I'll let you know. Not sure I can get away. I'm in *Tosca*."

"So I read. You really enjoy being in operas, don't you?"

"I wouldn't do it if I didn't. Take care, Carl."

As Pawkins began to walk away, Berry said, "Hey, Ray."

"What?"

"I almost forgot. Remember the Musinski case you worked on six years ago?"

"Sure."

"They're reopening it."

"Oh?" Pawkins said, his eyes narrowing.

"Yeah. Forensics has come up with something that might link that grad assistant to the scene."

"That's interesting," Pawkins said.

"Cole said he'll be wanting to talk with you about it."

"Anytime."

☙

At approximately the time that Annabel Lee-Smith met with the Opera Ball committee, and Berry and Pawkins conferred, Milton

Crowley wearily exited the plane that had brought him from Amman, Jordan, to Washington. He hated flying, especially long trips that crossed time lines, and found airport security procedures to be unnecessarily burdensome and most likely ineffective. Most of all, it was the flights themselves that turned his mood foul, the dispirited flight attendants, uncomfortable seats that seemed deliberately designed to cause discomfort, and what passed for food served in-flight. As he tried to sleep—he was tired, but also wanted to avoid talking with his seatmate, a gregarious woman whose voice was like a cracked bell—he thought of better days in air travel, when he was younger, when flying to exotic lands was a special privilege and people dressed properly for their flights and . . .

He went through Customs and stood in a line of people waiting for taxis. His turbaned driver drove a vehicle that reeked of stale tobacco and whose rear seat was lumpy and confining; he thought of spacious London cabs and their intelligent, gentlemanly drivers and . . .

And he thought of his cottage in Dorset, where he would soon retire and flip a bird at the whole bloody world of intelligence, politics, and governments, and the insane men who governed them. Always, it was the vision of the cottage that salved his otherwise cranky disposition.

He handed the driver a slip of paper on which he'd written the address of a building on Ward Circle, closed his eyes, and prayed that the ride would be quick.

It wasn't.

He was eventually deposited outside a gate and fence. The driver was told to leave. Crowley showed his identification to a military guard, who placed a call. Crowley was allowed to pass through the gate and enter the building. The soldier at the desk reviewed his credentials, and he, too, made a call. A few minutes later, with a visitor's pass hanging from his neck, he was escorted by a uniformed young woman to a staircase. He had to stop halfway. His right hip had been acting up and a stabbing pain caused him to wince and to let out a small verbal protest. He'd been told he should have the hip replaced, but he wasn't about to let any surgeon cut into him, thank you very much, unless it became an absolute necessity. It flared up only now and then. Once he was at the cottage, things would be better.

"Sorry," he told his escort, who stood a few steps above him and looked unhappy at the delay.

She led him to a room at the end of a long corridor. Two armed, uniformed young men stood watch. The female officer said something in a guarded voice, which prompted one of them to open the door. Crowley entered. The room was a rectangle. Large windows had been sealed and painted, the color a slightly different pale green from the walls. A man in a three-piece suit seated at a long table in the center of the room stood and shook Crowley's hand. "Good trip?" he asked.

Why do people always ask that? Crowley wondered.

"Yes, quite, thank you, Joseph."

"Please, sit down," Joe Browning said, indicating a chair to his left, which Crowley gratefully took, relieving the pressure on his hip. "I appreciate your coming here on such short notice."

"It seemed necessary," Crowley said.

"That's an understatement," Browning said, underlining it with a chuckle. "So, fill me in. As you can imagine, our people are anxious to be brought up to speed on what you and your colleagues have uncovered in Jordan."

Crowley cleared his throat and looked to where a window once was. He wished it were still there. The room was claustrophobic. "I'm afraid we've gotten only so far," he said. "I don't know whether you are aware that our source in Amman was killed."

Browning nodded.

"Without that source, we've reached a bit of a standstill, I'm afraid."

"Sorry to hear that. Actually, we've been receiving intelligence through other sources that helps fill in some of the gaps."

"That's good," Crowley said.

"Interesting, the way terrorists' minds work, isn't it?"

"I suppose it is, although I prefer to think of their so-called minds as more depraved and immoral than interesting."

"Of course. What our people found especially probative was this shift in their thinking. What's your take on it?"

"I'm really not paid to analyze information, Joseph. I simply arrange for it to be gathered. But off the record, I would say that there is a certain wisdom to their new approach. It will certainly be easier to carry out, and the impact could be substantial."

"If it's what they're really intending. Tell me, Mr. Crowley, did your source in Jordan—I understand he had a pretty direct line into the insurgents through a family member—"

"That's right."

"Was there any hint as to the sort of high-profile target they might choose?"

"That's what we were hoping to find out," Crowley replied. "According to the source, they were in the process of drawing up their hit list. I suppose it had to meet with bin Laden's approval."

"If he's still alive."

"Yes, if."

"But it was ascertained that it would be centered here in Washington."

"That was our information, which we passed along."

"Yes, and we appreciated that. The secretary made an announcement right after we received that info. We've raised the terrorist alert level to Orange-Plus."

A tiny smile crossed Crowley's lips. *Americans and their fondness for anything technological, colorful—and useless.* A vision of sitting on a white wrought-iron bench at riverside in Dorset came and went.

"Do you have anything else to report?" Browning asked, opening a file folder on which TOP SECRET was stamped in red.

"Only one thing," Crowley said.

"Which is?"

"I met with the source's handler in Amman before coming here. He mentioned something about a Canadian connection."

"Canadian connection? That's intriguing. What sort of connection?"

"I don't know, nor did the handler. He hadn't mentioned it in previous messages. I assume it was simply an oversight."

"Oversights, like loose lips, can get us killed," said Browning.

Crowley said nothing. He wanted the meeting to be over.

"Well," Browning said, "this was a long way for you to come with so little new to offer."

Criticism or sympathy?

"I wish I had more."

Browning walked him to the door. "Will you be staying in Washington long?" he asked.

"A day or two. I can be reached through our embassy."

"I thought you might enjoy taking in a baseball game while you're here. We have a new team, the Nationals. I know you don't have baseball in the U.K. and thought it would be a new experience. Have you ever been to a game?"

"No, I haven't." *Nor do I have any interest in doing so.*

"Give me a call if you'd like to go. They're playing at home tomorrow night."

◦෴◦

As Crowley headed for his hotel, where he intended to order a bottle of good Scotch and have it and dinner sent to his room, Joe Browning met with his superiors at Homeland Security.

"So he had nothing new to offer," his boss said.

"Right, except for some vague reference to a Canadian connection."

"We'll follow up on that."

"All we know at this juncture," said Browning, "is that the terrorists, presumably with bin Laden's blessing, have decided to forgo hitting big targets and concentrate on assassinating top political leaders here in D.C."

"Maybe claiming that Washington is the focus is a red herring. Maybe they intend to strike elsewhere."

"Where else?" Browning said. "If you're out to kill top political leaders, this is the place to do it."

"I'll run it past the secretary. Are you impressed with Crowley?"

"He's old."

"I mean, does he seem to know what he and his sources are talking about?"

"I suppose we'll see," Browning responded. "Right now, he's pretty much our only conduit to this new initiative by the terrorists. He still has someone in Amman, who's working on developing new sources. The original was assassinated."

"Unfortunate. See me later."

It had been a long, tough day for M.T., whose undercover code name was "Steamer." He'd spent the day supervising the installation of boilers in an Amman factory. He was hot and dirty, and wanted a hot shower and a hearty dinner at one of Amman's fancy restaurants, preferably with a member of the opposite sex. It wasn't easy making connections with attractive females. He wasn't the handsomest of men, and his belly—which hung over his belt, no matter how hard he tried to suck it up—was a turnoff, he knew, to many women. Maybe if he could reveal his second, clandestine life, he'd have more appeal.

The problem this night was that he had an appointment to keep, and it wasn't with a ravishing, dark-eyed Jordanian, or a buxom, red-headed employee of the British Embassy or British companies doing business in Jordan. Tonight's rendezvous was with an Iraqi he'd begun cultivating as a source to replace Ghaleb Rihnai.

He hadn't told Crowley about this new potential source of information from inside Iraq, or the terrorist cells that existed in Amman. This Iraqi, whom M.T. had met on one of his boiler installations, professed to suffer shame for the acts of Arab terrorists, and claimed to have contacts within Iraq who were privy to the insurgency's inner councils. M.T. wasn't sure whether to pursue the relationship. Rihnai's brutal murder had shaken him. Maybe it was time to sever ties with Crowley and the others who'd recruited him with the lure of money and an appeal to his innate sense of patriotism and decency.

He left the job site and grabbed a fast bite from a sidewalk vendor before driving out to the appointed meeting place, a deserted, dilapidated barn on an abandoned farm. The Iraqi was there when he arrived. Inside the barn, the smell of decaying wood and fermenting grain was pungent. Steamer suggested going outside, but the Iraqi said he felt more secure inside.

They discussed what M.T. expected of the Iraqi. He wanted to know everything that was discussed by the terrorists, especially their future plans. The Iraqi assured M.T. that he could, and would, deliver.

"How much will I be paid?" the Iraqi asked.

"That depends on how much useful information you deliver."

"I want money now," the Iraqi said.

M.T. had started to explain the realities of how money was paid for such information when a sound from behind caused him to stop in mid-sentence and to turn. Four young men wearing stocking masks leaped on him. One wielded a long, curved knife that he plunged into Steamer's thick neck. His assailants, slight of build, had a difficult time subduing the large and strong Brit, but as blood poured from his neck, he weakened and fell helplessly to the hard dirt floor. The Iraqi whom he'd befriended—or thought he had—pulled a small, silver revolver from his waistband and fired two shots into Steamer's forehead.

The Brit was dead, and the five young men left the barn to celebrate their coup.

TWENTY-ONE

Director Anthony Zambrano held court at the beginning of that night's rehearsal of *Tosca* at the Takoma Park facility. He was in an expansive mood, telling tales of various productions of that opera he'd directed around the world, and of some of the "Toscas" with whom he'd worked.

"You all know the story of Floria Tosca," he said, "and of her calamitous love affair with the doomed revolutionary Cavaradossi." He looked at Mac Smith and his colleagues from academia. "But for those of you unfamiliar with this remarkable tale of love, lust, and betrayal, let me give you a synopsis.

"It takes place in 1800, and begins in the Church of Sant'Andrea della Valle in Rome, where the painter Cavaradossi works on a canvas, unaware that a political prisoner, Angelotti, has escaped and is hiding in the chapel. Cavaradossi's lover, the famed diva Floria Tosca, arrives and sees that the beautiful young woman in Cavaradossi's painting has blond hair and blue eyes, unlike Tosca. She suspects that he has been unfaithful to her and rants. He eventually calms her down and assures her of his fidelity, which gives them the excuse to sing a lovely duet. Satisfied, she leaves after agreeing to meet later that evening. Her line as she leaves is absolutely beguiling: 'Change the eyes to black!'

"Angelotti emerges from where he's been hiding, and his friend Cavaradossi takes him to his villa, where he'll be safe from the police who are hunting him. Tosca returns to meet her lover but finds him gone. Instead, the sinister, lecherous Baron Scarpia, head of the Roman police, is there with his men in search of Angelotti. He reinforces Tosca's doubts about Cavaradossi's fidelity, and sends her on her way. Little does she know, Scarpia has instructed his officers to follow her, certain that she'll lead them to Angelotti."

Zambrano lowered his voice and twisted a nonexistent handlebar moustache. "And we learn that Scarpia desires the lovely Tosca for himself."

There were a few "Ooohs" and "Aaahs," and a solo giggler.

Zambrano continued. "Angelotti is still at large when Act II opens, but Cavaradossi is in custody for having aided his friend's escape. When he refuses to reveal Angelotti's hiding place, he's taken to the torture chamber. Tosca arrives. Hearing her lover's tortured moans, she tells Scarpia where he can find Angelotti. Cavaradossi is brought bloody but defiant from the torture chamber and curses Scarpia and his methods. Cavaradossi is again arrested, led away, and sentenced to die."

Zambrano rubbed his surprisingly small hands together and his eyes widened. "Aha," he said, "now comes the best part. Tosca pleads for Cavaradossi's life. Scarpia, scoundrel that he is, says he'll pardon Cavaradossi if Tosca will go to bed with him. She agrees. Scarpia tells his second in command, Spoletta, to stage a mock execution of Cavaradossi, and writes an official note granting Cavaradossi and Tosca safe passage from the country.

"He finishes writing the note and hands it to Tosca, who slips it into her bosom. Then she stabs him to death, and places a crucifix on his breast and candles at his head and feet. She slips away."

Smith's boss, Wilfred Burns, laughed and said, "Looks like she could have used a good defense lawyer like you, Mac."

"And I'd take the case," Mac said lightheartedly. "I'd put the victim, Scarpia, on trial, and get the jury to view it as justifiable homicide."

"Might make a good exercise for your students," Burns said, "how they'd defend Ms. Tosca."

"*Madame* Tosca," Zambrano corrected, obviously anxious to continue with his story. "The third act takes place at the Castle of Sant'Angelo. Cavaradossi bribes a jailer to let him write a final note to Tosca—you see, he doesn't know that the execution will be for show only, and that he will live. Tosca arrives and tells Cavaradossi about having murdered Scarpia, and that it will be a simulated execution. She instructs him how to fall realistically when the shots are fired.

"She leaves, and Cavaradossi faces the firing squad. He falls! She rushes to his side and is horrified to see that the execution was real after all. He's dead! She hears shouts in the distance announcing that Baron Scarpia has been murdered. As the police rush in to arrest her, the despairing Tosca, vowing to avenge herself before God, leaps to her death from the parapet."

Some of the supers applauded Zambrano's telling of the tale.

The director checked his watch. "We'd better get on with the rehearsal," he said. "Before I do, though, I should mention the famous story of the bouncing Tosca."

"I love this story," a super announced. "I wish I could have seen it."

"We all wish that," Zambrano said. "When Tosca flings herself to her death, it's supposedly into the Tiber River, although anyone who is familiar with Rome knows that it would be impossible for her to reach the river. In reality, I think she simply flattens herself on the cobblestones below. In any event, Toscas throughout eternity have made that leap onto a mattress positioned just out of sight of the audience and held by stagehands. This one particular Tosca, Rita Hunter, an especially stout woman performing in Cape Town, South Africa, complained that the mattress was too hard. The stage crew, accommodating fellows that they were, substituted a trampoline for the mattress. Our complaining diva landed on the trampoline and then bounced back up for all in the theater to see."

There was much laughter.

"There have been a few Toscas, usually the heavier ones, who have refused to make the leap and simply toddle off the stage, much to the directors' chagrin."

"Ever had that happen to you?" Mac asked.

"No," Zambrano said, "but if it did, I would personally and with pleasure fling that Tosca to her death."

Zambrano's anecdote prompted others, including one that took place at a regional opera house outside Rome. An aging tenor, not up to the role he'd wangled for himself, elicited boos and shouts of displeasure and whistles from the Italian audience. In the third act, while singing "Di quella pira," his voice cracked on a high note. The audience went into a frenzy, standing on their seats and hurling curses at him along with accusations of him being a beast, a criminal, and a murderer. The tenor became so enraged, he stomped downstage, sword in hand, and yelled, "All right, you morons, you come up here and sing the high note." The curtain was drawn and the rest of the final act was never performed.

Zambrano indicated he was aware of that episode, thanked them all for being there, clapped his hands, and snapped, "Places, everyone!"

An hour later, Zambrano called an end to the supers' walk-through and reminded everyone of the upcoming rehearsal schedule. He'd become agitated when he realized that two supers had failed to show, the pianist Christopher Warren and former detective Raymond Pawkins. His assistant called Genevieve Crier, who said that Warren was ill and that Pawkins had another commitment, which he couldn't change, but he would try to be there before rehearsal ended.

Mac was about to leave when Genevieve came bursting through the doors. She was always bursting through doors, never simply walking through them, and Mac wondered if she sometimes went through walls. Her energy reservoir seemed perpetually topped off with high-octane fuel.

"Ah, Mac," she said. "How did rehearsal go?"

"Fine. I learned all about the opera from the director. Fascinating stories behind *Tosca*."

"That's why it's always being staged somewhere. Where's Annabel?"

Mac looked up at a clock. "Waiting for me at a restaurant and wondering why I'm late. Join us?"

"I don't know if I can." She, too, looked at the clock. "Where are you meeting?"

"Cafe Milano."

"You devils," she said. "How can I pass up *that* invitation? I need ten minutes to soothe Anthony at two of my supers not showing and I'll be on my way. Do you have a reservation?"

"Annabel does—she made it. She has clout there now that she's on the Opera board. I understand the owner is on the board, too."

"Franco. A charming man. Maestro Domingo has his own private room there. Ah, to be rich and famous. Go, go, don't keep your Titian-haired beauty waiting. I'll be there in a flash."

Mac had no sooner left the building and was heading for his car when Ray Pawkins called out, "Hey, Mac. Rehearsal over?"

"Yes. You were missed."

"Couldn't be helped. I was tied up and couldn't get away. Zambrano's angry, I'm sure."

"I suppose so. Look, Ray, I'm running late myself. Annabel's waiting for me at Milano."

"I'm impressed."

Genevieve joined them. "Anthony wouldn't talk to me, which is just as well. I'm not in the mood to be verbally assaulted. Good evening, Mr. Pawkins. I hope your newfound fame from *Washingtonian* hasn't gone to your head."

Pawkins laughed. "Of course it has," he said. "My days as a super are over. It's strictly leads now."

"You're still here," she said to Smith. "Annabel is probably on her cell phone to a divorce attorney as we speak."

"She doesn't have to be," Mac said. "She was a matrimonial lawyer, remember? Coming?"

"You're going with them?" Pawkins said to Genevieve.

"Of course."

"Want a fourth?" Pawkins asked.

"Sure," Mac said. "Why not? But if we don't go now, it'll be the three of us at a Burger King."

He walked to his car, followed by Genevieve and Pawkins, who decided to go together in Pawkins' car. Genevieve had to return to Takoma Park after dinner, and Pawkins said he'd be happy to drive her.

Cafe Milano, on Prospect Street in Georgetown, had replaced the Jockey Club as Washington's prime celebrity gathering and gawking spot since opening in 1992. Its owner, Franco Nuschese, an acknowledged master host, was capable of making everyone feel famous and at home. That skill, plus superb northern Italian food, made it the hottest table in D.C.

Like all good hosts, Nuschese recognized Mac by name as he came through the door, despite Mac having been there only a few times before. "Ah, Mr. Smith," he said, "it is good to see you again. The signora is waiting." He threaded a passage through a knot of people three deep at the bar, to another dining room, away from the bar's cacophony. Annabel sat alone at a table for four, set for two.

"I'm sorry I'm late," Mac said, kissing her on the cheek and taking his seat. "The rehearsal ran long, and I was waylaid by Genevieve and Ray Pawkins on my way out."

"I was getting worried," she said.

"Genevieve and Ray are on their way. They're joining us."

"Oh?"

"Glad you landed a larger table. A prime one, I might add, away from the bar."

"I mentioned to Bill Frazier that we wanted to have dinner here and he offered to make a call. Nothing like having the chairman of the Washington National Opera put in a good word."

They'd just ordered drinks when Genevieve and Pawkins arrived.

"If I'd known I'd end up here tonight," Genevieve said breathlessly, "I would have changed into something dishy. I felt like Mrs. Tiggy-Winkle, Beatrix Potter's matronly washerwoman, walking through that crowd at the bar."

Pawkins chuckled. "I'd say you look like anything but a washer-woman."

"Isn't he sweet?" Genevieve said.

"Sweet's my middle name," Pawkins said.

"I love the Domingo Room," Genevieve said, pointing in its direction. She referred to one of Cafe Milano's private dining rooms, named after WNO's general director. One night in 1996, shortly after Plácido Domingo had arrived in Washington, he stopped in to eat and suggested to the owner that a door be put on the entrance to a private room to cut down on noise from the bar. When he returned the next night, the door was up and the room renamed the Domingo Room. A few years later, Nuschese commissioned a Russian artist to create a ten-foot painting on the room's ceiling of Domingo in costume as Verdi's Otello. The maestro has looked down on all who dine there ever since.

Over a large platter of beef and spiny lobster carpaccio with baby arugula and apple citronette sauce, accompanied by a bottle of Chianti Classico Riserva, Podere Tereno, talk eventually came around to the Charise Lee murder. Naturally, most questions were directed at Pawkins.

"Is there any progress?" Annabel asked.

"Nothing yet," he replied. Had he still been with MPD, discussing an ongoing case would have been off-limits—officially. But like most cops he knew, that rule was frequently ignored. Besides, those sharing the table with him this evening were, after all, his clients. "I'm in touch with a contact at MPD. They're looking closely at her roommate, a pianist from Toronto named Christopher Warren. They're also questioning every student in the Young Artist Program, and a couple of agents from Toronto who represented the victim and Warren."

"Christopher called in sick today," Genevieve said. "He said he couldn't make tonight's rehearsal."

"Maybe you'd better get a sub for him," Annabel offered.

"That's a good idea," Genevieve said.

"No it's not," Pawkins said. "Let's keep him close. I might learn something from him."

"It couldn't have been him," Genevieve said, wrapping her arms about her as though the AC had suddenly been turned up. "He's a lovely boy."

"That may be," Pawkins said, "but MPD has a different take on him."

It was over cappuccino and a platter of small cookies and fruit that Annabel brought up the Musinski murder of six years earlier. "I was fascinated to read that you were the lead on that case, Ray," she said.

"All part of my illustrious past," he said lightly.

"They never found those scores, did they?" Mac said.

"No" was Pawkins' reply.

"Or arrest anyone," Annabel said.

"They had a prime suspect," Pawkins said casually, "a grad student at the university. We all knew he did it, but we could never come up with enough evidence to convince the prosecutors to charge him."

"This grad student knew the deceased, Professor Musinski?" Mac asked.

"Oh, yeah, he sure did," Pawkins said. "He worked closely with him as an assistant. We grilled him pretty hard, but he never broke."

"Where is he now?" Annabel asked.

"Still at the university," Pawkins said. "My MPD source says they might reopen the case based on new forensic evidence."

"That's good to hear," Mac said. "Do you think this grad student killed the professor to get his hands on the musical scores? What were they—Mozart?"

"Musinski was a Mozart expert, wrote books about him and his music," Pawkins said. "But his primary interest was some string quartets supposedly written with Joseph Haydn."

"Supposedly?" Genevieve asked.

"No one's ever seen them," Pawkins said, leaning back in his seat and dabbing at his mouth with his napkin. "They only exist because

Musinski's niece claims her uncle said he'd brought them back from overseas a couple of days before he was murdered. Know what I think?"

"What?"

"I don't think those musical scores ever existed in the first place."

"Then why was Musinski killed?" Annabel asked. "The scores would provide the motive."

Pawkins laughed. "Maybe the kid got a bad grade from the prof and decided to even the score. This was great, but I have to get going." He reached for his wallet.

"On me," Smith said, waving him away.

"Not on your life. My turn."

"Yes, but this is Cafe Milano," Mac said.

"That makes it more special for me to treat," Pawkins said, pulling a credit card from his wallet and motioning for the waiter.

"What an unexpected surprise," Genevieve said as they parted outside the restaurant. "Thank you so much."

"Thank Mr. Pawkins here," Mac said.

"Yes, thank you, Raymond," Genevieve said.

"Come on," Pawkins said to her, "I'll drive you back to Takoma Park."

At home in their Watergate apartment, Annabel said, "Mr. Pawkins does quite nicely on a retired detective's salary."

"I didn't want him to pay," Mac said, "but he seemed determined. Bad form to argue over it."

"Did you notice what he was wearing?" Annabel asked as they dressed for bed.

"He carries clothes well," Mac said.

"That suit came straight from Savile Row," she said, "and those shoes were custom-made, too."

"Maybe he won a lottery we don't know about," Mac suggested, "or had an unmarried rich uncle who died and left his fortune to his only nephew."

"Maybe," Annabel said. "I think Genevieve is smitten with him."

"No."

"Yes. I can sense it."

"Not a bad match-up," Mac said. "She's attractive and a culture-vulture, and he's not without his own brand of erudition. They both love opera. By the way, Zambrano told us the story of *Tosca*. He had this wonderful tale of when a soprano playing Tosca jumped to her death, landed on a trampoline, and bounced back up for the audience to see."

"I've heard it," Annabel said with a laugh. "That's a staple. Opera is full of such stories, real or imagined. I think that's why everyone thinks operas, and the people who perform them, are crazy."

"Well," he said, "I like the soprano bouncing off the trampoline. Should go over well with my students, a few of whom I'd like to bounce off a trampoline—or a brick wall."

"Good night," she said, kissing him sweetly on the lips.

"It's early," he said.

"Not for me," she said. "Meetings exhaust me."

The strains of *Tosca* drifted into the bedroom from the den where Mac had put on the CD. Annabel turned over, fluffed up her pillow, and fell asleep, a contented smile on her face.

TWENTY-TWO

"**B**ut you can at least *try* to eat healthier, Willie."
Portelain and Sylvia Johnson had decided at the end of the day to have dinner together. He'd suggested a steak house; he was in the mood for a porterhouse and a baked potato with plenty of sour cream. Sylvia, while always enjoying a good steak, was aware of what the doctors had told Willie about the need to change his eating habits, and convinced him to try Bistro Med, a small, popular restaurant on M Street that featured "Mediterranean" food, much of it low calorie.

"You don't need a beer, Willie," she said. "Have a glass of red wine. It's good for you. The French live a long time."

"I'm not the wine type," he protested, holding up a hand with his pinky extended.

"There is no such thing as a wine type, Willie," she said, and ordered a bottle of inexpensive Cabernet from the waitress.

"Nice spot," he said, looking around the small, functionally furnished and decorated room.

"It's good food," she said. "How are you feeling?"

"Feel good—only, this body of mine is telling me it needs nourishment."

"The food here is nourishing," she said.

"Filling, too?"

"If you eat enough of it."

"So," he said after the wine had been poured and he'd clinked his glass against hers, "what's your take on those two clowns this afternoon?"

It had taken them most of the day to catch up with Melincamp and Baltsa.

Their first stop had been the apartment, where they encountered only Christopher Warren. He was watching TV when they arrived, and upon seeing Willie through the door's peephole, said loudly, "No way, man. You're not beating up on me again."

"Hey, son," Willie said in a loud voice, "we're not here to see you. Your agents in there with you?"

"No."

Willie banged on the door, louder this time.

"Let's go, Willie," Sylvia said.

"Man's not going to dis me," Willie said, his large fist striking the door again.

The door opened.

"Well, well," Willie said, "look who's here. Got yourself a shiner there, boy. Walk into a wall or somethin'?"

Warren stepped back, out of Portelain's range. An old black-and-white movie played on the TV behind him.

"Calm down, son," Willie said. "Sorry that we had that little run-in. Fact is, you shouldn't have taken off like that."

"Come on, Willie," Sylvia said, afraid that things would escalate.

"Where's your agents?" Willie asked.

"I don't know," Warren said.

"They been here today?"

"No. Yes. Zöe was here earlier."

"Where'd she go?"

Warren shrugged. "Maybe back to her hotel."

"Hotel Rouge?" Willie said.

"Right. Look, Detective, I'm sorry I ran like that. I was scared, that's all."

"We didn't mean you any harm," Willie said. "Next time, keep your wits about you. A fine piano player like you must have plenty of wits, huh?" He flashed a wide grin.

Warren, too, smiled. "I guess I do."

"All right, son," Willie said, "no hard feelings. But don't go no-where."

"I won't."

Willie looked past him at the TV set. "Humphrey Bogart," he said. "One a my favorites. You take care."

Back in the car, Sylvia asked, "Why did you bother getting into all that talk with him?"

"I don't know. Feel bad about what happened, his face getting busted up like that. Put me in the hospital, too."

"Speaking of that . . ."

"Rather not. Let's get over to that hotel and see if those agents are there. Hope one a them doesn't decide to run. Don't look forward to another night wearin' one of those little gowns that don't cover Willie's black butt, and gettin' stuck with needles. Man, how can any-body get into drugs, stickin' themselves with needles? Got to be sadists is the way I read it."

"Masochists," Sylvia said with a laugh.

"Yeah, them, too."

The Hotel Rouge, on 16th Street NW, was one of many smaller, upscale boutique hotels that had recently sprung up around Washing-ton. A former apartment building, which the Kimpton Hotel Group had converted into a trendy property, with the color red, of course, dominating everything. It had become especially popular with visiting celebrities, notably musicians and actors.

Sylvia used a house phone in the small lobby to call Zöe Baltsa's room. The agent answered.

"Ms. Baltsa, this is Sylvia Johnson, Washington MPD. My partner and I would like to talk with you."

"I've been expecting you," Baltsa said. "I meant to contact the police and offer to come there for an interview."

"Well," Johnson said, "we've saved you cab fare. May we come up?"

"Of course."

"Is Mr. Melincamp with you?"

"As a matter of fact, he is."

"We'll want to interview each of you separately. Perhaps Mr. Melincamp has a few errands to run while we speak with you."

Sylvia heard Baltsa pass along that message to Melincamp, who said, "Sure. Why not?"

They rode the elevator to the third floor, where Melincamp was waiting to ride downstairs.

"Hello there, Mr. Melincamp," Willie said. "This is my partner, Detective Johnson."

"Hello, Detective. How long do you want me to be gone?"

"An hour?" Johnson said.

"Sure."

The room occupied by Zöe Baltsa was surprisingly large for a hotel, probably someone's living room when the building was apartments. Red was everywhere, on the walls, in the carpet, on a floor-to-ceiling faux-leather headboard, on the bedding and velvet drapes. Soft mood lighting gave it the appearance of an elegant brothel from another era.

Sylvia pegged Baltsa as a woman who thought highly of herself and worked hard to maintain that self-image. The agent exuded sexuality, not in an obvious, glamorous way, but through a look in her eyes and the way she manipulated her full, red lips. She wore a pair of tight jeans, a lightweight orange sweater cut short to expose her bare midriff—*it clashes with the red in the room*, Sylvia thought—and sandals. Her hair was pulled back into a chignon, secured in back by what looked like a piece of American Indian jewelry. After introductions, she invited Willie and Sylvia to take the red love seat in front of the flat-screen TV.

"So," she said, "I am glad to be able to talk with you. I can't tell you how upsetting Charise's brutal murder has been for me and for Philip. It's like having lost a daughter. That's how close we were."

Had Sylvia and Willie spoken to each other at that moment, they would have said the same thing: *Take everything this lady says with a grain of salt.*

"I imagine it was quite a shock when you got the news," Sylvia said, a notepad on her lap, pen in hand.

"To say the least," Baltsa said, slowly shaking her head. "I mean, here she was, this immensely talented and beautiful young woman, in Washington to study with the best there is in the opera world, and to have some madman take her life and dreams from her in an instant. That's what it had to be, a madman. No one in their right mind could do such a thing."

Willie asked, "Where were you the night Ms. Lee was killed?"

"I was . . . Let me see. I believe I was right here at the hotel."

"All night?"

"Most of it. I went out for dinner."

"Where?"

"Oh, Lord, can I remember? Oh, yes, I had dinner at a lovely Thai restaurant. What's the name? Oh, yes, Bua. It isn't far from the hotel."

"Were you with anyone?" Sylvia asked.

"No. I dined alone. Do you like Thai food?"

Sylvia shot a glance at Willie, whose expression said it all.

"Did you see Ms. Lee that night?" Sylvia asked.

"No," Baltsa answered immediately.

"When did you arrive in D.C.?" Willie asked.

"On the afternoon of that fateful day. Tell me, have you made any progress in finding her murderer?"

"How come you didn't get together with Ms. Lee?" Willie asked, ignoring her question. "Isn't that why you came to D.C.?"

"Yes, of course it was. I—we couldn't find her."

"Nobody knew where she was?" Sylvia said.

"No. We checked with her roommate, Christopher Warren. He's a pianist, another of our clients."

"Yeah, we've met," Willie said.

"He hadn't seen her all day."

"You flew in with your partner?"

"No. Philip came here the day before. He had some business at the opera that didn't involve me."

"He stays at the apartment Ms. Lee shares with the piano player."

"That's right."

"How come he doesn't stay here?"

"You'll have to ask him." Her nicely plucked eyebrows went up. "We're not lovers," she said. "We're business partners, that's all."

Talk turned to the victim and the sort of person she was. Baltsa had only praise for the young opera student, personally and professionally. Toward the end of her soliloquy, she mentioned Charise's parents. "Her father is a horrible man," she said. "He abused Charise terribly."

"Physical abuse?" Sylvia asked. "Sexual?"

"I don't know about sexual," she replied, "but he was physically abusive. Psychologically, too. It's a miracle she turned out the way she did. That's why she moved out of her home and in with us."

"Us?"

"Me. I took her in and provided a safe and secure home, a nurturing one in which she could focus on her talent and future in opera, voice and acting lessons, fitness training, anything she would need when she launched her professional career."

Willie stood, stretched, and strolled around the large room. "Don't mind me. I've got a bad back that acts up when I sit too long."

"Bad backs," Zöe said, exhaling as though to expel the thought. "Nothing worse. I've suffered with one for years. Thank God for my chiropractor, Dr. Tim. I see him almost daily when I'm in Toronto."

The hour passed quickly, and was interrupted by Melincamp's arrival.

"Stay away long enough?" he asked.

"We're just about finished," Sylvia said.

"And now I suppose you want me to leave," Zöe said.

"If you wouldn't mind," Sylvia replied.

She gathered her purse and was about to leave when Willie,

who'd just come out of the bathroom, said, "How did you pay for your dinner at that Thai place? You use a credit card?"

"I think I did."

"Got the receipt?"

She rummaged through her bag, found it, and handed it to him. "Satisfied?" she said, annoyed.

"Thanks," he said. "Anybody with you at the hotel after you came back from dinner?"

"No. I exercised here in the room, watched part of a dreadful movie, and—oh, I'm sure you want the name of the movie. I have no idea what it was. You can check the TV listings in the paper."

She left, less sanguine than she'd been during the interview.

They went over the same ground with Melincamp.

He'd met with an administrator from the Domingo-Cafritz Young Artist Program on the day of Charise's murder, and provided a name to the detectives. That night he'd had dinner at Tosca.

"Tosca?" Willie said. "That's the opera."

Melincamp laughed. "Yes, I know," he said. "I'd not been there before and thought I had to try it, considering the name. The chef's daughter, I was told, is named Tosca. I just hope she doesn't meet the same fate as Madame Tosca in the opera."

A receipt? "No, I paid cash." Unusual to be on business and not document a meal with a credit card. "I try to pay cash whenever I can." No receipt for your files? "I don't remember whether I asked for one or not." Anyone likely to remember you there? "Absolutely. I engaged in conversation with a few members of the staff." The rest of the evening? A sheepish grin. "I went to a topless bar—please don't tell Zöe, she wouldn't understand. I find such places interesting. The sort of people who frequent them are fascinating."

"I know what you mean," Willie said. "And I always buy *Playboy* for the articles."

Sylvia smiled at the ironic comment as she said, "Mr. Melincamp, about Charise Lee. What sort of young woman was she? Did you know her friends and boyfriends? Was Mr. Warren a lover?"

Melincamp turned to Willie, who stood by a window. "I believe I already told you, Detective, that Chris and Charise were far too busy pursuing their careers to become romantically involved."

Portelain nodded. "Yeah, he told me that, Sylvia."

"What about her family life?"

Melincamp raised his eyebrows. "Not a very wholesome one, I'm afraid. It got so bad that we had Charise move in with us."

"You and Ms. Baltsa?"

"Well, she actually moved in with Zöe."

"I see. What was wrong with her family life?"

The agent painted a picture that was basically in tune with what his partner had told them. But he added, "Frankly, I never really believed that Charise's father abused her. I mean, he's an old Jewish guy with old-world ideas and values. Always citing the Holocaust. At least that's what Charise said. I think he tried to impose strict standards on Charise and she rebelled, like kids do. I mean, that's my own personal opinion. Zöe, she—well, she wanted Charise to live with her so she could keep an eye on her night and day, so she bought her claims that the father was abusive. I'd just as soon Zöe not know I said that. Look, Charise was high-strung, as most gifted artists are, especially female artists. She was hanging around with the wrong crowd and . . ."

"And what?" Johnson said.

"I shouldn't be talking this way," Melincamp said.

"Why not?"

"I don't like to be judgmental."

They continued the interview until Baltsa returned. "Did he say nice things about me?" she asked pleasantly.

"We didn't talk about you," Willie replied. "Thanks for your time. We'll be in touch again."

"Are we now free to leave Washington?" Baltsa asked.

"You always were," Johnson said.

"We have no intention of leaving," Melincamp said, eliciting a harsh look from Baltsa. "The least we can do is stand by to be of help to law enforcement in every way possible. We owe that to Charise."

"Well," Sylvia Johnson said, "that's admirable. Have a nice evening."

⌐

"Let me order for you," Sylvia offered when Willie complained that nothing on the menu at Bistro Med appealed. She ordered an appetizer—to share—of fried zucchini pancakes with yogurt garlic sauce; two entrées of steamed pinto beans tossed with carrots, celery, tomatoes, and fresh dill; and "Very Berry and Apple Kiwi" salads. Willie's face indicated his unhappiness.

"I know one thing," he said when the waiter left to put in their orders and they returned to discussing their interview with Melincamp and Baltsa, "claiming they don't get it on together is bull. You pick up on all those slips? 'We' instead of 'me'? 'Us'?"

"Yup."

"Besides, there's men's clothing in the closet. I checked."

"I knew you would."

"And his not wanting her to know he hit a topless joint after dinner. Why would she care if they're just business partners? There's lots he doesn't want her to know. You pick up on that?"

"Yes, I did."

"Also took a look in the bathroom. Man, that lady's got enough makeup stuff to do a thousand clowns."

"Don't exaggerate, Willie."

"I'm not. Whoever killed that Ms. Lee shoved a sponge in the wound to keep her from bleeding all over everything. Am I right?"

"Of course you're right."

"So, that Ms. Baltsa has got herself a few sponges of her own."

"So what? Lots of women have some sort of a sponge to apply makeup."

"You use a sponge to put on your makeup?"

"No."

"See what I mean?" He pulled a large sponge from his raincoat pocket and handed it to her. "I figured it wouldn't hurt to check hers against what was stuffed in that poor kid."

"Willie, you didn't!"

"Sure did. Let me tell you something else. Somebody's lying

about when Melincamp arrived in D.C. He told me the first time I talked to him that he flew in the day she was murdered. Baltsa says he came a day before."

"Why didn't you bring it up with him?"

"Didn't think of it until just now. Here's the appetizers. Looks . . . uh, good."

He tried to kiss her good night when he dropped her in front of her apartment building, but she evaded his lips. "Cool it, Willie," she said.

"Invite me up for a nightcap?"

"Sorry," she said.

His laugh was more of a growl. "Like I always say, pretty lady, when Willie's body says it needs something, I always try to accommodate."

"Well, you'll just have to accommodate it with someone else. Thanks for picking up the tab for dinner. Enjoy it?"

"I feel healthier already."

As she watched him drive away, she wondered whether he'd turn the corner and pull into the first fast-food restaurant he could find. She had to smile. She liked Willie Portelain, liked him a lot. He was a good man and a good cop. Not her type, but she'd been having trouble lately finding "her type."

She dressed for bed and settled in a chair in the living room to watch television. She was restless. She would have liked to find her soul mate and settle into a long-term, loving relationship, maybe get married and have a couple of kids before it was too late. She'd recently met a couple of men who were her type—at least they seemed to be at first blush—but the minute she mentioned that she was a cop, things changed. Out came the lame jokes about a female packing heat (Ho, ho, ho), and dumb questions about what it was like to shoot somebody. Truth was, she'd never even unholstered her weapon since becoming a cop, at least not with the serious intent of shooting someone.

Tired of such ruminations, and hungry, she went to the kitchen, where she smeared peanut butter and jelly on Ritz crackers and poured a glass of milk. Like Willie Portelain was fond of saying, when your body says it needs something, you have to oblige.

TWENTY-THREE

Arthur and Pamela Montgomery, president of the United States and first lady, returned to their living quarters in the White House after having hosted a state dinner for Canada's prime minister. The first couple enjoyed such events. President Montgomery was a gregarious host who took pleasure in bantering with guests, especially peers from other nations. His wife was equally at ease with a roomful of strangers. Her social secretary was adept at preparing a talking points list for the couple prior to social affairs, complete with a dossier on each guest that included special interests to be woven into conversations. The White House hadn't had as smooth and erudite a couple in decades, or one as good-looking. Montgomery was movie-star handsome, his wife possessing the sort of quiet, staunch beauty that graced films in the forties and fifties. A formidable pair.

The evening featured Canadian whiskey (a martini for the president) and Canadian wines from its Okanagan Valley, a 2002 Township Chardonnay, and 2001 red Jackson-Triggs Grand Reserve Meritage. A

Canadian wine expert was on hand to discuss the merits of the wines: "Because the wines are produced in a cooler climate, they tend to be lighter and fruitier, whereas hotter regions produce less fruity, heavier wines." Whether that was true or not, the first lady proclaimed them delightful, which was good enough for other wine drinkers at the black-tie affair, who perhaps thought otherwise.

The cocktail hour was to begin at seven. But at six, the president and Prime Minister Bruce Colmes met in a hastily scheduled session in a small room off the family quarters, a meeting arranged at the last minute by their staffs.

"I appreciate you taking the time to meet like this on the spur of the moment," Montgomery said to his counterpart.

"No inconvenience," Colmes said. "I'm here at the White House anyway, thanks to your hospitality, Arthur. Let's just say that this lovely evening has started a little earlier."

Colmes was a large, rough-hewn man with red cheeks, a shock of red hair, and the beefy, calloused hands of a working man, which he wasn't except for well-publicized outdoor chores on his ranch when on vacation. He wore his tuxedo like a sack.

These two governmental leaders had forged an easy, comfortable relationship since taking office, and enjoyed a first-name relationship when out of the public eye. Roughly the same age—Colmes was a few years younger than Montgomery but looked older—they shared, but only in private moments like this, a reasoned, albeit cynical view of politics, politicians, political consultants, political commentators, political pundits, political bosses, and everything else to which they'd successfully devoted their adult lives. Their bond, of course, was strengthened by the geographical and cultural boundaries of their two nations.

"The family is good?" Montgomery asked.

"Very much so," Colmes replied. "Yours?"

"Fine. Our youngest son is giving us a hard time, but that's just his hormones erupting. He hates living here in the White House, but someday he'll look back and appreciate the experience, probably by writing a scathing exposé of my administration. I'm sure you're aware,

Bruce, that our press has been making hay out of the tragic murder of your young opera singer from Toronto."

"I've been kept abreast," Colmes said, his sizable frame filling a crimson armchair. "The spotlight seems to be focused on another of our citizens, also a student at your opera school."

Montgomery, who consumed less of the matching chair, nodded. "I've had some briefings on the case from our Justice Department. One thing we don't need is for the press to make an international incident out of it."

Colmes laughed heartily. "They are capable of that, aren't they? Before we know it, one of your television commentators will find something untoward about our meeting like this before the dinner."

"I wouldn't doubt it. I do want you to know that our local police are doing everything possible to find the murderer and bring him to justice. I'm told the young lady was quite a promising singer."

"My understanding, too. You enjoy opera, don't you, Arthur?"

"Yes, I do, not to the extent Pamela does, but I respond to the spectacle onstage, the incredible voices, the drama of it all. It's a little like politics, I suppose."

"I've never developed a taste," Colmes said. "I prefer country-and-western music. At least I like the voters to believe that's my musical choice. The common man and all."

"That was the problem with Adlai Stevenson when he twice ran for president," Montgomery said. "Maybe if he'd played the fiddle, he would have done better."

"I'm sure he would have," Colmes said, eliciting a smile from the president, who was well aware that his Canadian counterpart was a lot more sophisticated than he let on.

Montgomery checked his watch. "Let's get to the meat of this little get-together, Bruce. My intelligence people tell me that this latest al-Qaeda threat has what they're terming 'a Canadian connection.' What the hell is that all about?"

"We're trying to ascertain the same thing on our end," Colmes said. "Our people have been in close contact with your intelligence agencies, unlike the way your FBI and CIA function together."

"We're getting better at it," Montgomery said, knowing that the jibe was without barbs. They'd discussed this subject on earlier occasions.

"So I hear. I was briefed on the situation this morning before coming to Washington. It's the considered opinion of our intelligence that al-Qaeda has decided to forgo large, bigger-than-life strikes, as happened on your nine-eleven, and concentrate on smaller but symbolic targets—namely, people like you, Arthur."

"I should be flattered."

"And concerned."

"The president is always a target. History proves that. Goes with the job. Security is good around here, and has been enhanced since the latest raising of the threat level."

"Still."

"I know, I know. If someone really wants to get you, they probably will. But I'm not concerned. Have they named me specifically?"

"What do your people say?"

"Nothing so specific, except . . ."

"Except that the threat might come by way of Canada," Colmes said.

"That's what I'm told," the president said. "Makes me wonder whether an assassin will come riding into the White House wearing a red Mountie uniform and pronouncing 'roof' funny."

"Pronouncing it differently, Arthur. Differently."

Montgomery laughed. "I stand corrected."

"Obviously," Colmes said, "we need more specifics. Hopefully, there'll be additional intelligence to provide it. Right now, all your people and ours know is that al-Qaeda plans to assassinate high-profile leaders here in the States rather than attempt to hijack airplanes again. I suppose they could coordinate such an attack for maximum impact—you know, target a dozen government leaders for a simultaneous strike, one or two of your governors here or there, a few of your senators, a cabinet member." He hesitated. "The children of a prominent figure."

Montgomery's eyes narrowed and his jaw worked. That same scenario had been presented to him only a few days earlier during an intelligence briefing, a what-if? exercise, one of three offered by his briefers.

"The British have been helpful," Montgomery said.

"They sometimes are," Colmes said.

"Our Homeland Security people have been briefed by British go-betweens," Montgomery said. "The border with you has been beefed up. In the meantime, life goes on."

"As it must. I want you to know that we're doing everything we possibly can to ferret out potential assassins from our Muslim population. That's what makes it so damn difficult, distinguishing madmen from good, decent, law-abiding Arab folks. They're good at assimilating into those communities."

Montgomery stood and checked his bow tie in a mirror. "We're making an interesting, and possibly fatal, assumption, Bruce," he said.

"Which is?"

"That these assassins, if they exist and this plan exists, are of Arab extraction. I'm sure you have as many homegrown nuts in Canada as we do here in the States."

"Sometimes I think we have even more," Colmes said, rising from his chair and slapping Montgomery on the back. "In the meantime, Mr. President, our better halves await us. And if you insist on having your usual martini when so much excellent Canadian whiskey and wine is available, the press will have another sinister plot to conjure."

TWENTY-FOUR

Ray Pawkins awoke with a start. A shaft of light had managed to find a slit in the drapes and hit him in the eye like a laser. He turned away from the brightness with the intention of dozing off again. But the body next to him moved, causing him to push up against the headboard and to rub sleep from his eyes. He glanced over. The woman snored softly and wrinkled her nose. He'd forgotten she was there.

They'd enjoyed dinner together following the supers rehearsal and had returned to his house to sample a new port that had been touted by a salesman at Rodman's, Pawkins' favorite wine shop, and to listen to opera. They'd argued, but only briefly, over which opera to choose from his expansive collection. She preferred a recording of Bizet's *Carmen* with Leontyne Price and Franco Corelli, which she'd heard and enjoyed before. But Pawkins said, "If we must listen to *Carmen*, I prefer the Callas version with Georges Prêtre conducting. Frankly, though, I'm not in the mood for *Carmen* tonight." He chose instead *Satyagraha*, written by Philip Glass and performed by the New York City Opera Orchestra and Chorus.

"I don't know that one," she said, the corners of her mouth turned down at having her selection dismissed.

"A gorgeous work," he said. "It deserves a better recording than this one, although the singing is first-rate. Unfortunately, the orchestra sounds uninspired, thanks to a lackadaisical conductor. Come. Sit next to me on the couch. Your lesson is about to begin."

Now, he continued to look down at her in bed. Her hair was long, and cascaded over the delicate yellow pillowcase. Pawkins was always impressed with the inky blackness and luxurious texture of Asian women's hair. Her eyes fluttered open and closed immediately. Her hand went to her nose to swipe away an itch. Pawkins noted her fingers, tipped with polish the color of castor oil. *Too short*, he thought, referring to her fingers. The rest of her was longer. She stood as tall as he did.

They'd first met at a record store, where he purchased the latest opera CDs while she selected from the classical section. Their initial conversation confirmed that she knew something about opera, but only in a popular sense, familiar arias and the biggest names—"*La donna e mobile*" from *Rigoletto*; "*Un bel di, vedremo*" from *Madame Butterfly*; "*Che gelida manina*" from *La Boheme*; and Domingo, Anna Moffo, Brigit Nilsson, Richard Tucker, Caruso, Kiri Te Kanawa, and, of course, Pavarotti. But that was enough for him. So few women he met had ever even attended an opera, let alone had a working knowledge of that most elegant and complex of entertainments.

Their date last evening had been their second; the first involved dinner and a movie, and Pawkins had been certain that an encore would result in sex.

He slipped out of bed and walked naked to the bathroom. When he returned wrapped in a terry-cloth robe, she still slept. He sat in a chair by the window and parted the drapes. It was gray outside, as gray as his mood. He looked across the room at the yellow hills and valleys her body created beneath the sheet and sighed. This was the trouble with bedding a woman. They were there in the morning. He'd considered driving her home after their lovemaking, but by that time he wasn't of a mind to get dressed, let alone end up in an argument. She'd said with a knowing smile as she was about to fall asleep, "It feels so good in the morning."

Actually, she'd fallen asleep much earlier, a half hour into the playing of *Satyagraha*, which annoyed him. He'd been telling her about the opera and Mohandas Gandhi's influence on the composer; how "Satyagraha" was the name Gandhi had given to his nonviolent resistance movement; and how Glass's first opera, *Einstein on the Beach*, had been a success but had left the composer broke and driving a New York City taxi. He wanted to tell her these things — educate her — but she'd nodded off on his shoulder. He especially enjoyed the opera's final scene and wanted her to appreciate it with him, but she was long gone, her small guttural sounds in his ear not enhancing the musical score.

She was wide-awake, though, once they'd undressed and were beneath the sheets, skin to skin, electrical pulses jumping the gaps, male and female sounds of sexual bliss creating their own aria.

"Good morning," she said now, propping a pillow behind her and pulling the sheet up over her breasts.

"Good morning. Sleep well?"

"Very. You?"

"Yeah, fine."

She smiled and motioned with her index finger for him to join her in bed.

"Love to," he said, standing and tightening the robe's sash, "but I have to get to an early appointment downtown. Sorry. We must do this again sometime."

She showered first. When he emerged from the bathroom, she was dressed and watching the news on TV.

"Can you believe it?" she said. "Terrorists are planning to kill American big shots, maybe even the president."

Pawkins stood behind her and watched the TV report. An anonymous but "highly placed" source in the government's intelligence apparatus had leaked the news of al-Qaeda's alleged plan to assassinate American political leaders. The reporter, whose breathlessness was a little too over-the-top, continued the story as BREAKING NEWS flashed at the bottom of the screen. Everything these days on cable news shows seemed to be "breaking news."

"Intercepts of terrorist chatter have, according to this highly credible source, indicated that al-Qaeda and affiliated terrorist groups have decided to forgo large, spectacular targets like September eleven and focus on symbolic assassinations of American political leaders. In addition—and this has not been confirmed—there appears to be a connection between al-Qaeda and unspecified Jihadist cells in Canada. Stay tuned for further developments as they unfold."

"You'd never think Canada would be involved," she said as Pawkins used the remote to turn off the television. "They're our friends."

"He didn't say Canada was involved," Pawkins said. "And there're terrorist groups in every nation in the world. Come on, I'm running late."

He drove her to her apartment building, where a chaste kiss on the cheek sent her from the car. "I'll call," he said, not sure he would. No pox on her. She was attractive and sexy, aside from short fingers, and their bedtime tussle had been satisfactory.

But at the moment he had other, more pressing things on his mind. He had work to do.

He'd called a friend in Toronto a few days ago, a private detective for whom he'd done a few favors over the years, including having rescued a small Raphael still life that had been stolen from a Canadian collector, who'd hired Pawkins' Toronto buddy to get it back. The thief, a barbarian with no appreciation of art, had cut the painting from its frame on the wall, which in Pawkins' mind raised the crime to a capital offense, punishable by lethal injection. Pawkins traced the painting to a fat cat in Bethesda known to have a particular fondness for Raphael. Pawkins confronted the Bethesda collector and cut a deal: Give back the painting or face jail time. He delivered the work to his Toronto colleague and split a hefty fee with him. Of course, this was after Pawkins had retired from the MPD. It would have been a dicey deal had he still been a D.C. cop.

Pawkins had asked his Canadian friend to dig into the background of Charise Lee. He'd learned over his years as a Homicide detective that it was usually the victim who gave up the most useful clues. Know the victim and you know why someone would want him—or in this case, her—killed.

"Ms. Lee was an interesting young lady," his friend reported on the phone. "Little girl, big talent—and a fiery disposition."

"Fiery? How so?"

"Big on causes. Hung around with a group of like-minded wackos. Attended protests, carried signs, wants world hunger ended, protested your government's invasion of Iraq. By the way, Ray, I agree with *that.*"

"Go on."

"Had her share of boyfriends, none of whom she was likely to bring home to meet Daddy. Had a thing going with a piano player who, I've learned, went with her to Washington to study in this opera program you've got down there."

"Christopher Warren."

"Right. Anyway, after she played footsie with this Warren guy, she hooked up with an Iranian student at McGill U. He's been linked to some organization that our government considers a possible terrorist sympathizer, fundraiser—feed the children but make sure there's a little left over for belts that blow up. Of course, our government still hasn't figured out what to do with mad cow disease, so its so-called war on terror is suspect."

Pawkins was silent.

"Ray? You there?"

"Yeah, I'm here. I'm trying to process all this. What the hell is a beautiful, young future opera star doing with that bunch of losers?"

"Hey, I don't analyze. I just report. Just the facts, ma'am, like your TV guy Webb used to say on *Dragnet.* I loved that show."

"So did I. What about the agents I told you about, Melincamp and Baltsa?"

"I'm working on that. I only have two hands, you know."

"Was Christopher Warren involved with these wackos, too?"

"Evidently. By the way, you made this Charise Lee out to be a young kid. Young, hell. She was twenty-eight."

"That's young from my vantage point," Pawkins said.

"I mean," said his friend, "it's a little old to still be marching for old left-wing causes."

"No it's not," Pawkins said. "Lots of domeheads and guys with artificial knees marching these days. Gives them something to do, I suppose, makes them forget they have one foot in the grave. Thanks, buddy. Get back to me when you check out the agents."

∞

"They're *both* coming!"

"Who?"

"The president and first lady."

"We already knew that."

"No, no, no, I don't mean opening night for *Tosca*. They're both coming to the *ball*."

Annabel was one of a dozen women that morning attending a meeting of the Opera Ball committee, at which the announcement was made by chairwoman Nicki Frolich.

Frolich's enthusiasm wasn't shared by everyone else in the room. One spoilsport was the chair of the executive committee, Camile Worthington. "I'm not sure I'd be so excited about it," she said. "Do you realize what it will mean having the president there? It was enough of a security nightmare with the first lady making an appearance. The president? It will be chaos, sheer chaos."

"We can handle it," Frolich said.

"We'd better handle it," Laurie Webster, the opera company's PR director, chimed in. "This is great. No president has ever attended the ball. We'll get tremendous press out of it."

"And have Secret Service people tasting all the food," Camile said. "Look, I know this represents a coup of sorts, and we don't have any choice but to make it work. But I'm an old hand at these things.

I've been involved before in events at which the president showed up. You have no idea what it entails."

"I've had my share of those experiences, too," Nicki said, not about to be trumped. Camile Worthington wasn't the only woman in the room to have partaken in affairs important enough for the president to lend his name and presence. "It just involves more planning, that's all, and coordination with the White House. Let's not put blinders on. Laurie is right. We'll have wonderful press coverage."

"Sell lots of tickets, too," someone offered.

"We're already sold out," said another.

"What do you think, Annabel?"

Annabel laughed. "I don't think it matters what anyone thinks," she said. "If the president of the United States says he's coming to the Opera Ball, you can't very well call and uninvite him. He's coming, we know he's coming, and that's that. I'm sure he and the first lady will make every attempt to disrupt as little as possible."

"Annabel is right," Nicki said. "Let's view this positively and enjoy the honor it means to us and the opera. I also suggest that we immediately select someone to coordinate the president's appearance. Annabel? It sounds like a job you'd be more than qualified to handle."

Annabel started to demur, but others seconded the suggestion.

"Will you do it, Annabel?"

"I'll give it my best," she said.

"All right, then," Nicki said, "let's get down to the other business at hand. I'm pleased to announce that the strike has ended at the manufacturer of our velvet goodie bags. He's confident he'll be able to meet our deadline. I might also say that . . ."

స్

Pawkins headed for Takoma Park, where he found Chris Warren accompanying a young, black soprano from the Domingo-Cafritz Program. Pawkins sat quietly in a corner of the otherwise empty rehearsal room and listened to her tackle *"Marten aller Arten,"* a challenging aria from Mozart's *Abduction from the Seraglio. Not bad,* he thought, although he considered her voice to be characteristically light. Too many light voices being developed in America, he mused, too many young sopranos being fed a diet of Mozart arias to develop airy, nimble voices; constricted, compacted voices; "sausage sopranos," as they were snidely called. He preferred bigger voices, the kind European opera audiences responded to, older voices—but not too old—capable of filling a large opera house while plumbing the depths of their roles.

When the soprano and Warren finished the piece, Pawkins applauded, startling the performers and causing them to squint to better see into the dark recess where he sat. He approached. "Bravo!" he said, his hands still coming together.

"Thank you," the singer said.

"I didn't mean to interrupt," Pawkins said.

"You aren't. I'm off to a class."

Warren started to walk away with her, when Pawkins said, "Got a minute, Mr. Warren?"

The pianist turned. "Who are you?"

"Raymond Pawkins," he said, extending his hand. "I'm investigating the murder of Charise Lee for the Washington National Opera."

"I've already been interviewed by the police," Warren said.

Pawkins cocked his head and leaned a little closer to Warren. "Accident?" he asked, referring to Warren's facial bruises.

Warren shook his head.

"I'm a private detective, former Washington MPD. Let's sit over there." He indicated a well-worn, red velour couch against a wall behind the Steinway.

"I have nothing more to say," Warren protested.

"Maybe, maybe not," replied Pawkins. "Come on, indulge me a few minutes."

They sat side by side on the couch. Warren's nerves were on the surface. He kept intertwining his long fingers, and there was a tic in his right eye. Pawkins said nothing, allowing the pianist's nerves to come full-blossom. Finally, he said, "So, Mr. Warren, tell me about this radical group you and Ms. Lee were involved with back in Toronto."

Warren's expression was a mix of surprise and confusion.

"You know what I'm talking about, and I know about it, too. So, let's make this a short and sweet conversation. How involved was Ms. Lee in the group's activities?"

"She—she was into it, I suppose."

" 'Into it'? Be a little more specific."

"She was always latching on to some new cause. Seemed like whoever she talked to last was the one she listened to."

"A Dionysian personality," Pawkins said.

"Huh?"

"Easily influenced, probably easily hypnotized, too. What was her latest cause before coming here to D.C.?"

Warren shrugged. "The war, I guess."

"Iraq."

"Yeah. She was really hot over that. Look, I have to go. I have a class, too, and—"

"Sure," said Pawkins. "You go ahead."

Warren stood, cradling sheet music to his chest, and took a step away.

"One last thing," Pawkins said.

Warren turned.

"How did you react when Ms. Lee dumped you for the Arab guy?"

"She didn't—I didn't—I wasn't dumped."

"I hear different."

"Oh, man, I can see where you're going with this," Warren said. "For your information, I was the one who broke off the relationship, not Charise."

"Because she was seeing the Arab guy behind your back?"

Warren seemed to be searching for something intelligent to say. Failing, he left the room, causing Pawkins to grin. He'd gotten to him, and he had no doubt that there had been bad blood between the pianist and Charise over the breakup of their romance. Motive to kill her? You bet. Hell hath no fury like a piano player scorned.

He called Carl Berry's office at MPD and was told the detective was unavailable. "Tell him Ray Pawkins called and was hoping to have lunch with him. I'll try again later."

꜀꜀

Mac Smith had arisen early in order to catch up on paperwork, professional and personal. Annabel had gone off to yet another meeting of the Opera Ball committee—her life was consumed by meetings these days. He was hard at work in his study at eight that morning when the phone rang.

"Mr. Smith?"

"Yes."

"My name is Marc Josephson, sir. We met a couple years ago when you and your lovely wife were in London. Lord Battenbrook introduced us."

"Of course, Mr. Josephson. What a pleasant surprise hearing from you. I trust you are well."

"Quite well, thank you. You and Mrs. Smith?"

"Busy, happy, and healthy."

"Splendid. I hope I'm not disturbing you."

"Just shuffling papers around," Smith said, laughing. "The computer age was supposed to create a paperless society. Quite the opposite has occurred."

"Yes. I'm calling from London, Mr. Smith, at the airport, actually. I'm about to board a plane for Washington."

"Oh? Please, call me Mac."

"All right. I apologize for this last-minute call, but my trip is last-minute, I'm afraid. I was hoping to get together with you when I arrive."

"Annabel and I would enjoy seeing you again. How long will you be staying?"

"Only a few days. Let me be direct. I need legal counsel."

"You do realize that I no longer practice law," Mac said. "I teach it."

"Oh, yes, I'm quite aware of that. You discussed your change in careers when we met. Frankly, I need to speak with someone with a knowledge of your laws, not necessarily to engage an attorney. Lord Battenbrook spoke so highly of you and—"

"Aside from the pleasure of seeing you again, I'd be more than happy to provide answers to your questions, provided I know the answers."

"I can't ask more than that. Would it be possible to see you this evening?"

"This evening? I—"

"I realize that this is terribly short notice, but I would sincerely appreciate getting together with you at the earliest possible moment."

"Mind telling me what this is about, this legal question you have?"

"I'd prefer to not discuss it on the phone, but I will say that it involves the murder of a friend and colleague a number of years ago."

"A murder?"

"Yes, in Washington. His name was Aaron Musinski."

After a moment of silence, Mac said, "I see."

"I only have a few minutes before my plane leaves," Josephson said. "I'll be staying at the Watergate. My flight is due into Washington at four o'clock your time. If I could possibly buy you dinner tonight, I would be most appreciative. Oh, and please don't mention to anyone that I am making this trip."

"All right," Mac said.

"Thank you, Mac. You must excuse me. They've announced my flight. I look forward to hearing from you this evening."

Mac hit the "Off" button on his cordless phone, lowered it into its charging cradle, and sat quietly for a few minutes, reflecting on the conversation that had just taken place. He tried to recall what he'd read on the material about the Musinski case that Annabel had pulled up from the Internet. Had a Marc Josephson been mentioned? He didn't think so. Josephson had termed Musinski a friend and colleague. A colleague in what? Oh, yes, Josephson had been introduced to him and Annabel in London as the owner of a shop specializing in rare manuscripts and art. They'd visited his Mayfair shop two years ago, four years after the Musinski murder. Josephson had never mentioned Musinski or his murder during that visit. Mac and Annabel had been in London so Mac could take part in a series of legal seminars hosted by the British Bar. Now, two years later, this phone call comes from out of the blue.

He called Annabel on her cell. "We have an interesting dinner on tap tonight," he said.

"Sounds intriguing."

"That's why we're doing it." He filled her in on Josephson's call.

"The Musinski murder? What does he have to do with that?"

"I don't know, although my assumption is that it has to do with those missing Mozart musical scores. Allegedly missing."

"Sure you want me to come along?"

"Yes."

"You have a supers rehearsal tonight," she said.

"I know. I'll call Mr. Josephson and see if we can get together after it. It should be over by eight thirty or nine."

"Most likely. Have to run. We'll talk later. Oh, Mac . . ."

"Uh-huh?"

"Maybe you should call Ray Pawkins and tell him about it."

"I considered that, Annie, but don't think I will. Let's find out what this is all about before bringing in Ray. Okay?"

"Whatever you say. Love you. Bye."

Mac put aside the Josephson call as he went back to the pile of papers on his desk. At eleven, the phone rang.

"Hope I'm not disturbing you and the missus in something sensuous and pleasurable," Pawkins said.

"If you were, I wouldn't have answered the phone, Ray. What's up?"

"First, I thought you looked splendid last night at the rehearsal."

"I'm getting into my role, as the thespians say. You looked okay yourself. So did that lovely woman who was waiting for you."

"Yes, very nice. I love the idea of there being two sexes, don't you?"

"I wouldn't have it any other way," Mac said with a chuckle.

"Thurber's view precisely. Free for lunch?"

"As a matter of fact, I am."

"Good. I have a few things to report on the murder. I'm at Takoma Park now. It's been an interesting morning."

"Looking forward to hearing all about it," Smith said. "Twelve thirty?"

"Sounds good. I'll come to the Watergate."

"I'll make a reservation downstairs at Aquarelle."

"Shame Jeffrey's closed there. Must have broken the Bushes' hearts when they were in D.C."

"Nothing's forever, including administrations and restaurants—especially restaurants. They can enjoy their Tex-Mex meals back in Austin. Twelve thirty."

Pawkins was in his car and heading for the Watergate when his cell phone rang.

"Ray. It's Carl Berry."

"Hey, buddy, good to hear from you."

"I got your message about lunch. No can do. But can you find time this afternoon to swing by here?"

"For you, I have all the time in the world. What's up?"

"The Musinski case."

"Oh? Making progress?"

"I think so. I need to go over your reports from when you investigated."

"Nothing I can add," Pawkins said. "Everything I know is in those reports."

"Yeah, I'm sure," said Berry, "but there are some loose ends we'd like to tie up before we go any further."

"Like what?"

"Not over the phone. What's good for you?"

"Since you didn't get back to me until now, I found someone else to break bread with. Three?"

"I'll be waiting."

Aquarelle was busy, as usual, when Pawkins walked in, spotted Mac at a window table overlooking the Potomac, and took the seat opposite him. Remembering Annabel's comments about the way the ex-detective dressed, Mac made a point of taking in what his luncheon companion wore that day—British tan chinos with razor creases, blue button-down shirt with a collar slightly higher than those bought off the rack, an intricately patterned tie in gold and browns, and a coffee-colored corduroy sport jacket with leather elbow patches and buttons. Whether his outfit was expensive to put together escaped Mac. All he knew was that Pawkins wore whatever he happened to have on extremely well.

"I haven't been here since they reopened," Pawkins said, indicating the dining room with a sweep of his hand.

Aquarelle had opened in the Watergate in 1996 and was a favorite of President and Mrs. Clinton during their White House days, although Jean-Louis' Palladin saw its share of the first couple, too. The Kennedys had a special fondness for the Jockey Club, a distinctly nonpartisan choice since the Republican Reagans also were regulars there. President and Laura Bush made it known when they arrived on the Washington scene that they missed the Texas-based restaurant Jeffrey's, and so Aquarelle gave way to that Tex-Mex establishment until 2003, when it closed, in part due to the stay-at-home Bush family's lack of presence. Aquarelle was brought back, much to the delight of many Washingtonians, particularly those residing in the Watergate apartments, for whom Southwestern food was not the be-all, end-all.

"Consistently good," Mac offered as a waiter placed menus before them. "Crab cakes?"

"Why not."

"So, Ray, you say you have some interesting developments in your investigation of the murder. I'm anxious to hear."

"Where do I start?" He motioned for a waiter and ordered a Bloody Mary. Mac declined a drink. "I spent time with the victim's friend from Toronto, the pianist, Christopher Warren. In fact, I just left him at Takoma Park."

"And?"

"He's high on my suspect list."

"Based on what?"

Pawkins laughed. "You sound the way you did when you were trying cases and grilling me on the stand."

"Old habits die hard. Tell me more about this pianist."

"He's a former boyfriend of the deceased. Toronto. She jilted him for some Arab stud, which would make any guy angry, maybe enough to kill."

"You got that out of him?"

"I had a little advance info that greased the skids."

"What about those agents?"

"They're next on my agenda, Mac. And there's a guy at the Kennedy Center I'm taking a closer look at."

"Who's that?"

"No names at this point. Let's just say that he's known to have a thing for Asian women."

Smith's immediate thought was of the attractive Asian woman who waited for Pawkins at the supers rehearsal the previous night, but didn't comment. Most men, he knew, tended to gravitate to a certain type of woman—blonde, redhead (certainly true in his case with Annabel), brunette, tall, short, plump, skinny. Second wives tended to mirror in some fashion first wives, although not always. Smith's first wife, who'd died along with their only son in that dreadful auto accident, had been a brunette and considerably shorter than Annabel. No hard-and-fast rules, but tendencies.

"Was he there the night Ms. Lee was killed?" Smith asked.

"What? Oh, sorry, My mind wandered. It tends to do that more these days."

Pawkins was thinking of his meeting later that afternoon with Detective Berry.

"The pianist," Mac repeated. "Was he there the night she was killed?"

"Sure he was. Genevieve pressed him into duty as a super."

"Yes, I remember him at the first get-together."

"I'll know more about him later today. I'm meeting with MPD after I leave here."

As they ate, Pawkins said, "So, tell me, Mac, how your first brush with opera is going."

"Going well," he replied.

"Good. I'd hate it to be an unpleasant experience for you. Heard the latest bit of scuttlebutt?"

Mac's raised eyebrows called for an explanation.

"Seems our diva in this production is unhappy with the soft drinks. They're using Coke onstage for the drinking scenes. She's a Pepsi fanatic and refuses to go on unless they change to Pepsi."

"So," Mac said, enjoying a final bite of crab cake, "give her Pepsi."

"My thought exactly," Pawkins said. He looked at his watch. "I'd better go. I've got a busy afternoon on tap."

"Don't let me stop you."

Mac's cell phone rang. It was Annabel. When the brief conversation was over, Mac said to Pawkins, "Annabel has just come from a meeting of the Opera Ball committee. I have a bit of scuttlebutt to report, too."

"Oh?"

"Not only are the president and first lady attending the opening night of *Tosca*, they plan to make an appearance at the ball."

"How did the ladies get so unlucky? It'll be crawling with Secret Service."

"I'm sure they'll manage. Go ahead and run, Ray. I'm going to have coffee. The check is mine."

"If you insist." He started to get up, but sat down again. "Mind a word of advice, Mac Smith?"

"Depends on what it's about."

"Opera," Pawkins said. "I couldn't help but notice that purple sweater you wore last night at rehearsal."

"Actually, it's plum-colored, but go ahead."

"It looked purple to me," Pawkins said. "At any rate, purple is considered bad luck in opera."

"Why?"

"I feel like I'm back on the witness stand," said Pawkins. "But to answer your question, Counselor, purple denotes religion, and operas were not to denote religion in their themes and stories. *Samson and Delila* broke through that prohibition, but purple is still considered bad karma onstage."

"I'll certainly keep that in mind, Ray. I have a wonderful pair of purple cashmere socks I intended to wear on opening night. I suppose that's out of the question now. Any other admonitions?"

"Just one. Never whistle when you're on the deck."

"More bad luck?"

"Right."

"Why?"

"I plead the Fifth, meaning I don't know. Thanks for lunch, Mac. See you at rehearsal."

Smith watched the former detective stride from the restaurant, turning a few female eyes as he passed their tables. Mac's feelings were mixed. On the one hand, he enjoyed Pawkins' company and respected what the man had accomplished—decorated cop elevated to detective status early in his career, and the lead investigator in high-profile cases; successful private investigator specializing in stolen art; and myriad personal interests, including opera to the extent that he volunteered to be an extra—a super—in various productions. All in all, a full and diversified life made richer.

On the other hand, there was a piece missing, one that Mac couldn't identify at the moment. Annabel had picked up on it even sooner. The self-assuredness and easy banter seemed, at least to Mac, to cover up a void of some sort. An emotional vacuum? Possibly. Pawkins had never married. Did that indicate an inability to truly connect with another person, to engage in the give-and-take necessary for successful relationships, whether heterosexual or homosexual? Mac wasn't a fan of cheap-shot, pop psychology and avoided indulging in it. But understanding other human beings was crucial to his success as a criminal lawyer. That's what trial law was all about, anticipating the opposition's moves and preempting them, getting under the skin of a witness by pushing his or her right psychological buttons, knowing what made people tick and how to throw them off their stride. He was good at it, sometimes so good that it caused him moments of guilt. Justice wasn't always served in a courtroom, not when good attorneys plied their trade and used the system as advocates for a side or point of view, even if it represented a miscarriage of justice. But that was the game, the profession, and Mackensie Smith had played it as well as any lawyer ever has.

Ray Pawkins. What was it that had stirred Annabel's interest and extended her antennae? What was it that caused Mac a minor-league discomfort as he sipped his coffee and abandoned his resolve against dessert for warm flourless chocolate cake?

He'd been tempted more than once during lunch to mention the call from Marc Josephson, but didn't. He had no reason to think that Josephson's sudden trip to Washington had anything to do with Pawkins. But something inside said it might well involve the retired detective, and he walked back to the apartment with that unsettling thought very much on his mind.

TWENTY-FIVE

It had been a busy and frustrating morning at MPD for Carl Berry. His superior, Cole Morris, had informed him that he was being pulled from the Charise Lee case, at least for the time being.

"Why?" Berry had asked. "I think we're making progress."

"I'm sure you are," Morris said, "but I take orders like you do. They want a task force assembled to focus on the Lee case."

Berry started to respond but Morris waved him off. "I know, I know," he said, "it's all PR. But we're getting pressure from Justice and the Canadians to solve this thing, to say nothing of the press. A task force sounds like it'll make a full-frontal assault, waves of cops swooping down on the culprit. At least that's the way the public will perceive it. Let them make the announcement, enjoy the accolades, and things will get back to normal. Meantime, I want you to bring in Grimes."

"He's being charged with the Musinski murder?"

"He's being told he's being charged. We'll see if that breaks him. I don't know, Carl, the new forensic evidence is shaky. A good lawyer will poke holes in it like Swiss cheese. But it's better than what we had before. Bring him in and we'll see what falls."

"I'll send Willie and Sylvia, now that they're off the Lee case."

"Good, but tell Willie to go easy. I don't need the threat of another brutality charge hanging over us."

At one, Berry, Johnson, and Portelain sat in an MPD interrogation room with Edward Grimes, an adjunct professor of music history at Georgetown University. Grimes was, he claimed, thirty-six years old, but he looked older. He was of medium height, and deathly pale. Totally bald on top, he'd grown his hair long on the sides and back and secured it into a ragged ponytail, which only highlighted his baldness. He wore wrinkled chinos, sandals over white sweat socks, and a burgundy T-shirt with GEORGETOWN U on it in white. His rimless glasses were round, thick, and too small for his face. All in all, Berry decided, he was not a college professor out of Central Casting. He looked positively frightened as he sat across the scarred table from the three detectives. Johnson and Portelain had found him in his office at the school and brought him in without incident.

"I appreciate you coming in like this to talk to us," Berry said pleasantly, as if welcoming a long-lost friend into his home.

"I don't understand," Grimes said. "This is very embarrassing. My colleagues saw me being led from my office by two detectives. I just don't understand why I'm here."

"Well," said Berry, "we just wanted to ask you a few questions about Professor Musinski."

"I knew it," Grimes whined, wringing his hands. "I knew it. Why do you want to talk to me again about that dreadful thing? Professor Musinski was my friend. He mentored me. I loved him like a father."

"I'll be straight with you, Mr. Grimes. Or is it Professor Grimes?"

"I am a professor. Adjunct."

"Not full," Johnson said.

"That's right. Next year. If things go well, I'll be offered a full professorship. That's why this is so terrible, bringing me here like this. What will they think of me at the school?"

"They won't think nothin' of you if you didn't kill Musinski," Portelain said flatly.

An anguished groan came from Grimes.

"Did you?" Berry asked.

"What? Kill Professor Musinski? Of course not. I swear to you I had nothing to do with it. He was revered. I loved him —"

"Like a father," Johnson finished the thought. She was unsmiling.

"Yes. Why won't you believe me?"

"It isn't that we don't believe you, Professor Grimes," Berry said. "We *want* to believe you. But there's new evidence that causes us to have some doubts."

"What evidence?" Grimes asked. "What new evidence could there possibly be?"

"DNA," Berry replied. "We've found some on the fireplace poker that killed the professor."

"It isn't mine," protested Grimes. "It can't be mine. You tested everything six years ago when *it* happened. You said you found nothing to link me to his death."

"True," Johnson weighed in, "but that was six years ago. We were looking for prints back then and couldn't match the partials on the weapon with you or anyone else."

Berry added, "But new and more sophisticated DNA tests now tell us that you had contact with that poker. Why would you have had contact with it?"

A small, crooked smile suddenly came to Grimes' lips. "You're lying to me," he said. "Even if I had touched that poker, my hands wouldn't leave any DNA traces."

"Maybe you drooled on it," Portelain said.

"Sweat," Johnson added.

"Why would you be handling a fireplace poker in that weather?" Berry asked.

"Unless —" Johnson said.

"I probably touched that poker other times when I visited with Dr. Musinski. Don't you understand? I did not do this!"

"Some of your colleagues at the school say you and Musinski didn't get along too good," Willie said, basing the claim on nothing.

"Who said that?" Grimes asked.

"You read Professor Grimes his rights?" Berry asked.

"Yup," Willie grunted.

"You want a lawyer, Professor Grimes?"

"Please, don't do this to me," Grimes said, and began to cry.

"Yeah, I think you need a lawyer," Berry said, standing. "You think about it, Professor. We'll be back." The detectives left the room and joined their boss, Cole Morris, behind the one-way mirror.

"That dude did the deed, man," Willie said. "Bet my pension on it." He started to walk away.

"Where are you going, Willie?" Berry asked.

"Get something to eat, a candy bar or something. I'm feeling dizzy. Must have low blood sugar or somethin'."

Berry shook his head. Johnson laughed.

"Next time you're in there with him," Morris told Berry, "ask what he did with that music Musinski's niece claims was stolen. There's our motive, a million dollars' worth of little black notes on paper with lines. Damn, I'm in the wrong business."

Despite his request for a lawyer, the questioning of Grimes continued until one thirty, when a young attorney from Legal Aid arrived and put a stop to it. Grimes was held as a suspect in the murder of Dr. Aaron Musinski, over the objections of the attorney, who insisted that his client either be formally charged or released.

"That's up to the prosecutor," Berry told the attorney as he, Willie, and Sylvia returned to Berry's office, where Ray Pawkins had just arrived.

"Hey, Ray, have a seat," Berry said.

"A blast from the past," Portelain said. "How've you been, man?"

"Couldn't be better," Pawkins said. "You?"

"Tip-top, babe. 'Course, the man here has been working us into the ground. No rest for the weary."

"Still cracking the whip, huh, Carl?" Pawkins said with a gentle laugh.

"You know that's not true," Johnson said. "Carl uses a carrot, not a stick."

"And you're as beautiful as ever, Sylvia," Pawkins said.

"I'm not easily flattered," she said. "Say it again." They all laughed.

"What's new with the Lee case?" Pawkins asked.

"I was just telling Willie and Sylvia earlier today what you told me about the two agents, Melincamp and Baltsa. They interviewed them."

"Charming couple, huh?" Pawkins said.

"From what Carl tells us," Sylvia said, "they don't have the world's best reputation."

"That's for sure," Pawkins concurred. "I've got somebody in Toronto digging a little deeper into them and their operation. I'll fill you in when I get something."

"We'd appreciate that," Berry said. "How're things in the opera world?"

"Exciting. Nothing like the murder—a real one—of a beautiful young soprano to spice things up." To Willie and Sylvia: "You know I'm working for the Washington National Opera."

"Yeah," Willie said. "Got your picture in a magazine, too."

"How'd I look?"

"Ugly as ever," Willie said, guffawing to take the edge off his comment.

"Willie and Sylvia brought in Grimes this morning, the professor over at Georgetown U," Berry said. "We've talked to him. Naturally, he swears he had nothing to do with Musinski's murder. Legal Aid sent someone to represent him."

"He say anything incriminating?" Pawkins asked.

"No," Berry answered.

"I say he did it," Willie offered.

"You're probably right," Pawkins said. "We had him pegged back when it happened, but we couldn't put him away."

"I know," said Berry. "Willie and Sylvia are going to work the case for a while."

"I thought you were on the Lee case," Pawkins said.

"Don't ask," Berry said, not attempting to keep the frustration from his voice.

"We're digging into Grimes' life, friends, whoever might know something." To Portelain and Johnson: "Speaking of that, you'd better get started."

"Good luck," Pawkins told the two detectives as they left the room.

"So, what's up?" Pawkins asked when he and Berry were alone. "You said you had some loose ends on the Musinski case."

"Yeah, we do, Ray. I've gone over all your reports from six years ago. You did a good job."

"Not good enough. He's been walking around free for six years."

"And never left D.C."

"Why should he? He was never charged."

"But you put a lot of heat on him. I don't know, if I were in his shoes, I think I'd look for a teaching job someplace far away."

"You can't figure people."

"Did you know him?"

"Sure. I must have done half a dozen interviews with him."

"No, I mean before the murder. You were taking courses at Georgetown around the time Musinski was killed, weren't you?"

"As a matter of fact, I was. I'd just started my master's program, thanks to the Metropolitan Police Department's largesse. That education program really helped."

"You never ran across Grimes while you were there?"

"No."

"But you must have known Musinski. He'd been there a long time, a high-profile guy."

"I might have met him once or twice. He was in the Music Department, I was art history. But yeah, I think I was introduced to him once."

"I never saw that in any of your reports."

"Never occurred to me to include it. Didn't have any bearing on the investigation."

"Right. Despite Willie's conviction that Grimes is guilty—you know Willie, he's never met a suspect who wasn't guilty—"

"Not a bad way to police," Pawkins said.

"That aside, what I can't figure is why Grimes would have killed Musinski."

Pawkins thought for a minute and shrugged. "Those missing musical manuscripts aren't a bad motive."

"I have a problem with that."

"Why?"

"A couple of reasons. To begin with, you indicated in your reports—and I remember having conversations with you about it— you questioned whether there ever were such manuscripts."

"I still do. All we had to go on was a letter from Musinski to his niece, and her claim that he came back from London with them. I never saw them. Neither did anyone else I know of."

"There was his partner over in Europe, wasn't there?"

Pawkins nodded. "I spoke with him a couple of times. He mentioned the scores but didn't press it. If anybody had a reason to raise hell about them disappearing, it was him. The fact that he didn't raise hell tells me that maybe they never existed in the first place."

"Maybe you're right," Berry said, "but there's something else that bothers me."

"I'm all ears."

"If anybody took those manuscripts—what were they, string quartets written by Mozart and Haydn?"

"So they say."

"If anybody took them, they would have sold them as fast as possible."

Pawkins pondered Berry's analysis. "Not necessarily," he said. "There are art lovers who steal paintings, or pay to have them stolen, who just want them to look at them every night over a snifter of brandy. Gives them some sort of solace."

"I can understand that with works of art, Ray, but musical scores? Not much to look at there, brandy or no brandy. I could understand recordings, or if whoever stole them plays the piano. By the way, Grimes doesn't play—the piano, that is."

"Still."

"I'm not ruling out what you said."

Berry did a decent impression of TV's Columbo about to leave a scene but having a sudden new thought. "What bothers me, Ray, is that Grimes doesn't live like a man who's sitting on a million dollars' worth of rare manuscripts. He, his wife, and two kids live in university-subsidized housing, nothing fancy. He drives a beat-up old car. His bank account gives him maybe a couple of months of living expenses. No savings, aside from a self-funded pension plan at the university. If he murdered Musinski to get his hands on those scores, what the hell did he do with them?"

"Beats me," Pawkins said. "What about the niece? Maybe she grabbed them the night she reported her uncle murdered."

Berry shook his head. "We checked her out, too, recently. Another modest liver, nothing to point in her direction."

"If I were you, Carl, I'd forget about these so-called Mozart-Haydn scores and concentrate strictly on the forensics where Grimes is concerned. I'd love to see you nail him. That case has bugged me for six years, the fact that we couldn't bring it to a conclusion. Grimes did it." He laughed. "Hell, even Willie knows that. Well, got to run. Great seeing you again. If I come up with anything in the Lee case, you'll be the first to hear—no, the second, after my esteemed client, the Washington National Opera."

TWENTY-SIX

Milton Crowley decided to extend his stay in Washington for a few days. He didn't feel well, chalking up his general malaise to the fatigue of the traveling he'd endured over the past week. He was staying at the Hotel Monaco, a relatively new boutique hotel in what once had been a post office and the home to the Tariff Commission. It had been recommended to Crowley by a colleague who'd recently visited Washington: "It's a small oasis of sanity, Milton, in an otherwise insane city."

Crowley dismissed his friend's characterization of D.C. Truth was, he liked Washington, and enjoyed strolling its wide avenues and seeking out unusual shops on its side streets. He also found the hotel very much to his liking, particularly its restaurant, Poste, with its pleasant outdoor terrace, where he enjoyed sitting, a single-malt Scotch and crab cocktail with papaya on the table, along with an ashtray. Crowley was a smoker—a discreet one, to be sure, but genuinely fond of the pleasure it gave him, the crusading fanatics be damned.

This day, after checking in with the British Embassy, he decided to spend a portion of the day leisurely strolling the National Gallery of Art's West Building. He'd visited the museum on earlier trips to Washington, marveling at its size and the scope of its collections; truly, the entire history of Western art from the 12th century to the present was contained in the building's half-million square feet of interior space, one of the world's largest marble structures. He was particularly fond of the Italian collection, which included *Ginevra de' Benci*, the only work of Leonardo da Vinci's on permanent display in the Americas. During his last visit, Crowley stood in front of that portrait of a young merchant's wife and wept. He saw in the woman's face the face of his own wife, Cora, who'd died a dozen years ago of cancer. It had been a childless marriage, which had suited them fine. Now Crowley sometimes wondered what it would be like to have a son or daughter bearing his name and carrying his blood. He'd never remarried, nor had he seriously pursued a new mate. His work became his mistress and spouse, but that, too, had provided less compensation in recent years. Whoever had invented the concept of retirement had done so with Milton Crowley in mind.

Soon.

Rather than begin in the Italian gallery, he stopped first in the East Hall, off the Rotunda, where 17th and 18th century French paintings were displayed. Renoir's *A Girl with a Watering Can* captivated him, and he spent many minutes taking pleasure from it and recalling what Renoir had said about the work: "A painting should be a lovable thing, gay and pretty; yes, pretty. There are enough things to bore us in life without our making more of them." *How true*, Crowley thought as he moved from Fragonard to Manet, Cézanne to Monet, and Renoir to Seurat before exiting that space and going to the West Hall, home of Italian art, of *Ginevra de' Benci*, which he now almost considered a portrait of his beloved Cora.

His cell phone rang. A guard gave him a stern look.

"Sorry," Crowley muttered, cupping his hand over the phone and speaking in whispered tones. "Now?" he said. "Can't it wait?" He was told it could not. "All right," he said. "I'll come immediately."

Sour over having been deprived of spending time with Cora, he replaced the phone in his pocket and abandoned his leisurely pace for a faster one in the direction of the main entrance, where taxis would be waiting. He grimaced against a stabbing pain in his hip and leaned against a wall for a moment to allow it to pass. He squeezed into the back of a cab and gave the address of the British Embassy on Massachusetts Avenue—Embassy Row, as it is known.

He closed his eyes as the driver lurched from the curb and executed a tight U-turn. What could be so important that he had to be there immediately? he wondered. They knew he'd elected to take a few days off before heading back to his post at the British Foreign Service's Baghdad office. He'd discharged his responsibilities by briefing Browning at Homeland Security. He was now sorry that he'd decided to extend his stay. Better to be on an airplane, where no one could reach you.

He was deposited at a small brick guardhouse at the gated entrance to the sprawling embassy, arguably the most stately in a city of stately embassies. The guard confirmed his credentials, called inside the main house, and allowed Crowley to enter. He was met at the front door by the embassy's head of chancery. "Mr. Crowley," he said in a pinched tone, "right this way."

They went down the main hallway, a long, wide corridor with bloodred walls and a checkerboard floor of white Vermont marble and black Pennsylvania slate. Huge portraits of British leaders past and present peered down at them as Crowley was ushered into a room with unmarked double doors. Heavy maroon drapes covered whatever windows were behind them. A large Tabriz carpet dominated the small, square room whose furniture was distinctly in the Louis XVI style, chairs and side tables all gold and blue. On the walls were four carved plaster friezes of Grinling Gibbons motifs, interspersed with landscapes by the hand of an artist unfamiliar to Crowley. Maybe Constable, he mused as the other men in the room stood at his entrance.

He knew two of them. Joseph Browning, replete in a three-piece suit different from what he'd worn when they'd last met at the Department of Homeland Security's headquarters, offered his hand. The second face familiar to Crowley was Jillian Thomas of the British Foreign Service home office in London. *What is* he *doing here?*

The third man, a stranger to Crowley, introduced himself: "Wendell Jones, Mr. Crowley, Canadian Security Intelligence Service."

"Pleased to meet you," Crowley said after shaking Jones' hand. The representative of the CSIS was a portly man, probably in his mid-fifties, Crowley judged, with a round, shiny face, gelled black hair, and heavy lips defined by a too narrow black moustache above them.

Thomas, tall and as slender as a javelin, was slightly hunch-backed, referred to in his circles as a "socialite slouch." In his sixties, he possessed a full head of flowing silver hair in which he obviously took immense pride, judging from the care with which it was arranged. An almost perpetual sneer, like his curved back, would be considered a sign of world-weariness and keenly honed cynicism. Crowley did not like him and never did, although his subservient position in the Foreign Service's hierarchy precluded him from demonstrating it.

"Enjoying your holiday?" Thomas asked Crowley after everyone was seated in a circle in their gold-and-blue chairs.

"I hadn't considered it a holiday," Crowley said, not pleased with how defensive he sounded. "Just a day or two between assignments."

"Yes, quite," Thomas said. "Well, I see no reason to delay the topic of our gathering. Mr. Browning, please."

The American reached into the recesses of a large, battered, top-opening briefcase and extracted a sheaf of papers. He looked through them, chose one, and handed it to the Canadian, Jones, who slipped on a pair of half-glasses and frowned as he read. Crowley waited patiently, adjusting himself in the lovely-to-look-at, uncomfortable-to-sit-in chair to accommodate his nagging hip.

"Yes, this matches what we've been told," Jones said, handing the paper back to Thomas.

"May I ask what this is about?" Crowley asked, after first clearing his throat.

"It's about what the bloody terrorists are planning, Milton," said

Thomas. "It's about what your people in Amman have been hinting at for months but never quite delivered."

Crowley extended his hand to Thomas. "May I see what is of such interest?" he asked.

Thomas grimaced, ran fingertips down his prominent nose, and handed Crowley the dispatch. Milton was aware that six eyes were trained on him, awaiting a response. He read slowly and deliberately, ignoring the tendency to want to accommodate them by reading faster. Finished, he looked up and said, "Yes, the Canadian connection is very much in line with what my people in Jordan were able to gather from their Iraqi sources."

"Hardly a great revelation," Thomas said. "The question, Crowley, is why these gentlemen's intelligence agencies were able to pinpoint with greater specificity the threat, while your people only pussyfooted around it. You run a flaming expensive operation. A king's ransom. And for what?"

Crowley began to respond, but fell silent.

"I might also say," Thomas added, "that the leaks coming out of Amman are enough to sink the *Queen Mary II*."

Many thoughts ran through Crowley's mind. If he was being made a scapegoat, it wouldn't be the first time. It occurred to him that the three intelligence agencies represented in this faux Louis XVI room were competing with one another for dominance, or at least for the most slaps on the back. He found it distasteful, at best. Terrorists were out there planning to kill as many non-Muslims as possible, and here they were, men jockeying for political position and kudos. Thomas, his boss at the Foreign Service, was not a man to take criticism with aplomb, Crowley had learned over the years. *Of course!* Crowley thought. Thomas, and the British intelligence services he represented, had been made to look, at best, inept. How handy for Thomas to have Crowley on hand to take the blame in front of his bosses' counterparts. The Canadian, Jones, was cheeky to sit there and claim success. From what Crowley knew, the Canadians had squandered much of their counterintelligence resources worrying about foreign governments spying on Canadian industry, money obviously of a higher priority than lives. *Bastards! How dare they subject me to such embarrassment? I've given the best years of my life to the fugging Foreign Service, and have done a damn fine job, to boot.*

A vision of the cottage in Dorset came and went.

"You've lost two of your so-called sources in Amman," Thomas said. "Obviously the enemy knows only too well what's going on within your operation."

"Two?" Crowley said.

"You haven't heard, Crowley?" Thomas said. He was showboating, performing for the others' benefit. "Your man, Steamer—I believe that was what he was called—got it in the neck, in a manner of speaking."

"I didn't know," Crowley said. "I've been here and . . ." His stomach churned at the thought of the big Brit with the code name "Steamer" no longer being alive.

Thomas' sigh was loud and said much.

"If I might, I'd like to narrow down this conversation to some pertinent matters in these intercepts," Jones said, removing his glasses and leaning toward Crowley. "Mr. Crowley, as you read, it seems that the terrorists—presumably led by al-Qaeda, although that's not set in stone—intend to press forward with their plans to assassinate political leaders. It's my understanding that you had said as much in briefings you've given Mr. Browning and Mr. Thomas."

"It was only, as Mr. Thomas said, hinted at. Attempts were made to gather more specific information but—"

"You might be interested in this, Crowley," Thomas said, handing his subordinate another piece of paper.

Crowley read it, quickly this time, and handed it back. "The same intent, a different target," he said.

"The question is," Jones said, "whether anything your sources in Amman told you might have forecast such a shift in their targeting."

"No, nothing."

"You can understand my government's interest in this shift, which we've gotten through intercepts—the terrorists' chatter, as it were," said Jones.

"Of course," Crowley agreed. The paper he'd just read indicated that rather than attempt the assassination of American political figures, the emphasis would now be on Canadian and British leaders.

"I might echo what my distinguished friend from Canada has just said," Thomas intoned. "We're now talking about terrorism on our home front, Crowley. The stakes have been raised considerably."

Why? Crowley wondered. Were Canadian and British leaders more important than Americans? They were, of course, to those charged with protecting them. *But in the larger scheme of things?*

Besides, he thought, putting so much credence in the babble of Arab terrorists was misguided. If al-Qaeda knew that the Americans had been alerted to their plans to assassinate their top political figures, it would be easy to "chatter" about a change of targets, whether it represented the truth or not. The terrorists might be ruthless and bloodthirsty, but they weren't stupid.

The security of the Western world was not, he decided on the spot, in especially competent hands.

"Is there anything else?" Crowley asked, anxious to bolt. "I think it best that I leave Washington immediately and return to Baghdad."

His superior coughed politely into his closed fist.

"One other thing, Mr. Crowley," Jones said. Browning handed Jones yet another communiqué, which was passed to Crowley. Again, he read quickly, but stopped midway and focused more attention on the words. When he was finished, he removed his glasses, rubbed his eyes, and shook his head. "This means nothing to me," he said.

"These names never came up in all the months you've been handling sources in Amman?" Thomas asked, forcing incredulity into his voice. "Never?"

"Never."

"They've only recently captured the attention of our people," the Canadian intelligence operative, Jones, said. "We'd been aware of the potential of their involvement with terrorist organizations, but it's so damned difficult to trace these things, especially when the company does everything aboveboard, or appears to."

"Who are they?" Crowley asked.

"Talent agents," Browning answered. "They represent opera singers and such. Offices in Toronto."

"They represent many foreign singers, mostly operatic," Jones added. "Their reputation isn't pristine, I might say, some shady dealings alleged, pocketing fees belonging to clients, bringing young performers to Canada from other countries on the pretense of finding them training and work, taking their money, and leaving them high and dry. Not unusual, I suppose, for people in that line of work."

"They represented that young opera singer who was murdered at the Kennedy Center," Browning said.

"They've had dealings with Middle Eastern groups, we've learned. It all seems kosher, if that's an acceptable way to put it considering the circumstances, but the name did come up in one of our intercepts."

Crowley again shook his head, and groaned.

"Problem, Crowley?" Thomas asked.

"My hip," Crowley said. "Acts up now and then."

"You sound like a candidate for a hip replacement," Browning offered.

"Perhaps," Crowley replied, finding it strange for this discussion of terrorism and planned assassinations of political leaders to morph into talk of his hip. "If that's all," he said, standing, "I'd best be going."

Without anyone saying anything, Jones and Browning shook Crowley's hand and walked from the room, leaving him alone with Thomas. Crowley started to leave, too, but Thomas said, "A word with you, Milton," indicating with his hand for Crowley to again take his seat. When he had, Thomas said, "I'm quite sure it's evident, Milton, that we've fallen behind our colleagues in the gathering and assimilating of useful intelligence on the ground in Iraq."

Crowley didn't respond; his jaw moved silently.

"Somewhat embarrassing, I'd say," Thomas said, examining his fingernails. "Let me cut to the chase, Milton. Hunting down these bloody savages is a young man's game, wouldn't you agree?"

"I hadn't given it much thought, Jillian."

"Well," Thomas said, forcing a smile, "I think it's time you did.

As a matter of fact, I've been giving it considerable thought for some time now."

"And?"

"And, Milton, I believe it is time to relieve you of your duties in Baghdad. Collinsworth will take over for you there, effective immediately."

"Collinsworth?"

Adrian Collinsworth, in his early forties, had been transferred to Baghdad from Cairo six months earlier as Crowley's second in command. He was, as far as Crowley was concerned, a thoroughly dislikable man, skilled at boot-licking but lacking even rudimentary skill at intelligence analysis.

"I suppose I don't have a say in this," Crowley said, successfully masking a small smile behind his hand.

"Afraid not, old chap. It's for the greater good, you understand. Nothing personal. Time marches on. A new guard is always waiting in the wings to pick up where we leave off. It's the way of the world, Milton. Happens to the best of us. At any rate, my friend, your early retirement—I might say immediate retirement—has been arranged. No need to worry about your personal items. Your things will be shipped from Baghdad forthwith, to that cottage of yours, I assume. Where is it? The Cotswolds?"

"Wareham, Dorset."

"Yes, Wareham. Lovely spot. I know, I know, you'll find it an adjustment to be a gentleman of leisure after the excitement and intrigue to which you've been accustomed all these years. But think of it this way, Milton, you'll now have a leg up on your golden years, enjoying the sort of civilized comfort that's been lacking in that hellhole Baghdad. Good food, good drink, and perhaps even a good woman with whom to commune." His laugh was annoyingly lascivious. "Well, my friend, no need to prolong this. Any questions?"

Crowley fought to keep his face from reflecting what he was thinking and feeling at that moment. He remained stoic as he said, "No, Jillian. As disappointing as this is, I must agree with you. There is a greater good to be considered. All I can say is that my years of service have been highly satisfactory, and I trust my contributions have not gone unappreciated."

They stood. Thomas placed his arm over Crowley's shoulder and smiled broadly, displaying a large set of dull teeth. "You've been a true patriot to the Crown, Milton. The nation is in your debt. Make your travel arrangements through the embassy." His laugh was accompanied by a deep, rattling cough. "And for God's sake, man, remember to book a flight to London, not Baghdad. Cheerio, Milton. See you back home." A firm slap on the back ended the meeting.

Crowley left the embassy with a spring in his step that hadn't been there in quite a while. His hip was pain-free. Had he dared, he would have attempted to leap into the air and click his heels the way Russian dancers do. He enjoyed a cigarette outside the building before hailing a passing taxi. "The National Gallery," he told the driver. Once inside the museum, he went directly to the Italian gallery and stood before Leonardo's *Ginevra de' Benci*, a smile on his face.

"Good news, Cora, darling," he said. "We'll be back in Dorset before we know it."

TWENTY-SEVEN

Annabel Lee-Smith met the Secret Service's four-man advance team at the Brazilian Embassy at four that afternoon. They lived up to the image of Secret Service agents as depicted in motion pictures and on television—taciturn, steely-eyed, short haircuts, dressed in nondescript off-the-rack suits, and all business, but not without a smile when appropriate.

"This is where the event will take place?" one of them asked Annabel, referring to fact sheets that had been provided earlier that day.

"Yes. This is where all the guests will gather after their more intimate dinners at various embassies around the city."

She followed as they slowly walked the interior perimeter of the huge tent that was in the process of being erected on the embassy's grounds.

"There will be a band over there," Annabel said, consulting a sketch she'd been provided by Nicki Frolich. "And over there, too. The bars will be in those corners, and the food services—desserts, really—will be where those tables are being set up."

The agents said nothing as they continued their stroll, eyes taking in everything, including rooftops of nearby buildings, bushes and trees on the property, and other potential locations from which an attack could be launched.

"The president and first lady won't be eating or drinking," Annabel heard one say to the other.

An agent turned and asked Annabel, "What about the band? Who are they?"

"Actually, there are three bands," she replied. "One is being booked through a talent agency here in Washington. That band will play American music. The other two are Brazilian bands."

"Which talent agency?"

"I don't know, but I'll find out."

"The Brazilian musicians. Where are they coming from?"

"Brazil," said Annabel. "The embassy has made those arrangements."

They proceeded to what would be the portal through which invited guests would arrive. "What do their invitations look like?" one of the agents asked Annabel.

She handed one to him.

"They'll have to show ID besides this," he said. "We need the guest list."

"It's on its way over," another agent said.

"Will you have time to—?" Annabel started to ask.

"The boss tossed us this last-minute," one of the agents said, flashing a grin. "He's known for that. But we'll manage." Then, as though he might have told a tale out of school, he looked away from her and made a call on his radio.

Being summoned to meet with them was last-minute for Annabel, too. She'd called a number given her by Nicki Frolich and was connected to the person in the Secret Service responsible for the president's forays outside the White House. She was also put in touch with an officer from the thousand-strong Capitol Hill police force, whose mission was to protect the foreign diplomatic corps in Washington. He made an appointment to meet her there at five that afternoon, along with the head of security for the Brazilian Embassy. According to Frolich, there were mixed emotions at the embassy about the president's sudden decision to attend the festivities following the private dinners. The ambassador was delighted. His staff was not.

The agent with the fact sheet went over it with Annabel. They discussed the number of embassy staff that would be working the ball, as well as the outside catering services and their people.

"What about these opera performers?" he asked.

"The Washington National Opera will provide musical entertainment. Some of the students in the Domingo-Cafritz Young Artist Program will perform."

"We'll need their names."

"Of course."

"These supernumeraries?" the agent said. "What's their role?"

"They'll be in costume and dress up the party, give it the right opera theme."

"Costumes?"

"Yes. From famous operas."

"That include masks?"

"For some, I'm sure."

He noted that on the sheet.

"The president and first lady are due here at ten sharp," the agent said.

"Yes," Annabel said.

"They'll stay a half hour."

"That's what I've been told."

"He'll make a couple of remarks."

"We'll be anxious to hear them," said Annabel.

"Well, thank you, Mrs. Lee-Smith. We appreciate the cooperation. We'll be back tomorrow morning and probably spend most of the day here."

"Will I be needed?" she asked.

"Not the whole time, but we will want to speak with you from time to time. May I have your cell number?"

She gave him the number and watched the agents walk away,

stopping every few feet on their way out to Massachusetts Avenue, making notes as they went; one wielded a small video camera with which he taped the entrance to the embassy grounds.

Nice young men, she thought as she awaited the arrival of the next security detail. She was aware of the enormity of their job, protecting the free world's most powerful leader from harm. She was certain they weren't pleased at the president's decision to make an appearance. Leaving the secured confines of the White House compounded their problems, she knew. That there were nuts out there, either acting alone or in concert with others, who would take pleasure in assassinating a president of the United States was an unfortunate reality.

❧

Following his lunch with Pawkins, Mac Smith went to the computer in the apartment and Googled the Musinski murder. He and Annabel had pulled up only a fraction of the hundreds of articles that appeared, and Mac quickly accessed many others, until finding a few that mentioned Marc Josephson, from newspapers and magazines in Great Britain. Josephson had been interviewed in the months following the murder. In these pieces he talked of how he and Musinski had discovered the Mozart-Haydn string quartets after years of searching. The scores had been, he claimed, in the attic of a home on London's outskirts. The home's owner, a doddering old man, had died, and his daughter had held a tag sale to dispose of the house's contents.

❧

"At first," Josephson said in one of the articles, "I didn't realize what I'd come across. Aaron (Musinski) and I had come to this suburb of London that weekend to spend a few days with an old, dear friend, and we did what we often did, stopped in at private house sales with the whimsical notion that we might find something of great value among the junk being offered. I'd chatted with the daughter upon arriving and learned that her father had been an inveterate collector of memorabilia on his many travels, which included frequent trips to Vienna. I was strolling through the front yard, where tables had been set up, and spotted a stack of scores, yellowed with age and curled at the corners, sitting on a table with piles of old magazines and newspapers. I called Aaron over and we perused them.

"I could literally feel Aaron begin to tremble as he picked up each score and examined it. 'I don't believe what I'm seeing,' he said to me. There were no names on the music, but the dates of composition were there, along with a numbering system that was unmistakably Mozart."

"Numbering system?" the interviewer said. "Please explain."

"Mozart's compositions are often identified by the letter 'K,' followed by a number. The 'K' stands for 'Ludwig von Köchel.' He created a catalog of Mozart's works in 1862, listing them in the order he thought they had been written. Remarkably, the scores Aaron and I found that day in the front yard of the home contained the 'K,' but had handwritten next to it the letter 'H.' "

"For Haydn."

"Yes. Of course, the date was significant, too. Mozart met Haydn in 1781 in Vienna. Haydn was somewhat older than the young maestro and was Mozart's idol. The string quartets were written during that period."

"And you and Professor Musinski knew what you had come upon?"

"Oh, yes. I was convinced of it because of my lifelong immersion in rare manuscripts, including musical scores. Aaron was the acknowledged expert on Mozart and his compositions. Between us, we were sure we had the string quartets."

"You must have been ecstatic."

"An understatement."

"What happened next?"

"We quietly debated whether to inform the daughter that the scores were worth considerably more than what she was asking for them."

"Which was?"

"Thirty pounds."

"And you judged their worth to be?"

"A million pounds, perhaps more."

"What did you pay her?"

"We decided to not reveal what we were convinced we'd found, but to be more generous than her asking price. We bought some other items to mask our intentions and paid her two hundred pounds, explaining that the scores, as ragged as they were, were perfect for framing and decorating my study. She seemed quite pleased."

"But you weren't being honest with her. Did you feel any guilt?"

"Oh, yes, and I still do on occasion."

"The Mozart-Haydn scores have disappeared, as you've announced. Professor Musinski took them back to the States?"

"Yes. He'd developed a highly sophisticated computer program into which most of Mozart's compositions had been inputted. His intention was to compare these compositions with the vast array of other Mozart works in style and technique, using the powerful program he'd developed. He never had the opportunity to do that, I'm afraid. He was killed shortly after arriving back in the United States. The scores haven't been seen since."

"Stolen by whomever killed him."

"I would say that is a logical conclusion."

Smith read other articles in which Josephson was quoted. In one, he was asked about what he thought of the job the Washington, D.C., police were doing searching for Musinski's murderer and recovering the Mozart-Haydn scores.

"I suppose they are doing what they can, but with so many murders in that city, it would be unreasonable to expect them to devote all their energies to this. I'm afraid that neither the murderer nor the scores will ever be found."

A *hell of a reputation to have*, Mac thought as he exited Google and read the printouts he'd made of the articles. He called Annabel on her cell.

"I'm still at the Brazilian Embassy," she said, "and I'll probably be here quite a while longer. Why don't we meet up at the Kennedy Center."

"Okay."

"Are we still on for dinner with Mr. Josephson?"

"I haven't actually made dinner plans with him. I'm supposed to call. He should be arriving here at the Watergate about now. I'll give him a try. Have you checked in at the gallery?"

"Many times. Margo has everything under control. She sold that small Aztec incense burner."

"Good. We get to eat again."

"I have to go, Mac." She puckered a kiss into the phone and was gone.

"Mr. Josephson?" Mac said when the hotel operator put him through to the room occupied by Josephson.

"Yes. Mac Smith?"

"Right. If we're to meet for dinner, it will have to be a late one, say nine? I have a rehearsal earlier in the evening."

"A rehearsal. Are you a thespian as well as a professor of law?"

"No. It's a long story. Actually, it's a short story. Sorry it will have to be so late."

"It's fine with me," Josephson said. "I'll nap till then."

"A preference in food?" Smith asked.

"Anything not too spicy, please."

"I'll keep that in mind. I will be bringing my wife. I trust that's all right with you. As you might remember, she's a former attorney, too."

"It will be a pleasure seeing her again."

"One question before we get together."

"Yes?"

"Is this about those missing musical scores that were allegedly in Professor Musinski's hands when he was murdered?"

"You've been doing your homework," Josephson said. "As a matter of fact, my trip here is precisely about that."

"I'm at a loss as to how I might be of help in that regard."

"That, I believe, is a topic better reserved for over a dinner table. Let me just say that if you can assist me in this matter, I can make it worth your while. You see, Mac, the scores are no longer missing."

TWENTY-EIGHT

Despite Sylvia Johnson's mild protest, Willie Portelain insisted upon stopping for a slice on their way to Georgetown University. She'd decided that her nagging about his eating habits only put her in the position of sounding like a wife, a role she wasn't anxious to play. Besides, it didn't seem to do any good. Maybe not mentioning it would be more effective. Her not wanting to stop this time had more to do with schedule than concern over Willie's health. She had a date that night with a handsome young lawyer from the Department of Homeland Security and wanted time to get ready before he picked her up.

She stayed in the car while Willie gobbled his slice of pizza and washed it down with a Mug root beer. She checked her watch every few minutes. He was back in the car in seven minutes. Not bad.

"Good?" she asked as she backed out of the parking space and headed for 37th and O Street, the main entrance to the university.

"I've had better. Not enough cheese. Should have asked them to put on some extra."

"How have you been feeling?" she asked.

"Good. Real good."

"Taking your medication?"

"When I remember. Maybe I ought to buy one of those little pill boxes—you know, with the days on it. That'd help me."

She made a mental note to buy him one. He wouldn't.

Sylvia wasn't Catholic, but she had a special fondness for the Jesuit university, founded in 1789, making it the oldest Catholic university in the country, although approximately half of its student population was not of the Catholic faith. The first black person to earn a doctorate in the United States, Reverend Patrick Healy, had once been its president, making him the first black president of a predominantly white university in America. Sylvia took pride in the accomplishments of African Americans and had read a number of books about those who'd left their mark on American society. She'd spent an occasional Saturday or Sunday strolling Georgetown University's shady cobblestone streets, stopping now and then to rest on a bench and read whatever book she was into at the moment, soaking in not only the sun and fresh air, but the aura of the place, as though absorbing an education through her pores.

They bypassed the Visitor Information Center and went directly to the building in which Edward Grimes' office was located. The young woman who'd been at the receptionist desk when they'd taken Grimes away looked positively panic-stricken when they walked through the door.

"Hello again," Willie said, flashing a broad smile.

"Hello," she said in a shaky voice. "How is—how is Professor Grimes?"

"He's just fine," Willie said. He pointed to a series of doors. "We thought we'd have a chat with some of the professors who work with him."

"Is he—?"

"He's just fine," Willie repeated. "Not to worry. We're just asking some questions, that's all." He pointed to doors along a corridor. "This where some of his colleagues work?"

"Yes, but—"

"Who is his superior?" Sylvia asked.

"The dean."

"Could we speak with him, please?"

"Just a minute."

She placed a call. A few minutes later, a tall, patrician man wearing a maroon cardigan sweater over an open collar, blue, button-down shirt appeared in the hallway. He introduced himself as Warren Eder. "Can I help you?" he asked.

Johnson and Portelain explained their presence, and asked if they could speak with him privately. "Of course," he replied, and led them into his office, a large space with windows overlooking the campus. They took chairs across the desk from him. "I have to admit I was shaken when Professor Grimes was arrested earlier today. Is he being charged with Dr. Musinski's murder?"

"He's being questioned about it," Sylvia said.

"I thought that was all resolved six years ago," said Eder. "We were all so relieved when Professor Grimes was cleared."

"Still an open case," Willie said. "Tell us about Professor Grimes."

"We understand he's not a full professor," Sylvia said.

"That's right. He's up for appointment next year."

"He worked with Musinski, right?" Willie said.

"Dr. Musinski had a number of people involved with his research, including Ed Grimes. Dr. Musinski had a unique situation here at Georgetown. We're not known as a liberal arts school, although that department has developed significantly over the years."

And I bet you think it's thanks to you, the cynical Willie thought.

"We've always been known for our schools of diplomacy, government, medicine, and law. I believe our law school receives more applications than any other law school in the country."

"What was Professor Grimes' relationship with Dr. Musinski like?" Sylvia asked.

"It was . . ." Dean Eder laughed. "Dr. Musinski was a remarkable character, not an easy man to understand, much less get along with. As I said, his situation here at the university was unique. It would have been more logical for him to have established himself and his research at another university, one more immersed in the arts, particularly music. But his Catholic background caused him to come here, and we were privileged to have a man of his stature on our faculty."

"About Professor Grimes," Sylvia said, having stolen a peek at her watch.

"He and Dr. Musinski got along as well as anyone. What I mean is, working closely with Aaron could be frustrating, at best. He wasn't a tolerant man. He tended to berate his staff on occasion for what he felt was a lack of academic commitment. Finding those lost Mozart-Haydn musical manuscripts represented another feather in his cap. How tragic that not only did he lose his life in such a brutal way, but the thing he'd pursued for years was gone with him." He leaned forward, elbows on the desk. "Has new evidence surfaced implicating Ed Grimes again?"

"We're not at liberty to say," said Sylvia. "Let me ask you this question, Dean Eder. In the months and years following Dr. Musinski's murder, did Professor Grimes show any difference in his lifestyle?"

"In what way?"

"Did he seem to live a little more lavishly than before?"

"Ed? Gracious, no. He's a very modest man. Have you met his family?"

"We intend to."

"A nice family. I just pray he wasn't involved in the murder. It would be devastating to his wife and children, and to the university."

"You said he and Musinski got it on sometimes," Willie said.

"Got it on? Oh, you mean had their differences. As I said, Dr. Musinski could be difficult to get along with. I do remember one time when Musinski berated Grimes something fierce. I was appalled at the vehemence of his attack and spoke to Aaron about it. He was aware of his volatility and tried to curb it. I admired him for that."

"When was that?" Sylvia asked.

"I can't recall specifically. Maybe six years ago."

"Around the time of the murder," Willie said.

"I suppose," Eder said.

"Let me ask you another question," Willie said.

"Yes?"

"If Musinski was so tough to get along with, how come you kept him around?"

"As I said, Detective, any college or university prides itself on the professional credentials of its faculty. Musinski was a giant in his field. His computer program, through which the compositional techniques of the masters from generations ago could be compared to newly discovered works, was groundbreaking. And it should go without saying that men of his stature invite considerable donations to an institution of higher learning."

"Yeah, I imagine," Willie said.

"We'd like to see Professor Grimes' office," Sylvia said. "Has anyone been in there since he left with us?"

"I don't believe so."

She said to Willie, "Let's get some help over here and clean out his office."

"Yes, ma'am," Willie said.

A call to MPD resulted in two uniformed cops and an evidence tech arriving in a panel truck and removing files, papers, and Grimes' computer. Sylvia and Willie helped, but another look at her watch told Sylvia she was running late.

"I have to go," she whispered to Willie. "I'll drop off the car. You can get a ride with them. Will you stay here until they're done?"

"Where you going?"

"Not that it's any of your business, but I have a date."

"Oh, ho," he said. "Cheatin' on Willie, huh?"

She looked at the officers unloading things from the office to see whether they'd overheard the exchange. "See you in the morning," she said.

"You have trouble with this dude, you call me," Willie yelled after her, to her chagrin.

TWENTY-NINE

Mac Smith walked through the stage door to the Kennedy Center's Opera House and signed in as "talent"—he had to admit he was getting a kick out of doing that—and was met by Genevieve Crier.

"Mac, darling," she said, planting a kiss on his cheek—everyone in opera seemed to kiss one another on the cheek. "There's been a change in the rehearsal schedule. Anthony is so pleased with the way the supers and chorus have been performing that he's decided to use tonight for a *Sitzprobe.*"

"Is that like a sitz bath?" Mac asked, mirth in his voice.

"No, silly, it's a special sort of rehearsal. *La prova all'italiana* in Italian. A sitting rehearsal. The singers will go through their music with the full orchestra, rather than with just piano accompaniment."

"A dress rehearsal," he said.

"Hardly," she said. "No costumes, no props, no stage business. The singers simply sit in chairs, or stand, and sing with the orchestra.

It's my favorite type of rehearsal. It was supposed to be night after to-morrow, but Anthony pushed it up to tonight. You'll love it!"

"I have some things I can be doing at home," Mac said.

"Not on your life," she said, grabbing his arm and propelling him down the corridor and into the theater. "We'll sit here. Is Annabel coming?"

"Yes, but we can't stay for the entire rehearsal. We're meeting someone for dinner."

"Ah, the life of a favored couple in a city of favored couples. Anyone I know?"

"I don't think so. That reminds me. I have to call him. Back in a minute."

He went to the lobby, called the Watergate Hotel, and asked for the guest room of Marc Josephson, who answered on the first ring.

"Mac Smith here."

"I've been waiting for your call. Is dinner still on the agenda?"

"Oh, yes. I'm here at the rehearsal I mentioned to you. My wife will be joining me shortly. We can be free by eight-thirty."

"That sounds fine. Where shall I meet you?"

"Enjoy fish?"

"Very much."

"Good. I'll make a reservation at Kinkead's. It's on Pennsylvania Avenue, a fairly good walk. Take a taxi. Every driver knows where it is. See you at eight thirty."

When he returned to his seat after calling the restaurant and securing a table on the quieter second level, he saw that Ray Pawkins had joined Genevieve.

"We're in luck," the retired detective said as he and Mac shook hands. "You'll finally get to hear the voices you'll be enjoying every night when the show goes on."

"Looking forward to it," Mac said, turning to see whether Annabel had arrived.

"Where's your lovely wife?" Pawkins asked.

"Helping protect the president," Mac replied.

"How exciting," said Pawkins. "She packing heat these days?"

Mac thought of a double entendre, but stifled the urge. "She's conferring with the Secret Service about the president's visit to the Opera Ball."

"I am impressed," Pawkins said. "The fate of the free world rides on your wife's beautiful shoulders."

Genevieve bounded away to take care of something backstage.

"Hopefully, they won't just be marking," Pawkins said, his eyes on where a row of chairs was being set up. The musicians in the pit went through their ablutions, the tuning of the myriad instruments creating a cacophonous, atonal wash of sound, but not unpleasant.

"Marking what?" Mac asked, feeling he had to.

"Not giving it their all vocally. Going through the motions. I understand the soprano, our Madame Tosca, is fighting a cold, although I'm told she always claims to be on the verge of a terminal head cold. Never misses a performance, though. Likes the attention, I suppose."

"Anything new on the Lee murder?" Mac asked.

"No, but I'm on the case. It looks more and more like Chris Warren is taking center stage."

"And the Musinski murder? You said new evidence has shed light on it."

"For me, Grimes, the guy who was a grad assistant to Musinski, is the culprit." He laughed. "I sound more and more like a private eye, don't I, 'packing heat' and 'culprits'? Next I'll be talking about gats, gams, and molls."

Genevieve returned with some of the other supers in tow, including Mac's boss at GW, Wilfred Burns, who said he was taking advantage of the change in schedule to catch up on things back at his office.

"Where's the young pianist, Warren?" Mac whispered to Genevieve.

"I told him earlier of the new schedule and he's opted to stay away," she replied in her own low voice. "Is he—?"

Mac finished her thought. "A suspect?" he said. "Everyone is, Genevieve."

As Burns was about to leave, he leaned close to Mac and asked, "Is there anything new?"

"No," Mac said, uncomfortable at having ended up the conduit for such information. He looked to where Pawkins was chatting with another super, the navy commander. He'd been tempted since seeing Pawkins to mention the call from Josephson and to relay the final line of their most recent phone conversation: *"The scores are no longer missing."* Certainly, Pawkins would be interested in this development, and by extension so would the detectives working the Musinski case. But Mac had determined that until he knew more, there was nothing to be gained by passing along Josephson's offhand comment. Maybe it wasn't true. All Smith had to go on was what a man he hadn't seen in two years had said to conclude a telephone conversation. Yes, if the Mozart-Haydn string quartets had surfaced, they might help point a finger in the direction of whomever had killed Musinski. If Mac decided there was credence to what Josephson had to say, he wouldn't hesitate to share it with Pawkins. So for now, and until after his dinner with Josephson, he'd keep it to himself. It wasn't easy.

Annabel arrived shortly after the *Sitzprobe* had started, and the singers, including the soprano and tenor leads and lesser characters, had begun running through the music with the orchestra. During a break, when the conductor stopped the aria being sung to adjust something in the orchestra's score, Annabel said quietly to Mac, "What's this dinner tonight all about?"

He started to respond, but the rehearsal resumed, and they fell silent. The music was lovely, the power and richness of the voices sending chills up Mac's back at times. He was torn; he wanted to be there to enjoy the music, but at the same time he wanted to be where he could fill in Annabel about Josephson before meeting with him.

A natural pause occurred a few minutes past eight when the soprano announced she wasn't feeling well and would not be able to continue the rehearsal. Her "cover," a younger soprano, who'd been sitting quietly onstage along with the others, said she was ready to pick up where the diva had left off.

"Maybe they gave her Coke instead of Pepsi," Mac said.

Genevieve gently punched his arm.

Mac said, "Annabel and I have to run. That dinner I mentioned."

"I'll walk you out," she said.

As they headed up the aisle, Pawkins fell into step with them. "You'll miss the best part," he said cheerily. "The cover has real *pastoso*. She sings '*Vissi d'arte*' better than the lead."

" '*Pastoso*' is an Italian term for singers with a warm, mellow voice," Genevieve translated for Mac and Annabel's sake.

"Thanks," Mac said. "Sounded like lunch."

They reached the exit and stepped out into a night illuminated by a full moon. A lone taxi stood waiting at the curb across the street.

"I enjoyed that," Annabel said. "I hope the soprano feels better."

"She will," Pawkins said. "But if she doesn't, her cover will do just fine. I've heard her before. She's wonderful."

The cab did a U-turn and pulled up to them. Mac opened the back door and Annabel climbed in. As he started to join her, he asked Pawkins, "Will you be around tomorrow?"

"Plan to be. Why?"

"I may want to catch up with you."

"Oh? What's the occasion?"

"Nothing specific. I'll call."

As the cab pulled away and Mac gave the driver the name of the restaurant, Annabel said, "Okay, we're alone. Tell me what this is all about."

Mac gave her a thumbnail sketch of Josephson's call. "The last thing he said to me was, 'The scores are no longer missing.' "

"Wow!"

"I'm not sure what he means by it—whether he actually has them in his possession, or knows where they are. At any rate, I couldn't resist taking him up on his suggestion to have dinner."

"Of course not. Did you mention it to Ray?"

"I almost did a few times, but thought better of it. Let's see what's really going on before we do."

The lower floor of Kinkead's was bustling, elbow-to-elbow patrons at the bar, their conversations livened up by jazzy tunes from a spirited pianist. The restaurant had consistently been considered among Washington's finest, a seafood mecca that always ranked high on reader polls. Josephson, who sat on a chair by the entrance, saw them, and got to his feet.

"Ah, Mr. and Mrs. Smith," he said, extending his hand. "How wonderful to see you again."

Josephson was a slight man with a deeply lined, chiseled face, his sparse, unruly hair tinted a rusty red. He wore a tan, black, and pale green plaid sport jacket, a white shirt, and a small, Kelly-green, clip-on bow tie. He carried a large, bulging manila envelope with myriad scribbles on it.

"It's our pleasure," Mac said. "We have a table reserved upstairs. It's less noisy there."

Bob Kinkead, the owner and an old friend of Mac's, greeted them at the top of the stairs and led them to a prime table. Once seated, and the initial exchange of pleasantries completed, Mac said, "I have to admit, Marc, your call came as quite a surprise."

"I didn't mean to call like that at the final minute before boarding my flight, but I'd been trying to summon the courage for some time now."

Annabel laughed. "Summon courage to call Mac? He's the most accessible person I know."

"Oh, I can see that," said Josephson. "I knew it the time we met at my shop in London. But this is—Well, how shall I say it? My reason for calling is a bit unusual. I'm here to ask a rather large favor."

Mac thought for a moment, glanced at Annabel, and said, "A favor concerning the Mozart-Haydn musical scores?"

Josephson nodded, his eyes fixed on the table. He looked up, smiled at Annabel, and asked Mac, "You've told Annabel about it?"

"The little I know," Mac said. "You said that—"

A waiter took their drink orders and left menus in front of them.

"Mac said that you told him the scores are no longer missing," Annabel said.

"In a manner of speaking."

Josephson's response disappointed Mac. For some reason, he almost expected that Josephson would have the scores with him. What was in that full envelope he'd placed on the empty fourth chair?

"I'm not sure where to begin," Josephson said.

"Why don't we order," Annabel suggested. "Let's get that out of the way first."

They shared a platter of fried clams—"The best Washington has to offer," Mac said—and pepita-crusted salmon over a ragoût of crab, shrimp, corn, and chilies for the three of them. The drinks and the succulent food cast their comforting spell, and conversation touched upon everything except the missing scores. Finally, after coffee and crème brûlée, Annabel brought the topic back to the reason they were there in the first place. She was aware that Josephson was edgy. Although he willingly participated in the small talk during dinner, he fidgeted a great deal, and a tic on the left side of his face, not evident earlier, was now constant.

Josephson glanced about the room. Confident that he could speak without being overheard by others, he began to explain, a clearing of his throat preceding his lengthier comments.

"You see, when Aaron—he was a close friend and a colleague, of sorts—when he first told me of string quartets that had been written by Mozart in collaboration with his idol, Franz Joseph Haydn, I was naturally excited. I'd not heard of them before but had no reason to question Aaron's belief that they existed. He was, after all, an acknowledged expert on Mozart and his works."

"How had he learned of their existence?" Annabel asked.

"Through sources. He had many around the globe. Of course, there was also his disciplined academic research."

"Why had he decided to work with you?" Mac asked. "Surely he could have sought the scores himself using his sources."

Josephson smiled self-effacingly. "I have my sources, too," he said, "in the world of rare manuscripts. Aaron felt that between us we stood a better chance of successfully finding the scores." He looked at Mac, his eyes narrowed. "Are you questioning my expertise in this area?" he asked.

"Of course not," Mac said. "I just want to fully understand."

"Well," Josephson, said, "Aaron could be a generous man when it came to friends."

Not from what I've heard, Mac thought.

"I read," Mac said, "that you and Dr. Musinski found the manuscripts quite by accident, at a tag sale."

"Where did you read that?" Josephson asked.

"An interview you gave to a British publication," Mac replied, smiling. "The joys of the Internet."

Josephson cleared his throat. "Yes, that's precisely the way it happened. Life is funny. You work for months, years, seeking something, and there it is, right under your nose, in an unlikely place. Sheer good fortune."

Annabel indicated she wasn't aware of the story, and Josephson recounted it for her.

"Remarkable," she said when he'd finished.

"It certainly was remarkable," Josephson said. "I couldn't contain my glee when Aaron and I left that yard sale and returned to my shop with the scores in hand. Aaron was—well, Aaron was more stoic than I. He was anxious to get back to Washington and start the authentication process in his laboratory at the university. That's the last I saw of the scores, or of Aaron. Dreadful what happened to him. Such a cruel way to die. They've never found the murderer, have they?"

"No, but they might be getting close."

Mac's comment caused Josephson to straighten in his chair. A puzzled expression crossed his face. "Do you know who killed Aaron?" he asked.

"No," Mac said, "but there might be new evidence that will help the police solve the case. But wait, we've come up to the point where Dr. Musinski returned to Washington with the scores and was killed. You told me on the phone that you've found the scores. We're listening."

Josephson drew a breath and sipped his coffee, which had gotten cold. Annabel ordered a fresh pot and Josephson continued.

"In the months after Aaron's murder and the disappearance of the scores, I was in a state of shock. My friends were concerned for my health and well-being. I was numb. Not only had my friend and associate been cruelly killed, rare manuscripts worth a million dollars, perhaps more, had vanished. It took me years to gather my senses and decide to pursue those Mozart-Haydn masterpieces."

"If they were," Mac said.

"If they were what?" Josephson asked.

"Masterpieces. Dr. Musinski hadn't had a chance to examine them to ascertain their provenance."

"Oh, no," Josephson said, slowly shaking his head. "I never doubted for a moment their validity, nor did Aaron." He sounded angry at Mac's comment. "Verifying their origins was necessary, of course. Potential buyers would expect no less than authentication by someone of Aaron's stature. No, they were what we believed they were. Do you doubt that?"

"Not at all," Mac said, now taken slightly aback at Josephson's apparent anger at being challenged.

"All right," Annabel said. "Let's assume the scores are authentic. You say you woke up, in a matter of speaking, and started to pursue them. What did you do?"

Josephson sat back, his hands laced on his small potbelly, and gathered his thoughts. He came forward again. "I began by making inquiries of friends around the world. Those of us who deal in rare manuscripts form a tight-knit fraternity, as you can imagine. Of course, no one knew at that juncture that we'd unearthed the string quartets. Everything had happened so fast. Many of my friends were flabbergasted when I told them what Aaron and I had found. Some were skeptical, especially those who also have an interest in missing musical material. They doubted whether Mozart and Haydn had ever collaborated on string quartets. Others accepted that those two towering geniuses had, indeed, written together, but were cynical about my tale of having uncovered the material in a yard sale. I suppose I can't blame them. It was an unlikely scenario. But a true one!" He slapped his hand on the table.

Annabel said, "You saw those manuscripts, Marc, and they looked to your trained eye as though they came from the period in which Mozart and Haydn were known to have been together."

"Yes, they did. I had only a cursory look at them on that table in the yard, but when we returned to my shop, I had the opportunity to sit down with a magnifying glass and study them closely. Of course, I'm not a musician or musical scholar, so their musical structure escaped me. But from the standpoint of the paper on which they were written, the ink used, and other factors, they were definitely of that era."

Mac finished his second cup of coffee and suggested they go back to their apartment to continue the discussion. A half hour later they sat in the Smiths' living room. Rufus, their blue Great Dane, took a liking to Josephson. "Lovely animal," he said, not sounding as though he meant it.

Mac poured them snifters of cognac. "So," he said, "where did you leave off?"

"The manuscripts and their authenticity," said Josephson.

"I suggest we accept that they are what Marc and Musinski believed they were," Annabel offered. "Let's get to the reason we're here. You told Mac the scores are no longer missing. Where are they? How did you find them? Why are you sharing this with us?"

Mac laughed. "Annabel has a talent for getting to the point."

"Yes, I see that," Josephson agreed, but not sounding particularly pleased. "As I said, I contacted friends around the world once I'd come out of my doldrums. Surely, I thought, someone would become aware of the manuscripts being sold on the black market, perhaps even have them offered to them as potential buyers. No such luck. That's when I hired Mr. Poindexter."

"Who's he?" Mac asked.

"A private investigator, and a very good one, I might add."

"In London?"

"The firm for which he works is London-based, but they have offices in other cities around the world. I contacted that firm and was assigned Mr. Poindexter as my investigator."

"I'm sure he didn't come cheap," Mac commented.

"No, he certainly didn't. I invested my life's savings in his services, but I reasoned that it was worth it when compared to the value of the manuscripts."

"Go on," Annabel urged.

Josephson picked up the manila envelope from where he'd perched it on the floor next to his chair, opened it, and withdrew a sheaf of papers. He looked through them until finding the one he sought. "Ah, here. We can start here," he said. "Mr. Poindexter used his firm's vast network of investigators to identify certain individuals who in the past had shown keen interest in such material. One in particular stood out from his report, a wealthy gentleman in Paris, Georges Saibrón, who was known to have purchased valuable Mozart scores, some legitimately, some not so legitimately. Using a fellow investigator in Paris, Mr. Poindexter closely monitored Mr. Saibrón's activities over a four-month period." He dropped that sheet of paper to the floor and replaced it with another. "Something interesting developed toward the end of the investigation into Saibrón. He was visited by someone, an American, who claimed he had the scores and was willing to sell them."

"How did this investigator, Poindexter, learn about this?" Mac asked.

"It's my understanding that he'd enlisted the services of an individual who worked for Mr. Saibrón. Saibrón is a successful exporter of French wines and has quite a large staff. I gather it wasn't difficult to find someone on that staff willing to exchange information from inside the company for a fee. I learned while working with Mr. Poindexter to not question his methods."

Not necessarily a prudent decision, Mac thought.

"Go on," Annabel urged. She'd slid to the edge of her chair.

"According to Mr. Poindexter, this American and Saibrón struck a deal, and the scores were ultimately delivered to Paris by the American."

"I see," said Mac.

Rufus yawned loudly, startling Josephson. "Everything is big about Rufus," Mac said, "even his yawns. So the scores are now with this Georges Saibrón."

"No," Josephson said.

"No?" Annabel repeated. "Then where are they?"

"In Vienna. Mr. Saibrón quickly sold them to a collector there. I have his name."

"That's not important for the moment," Mac said. "This American. Who was he?"

Josephson sighed, sat back, and rubbed his eyes. "Sorry," he said. "Long flights tire me."

"Me, too," said Mac.

"The American?" Annabel said.

"At first, I couldn't believe it," Josephson said. "To think a man in his position would stoop to such a thing."

Mac and Annabel looked at each other. Their thoughts were identical at that moment, unpleasant thoughts confirmed by Josephson.

"It was the detective who'd investigated Aaron's murder, Mr. Raymond Pawkins."

THIRTY

Mac walked Josephson back to the hotel.

"I must admit, Marc, what you've outlined for us this evening is—well, let's just say it's as troubling as it is shocking." They stood in the lobby exchanging final words.

"You can imagine my reaction when the final pieces were put together for me by Mr. Poindexter," Josephson said. "At first, I didn't believe it. But once I did, I was angry. To think that someone in law enforcement would kill to obtain the scores was unfathomable."

"Let me caution you again, Marc, we don't know if Detective Pawkins killed Dr. Musinski. You've traced the route the scores took, that's all."

"Can it be any other way?" Josephson said. "Whoever took those scores must have murdered Aaron."

Mac didn't prolong the debate, although what Josephson had deduced made sense—too much sense.

"You will think about what I've asked of you?" Josephson said.

"Yes, of course, but no promises. Frankly, I'm not sure what you've asked is the right approach."

"I leave the approach to you, Mac. I knew I made the right decision in calling you. I feel so much better being in your capable hands."

Mac said nothing.

"Thank you for a splendid dinner. Your wife is as lovely as I remember. I look forward to hearing from you in the morning."

Mac hurried back to the apartment, where Annabel had been busy in his absence making notes of everything she could remember from the evening. They'd asked Josephson if they could make copies of some of the reports on their home photocopy machine, but he declined to do so despite their assurances that the copies would not leave their possession.

"I need a drink," Mac said, heading for the kitchen. "You?"

"I already have one," Annabel called after him.

"So," he said after he'd joined her on the couch, "what now?"

She shook her head and sipped. "I don't want to believe him. I've been sitting here conjuring all the reasons *not* to believe him."

"Lay them out for me."

"All the evidence he has comes from this Poindexter character. Is he to be believed?"

"The agency he works for is respected, Annie. I don't see what Poindexter or his agency would have gained by giving Marc false information."

"Maybe not deliberately false, Mac, but possibly erroneous. They wouldn't be the first private investigatory agency to phony up results to satisfy a good-paying client."

"No, but let's view them in a positive light and take a look at what you've written."

Based upon what Josephson had allowed them to see, there wasn't any doubt that the private investigator, and those working for him, had done a thorough job of building a case against Pawkins. According to the reports, Pawkins had visited Georges Saibrón two months after the murder of Aaron Musinski. A series of receipts were attached to the report, Air France records of the trips Pawkins had taken, and hotel bills. There had been three trips within six weeks of one another. Poindexter's source inside the Saibrón organization told him that the Mozart-Haydn string quartets had been delivered during that third trip.

The next report traced Pawkins' movements following his final trip to Paris. He'd flown to the Grand Cayman Island, where he'd opened an account at one of that island's numerous private banks, their existence marked only by small, nondescript placards on their doors. Two days later, according to Poindexter, Georges Saibrón wired Euros equivalent to a half-million U.S. dollars to that account.

"So much for the famed secrecy of Cayman Island banks," Annabel said.

"Happens all the time," Mac said. "You can always find someone willing to give out a little information about accounts in return for a payoff. I did it myself once or twice when I was practicing criminal law. The important thing is that if this information is true—and I don't see any reason to doubt it at this juncture—Ray Pawkins is not the man I thought he was. He might be not only a thief, he could be a murderer."

"A cop investigating a murder he committed."

"Convenient. But as I told Marc, there's nothing in these reports pointing directly to Ray as Musinski's killer."

"One and one add up to two, Mac."

"Not always. Look, what we have to hash out is what Marc wants me to do."

"You aren't considering it, are you?"

"There was a moment when I was open to it. Not anymore."

"Good."

"I'm listening. I always do—listen to you, Annie. Go on."

"You should go to the police with this, Mac."

"And tell them what, that I've met with a gentleman from London who claims he knows that Ray Pawkins took the musical scores from the apartment of a murder victim?"

"A victim whose murder he investigated."

"Marc Josephson has his own agenda in this, Annie. He's more interested in having Pawkins return the money he lost than the possibility that Pawkins murdered his friend. Ray says MPD has reopened the Musinski case based upon new forensic evidence. The focus is back on the fellow who worked with Musinski at the university." She started to respond but he added, "I don't feel it's right to simply go to the police with what Marc has told us. Yes, it looks like Ray probably took those scores from Musinski's home and peddled them to this Frenchman, Saibrón. That's bad, if it's true. But to paint him as a murderer is premature. Josephson is the one to contact the authorities. He's got the evidence. But Pawkins deserves a chance to clear this up before that step is taken."

"Mac, do you know what you're sounding like?"

"Tell me."

"You're sounding like a criminal defense attorney again. You're sounding as though Ray Pawkins is your client."

"He may need an attorney."

"But not you."

"Of course not. I don't defend clients anymore. But I do believe in giving him the benefit of the doubt. I believe in that for anyone. By the way, Marc offered me a fee. Ten percent of what he collects from Ray."

"Which you turned down, of course."

"Of course. As I said, I think Ray Pawkins deserves the benefit of the doubt."

"I suppose he does. What do you intend to do, take him to lunch and ask if he murdered Aaron Musinski?"

"That's a possibility."

"And what if he says, 'Yes, I killed him, and I stole his musical scores and sold them to some Frenchman for a half-million dollars.' Then what?"

"A bridge to cross."

"Well, Mac," she said, "I'm not as sanguine about this as you seem to be. If Raymond Pawkins is a murderer and a thief, I certainly don't want him investigating the Charise Lee murder for the Washington National Opera. Oh, my God!"

"What's the matter?"

"What if he . . . ?"

"I see where you're going with this," Mac said, placing his hand on hers. "What if Pawkins killed Charise Lee."

"And ended up investigating that murder, too."

Mac's thoughts went to the attractive Asian woman who'd waited for Pawkins at the supers rehearsal. He also recalled Pawkins saying that he was looking into a worker at the Kennedy Center who "has a thing for Asian women." Was Pawkins talking about himself?

He didn't express these musings to Annabel. It was all circumstantial, all speculation based on nothing. Instead, he said, "Tell you what, Annie. Let's sleep on it. We'll discuss it again in the morning after we've had time to let what we've been told tonight settle into some sort of logical pattern. We'll decide then what to do."

"Including what Marc Josephson has asked you to do."

"That's not in question, Annie. I don't want any part of what Marc has asked of me."

Josephson's request of Mac had been simple. He wanted him to act as a go-between with Pawkins to try to convince the retired detective to pay Josephson the money Pawkins had received for the Mozart-Haydn scores from Georges Saibrón. "Use the threat of going to the authorities if you must," Josephson had said as they stood in the Watergate lobby an hour earlier.

Annabel kissed her husband on the cheek, then on the mouth. She pulled back and exhaled a stream of air. "I was actually afraid you were considering doing it," she said.

In bed, she reminded him, "Don't forget the tech rehearsal tomorrow night, dress rehearsal the night after that, then opening night. And, of course, there is the ball following that."

"It looks like there are two operas going on at once," he said, "one on the stage, and the other offstage."

"And murders taking place in both," she said, tightly wrapping her arms about him, as though to squeeze such thoughts away.

THIRTY-ONE

Marc Josephson was not pleased with the way the evening had gone.

After leaving the lobby, he sat alone in his Watergate Hotel room, an assortment of pills prescribed by his London physician for his nervous condition and a glass of water at his side, and pondered what the Smiths had said, particularly Mac.

He'd come to Washington convinced that Smith would eagerly rally to his cause and agree to broker a deal with Pawkins. After all, he'd offered Smith a fee for his services—a hefty one, considering how little he had to do to earn it.

But both Smiths seemed skeptical of what he'd presented. They'd asked so many questions, and he sensed that at times Annabel Lee-Smith found his answers lacking. How dare she? How dare they question his veracity? He'd gone to great expense building a case against Detective Pawkins. It was all there in black-and-white, supported by receipts from airlines and hotels. George Saibrón's employee had verified that Pawkins had delivered the scores to the Frenchman, and that he had wired money to the bank in the Cayman Islands. Another person with access to bank records had reported to Poindexter that Pawkins had opened an account there, and that Saibrón's money had been deposited into it.

What further proof could anyone possibly want?

Before placing his call to Smith, he'd considered simply coming to Washington and presenting his findings to the police. He'd quickly abandoned that notion. The minute the police became involved, whatever money that was left would be tied up forever. He was now in his dotage and not well. What good would the money be after he'd been planted in the ground?

Once he'd made the decision to avoid entanglement with the police, Mackensie Smith came to mind. Perfect! They'd been introduced by someone with impeccable credentials, a member of the House of Lords and a respected businessman. Yes! Lawyer-cum-professor Mackensie Smith was the right choice. As a lawyer, he would know how to negotiate with Pawkins. He would be discreet because of that attorney-client privilege Josephson had heard so much about. He'd offer Smith a decent fee for his services. What attorney, American or British, didn't respond to the lure of easy money?

There were times, although not many, when he wondered whether his decision to go after the money and ignore the fact that Pawkins had killed Aaron Musinski was immoral. Marc Josephson liked to think of himself as a moral man, although he tended to define it in a highly personal way, as most people do. The letters of Leon Blum that Josephson had once purchased and resold from his shop provided one of many rationalizations: "I have often thought morality may perhaps consist solely in the courage of making a choice."

And I've made a choice, Josephson thought, his conscience salved.

Too, there was his relationship with Aaron Musinski to consider. He didn't wish a premature death for any human being, especially at the hands of a brutal assailant. But he had to admit—to himself only of course—that Aaron Musinski had been a thoroughly despicable man. God, how he disliked him on a personal level, his arrogance and pomposity, his crudeness and insensitivity. There were times when

Josephson had secretly wished the famed musicologist dead. He'd suffered Musinski's insults and bad temper because the man was a genius. Besides, he was someone who had accepted him, Marc Anthony Josephson, into his professional sphere and was willing to share in whatever spoils might come from their explorations into artifacts from years gone by. He had no illusions about the willingness of Musinski to include him. It wasn't that Aaron had been a generous man. Far from it. But Musinski had been well aware that Josephson had access to many people in the British Isles who might lead them to treasures, particularly the Mozart-Haydn string quartets for which Musinski had been searching for years. How ironic that it took none of his British contacts to ultimately find the scores. There they were on a table with old newspapers and magazines, damp from the morning dew, yellowed, edges curled, on the verge of starting someone's fireplace to ward off the chill.

He barely slept that night, so consumed was he with the need to right a wrong and to be given what was, after all, his due. He and Musinski had been partners. Without him—he had led them to that London suburb on that fateful weekend and was the first to have spotted the papers on the table—the scores would never have been found. Close friends—he didn't have many—told him he'd become obsessed with recouping the money. Who were they to analyze his needs? Engaging Poindexter and his agency had cost him his life savings. The shop no longer supported him; his greedy landlord had tripled the rent in recent years. Yes, his dedication—his obsession—to find the scores and the money had diverted much of his attention from the shop and its business. But what was fair was, after all, only fair. That money was rightfully his.

At five the next morning, he again sat at the window, looking out over Washington. He'd made another decision while lying in bed. He had to be more aggressive. Was Smith going to act on his behalf? He needed an answer now.

Waiting until the Smiths might be awake and out of bed seemed an eternity. At seven, he called.

"Hello?" Smith said.

"It's Marc Josephson, Mac. I trust I didn't awaken you and your wife."

"Not at all. We've been up for an hour. Sleep well?"

"No, as a matter of fact, I did not."

"Strange beds. I always have trouble my first night in a hotel."

"It wasn't that," said Josephson. "Have you decided?"

"Decided what?"

"To confront Pawkins about the money."

"I've given it a lot of thought, Marc, and Annabel and I discussed it last night. You've asked for my opinion, which I'm happy to give you. You have no option but to contact the local authorities and present your evidence to them. I can give you the name of someone to—"

"I don't want to go to the police."

"But you should."

"I came to you for help," Josephson said, aware that his voice was getting higher and more strident as his frustration bubbled to the surface.

"I'm aware of that," said Smith, "but I'm afraid the only help I can offer is to give you my best counsel. What you're alleging is a police matter. You're talking about the theft of valuable items, and possibly that the person who took them is a murderer. This isn't a situation calling for a private negotiation. You have an obligation to see that justice is done. I realize that the money is important to you, but that's something to be dealt with later."

Josephson's voice now became a screech. "What sort of an attorney are you!" he demanded. "What sort of a man are you?"

Smith did not reply.

"I engaged you to handle this for me and—"

"Hold on a second, Marc," Smith said. "You haven't engaged me for anything. You called and asked to meet with me. We met. I listened. If what you claim is valid, you have an obligation to—"

The sound of the handset being slammed down reverberated in Smith's ear.

"I'll be damned," he said into the dead phone.

Annabel came from the bathroom. "Who called?" she asked.

"Josephson. I think the man is unbalanced." He recounted the conversation.

"I'd say you're right," she said. "What are you going to do?"

"Nothing."

"Nothing?"

"That's right. Let's see if Josephson takes my advice and goes to the police."

"How will we know if he does?"

"I'll give him a day or two and ask him."

"What about Ray?"

"We'll let that play out for a couple of days, too. I'd better shower and get moving."

She grabbed the sleeve of his robe. "Mac," she said.

"What?"

"I'm terribly uncomfortable having him working for us at WNO. And you have the tech rehearsal tonight. Frankly, I'm not anxious to be around him."

"There's nothing to be concerned about, Annie. He doesn't know we know. Better to keep it that way, at least for now."

A kiss and he was gone, the bathroom door closing behind him.

The last time Ray Pawkins had spoken with Marc Josephson was six months after the murder of Dr. Aaron Musinski, almost six years ago. He'd taken the call at MPD, where he was still a detective.

Josephson had introduced himself as a professional colleague of Musinski. He owned, he said, a shop in the Mayfair section of London dedicated to rare manuscripts, art, and musical scores. He was, he said, terribly dismayed at the death of his colleague and friend, and wondered whether Pawkins could shed some light on the circumstances surrounding Musinski's murder.

Pawkins had said he wasn't at liberty to discuss an ongoing case, but would be glad to take Josephson's phone number and call once he was free to release information. That prompted Josephson to thank the detective for his courtesies, and to ask about the disposition of Musinski's personal effects.

"His niece, a Ms. Felicia James, has taken control of Dr. Musinski's assets. She's his next of kin."

"Yes, I know of her," Josephson said. "Let me be candid, Detective Pawkins. Dr. Musinski and I were involved for many years in searching out rare musical manuscripts written by Mozart in collaboration with Joseph Haydn. They were string quartets."

"Well," Pawkins said, "I wouldn't know about such things. As I said, once we concluded our investigation at Dr. Musinski's house, Ms. James took control of anything that was in it. Sorry, but I'm afraid I can't be of any help to you."

"I've spoken with Ms. James," Josephson said. "She tells me that those musical scores had been in her uncle's home but disappeared shortly after his murder."

"Look," Pawkins said, "I'm a Homicide detective, not a music critic. I don't know anything about string quartets by Mozart and . . . who?"

"Joseph Haydn. I understand this is not your area of expertise, but I just thought you might have some information that would be helpful to me. You see, those scores are worth a great deal of money. Dr. Musinski had taken them with him when he returned to Washington from London, to begin the authenticating process. They've simply vanished into thin air."

"I doubt if they vanished into thin air, as you put it. Whoever killed Dr. Musinski undoubtedly took them," Pawkins said. "Maybe that's why he was murdered."

"Precisely my thought," Josephson said. "Well, sir, I've already taken too much of your time. Thank you."

❧

This second call from Marc Josephson woke Pawkins.

"Mr. Raymond Pawkins?"

"Yeah."

He looked over at the clock. Seven thirty. He'd been out late, hadn't gotten home until three. He'd been at a birthday party at a friend's apartment off Dupont Circle. His friend, whose birthday it was, had lived with his gay partner for the past twenty years and was part of a small circle of opera-loving friends. They'd consumed large quantities of wine, good wine—his friend had impeccable taste in almost everything, his collection of CDs rivaling Pawkins'. They'd listened to the complete recordings of Alban Berg's twelve-tone *Lulu*, with a spectacular performance by Teresa Stratas playing the amoral slut Lulu, who corrupts every man she meets until getting her comeuppance at the end from none other than Jack the Ripper; and to the Angel recording of Jules Massenet's *Werther,* with stirring performances by the lyric tenor Alfredo Kraus and the late Tatiana Troyanos, who played the doomed Charlotte. A spirited argument broke out among the fifteen guests about the significance of *Werther* in today's society, with no clear-cut winner.

Pawkins' head throbbed as he pushed himself up in the bed and held the receiver to his ear.

"This is Marc Josephson."

"Who?"

"Marc Josephson. You don't remember me?"

"Obviously I don't. Oh, wait a minute. Yeah. You were in business with Musinski."

"We were colleagues, Mr. Pawkins. I would like to speak with you in person."

"About what?" He didn't wait for an answer. "If you want to know how the investigation is going, you can call Detective Berry at MPD."

"I'm not here to speak with any detective, Mr. Pawkins," Josephson said, fighting to keep his voice under control. "I wish to speak with *you!*"

"Where are you?"

"I am here in Washington."

"Yeah, well, I'm really busy and—"

"You remember Mr. Georges Saibrón, of course," Josephson said.

The mention of the Frenchman's name caused Pawkins to swing his legs off the side of the bed and to focus more on the call.

"Mr. Pawkins? Are you there?"

"I don't know anybody named Saibrón."

"Oh, yes you do. And you know about your bank account in the is-lands and—"

"What the hell do you want, Josephson?"

"I want my money, Mr. Pawkins."

"What money?"

"Don't force me to go to the authorities, Mr. Pawkins. I have all the evidence."

"Look, Josephson, I . . . All right, I'll meet with you. But I'm telling you, you don't know what the hell you're talking about."

"I'm staying at the Watergate Hotel, and will be here for two more days. Come to my room this afternoon."

"I can't today. It'll have to be tomorrow."

Josephson's voice raised an octave. "Don't put me off, Pawkins. I want to see you today!"

Pawkins waited a beat before saying, "All right. What time?"

"Four o'clock. Don't disappoint me."

"Don't worry, I won't."

"And Mr. Pawkins, should Mr. or Mrs. Mackensie Smith call, please inform them that they no longer represent me. Good day."

Pawkins slipped the cordless phone back into its bedside cradle and went to his elaborate study, where he turned on the computer. He went to "My Favorites" and clicked on Google. It took only a few min-utes to find a photograph of Josephson from one of the interviews he gave to British media. Pawkins studied it, turned off the computer, and put a CD into the changer, Verdi's *Otello*, featuring opera's greatest modern Otello, Plácido Domingo. Music always helped him think.

He sank into a red leather recliner and processed what had just transpired on the phone. Josephson sounded ancient, his voice fee-ble. He said he had "evidence." What evidence could he possibly have? Whatever it was, Pawkins could handle it, and him, the old Englishman.

Mackensie and Annabel Smith were another matter.

THIRTY-TWO

This morning was not unlike most other mornings for Joseph Browning III.

He awoke before sunrise and took a cup of coffee and the newspaper to the small brick patio outside the kitchen of the Alexandria, Virginia, home he shared with Christine, his wife of thirty-two years. He'd been a Washington bureaucrat for twenty-seven of those years. Possessing a freshly minted Yale law degree, he'd gravitated to the nation's capital as a young attorney for the Department of the Interior before progressing through a succession of jobs, each with a higher GS rating and increasingly involving intelligence functions— State, Justice, the FAA, and now the Department of Homeland Security (DHS). Cynics might view his career as one in which he was incapable of holding a steady job. But Joe knew better. Surviving changing administrations was a talent unto itself, and Browning took pride in still being gainfully employed after seeing a string of presidents join the ranks of the unemployed.

The summons to assume a post at the newly created DHS represented, at least to family and friends, an important step up in his career. The safety and security of the United States of America, and the fate of its citizens, necessarily took center stage after 9/11. Being in the forefront of protecting the republic would be a heady experience, one that he'd attack with purpose and dedication.

But as DHS morphed into a larger and more unwieldy entity, assimilating twenty-two separate intelligence agencies under its umbrella, he found his enthusiasm waning. It wasn't that DHS's stated mission of protecting America had dimmed. Far from it. It was the way that mission was becoming increasingly compromised. This took some of the spark out of getting up in the morning, donning a cape and shield, and doing battle with the terrorists who'd so callously wiped out more than three thousand innocent American lives.

He'd ended up second in command of DHS's Information Analysis and Infrastructure Protection Directorate (IAIPD), which was to coordinate interagency counterterrorism efforts with members of the "Big 15," the fifteen major agencies comprising the U.S. Intelligence Community (IC)—the FBI; the CIA; the Defense Department's National Security Agency (NSA), National Reconnaissance Office (NRO), National Geospatial-Intelligence Agency (NGA), and Defense Intelligence Agency (DIA); the State's Bureau of Intelligence and Research (INR); the intelligence agencies of the army, navy, air force, and marines; as well as lesser known, shadowy, and seldom understood intelligence agencies, such as the Counterintelligence Field Activity (CIFA), the Defense Airborne Reconnaissance Office (DARO), the President's Foreign Intelligence Advisory Board (PFIAB), the President's Intelligence Oversight Board (IOB), the Pentagon Force Protection Agency (PFPA), and the intelligence community's internal overseer, the Defense Security Service (DSS). Add to that jumble of acronyms the newly formed Terrorist Threat Integration Center (TTIC), a CIA task force of analysts with plans to integrate with the CIA's Counterterrorist Center (CTC) and the FBI's counterterrorism division; plus the latest, the Office of the National Counterintelligence Executive (NCIX)—and Lord knew how many others that had sprung up under the now wider national security umbrella (even Browning didn't know, and he was an insider). Intelligence reports were modified for distribution to local law enforcement agencies around the country, including Washington's police department.

This had spawned another acronym among Browning and his colleagues, spoken only in private: BON, "Bureau of Noncoordination."

The truth was, Browning had learned that, despite all the promises, all the lofty rhetoric, and all the potential of creating a Department of Homeland Security as the first line of defense against further terrorist attacks—and despite the acknowledgment that a failure of sharing information had played a major role in the September 11 attacks—these agencies, and more, simply would not cooperate, and refused to cede turf and budgets, no matter how high the stakes for the nation and its trusting citizens.

Which was why Browning, in concert with his superior and others at DHS, had elected lately to deal directly with the British and Canadian intelligence services and not funnel such sources as Milton Crowley through the CIA and FBI. Crowley was but one of many sources whom Browning and his people had begun to deal with directly. The FBI had forged an agreement with DHS under which it was required only to provide the agency with summaries of its intelligence gathering, not the raw material. The FBI had hired two hundred new agents to do nothing but wade through hundreds of thousands of recorded phone calls and computer intercepts under the Patriot Act, using "trap-and-trace" surveillance techniques favored by the NSA. In addition, the FBI itself had begun monitoring the web-surfing habits of Internet users, resulting in thousands of "captures" that also needed to be analyzed each day.

Meanwhile, the CIA had long ago abandoned its mandate to conduct operations only outside the country, and had launched an aggressive campaign of domestic spying and eavesdropping on Americans.

This all resulted in a massive intake of information, most of it useless, but which had to be analyzed nonetheless.

Intelligence gathered by the FBI remained in the House That Hoover Built until someone got around to writing a report to send it to the Department of Homeland Security.

The CIA's treasure trove of intercepted communications remained in Langley, its importance to national security left in the hands of those who'd obtained it.

And information that a Toronto talent agency, Melicamp-Baltsa, might be sympathetic to terrorist aims, joined thousands of other bits of information that was eventually shared with the FBI.

Joseph Browning III finished his coffee and went back inside the house to shower and dress for the day.

"Good morning," Christine said as she came down the stairs to get her own coffee.

"Good morning," he said, accepting a feathery kiss on the cheek.

"Heavy day lined up?" she asked.

"The usual," he said, truthfully. It would be business as usual at DHS, and that was the problem. His frown said as much.

She disappeared into the kitchen as he started up the stairs.

"Oh, before I forget," she said, reappearing, "Rosie and George wonder if we'd like to go to the opera with them. They have two extra tickets—friends of theirs had to cancel."

"The opera?" he said from the landing, a smile on his face. "Chris, I appear in an opera every day I go to work."

"It's *Tosca*," she said. "We never go to the opera. I'd love to. The tickets are for opening night."

"Sure," he said. "Let's do it. I could use some original make-believe."

THIRTY-THREE

"So, how'd it go?" Willie Portelain asked Sylvia Johnson.

They sat in an interrogation room at headquarters, awaiting the arrival of Carl Berry and others. Their brief assignment to the Aaron Musinski murder was over, now that Grimes had been brought in and the contents of his office had been secured, his computer in the hands of forensic technicians capable of finding things on its hard drive that long ago had been assumed to have disappeared into the ether. They were back on the Lee case, joining the newly formed task force.

"How did *what* go?" she asked.

"Your date last night. Who is he?"

"Willie!"

"Just curious, lady. You have a good time?"

"As a matter of fact, I did. We had dinner at Georgia Brown's, and caught the last set at Blues Alley."

"He pay?"

"Of course he— How are you feeling?"

"Pretty good."

"You taking your medicine and cutting down on the calories?"

"What are you, my mother? Who'd you see at Blues Alley?"

"A young pianist, Ted Rosenthal, and his trio. He was wonderful."

"So, tell me about this dude."

The door opened, to Sylvia's relief, and Berry and the other detectives joined them.

"Okay, what've we got?" Berry asked.

They went around the table, each detective reporting.

"We've talked to every student in that opera school they run out of Takoma Park," one said.

"Not for the first time," said another. "We compared reports of the previous interviews with them with what they had to say this time around. Nothing new."

"What about Christopher Warren?" Berry asked.

"Yeah, we talked to him again, too. Surly bastard." He punched Willie in the arm and laughed. "He's the one you coldcocked, huh?"

"Ran into my arm, that's all."

"Yeah, right."

Another detective said, "There's one student who doesn't have an alibi."

"Warren."

"No, besides him." He consulted his notes. "A Korean named Lester Suyang. He was alone all night, he says, like he said in previous interviews. Nothing there. He doesn't strike me as the murdering kind."

"What is 'the murdering kind'?" Berry asked.

"You know what I mean."

"A couple of the other students say Suyang didn't like the deceased, that they had a few shouting matches."

"That's new," Berry offered. "What's he say about it?"

"He denies it, says he and the deceased were good friends."

"He's big, man," another detective said, "must go two-fifty, two-sixty. Got a voice like a one-man gang. If he doesn't make it as an opera singer, he can always become a sumo wrestler."

"Even bigger than you, Willie," one said. "But not as pretty."

The discussion continued. Eventually, it came around to Charise Lee's agents, Philip Melincamp and Zöe Baltsa.

"Willie and Sylvia have interviewed them a couple of times. Ray Pawkins—he's working as a PI for the Opera company—says Melincamp and his partner have a shady reputation back in Toronto."

"How shady?" someone asked.

"They run a smarmy operation, according to Ray. He says—"

The door opened and a uniformed officer working desk duty in the Detective Division entered. He handed Berry a piece of paper. "Thought you might want to see this," he said.

Berry read it and passed it to Sylvia.

"What's up?" Portelain asked.

"Joey pulled this from the latest intelligence report from Homeland Security," Berry said as it was passed around.

"Interesting," Sylvia said, "but what does it have to do with the Lee case?"

"Probably nothing," Berry said. "Any ideas?"

There weren't any.

"I want to run this by Cole," Berry said, picking up the intelligence report and ending the meeting.

Carl Berry's meeting may have just ended, but Annabel Lee-Smith's was just getting started.

Everyone on the Opera Ball committee gathered for a final run-through of the "Battle Plan," a thick book in which—hopefully—every conceivable base had been covered, and every possible contingency accounted for. Annabel willed herself to concentrate on the business at hand, but was unable to keep her thoughts from straying back to the dinner with Marc Josephson and what had come out of it. She still wanted to believe that there was something wrong with Josephson's claim, and his behavior with Mac on the phone that morning helped her in that regard. The man was certainly skewed;

hopefully, his claim and alleged supporting evidence was, too. But try as she might to take umbrage in that thought, she knew down deep, felt it in her heart and bones, that Ray Pawkins had stolen the musical scores from Aaron Musinski's home and . . .

Conceivably had murdered Musinski.

"You okay, Annabel?" someone asked as they prepared to break for an hour's lunch.

"Oh, sure. I'm fine. I never dreamed putting on a fund-raiser of this magnitude involved so much planning and detail. You all deserve a medal."

"*We,* you mean. It couldn't have been done without you. It's so good that you agreed to act as liaison with the White House. Isn't it wonderful that the president and first lady will be at the ball?"

"Yes, it's wonderful," Annabel said. As far as she knew, her meetings with the various security forces involved had gone well, and all was in place to ensure a safe visit by President and Mrs. Montgomery.

"Grab a bite?" Genevieve Crier asked Annabel as they filed from the room.

"Sure," Annabel said. "I'm famished."

"Meetings like this always make me hungry," Genevieve said, punctuated by her lilting laugh. "The tension eats away at your stomach lining."

Annabel laughed, too. "I hadn't quite thought of it that way, but I think you're right."

They popped into the nearest luncheonette and found a vacant booth, where both ordered salads and iced tea. Genevieve, always verbose, was especially talkative this day, and entertained Annabel with a succession of stories about her life, first as an actress in London and Hollywood, and more recently her job with the Opera.

". . . and finding supers for every production can be a bloody nightmare," she said. "I have my own techniques." A wicked laugh. "I haunt health clubs and gyms. I want my supers to be in good shape — so do most directors, and I try to accommodate. You might have noticed that many gays are particularly fond of opera. I've gotten some wonderful supers at the yearly Miss Adams Morgan Pageant. And, there's always church."

"Church?"

"I watch single men go up for Communion and make mental notes which ones would be good supers."

"You're a mobile talent scout, Genevieve."

"I suppose I am. Of course, when children are involved it can be really dicey. Thank God for our volunteers who are willing to play backstage nanny. And the parents!" She rolled her eyes and made a dismissive sound through pursed lips. "Most are okay, but some can drive you mad. Like last year when I was providing supers for *Die Walküre*."

"I saw that," Annabel said. "Were there children in it?"

"No. I'm not talking about children anymore. These were adults. I went mad, absolutely tore my hair out trying to please the director. Gawd, he was impossible. But I came through."

"You always do, it seems."

"Yes, and I love it!"

"Have you spoken with Ray Pawkins lately?" Annabel asked.

"That darling man? As a matter of fact, I have. Yesterday. We're grabbing a bite tonight before tech rehearsal."

"Do I detect a budding romance?" Annabel asked.

"No, silly. We're just good friends. How many men do you find in this city who love opera?"

Annabel thought of Mac. "Not many," she said. "Does he ever talk about his life as a Homicide detective?"

Genevieve screwed up her face in thought. "Hmmm. No."

"I'm fascinated with that famous case he investigated six years ago, the one involving the Ph.D. musicologist from Georgetown, Aaron Musinski."

"Wasn't that something? Everyone was buzzing about it."

"And Ray never mentions it?"

"No. I asked him once about that case. He said that was then, and this is now. I understand."

"Well, we'd better get back. The afternoon session will be starting."

They were approaching the entrance to the building when Genevieve stopped Annabel. "What do you think of Ray, Annabel?"

"Oh, I don't know. He certainly is . . . interesting. Why do you ask?"

"I just wondered if you or Mac have noticed anything unusual about him."

Was this an opportunity to share with someone other than Mac what Josephson had claimed? She thought not.

"He seems very self-confident," Annabel substituted.

"Yes, he is that. He seems to have two sides, two personalities. But maybe that's what makes him so attractive. Forget I even asked. Let's get inside."

∽

Speaking of Ray Pawkins.

He spent the rest of the morning at his home, music pouring from the speakers in his elaborate study, and through wireless ones he'd placed in other areas of the house—Verdi, Wagner, Mozart, and Strauss. The volume was loud, louder than even he was accustomed to. He paced from room to room, still in his robe and slippers, and sang along with the sopranos and tenors, stopping every now and then to gesture dramatically in a particularly strong or poignant section of the score. At times, he conducted the orchestra, holding an imaginary baton and urging the musicians to instill more spirit into their playing, pointing at the brass section for emphasis, lowering the volume with outstretched hands, palms down, nodding his head in approval at how they'd followed his directions. It was a fatiguing performance, and by the time lunchtime rolled around, he was bathed in sweat, and hungry. He showered and dressed in gray slacks, a lightweight black mock turtleneck, and black sneakers. He slipped into his shoulder holster, which hung in the closet, donned a tan cotton safari jacket, and went to his study. He opened a small wall safe and removed not his licensed 9mm Glock that was there, but an unregistered .22-caliber he'd confiscated years ago from a drug dealer during a raid. He secured it beneath his armpit in the holster, and checked that the cats had water and food in the kitchen before leaving the house and sliding behind the wheel of his silver Mercedes. His first stop was the 600 Restaurant, across from the Kennedy Center, where he enjoyed a shrimp cocktail, steak sandwich, and a Bloody Mary at the bar.

"You're looking fine, Mr. Pawkins, real fine," Ulysses said while serving him. "You look like you're in the game, and you've got to be in the game if you're gonna win."

Pawkins laughed at Ulysses' favorite bit of philosophy. "You are right, my friend. I am in the game, and I intend to win. Let me have the check."

Pawkins stepped outside. It was an unusually cool day for that time of year in Washington, with a cloudless, cobalt-blue sky, and a breeze light enough to ruffle hair but brisk enough at times to tease the cheeks. He left his car where he'd parked it in the Kennedy Center's underground garage and walked up New Hampshire to the Watergate complex, passing through the central open space with its gushing fountains, inviting benches, and tranquil greenery, until reaching the entrance to the hotel. He was greeted by the doorman. "Hello, sir."

"Hello," said Pawkins. "Beautiful day."

"Yes, sir, it most certainly is that."

He meandered the length of the lobby in the direction of the elevators, and beyond them the check-in desk on the left, the entrance to the bar on the right. He'd almost reached the elevators when he saw Josephson emerge from one. Pawkins pretended to admire a print on the wall, but his peripheral vision took in the little Englishman. Josephson came halfway to where Pawkins stood, his eyes going from one side of the lobby to the other. He kept checking his watch as he retraced his steps, then turned and again walked in Pawkins' direction.

Pawkins looked at his watch. Three forty-five. What was he doing in the lobby? Pawkins was expected at four. Josephson should be in his room awaiting a phone call.

Josephson passed Pawkins this time and stepped outside, where he leaned against a column and drew deep breaths. Pawkins took the opportunity to sit in a yellow slipcovered chair that afforded him a view of the lifts, but that was partially obscured by a large potted plant. He had to smile; he felt like a movie version of a hotel's house detective spying on a guest.

Josephson returned inside and walked to the elevators. Pawkins turned so that only his profile was visible. Not that the Brit would know what he looked like, although his photograph had made some publications at the height of the Musinski investigation. The doors slid open, Josephson stepped inside, and the doors closed behind him.

Pawkins waited a few minutes before going to a house phone and asking to be connected to Mr. Josephson's room.

"Hello?" Josephson sounded breathless. His voice was barely above a squeak.

"Josephson. This is Pawkins."

"Are you . . . ? Where are you?"

"Downstairs. I've been watching you."

"You have? Are you—are you coming up?"

"Yes. I know your room number. I'll be there in a few minutes. You are alone, I assume."

"Yes, of course I am. Why would I—"

Pawkins lowered the phone into its cradle and stepped into a waiting elevator, pressing his elbow against the holstered .22 as the doors closed. The doors opened at Josephson's floor. Pawkins walked down the long, red-carpeted hallway until he stood outside Josephson's door. Was the Brit observing him through the peephole? He smiled for Josephson's benefit, and knocked. The door opened.

"Mr. Pawkins," Josephson said.

Pawkins ignored the greeting and walked past him into the center of the room. He'd stayed at the Watergate Hotel on a few occasions. This wasn't one of its most expensive rooms. He went to the window and looked out over the city, aware of Josephson behind him. He heard the door close, and sensed Josephson nearing him across the thick carpeting.

"So," Pawkins said, not turning. "What is it you want?"

"My money. You stole my money."

"Is that so?"

Now the former detective slowly turned and faced Josephson, who stood only a few feet from him.

"Tell me how I stole your money."

"You . . . you took the musical scores from Aaron Musinski. He and I were partners. We were to share the money from them."

"I see."

Pawkins went to a small couch. "Sit down," he said, pointing to a chair across from a coffee table. Josephson did as he'd been told. Pawkins leaned forward, a smile on his face. "Let's get a few things straight here, Mr. Josephson. I don't care what you claim I did. I don't care whether you lost money, as you claim. I came here as a favor. No," he said, waving his hand, "I came because I was curious to see what a conniving little Englishman looks like. Now I know."

Josephson got to his feet. "I have the proof," he said, going to the manila envelope on the desk, extracting its contents, and waving them at Pawkins. "It's all here," he said, agitated, sweating, eyes darting back and forth from Pawkins to the window, to the door, back to Pawkins. "I know what you did. I hired an investigator. I know how you killed Aaron to get the scores and went to Paris to sell them to Saibrón, how the money went to your secret bank account in the Cayman Islands, how you—"

He stopped in mid-sentence as Pawkins calmly pulled the .22 from his holster. Josephson's eyes widened at the sight of the weapon, which Pawkins pointed directly at him. "Give me that stuff," he commanded.

Josephson pressed the papers to his chest and stepped back.

"Come on, come on, hand it over. I want to see this so-called evidence you say you have."

"Please, put that away," Josephson pleaded.

Pawkins looked down at the weapon. "This?" He laughed. "Nice little gun, Mr. Josephson. Doesn't make a lot of noise, and leaves a relatively small hole." The smile left his face. "Give me those papers, goddamn it, before I show you how small a hole it really does make."

Josephson tentatively approached the table and dropped the papers as though they were aflame.

"That's better," Pawkins said. He sat back, the papers in his lap, and scanned them, the .22 resting casually in his right hand. At one point he looked up and said, "Sit down, Mr. Josephson. Relax. You have anything to drink? Be a good host and pour us something."

"I don't have—"

"Sure you do, in the mini-bar over there. You have ice?"

"Yes, I—"

"Good. Scotch will be fine, just a few cubes."

"I can call security and—"

"You touch that phone and it'll be the last thing you ever touch. Add a splash of soda."

Pawkins kept his eyes going from the papers to Josephson, who'd taken a mini-bottle of Scotch from the self-serve bar and poured it into a glass. His hands trembled so much that some of the liquor ran down the outside of the glass. He approached Pawkins with the drink, but Pawkins said, "Ice, Mr. Josephson. And a little soda. Come on, now, you're an Englishman. You know how to make a proper drink, even for an American."

After sipping the drink and examining the papers, Pawkins tossed the sheets on the coffee table and stood. Josephson sat in the chair, rigid, small sounds escaping his throat, his eyes never straying from the weapon in Pawkins' hand. Pawkins came around behind Josephson, who also started to get up, but Pawkins' firm hand on his shoulder kept him pinned to the chair. He pressed the barrel of the .22 against Josephson's temple. "Nice drink, Mr. Josephson. Thanks."

"Please, I only wants what's fair," the Brit said. He was almost crying.

"What's fair, huh? I like that," said Pawkins. "I believe in fairness, too. I bet you didn't know that, did you?"

"I—I'm sure you're a fair and reasonable man," Josephson said, his voice quavering. "Don't you see, the money I would have enjoyed from selling those scores was for my retirement. I'm not a rich man. I have a small shop in Mayfair and wanted to be able to retire and live decently."

"That's a worthy goal," Pawkins said, pressing the barrel a little harder against Josephson's head. "That's what I want, too." He laughed. "We have a lot in common." He now faced Josephson. "So I'll make you a deal."

"A deal?"

"Yeah. Actually, I'm willing to make a deal for your life. How's that sound?"

"I . . . yes, I might be willing to make a deal with you."

"You *might* be willing? I'd like a little more assurance than that, Mr. Josephson."

"What is it you suggest?"

"That's better." Pawkins took the couch again. "Tell you what. I'd hate to see you not have the sort of retirement you've been looking forward to. I think when a man works hard his whole life he deserves to spend his so-called golden years in comfort, free from worry. So, here's what I'm offering. In return for me taking those silly papers you have and burning them—and in return for you promising me that you'll do the same with any copies you might have—I'm willing to pay you a princely sum. How's that sound?"

"I don't know. I suppose it's—"

"Hey, Josephson, I'm the one with the gun. Let's not forget that."

"I'm sorry."

Neither man said anything for a moment. Josephson broke the awkward silence. "How much?"

"Good. Now we're down to the nitty-gritty. I like that. How's fifty thousand sound to you?"

"Fifty thousand dollars?"

"Uh-huh."

"In American currency? The exchange rate and—"

"Right, right. Okay. I'm not an unreasonable man. A hundred thousand American. But that's my final offer."

Another silence.

"A problem?" Pawkins asked.

"No, it's just that—well, there will be taxes and—"

"You want it off the books, under the counter, cash in paper bags, huh? I can arrange that."

Pawkins watched as Josephson trembled and wrapped his arms about himself, tears streaming down his face.

"We have a deal?" Pawkins asked.

"Yes."

"Great. That deserves a drink to celebrate. I'll do the honors this time."

He made two drinks at the mini-bar and handed one to Josephson. "Here's to reasonable men resolving an issue the gentlemanly way." He lifted his glass in his left hand; his right still held the .22. Josephson touched the rim of his glass to Pawkins'.

"Now," Pawkins said, "I really must be going. You write down your address for me, and I'll see to it that a hundred large is delivered to you by hand. Put the papers back in the envelope and give them to me."

Josephson obeyed.

"*Gracias, señor*," Pawkins said. "You can rest assured that the money will be delivered to you, just as I've promised. It will take me a week or so to arrange for a transfer of funds, but you needn't lose any sleep over it. It'll be there."

"I trust you," Josephson said. He was calmer now; the shaking had stopped, and he actually managed a smile.

"And I trust you," Pawkins said, again making sure Josephson saw the weapon in his hand. "But we had a president once named Reagan who believed in trusting but verifying, too. I'll be verifying, Mr. Josephson, and if you were to decide to try this again, or go to the authorities, your retirement will be short-lived. Understand?"

"Perfectly."

"My advice to you is to get on the first plane back to jolly old England and wait for your pension to arrive. Agreed?"

"Of course."

As Pawkins holstered his weapon and walked to the door, Josephson said, "I don't wish to be bold in the face of such a generous settlement, Mr. Pawkins, but might I ask how much the Mozart-Haydn scores fetched on the open market?"

Pawkins frowned. "You have it right here in your reports."

"Oh, I know. Mr. Saibrón paid you a half a million dollars for them. I suppose what I'm asking is how much of that you've managed to save."

Pawkins grinned. "Let's just say I can afford a partner like you, Marc. You don't mind if I call you Marc, do you?"

"Of course not."

"Now I have a question for *you*."

"Yes?"

"What did you tell Mackensie and Annabel Smith about this?"

Josephson explained, haltingly, how he'd tried to enlist Mac Smith to negotiate a deal with Pawkins.

"And you showed them these papers?"

"Yes, but—"

"Don't sweat it, Marc. I'm just pleased to know it. Nothing I can't handle. Safe trip home, and enjoy your retirement. Do some fishing, read some good books. You like opera?"

"Very much."

"So do I."

The door closed behind him.

Back home, Pawkins rewound what had transpired.

Dillinger had been right. A gun and kindness got you further than a gun alone.

Of course, there had been plenty of kindness on his part, too. He'd committed a hundred grand to the little weasel. But that was okay. He had $350,000 left from Saibrón's money, enough to fund his own idyllic retirement, along with Social Security and his MPD pension, which was pretty generous. Just as long as he didn't have to lay out any more.

There was one problem left, however.

Mac and Annabel Smith.

"Hello?"

"Mac. It's Marc Josephson."

"I didn't think I'd hear from you again," Smith said from his study in the Watergate apartment.

"I understand why you would assume that," Josephson said. "I'm terribly sorry for my behavior this morning. I was upset and—"

"No apologies necessary," Smith said.

"At any rate, Mac, I'm about to leave for the airport and a flight home. I just wanted you to know that the matter we discussed has been settled."

"Oh?"

"Yes, and quite to my satisfaction."

"I'm happy to hear that, but there is the matter of the murder of Dr. Musinski. I'm not sure that's been settled."

"Oh, it has, I assure you. Please, put the entire matter out of your mind. Much ado about nothing, as the Bard said. I thoroughly enjoyed seeing you and the lovely Mrs. Smith again, and I thank you for a splendid dinner and drinks afterward. I will be in touch. Do I owe you anything for your counsel?"

"Of course not."

Except a better explanation, Mac thought.

"Well, then, cheerio, Mac. Until next time."

THIRTY-FOUR

That night's technical rehearsal at the Kennedy Center went well, with only minor lighting and sound miscues. The director, Anthony Zambrano, and his assistants functioned like a well-oiled machine. Even the two people recruited at the last minute by Genevieve Crier to replace Charise Lee and Christopher Warren as supers melded smoothly with the others. Mac Smith was helpful to them and took a certain pride at being an old hand at this supernumerary business.

But while Mac concentrated on where he was supposed to be, and what he was supposed to do under Zambrano's watchful eye, his attention seldom strayed from Ray Pawkins. Nor did Annabel's. She sat in the mostly empty theater with Genevieve and a few others from the Washington National Opera. At times, she sensed that Pawkins paid unusual attention to her, too, although she rationalized that her mindset might be making her paranoid. Knowing something about someone, while they don't know you know it, is always somehow absorbing.

Mac had filled her in on Josephson's call and the message he'd delivered, that "the matter" had been settled to his "satisfaction."

What does that mean? they'd conjectured over a fast dinner before the rehearsal.

"Do you think Ray paid him off?" Annabel asked.

"Could be, Annie. From the brief exposure we had with Josephson, it was obvious that money was what mattered most to him. The possibility that Ray murdered Musinski didn't seem to be important. I encouraged him to go to the authorities, but he obviously decided not to."

"Which leaves us in a quandary, Mac."

They were about to explore that subject when old friends on their way out of the restaurant joined them at their table and talked until it was time to leave for the rehearsal.

Now, as Zambrano called it "a wrap" and everyone scattered, Mac ended up in the supers' dressing room with Pawkins.

"I thought you were going to call me today," the detective-super said offhandedly.

"I intended to, but the day got away from me."

"What was the reason?"

"For the call? I don't remember. Couldn't have been important."

Pawkins fixed him in a hard, probing stare.

Mac laughed. "No, I mean it," he said. "I have no idea why I was going to call you. Maybe to further my education in opera."

He was desperate to get Pawkins aside and ask him directly about his involvement in the Musinski case, but knew he couldn't raise it at the moment, given the presence of the others in the cramped dressing room.

Pawkins secured his locker door and turned to Mac, his sport jacket open at the waist, enough for the Glock in its holster to be visible. He'd substituted it for the .22 at home before coming to the Kennedy Center. Satisfied that Smith had seen it, he closed the jacket and said, "Going to be a great production, Mac. Agree?"

"I'm sure it will be," Mac said. He lowered his voice. "Do you always arm yourself for opera rehearsals?"

Pawkins laughed. "Oh, that? You noticed, huh? No. But I've decided that with all the street crime in D.C. these days, especially with the weather getting warmer—it brings out the bad guys—I might as well tote some protection. By the way, it's registered."

"I'm sure it is," Mac said. "Wouldn't do for a former cop to carry an unregistered weapon." When Pawkins didn't respond, Mac added, "Would it?"

"No, it wouldn't, Mac. I see that Annabel is here. Feel like a drink? I promised Genevieve one. We were supposed to have dinner, but I bailed."

"I don't think so, Ray. It's been a long day for both of us. It's straight home."

Am I missing an opportunity? Smith wondered. He decided he wasn't. He and Annabel had more to discuss before confronting Pawkins with a question as serious as whether he was a thief and murderer.

"Well, see you tomorrow for dress rehearsal," Pawkins said. "If you remember what it was you wanted to call me about, I'll be home most of the day."

"Sure," Mac said as they went up the aisle to where Annabel and Genevieve waited.

"Good evening, Mrs. Smith," Pawkins said, his face creased with a wide smile. "Enjoy your husband's performance?"

"I think he made all the right moves," she responded. "Walked straight ahead."

"All the right moves," Pawkins repeated. "That's been the story of the counselor's life, hasn't it?"

The edge in his voice caused Annabel to meet his eyes without saying anything.

"Well," Pawkins said, "this lovely lady and I are on our way for a nightcap. Ready, Genevieve?"

"I'm always ready for a nightcap," she said brightly. "Especially in the morning."

"I invited you and your husband to join us," Pawkins said to Annabel, "but he claims advancing age. You two enjoy an early to bed. *Ciao!*"

Mac and Annabel decided to have a nightcap, too, but not at the Watergate Hotel bar or 600 restaurant, where Pawkins and Genevieve might have gone. Instead they walked up 25th Street to the River Inn's Foggy Bottom Café. The manager was in the process of closing, but invited them to have a drink, his treat. It was the perfect setting for a serious discussion. They were the only customers there.

"Did he have anything to say to you tonight?" Annabel asked after they'd been served and the manager had disappeared into the kitchen.

"Ray? No."

"He was acting strange."

"So I noticed. He's always smug, or a little strange, but there was an extra dollop of it tonight."

"I'm worried about Genevieve."

"Because she went out for a drink with him?"

"Yes." She gripped his arm on the bar. "Mac, the man may be a murderer."

"I'm well aware of that, Annie."

"You have to go to the police."

"With what? We've been over this before. I have nothing except the word of a slightly unbalanced Englishman. He took all his supporting evidence with him, every scrap."

"The police can call Josephson."

"To what end? If Ray paid Josephson off, he undoubtedly bought his silence. Josephson doesn't give a damn about who killed Musinski. He opted to not go to the police while he was here because that would muddy the waters about the money from the musical scores, and who it belongs to. Frankly, I wonder if he's even entitled to half of it. He never showed us any piece of paper between him and Musinski regarding the scores." He downed the remainder of his cognac. "There's only one approach," he said, "and that's for me to confront Pawkins."

"For *us* to confront him, you mean," she said.

"No, you stay out of it, Annie."

"Absolutely not. I was there when Josephson told his tale, and I've been in the loop ever since."

"Which doesn't mean you have to stay in it. If Ray is to be approached, I'm the one to do it."

"It was my idea to bring him into the Charise Lee murder."

"And I was the one who actually did it. Speaking of Charise Lee, I haven't heard another word about it except what the papers say, and that isn't much anymore."

She, too, finished her drink. "Maybe we should ask Pawkins about that—not what he's come up with, but whether he killed her, too."

"Let's not get carried away, Annie. We have no reason to suspect that of him."

A vision of the Asian woman waiting for Pawkins at rehearsal came and went.

They thanked the manager for the drinks and walked back to their apartment, where Rufus greeted them with rowdy enthusiasm.

"I'll call Ray tomorrow and try to set up a date with him," Mac said after returning from walking the "beast," the Great Dane.

"Maybe you should wait," she said.

His face mirrored his surprise. "I thought you were anxious for me to do it," he said.

"I was anxious for *us* to do it. But dress rehearsal is tomorrow night, opening night after that, and then the ball. I don't want to do anything to taint those things."

"All right," Mac said. "We'll give it a few days, let the show go on, and then deal with it. As long as he doesn't know we know, there's no reason to rush it."

They climbed into bed and Mac turned off the bedside lamp.

"By the way," Annabel said, "you looked splendid in your costumes tonight."

"Thank you. I have to admit, I'm enjoying it."

"I knew you would. Good night."

"Good night, Mrs. Smith."

Both slept fitfully that night.

THIRTY-FIVE

"How come we're pulling this duty, Carl?"

Willie Portelain and Sylvia Johnson sat in Berry's office. They'd been assigned to a contingent of metropolitan police working security for the Opera Ball at the Brazilian Embassy.

"Supply and demand, Willie," Berry said. "We have to provide X number of cops to the event, uniformed and plainclothes. That's the demand. We're shorthanded. That's the supply. Think of it this way. Plácido Domingo himself might spot you, recognize your talent, and make you an opera star."

Sylvia laughed. "You're sure built like one, Willie," she said playfully.

"Lost two pounds," he said proudly.

"Yeah, I noticed right away," said Berry, shooting a bemused glance at Sylvia, who lowered her head and smiled.

Before Portelain and Johnson had arrived, he'd been reading that morning's paper, including a long article about the production of *Tosca*. According to the writer, a relatively new addition to the *Post's*

Entertainment section, the dress rehearsal she'd been invited to attend gave promise of a spectacular production the following night.

Aside from a few rough spots that I'm sure the director, Anthony Zambrano, will smooth out before the opening, this particular reincarnation of the Puccini classic has all the trappings of greatness. The Washington National Opera has slowly but surely worked its way into the top tier of American opera companies. This Tosca *will go far to cement its well-earned, lofty position.*

"You read this?" Berry asked his detectives, pointing to the article.

"I don't read that section," Willie said.

"I read it," said Sylvia. "I'd like to see the opera."

"I'll call Ray Pawkins and see if he can arrange for a comp ticket."

"See if he can come up with two," she said.

"Got another date?" Willie asked.

"No, but I—"

"Take me," he said, grinning. "Like Carl says, we might get discovered and end up singin' those arias together."

"You'll be missed here," Berry said. "The opera world's gain, MPD's loss. I'll see what I can do. If Ray doesn't pan out, Public Affairs gets freebies from the Kennedy Center now and then."

He opened a thick file folder and passed out sheets of paper from it. "Here's everybody who was at the Kennedy Center the night Ms. Lee was killed. The check marks indicate they've been interviewed."

"A lot of missing check marks," Sylvia commented as she quickly went through the pages.

"Another case of supply and demand. We narrowed down the list into priorities, and ruled out certain people. They'll still have to be questioned, but we've left them for last."

"Wilfred Burns, the president of GW, huh?" Willie said. "I don't figure him for a killer."

"Or the other supers on there from universities," Berry said. "There's also a half-dozen people from the opera company we haven't talked to."

"Who's this Mackensie Smith?" Sylvia asked.

"One of the supers. Teaches law at GW. His wife's listed there, too. She's on the Opera board."

"Ray Pawkins," Sylvia muttered, still going over names.

"I've spoken with Ray a few times," Berry said, "but we should do a formal interview, cover all the bases."

"Cover all the butts, you mean," growled Willie.

"If you say so. I've got others tracking them down. I want you to interview those two agents again, Melincamp and Baltsa."

"What in hell for?" Willie said. "We've already questioned them twice."

"Maybe the third time will be the charm," Berry said.

"Does this have to do with that dispatch from Homeland Security?" Johnson asked.

"No," Berry said. "I ran it by Cole. It's strictly an FBI matter. Maybe if they lived here, we'd get involved, but *not our job*. You said they claim that the woman, Baltsa, took Ms. Lee in after her father had abused her. But Melincamp debates that. Right?"

"That's what he said," Johnson replied.

"And he lied about when he came to Washington. Right, Willie?"

"I don't know if the dude actually lied. Maybe he got a little mixed up."

"Yeah, well, getting a little mixed up in a murder investigation might mean something bigger. Check in with me this afternoon about the tickets, Sylvia."

Johnson and Portelain first stopped at the Hotel Rouge. Their call to Zöe Baltsa's room went unanswered. Willie asked the desk clerk whether he'd seen Baltsa that morning. Answer: no.

"Let's try the apartment," Sylvia suggested, heading for their car.

"Who's there?" Melincamp asked through the intercom.

"Police," Johnson said. "Detectives Johnson and Portelain."

"Just a moment."

Melincamp buzzed them in, and stood in the doorway to the apartment. He was dressed in a blue summer-weight suit, a blue-and-white checkered shirt, and a maroon tie.

"How are you?" Willie asked as they walked past Melincamp.

"I'm all right," he answered, not sounding at all sure. "Why are you here?"

"Just checking back, that's all," Willie said, his eyes taking in the room, where two suitcases stood in a corner.

"Taking a trip?" Sylvia asked.

"As a matter of fact, I am," Melincamp said. "I'm going back to Toronto."

"You and your partner?" Willie asked.

"No. I mean, she's already left." He wiped perspiration from his upper lip with the back of his hand.

"Is that so?" Willie said. "We just left the hotel. Nobody said she'd checked out."

"She probably hasn't yet. Her flight is later today. She's probably running last-minute errands. I don't know where she is. Look, I have to leave."

Johnson ignored him. "The reason we're here," she said, "is to see whether you've had any additional thoughts about Ms. Lee's murder, came up with anything you might not have told us the last time we spoke."

Melincamp screwed up his face in exaggerated thought. "No," he said, "I can't think of anything. Maybe I should ask you the same question. Have you come up with anything new about her murder?"

"We're making progress," Willie said. He grunted, and swung his left arm in a circle.

"You okay?" Sylvia asked.

"Yeah, yeah, just some arthur-itus."

"We've been going back over the notes of our previous conversations, Mr. Melincamp," Johnson said, "and there's a discrepancy we'd like to clear up."

"A discrepancy? What do you mean?"

"Well," she said, "when Detective Portelain first interviewed you—I believe it was here at the apartment—you said that you'd flown to Washington the day of the murder. But Ms. Baltsa said you came a day earlier than that."

"She did? I don't understand. What difference does it make when I arrived?"

"It could make a lot of difference. What did you do that first day in town?"

He forced a laugh. "How can I remember? There's always so much to do, so many people to see."

"Well, maybe you can try to remember," Willie said. "You know, put your mind to it."

"I'm sorry," Melincamp said, "but it's all a blank. Look, I've stayed here in Washington because I wanted to be of help in solving Charise's murder. But now it's time for me to get back to Toronto and my work. I don't want to miss my plane, so unless you have a reason for me to stay, I have to go."

"You're free to go, Mr. Melincamp," Johnson said. "Is something bothering you? You seem uptight."

"No, I'm fine. Excuse me." He grabbed the luggage.

"We might have to contact you again with follow-up questions."

"Good. That will be fine. I wish you both well in solving this horrific thing that's happened to Charise."

They followed him outside, where he looked for a taxi.

"Where's your other client, the piano player?" Willie asked.

"At Takoma Park, naturally, rehearsing the chorus for tonight's opening of *Tosca*. The director wants some last-minute changes."

A cab turned the corner and headed for them. Portelain and Johnson watched Melincamp toss his luggage in the backseat and climb in beside it. He waved as the driver pulled away.

"Waste of time," Willie grumbled.

"Most of what we do is a waste of time, Willie. But this wasn't. The guy's a nervous wreck."

"Those artsy types always are" was Willie's take on it.

Her cell phone rang. It was Carl Berry. "Where are you?" he asked, his voice tinny through the small speakerphone.

"At Warren's apartment, talking to Melincamp. He's on his way back to Toronto, just got in a cab."

"Yeah, well, you might as well head back here. We're on call. Oh,

Sylvia, Ray Pawkins came through with a couple of tickets for the opera tonight."

"That's great. Thanks."

"Thank him when you see him."

"Well?" Willie asked after she'd clicked off.

"Well what?"

"The man says Pawkins got you a couple a tickets. That means two. How about it, you take your favorite partner along? I've never been to an opera."

Sylvia knew what was coming. She didn't have a date that night; her latest romantic interest was out of town on government business.

"Sure, Willie, we'll go to the opera together."

His white teeth glowed against the contrasting blackness of his round face. "Damn," he said, "now I'll have to stay awake. I saw an opera once on TV. Can't remember what it was, but I know I fell asleep before the first act was over. And those suckers can be long, *real* long."

"I'll keep you awake, Willie," she said as they got in their green, unmarked MPD car. "And if you do fall asleep, and snore, I'll shoot you dead right there in the theater."

He insisted on stopping on their way back to headquarters for a take-out sandwich from Subway, which he started to eat during the ride. They parked in the lot reserved for MPD vehicles, then entered the station through a rear door as two detectives were exiting.

"What's up, man?" Willie asked one of them.

"Homicide over on 16th, Northwest. Hotel Rouge."

"Hotel Rouge?" Willie and Sylvia said in concert.

"That's what the dispatcher said."

"Let's go, Willie," Sylvia said, leading him and his half-eaten sandwich back to their car.

THIRTY-SIX

Willie and Sylvia arrived with the two detectives who'd originally caught the case. Two uniforms, who'd been waved down in their car by the doorman, were already at the scene, one standing guard just inside the door to the room, the other in the hallway keeping the curious away.

The four detectives stood in the middle of the room now, their eyes registering initial impressions. Zöe Baltsa's lifeless body was slumped on the floor at the foot of the king-sized bed, her back against it, her legs akimbo in front of her. Her head flopped to one side; drying blood seeped from the downward corner of her mouth onto the red carpeting. She wore yellow Capri pants and a fuzzy gold sleeveless shirt. She was barefoot.

Because Willie was the senior detective, he took charge of the crime scene. "You were the first in here?" he asked one of the cops in uniform.

"Right. A chambermaid discovered the body and notified the desk. We were driving by. A doorman—maybe he's a bellhop—hailed us."

"Nobody's been in here since you arrived?"

"Right. The maid who found the body is downstairs in the manager's office. She was pretty shaken up."

One of the detectives lit a cigarette. "Hey, put that out," Willie said. "This is a crime scene, man."

The detective, a tall, gangly young man, said, "Sorry," and went into the hall to find a receptacle.

Sylvia slowly approached the body, her eyes scanning the carpeting before stepping on it. There were slight indentations, but nothing that would provide substantial evidence of the shoes, or the feet inside them. She went to one knee and placed two fingers on the side of Baltsa's neck. The talent agent's eyes were open wide; the corneas had become milky, indicating to Sylvia that she'd been killed at least eight hours earlier. A gentle manipulation of the rigid jaw also pointed to an approximate time of death, between eight and twelve hours ago. Sylvia was fascinated with forensic science and had taken every course offered by MPD. She looked down to Baltsa's torso, where a small amount of blood had seeped through a tear in the front of her gold shirt from an area between her breasts. Sylvia leaned closer. She turned and motioned for Willie to join her. "Look," she said, pointing to the bloodstained edge of a sponge that had been wedged into the wound.

"I'll be damned," he said. "Maybe our killer is SpongeBob."

"She died between eight and twelve hours ago," said Sylvia. "Her skin's clammy, cold."

They turned at the arrival of white-coated evidence technicians, and an assistant medical examiner. Sylvia told the doctor her conclusions, and she and Willie went to where the original two detectives stood. "Check out everybody with rooms on this floor," Willie ordered. "Maybe somebody heard or saw something." To one of the uniformed cops: "Keep everybody away, and that means everybody. Got it?"

"Got it."

"Come on," Willie said to Sylvia, "let's go downstairs and talk to the maid."

The hotel's manager was in his office, along with the chambermaid, a middle-aged Hispanic woman who wept into a handkerchief, and two other hotel employees. Portelain and Johnson introduced themselves. Willie asked, "Is this the lady who discovered the body?"

"Yes," the manager replied. "Mrs. Cruz." He gave his own name and those of his employees. Sylvia asked the other two employees to leave, and she and Willie took the maid's statement. She spoke good English, and managed to pull herself together well enough to give a cogent account: She'd gone to the room to service it. There was no sign on the door indicating that the guest didn't want to be disturbed. She let herself in with her master key, and saw the woman on the floor.

"Did you do anything in the room?" Willie asked.

"No, *señor*. I run from there to here as fast as I can run."

"That's good," Willie said, patting her arm. He noted her name and the time she said she'd entered the room, and told her she was free to go.

"Who was on duty last night, say between midnight and six this morning?" Sylvia asked the manager.

"Our usual night staff," he said. He was a young man, dressed in a nice suit, and he had a boyish, freckled face. "Mr. Galberth was in charge of the desk."

"Galberth?"

"Yes. He was just in here. One of our morning desk clerks called in sick, and he volunteered to work a second shift. He told me something that you might find interesting."

"Would you get him back in here, please?" Willie said.

"You were on duty last night?" Sylvia asked the clerk.

"Yes, ma'am."

"Your manager says that you have something that we might be interested in hearing."

"Yes, ma'am. Around midnight, a man came here to see Ms. Baltsa."

"You say it was around midnight?"

"Yes, ma'am. We're always a little more interested in who comes and goes at that hour."

"That makes sense," Sylvia said. "He came to see Ms. Baltsa. How do you know that? Did he ask for her?"

"No, ma'am. He came in and went to the house phone by the desk. I wasn't eavesdropping or anything, but I couldn't help but hear him on the phone."

"What did he say?"

"He said—let me see, now; I want to be accurate—he said, 'Zöe, this is Chris.' "

"You knew who Zöe was?"

"Sure. That's Ms. Baltsa's first name."

"And you're sure he said his name was Chris?"

"Yes, ma'am. Absolutely."

"Did he say anything else?" Willie asked.

"No, sir. He hung up and went to the elevators."

"Did you see him come down?"

"No, ma'am."

"So you don't know how long he was up there in her room."

"No, sir, I'm afraid I don't."

"And you never saw him leave."

"No, sir, I didn't."

"What did he look like?" Sylvia asked.

"Gee, I don't know. Kind of average, I guess."

"Black? White? Hispanic?" Willie asked.

"White. Pretty tall, maybe six feet. He had on a T-shirt, a white one. It had some sort of music on it."

"Music?"

"You know, like sheet music, lines and little notes. It was on his chest."

"You'd recognize him again, wouldn't you?" Sylvia asked.

"Yes, ma'am, I'm sure I would. He was standing pretty close to me when he was on the phone, no more than a few feet away."

"Thank you," Sylvia said. "I'm sure we'll want to talk with you again."

"My pleasure, ma'am."

They returned upstairs to ensure that the crime scene was sufficiently secured, gave further instructions to the others, and went to their car, where Sylvia called Carl Berry.

"It's that talent agent, right?" were the first words out of Berry's mouth.

"Right. Ms. Baltsa." She gave him their initial findings and impressions. "That client of theirs, the pianist, Christopher Warren, evidently visited her last night at about midnight. Willie and I are on our way to pick him up. Baltsa's partner, Melincamp, is supposedly on his way back to Toronto. I suggest you dispatch officers to the airport to pick him up, too."

"Which airport?"

"I don't know, Carl. National, Dulles. I'm a cop, not a travel agent."

There was silence on his end, and she wished she hadn't responded so flippantly.

"Okay," he said. "I'll get on it."

THIRTY-SEVEN

Willie and Sylvia found Chris Warren at Takoma Park, where he accompanied *Tosca*'s chorus as it ran through the changes dictated by Zambrano. Their unexpected presence, one at each door to the vast rehearsal space, caused the chorus director, a rotund man with a shock of snow-white hair, to stop the run-through and approach Sylvia. "I'm afraid this is a closed rehearsal," he said.

"Sorry to interrupt," she said, "but we're here on police business." She showed her badge. "We need to speak to Mr. Warren."

The director turned and looked at Chris, who sat stoically at the piano.

"Can't it wait?" the director asked. "We're almost finished. We can't continue without him."

"Sure, we can wait," Sylvia said, "but not for long." She looked at her watch. "Fifteen minutes?"

"Yes, that should be sufficient time," he said, and returned to his position in front of the singers.

The voices filled the room, sending a shiver up Sylvia's back. The power and majesty of the music was breathtaking, and she looked forward to hearing it in context that night on the Kennedy Center stage—provided this new wrinkle didn't have them pulling night duty, too. She glanced at Willie, who leaned against the doorjamb, a smile on his face. The music was getting to him, too, transcending any cognitive understanding and reaching a spot far deeper and less tangible than the mind. Fifteen minutes later, the choral director applauded the singers: "Splendid. That was splendid. That movement has now come alive."

As everyone began leaving the room, Sylvia wondered what Warren would do. Certainly he knew that they were there because of him. Would he come to them, or make them go to him? It immediately became evident that it would be the latter. He gathered up sheets from the piano's music desk and started to walk away.

"Mr. Warren," Sylvia announced as she and Willie converged to block his path.

"What do you *want*?" he asked. "Why can't you leave me alone?"

"You'll have to come with us," Sylvia said.

"Why?"

"Because we say so," Willie said, taking a menacing step closer to the young musician, who wore a white T-shirt with a wavy black musical staff emblazoned across the chest. "Don't give us a hard time again."

Warren looked confused, as though contemplating his options. Submit? Run? He was obviously contemplating the last time he'd tried to flee and its ramifications.

"All right," he said, "but I want someone from the embassy with me."

"Sure," Willie assured, placing a large hand on Warren's bony shoulder. "We just have a few questions to ask. You answer them right, you're back here tickling the ivories in no time."

Annabel Smith was also at Takoma Park that day. She and Genevieve had spent the morning choosing costumes for a dozen supers to wear the following night at the Opera Ball. Genevieve had pulled out all the stops and tapped her list of past supers to come up with twelve volunteers. She'd inquired whether Mac and the other *Tosca* supers from academia would be willing, but they all declined, which she understood. Mac and Annabel would be guests at the ball by virtue of Annabel's position on the board and the ball committee; Mac's tuxedo had already been slightly let out by their tailor, and Annabel's gown had been purchased, fitted, and now hung in her closet, ready to go.

Annabel and Genevieve left at one that afternoon and went to WNO's administrative offices on Virginia Avenue, where yet another meeting of the ball committee was scheduled. That lasted until three. Individuals on the committee made plans to gather at various homes the following morning to read the reviews of the opening night of *Tosca*; Genevieve, Laurie Webster and her husband, Camile Worthington and her husband, and two other couples would join Mac and Annabel at their apartment for breakfast, ideally a place to celebrate how the critics received the production.

"Mind if Ray joins us for breakfast?" Genevieve asked as she and Annabel shared a taxi.

Annabel didn't respond.

"Is there a problem?" Genevieve asked.

"Oh, no, of course not," Annabel said, not admitting that she did have a problem. "By all means, ask him to come."

⁊

Chris Warren sat alone in an interrogation room, the same one in which he'd been questioned earlier. Berry, Portelain, and Johnson observed him through the one-way glass.

"He give you a hard time?" Berry asked.

"No," Johnson answered. "He balked at coming with us, but only verbally. Came along nice and peaceful."

"What did you tell him?"

"Only that we had some more questions for him. We didn't say what it was about. We didn't mention Baltsa."

"Good. I sent a team out to National Airport to look for Melincamp. We checked passenger manifests for flights going to Toronto today—Air Canada, United, and U.S. Air. No Melincamp booked on any of them."

"Maybe he flew someplace else," Willie offered.

"That's always a possibility," Berry said, "although why tell you he was going back to Toronto?"

"To confuse us," Johnson said.

"If so," Berry said, "I'd view that as consciousness of guilt. I put an APB out for him."

"He was a bundle of nerves when we talked to him," Johnson said.

"Like maybe he'd just offed somebody," Willie said.

Berry looked through the window at Warren again. "All right," he said, "you two lay it on the line for him, see if he breaks."

"What about his lawyer?"

"I'll notify the Canadian Embassy again, but I won't rush. See what you can get from him before I do."

Johnson sat across the table from Warren. Portelain stood behind him.

"Okay, Chris," Johnson said, her voice and smile friendly, "let me get right to the point of why you're here. When did you last see Ms. Baltsa?"

The question generated confusion on his face. "Zöe?"

"Why don't you let me ask the questions first?" Johnson said.

Warren looked nervously back at Portelain, who leaned against the wall, arms crossed over his massive chest, a scowl on his face.

"When did I see her? I don't know, maybe a day ago, maybe two."

"You're sure about that?" Johnson asked, her eyes confirming that the tape in the small machine on the table was running.

"Yeah, I'm sure. Why? Is something wrong with that?"

Willie pushed away from the wall and leaned over Warren. "You know what, dude?" he said. "You might be one hell of a piano player, but you suck as a liar."

"I'm not lying."

"The hell you're not." Portelain now pulled up a chair next to Warren. "Where were you last night, say around midnight?"

"I was—"

"Careful," Willie said. "You flunk as a liar, so you might as well start telling the truth. Where were you?"

"Home. At the apartment. I—"

"Chris," Johnson said softly, "we know you visited Ms. Baltsa at midnight at the Hotel Rouge. We've got a positive ID on you, and your prints are all over the hotel room."

"I forgot."

The slap of Willie's ham-hock hand on the table jarred both Warren and Johnson, and sent the small tape recorder an inch into the air.

"Look, my man," Willie said, "you don't seem to get it. You say you forgot going to see her at midnight last night. You forget stickin' her in the chest with a knife, too?"

"Oh, no," Warren said, jumping up from his chair and going to the room's only window.

"Sit down," Willie said.

"She's dead?" Warren moaned from where he stood.

"Yes, she's dead," Johnson confirmed. "Now, why don't you sit down and tell us all about it."

❧

Philip Melincamp vomited in a men's room at U.S. Air at Reagan National Airport before boarding a shuttle to New York City. He felt faint for most of the flight, his plight noticed by a flight attendant, who asked, "Are you all right, sir? Is there something I can get you?"

"No, no, nothing. Thank you. It's just a cold, maybe the flu."

She kept a wary eye on him for the duration of the short flight to New York's LaGuardia Airport. She kept a wary eye on everyone.

At LaGuardia Airport, he stepped in front of other passengers waiting in a taxi line, ignoring their shouts of protest, and gave the driver an address on Steinway Street, in the Astoria section of Queens, an area known as "Little Egypt." After some wrong turns that took them past dozens of Middle Eastern grocery stores, restaurants, and clubs, the cab pulled up in front of a café whose sign boasted AUTHENTIC ARAB CUISINE AND HOOKAH. He paid the driver, overtipping him, and dragged his two small, wheeled suitcases behind him into the restaurant. A short, swarthy man looked up from where he'd been counting money. "Can I help you, sir?"

Melincamp looked to the back of the long, narrow room, where four men sat drawing in *shisha*, fruit-flavored tobacco, through the water pipes known as hookahs, the smoke shrouding their faces and creating swirling patterns as it gravitated to recessed lighting fixtures in the low ceiling. "I came to see someone back there," Melincamp said, shoving his luggage into a corner of the entryway and walking to the rear. A young Arab man removed the pipe from his mouth and frowned up at Melincamp.

"Can we talk?" Melincamp said, aware of sweat running down his cheeks.

Without responding, the Arab placed the pipe in its holder and went to a door leading from the hookah room to an alley. Melincamp followed. They climbed a wooden set of exterior stairs to an apartment above the café, where another Arab male, considerably taller and heavier than the first, sat at a scarred, yellow kitchen table, an Arabic newspaper open in front of him. His swarthy face was deeply pitted from acne. He wore a traditional male Arab headdress—a keffiyeh—in a black-and-red pattern and secured by an *egal*, a thin rope circlet.

"Why do you come here?" the man at the table asked.

Melincamp turned to the man who'd led him upstairs. "Joseph said to come here if there was trouble."

"Is there trouble?" the man at the table asked.

"Yes."

Another large man stepped from behind curtains separating the small kitchen from another portion of the apartment.

"I can explain," Melincamp said.

"I am listening," said the man, who closed the newspaper and glared at Melincamp in a way that drained blood from the talent agent's face and turned his legs to jelly.

Melincamp grabbed hold of the back of a chair to support himself. He saw a glass half filled with water on the table. "Please," he said, "could I have some water?"

The man picked up the glass and threw its contents into Melincamp's face. Melincamp collapsed into the chair.

"It is too late for trouble," the man said. "The plan goes forward. Are you ready?"

"No, but there is a reason, a good reason," Melincamp said, his voice weak. "You see—"

He was struck from behind, and tumbled to the floor, unconscious.

THIRTY-EIGHT

There was a deathly silence as the dramatic, final minutes of Act II of *Tosca* played out. Twenty-three-hundred men and women in the Kennedy Center's Opera House watched intently, many barely breathing, as Tosca and the evil Scarpia performed Puccini's dramatic dance of lust and betrayal. Tosca has asked Scarpia in song how much he wants in return for sparing the life of her lover, Cavaradossi, who is in custody and scheduled to be executed.

Scarpia laughs and dismisses the notion.

"I want a higher payment," he sings in his rich baritone voice. "I want a much higher payment. Tonight is the night I have longed for. Since first I saw you, desire has consumed me, but tonight, though you hope to defy me, you can no longer deny me."

He stands and approaches her, arms outstretched. "When you cried out, despairing, passion inflamed me, and your glances drove me almost beyond bearing the lust to which you've doomed me. How your hatred enhances my determination to possess you. I may curse or bless you, but you must be mine. You *are* mine, Tosca!"

Willie Portelain stage-whispered to Sylvia, "I hope she sticks it to the bastard."

"Shhh," Sylvia hissed in return.

Tosca and Scarpia continue their "negotiation." Finally, Tosca agrees to his terms; she will indulge him in a night of passion in return for a mock execution of Cavaradossi, and a legal letter signed by Scarpia ensuring the lovers' safe passage out of the country. Scarpia writes the note and places his official seal on the envelope. As he does, Tosca sees a knife on the table and hides it behind her back.

He goes to embrace her: "Tosca, at last you are mine."

She rams the knife into his chest, eliciting a variety of muttered utterances from the audience.

"You assassin!" Scarpia shouts as he falls to his knees, his hands clutching the weapon in his chest.

"That is the way Tosca kisses," she spits.

"I'm dying. Help me," Scarpia implores her.

"Your own blood will choke you," Tosca sings, hatred in her voice. "It is Tosca who has killed you. Now you pay for my torture. Can you still hear me, Scarpia? Answer me! Look at me! Look, Scarpia, it's Tosca. Your own blood will choke you. Die in damnation, Scarpia. Die now!"

He draws his last breath as Tosca yanks the safe-passage letter from his hand and secures it in her bosom. She's about to leave, but changes her mind. She takes two candlesticks from the table, lights them, and places one on either side of Scarpia's head. She removes a crucifix from the wall and puts it on his chest. Satisfied, she leaves the room, the train of her gown trailing behind her, the sound of chilling chords and fatal drumbeats from the orchestra blasting a crescendo to end this act of murder.

The audience erupted into a loud, sustained, standing ovation as the curtain closed.

People eventually left their seats to enjoy a stretch during the intermission, or to indulge in a cigarette on the vast terrace outside the lobby doors, low-flying flights into Reagan National Airport joining the animated sounds of their excited voices. Annabel stood with friends from the Opera Board. "It's a spectacular production," one said, "one of the best *Toscas* I've seen, and I've seen plenty of them, all over the world. No one gives his leading ladies more dramatic entrances and exits than Puccini."

"The performers are wonderful," Annabel said. "It's almost spiritual listening to them, as though we're in a giant cathedral."

"Scarpia sure does a good death scene," a man said.

"I've seen other Scarpias take longer to die in different productions."

"What an added thrill to have Maestro Domingo conducting the orchestra. To be able to step in like that on a moment's notice when the scheduled conductor got sick is amazing."

"*He's* amazing," someone said of Domingo. "Nothing short of amazing."

Across the terrace, at a low wall beyond which the rippling waters of the Potomac shimmered, stood Willie Portelain and Sylvia Johnson.

"Isn't it wonderful?" Sylvia said.

"Yeah, I like it a lot. Never nodded off once."

"I can't imagine a better endorsement, Willie."

They had turned off their cell phones upon entering the theater. Berry had given them permission to be out of touch during the performance, but told them to call in during intermission, and again when the opera was over. Sylvia activated her phone and punched in Berry's direct-dial number. "Hi," she said. "It's between the second and third acts."

"Glad you checked in," Berry said. "Hate to do it to you, but you'd better get back here right away."

"And miss the third act?" Sylvia said jokingly.

Berry took her seriously. "We'll get you tickets for the next performance. Make it quick."

He clicked off.

"Let's go," Sylvia said.

"I heard him," Willie said. "You get those other tickets and forget about taking another dude with you. Remember, Willie here needs to see what happens to Tosca and her boyfriend. It was just getting to the best part."

"Okay," she said, and they headed out of the theater.

☙

"What's up?" Sylvia asked Berry.

"This." Her boss handed her a fax.

She read it quickly, then handed it to Willie.

"Damn," he said when he'd finished. "Can you believe it?"

"I think we'd better."

The fax was from the New York Police Department. Officers had discovered a male body dumped beneath the Whitestone Bridge, in Queens. The man's throat had been slit. Papers recovered from the body identified the victim as Philip Melincamp, the name of the individual for whom an APB had been issued by Washington MPD earlier that day.

"I wanted to wait until you got here before informing Mr. Warren of this development," Berry said.

"He still here?" Willie asked.

"Yeah. We're holding him as a person of interest."

"Man, I hate that term," Willie said as they went to the interrogation room where Chris Warren sat with a uniformed female officer. "You're either a suspect or you're not."

Berry laughed. "His lawyer didn't put up much of a beef," he said, referring to Warren's attorney. "The combination of the kid being there around the time Baltsa was killed and his lying doesn't look good for him. The lawyer recognized that, too."

They stood on the other side of the one-way glass and observed Warren. He looked almost complacent compared to his earlier volatility.

"How do you figure Melincamp getting it jibes with him?" Willie asked. "Me? I'd put my money on the talent agent offing his partner."

"You may be right," Berry said. "Let's go find out."

An hour later, they had their answer.

THIRTY-NINE

"**E**veryone, listen to this!"

A dozen people were gathered at Mac and Annabel's apartment the morning after *Tosca*'s opening. The reviews were in. Genevieve Crier held them in her hands and read them aloud. They were uniformly positive, but everyone waited for the one they feared—and treasured—most, which Genevieve had saved for last. What would John Shulson have to say?

Shulson was acknowledged as one of the opera world's most knowledgeable, insightful, and demanding reviewers. His reviews and commentary appeared in a wide variety of publications, always stylishly written but often with barbed criticism of some aspect of a production.

Genevieve stood on a chair.

"Come on, Genevieve," someone urged. "Is it bad?"

The coordinator cleared her throat, looked down at the review through half-glasses, and began reading.

"The headline is, 'Tosca Triumphs Over Double Murder.' "

"Charise Lee," someone said.

"Of course," responded a woman. "Some of the other reviewers mentioned it, too. It can't be ignored."

Genevieve continued in her best British stage-honed voice.

" 'The murder of aspiring opera singer Charise Lee, a promising member of the Domingo-Cafritz Young Artist Program, added heightened verismo to the Washington National Opera's opening night production of Puccini's tragic tale *Tosca*. The fact that the murder took place during rehearsals, and onstage, added substantial stir in the lobby of the Kennedy Center Opera House prior to the performance, as patrons speculated whether the dual deaths of Scarpia and Ms. Lee signaled a jinxed production.' "

"Oh, my God," someone said. "He's calling it a jinxed production."

"No, no," Genevieve said. "Listen!" She drew herself up to full height, which wasn't very high at all, and continued. " 'Not to worry.' " She looked up from the page. "That's what Mr. Shulson wrote. It's not what I'm saying."

"Okay, we get it," someone said. "Go on."

" 'Not to worry. True to form, the Washington National Opera's *Tosca* rose above the mayhem created by the incident, bringing added drama to the tale of lust, love, and, of course, murder. Literally leading the way to success was General Director Plácido Domingo, who stepped in as a last-minute replacement for conductor and music director Heinz Fricke. Fricke fell ill the afternoon of the opening, only adding to this *Tosca*'s turmoil. However, the maestro's strong hand and familiarity with the score, no doubt greatly enhanced by his having performed the role of Cavaradossi countless times, brought an unusually perceptive sense of drama, richness, and poignancy to the orchestra's performance, and to the production itself.' "

"He liked it," a few guests said, joy in their voices.

Genevieve continued: " 'Equally sure-handed was Anthony Zambrano's direction, although one suspects he never anticipated the notoriety he would receive from this production when he signed on. Despite the real-life drama surrounding the murder and this production, Zambrano's vision remained grounded and focused. Not surprisingly, Scarpia's murder in Act II sent chills throughout the full house as Tosca plunged the knife into his chest, uttering, "That is the way Tosca kisses." One wondered instinctively what the real-life murderer might have said when a similar knife was plunged into Ms. Lee's chest on that very stage, her blood symbolically mingling with the blood of the slain Scarpia in an eerie and ominous close to the act.'"

Genevieve surveyed her audience. No one moved, nor said anything. She read the rest an octave higher. "Listen to what he says next! 'Despite the high-pitched hype surrounding the murder-performance, the entire cast deserves considerable praise for performing under duress and distress. It was not just a case of rising above the occasion, but a ringing musical example of excellent preparation, singing, finely crafted characterizations, and a dedication to an art form not always thought of in terms of reality—except in the case of murder. Don't miss this *Tosca* at the Kennedy Center! Its power and majesty astounded even this reviewer.'"

Genevieve jumped down from the chair and curtsied as applause broke out.

Spirits were high at the Smiths' that morning because of the rave reviews, and appetites were whetted. But no one lingered once they'd enjoyed a bagel or croissant, some salmon, caviar, juice, or coffee. There was the Opera Ball that evening to prepare for, and the apartment soon emptied. Mac and Annabel cleared the table of leftover food and filled the dishwasher. That chore completed, they took coffee to the terrace.

"A success," Annabel proclaimed.

"Our parties are always a success," Mac said. "You're the perfect hostess."

"The host had something to do with it, too." She sobered. "So, Mac, what was your read on Pawkins this morning?"

"He seemed in good spirits, but that's not unusual for him. I'll face him about the Musinski murder once the ball is over with."

"The reviews were excellent."

"Yes, they were, although I was disappointed none of them singled me out for my performance."

"I thought you were an absolute star," she said, kissing his cheek. "My star." She got up from her chair. "I have to run. Another meeting."

"Your life is a series of meetings," he said, not being critical.

"Only until tonight is over."

Another meeting taking place that morning didn't involve reviews, and there wasn't a bagel in sight. It was held at the J. Edgar Hoover Building on Pennsylvania Avenue, headquarters for the Federal Bureau of Investigation. A top official from that agency chaired the meeting. Also present were Joseph Browning and two aides from the Department of Homeland Security, a representative from the CIA, and Detective Carl Berry and his boss, Cole Morris. Morris read from a lengthy report, copies of which had been handed out to the others. *Why is he reading it if we all have it?* Berry silently wondered. When Morris finished, the ranking FBI special agent in the room asked, "And you believe everything this young man says? What's his name. Warren?"

"Christopher Warren," Morris said. "Yes, we believe him. The pieces all fit."

"We have agents working with the New York police on this Melincamp murder," the special agent said.

"Any leads on who killed him?" Berry asked.

"Not at the moment," the FBI agent said. "Let's go over your report more closely."

The report was based upon an hour-long interrogation of Chris Warren following the fax informing Washington's MPD that Melincamp had been found dead in New York. That news had shaken Warren badly; Berry wondered whether he might have a breakdown before they could question him. But Warren pulled himself together and began to talk, and soon words and thoughts were flowing as though an internal dam had broken.

". . . and I'm glad that Philip is dead," Warren said, drawing in gulps of air. "He deserved to die."

"Why is that?" Sylvia Johnson asked.

"Because of what he did to people. I wanted to kill him myself, but I was . . ."

"You were what?"

"I was afraid of him. That's why I didn't say anything when he killed Charise. He told me that if I talked to anybody about it, the same thing would happen to me."

"If you talked about *what*?" Berry asked. "Charise's murder?"

"That, and the plan, too."

"What in hell plan are you talking about, Warren?" Willie asked, his impatience showing.

"The plan to kill the president or some other big shot. It was going to be part of a larger plan, a bunch of American political big shots killed the same day."

That statement brought a hush to the dimly lighted room. The tape recorder ran silently.

"Go on," Berry said softly.

The three detectives sat back and allowed Warren to continue, which he did for the better part of the hour.

He told of how Charise had fallen under the spell of the young Arab student she'd started dating, and how that student had introduced her to a terrorist cell in Toronto with plans to strike another blow against the United States. Melincamp, he said, also exerted a strong hold over Charise, and she brought him into her new sphere of terrorist friends.

"What was in it for Melincamp?" Sylvia asked.

"Money. He wanted out of the partnership with Zöe and needed money, big money to buy her out. He and Zöe had some kind of agreement that gave him the right to do that. The terrorists promised him and Charise a ton of money if they would assassinate someone when they were in Washington."

"When did you learn about this?" asked Berry.

"After we got here. I owed Melincamp money. He kept giving me advances. When it got to be a lot, he said he'd drop me and see to it that I didn't have a career as a pianist. I believed him."

"Whoa, whoa," Willie said. "Hold on a minute. Are you telling us that you kept your mouth shut because you owed this slimeball money?"

"In the beginning," Warren responded. "But it was more than that. When Charise told him she wasn't going through with it, he—"

"She decided not to cooperate?" Berry asked.

"That's right. She got cold feet. I don't think she ever intended to do it. She might have been a little screwed up, preaching how the U.S. is out to conquer the world, keep people in poverty, dumb stuff like that. But she wouldn't have tried to assassinate anybody." He shook his head. "Man, when she told me about the plan, I just laughed. At first. She was supposed to get close to the president whenever she could and—and kill him. Kill somebody. Charise told me that the president and his wife were opera lovers, and attended a lot of operas. Melincamp and the terrorists figured she'd have it easy getting close, being young and pretty and Canadian, maybe even get to sing for them, and then shoot him."

"She had a gun?" Willie asked.

"Melincamp did. He showed it to me whenever he threatened me about talking to people."

"When did Charise confide in you about the plot, Chris?" Sylvia asked.

"Just before she was killed. I told her we should go to the police or Secret Service or somebody, but she said she wanted to talk to Melincamp first. She was supposed to meet him at the Kennedy Center the night he killed her."

"And Melincamp admitted to you that he'd murdered her?" Berry asked.

Warren nodded. "That's when he said the same thing would happen to me if I talked about it. He tried to get me to take her place and kill the president, but I told him no way. If Melincamp didn't pull it off, they wouldn't pay him the money he was promised."

Berry halted the session to see whether Warren wanted anything to eat or drink.

"No. I just want to get this over with."

"Fair enough," Berry said. "Now, what about last night? You went to see Melincamp's partner, Ms. Baltsa."

Another nod from Warren. He kept his head lowered, his eyes focused on the table as he spoke. "I went to the hotel to tell her I wanted out of the program at Takoma Park, and was going back home."

"Did she know about this scheme of Melincamp's to kill an American official?"

"No."

"Did she know he'd killed Ms. Lee?"

"She suspected, but didn't know for sure until I told her last night. She said Philip was coming to see her later, after I left. I didn't kill her. I swear I didn't."

The detectives said nothing in response; they knew that he was telling the truth.

⁊

"You still have him in custody?" the FBI agent asked Cole Morris.

"Yes. He's in protective custody."

"We'll want to talk to him."

"Of course."

"Did he give you the names of this Arab boyfriend back in Toronto, and his terrorist friends?"

"Yes." Morris provided another piece of paper with that information.

"We'll take it from here," Browning said from his spot at the end of the long table. "This goes far beyond just the murder of some opera singer. There's national security at stake."

"Until we're told otherwise," the FBI agent said, "it's our jurisdiction."

"I'll get a reading from Justice," Browning said. "This young man aided and abetted a terrorist plot to kill the president of the United States. He can be held as an enemy combatant until all the links have been explored, all the dots connected."

Berry looked at Morris and raised his eyebrows.

"We're happy to help in any way we can," Morris said, "but until I get a reading from Justice that says otherwise, Mr. Warren will stay with us. He's a material witness to two murders that occurred in *our* jurisdiction."

"Maybe this will help you with the murder of the opera singer at the Kennedy Center," Browning said, sliding badly wrinkled and folded sheets of yellow legal-size lined paper to Morris.

"What's this?" Morris asked.

"Read it," Browning said. "It was found on Melincamp in New York."

Morris carefully unfolded the pages and ran his hand over them on the table to straighten the creases. Most of the handwriting was crude and in blue pen, difficult to read. A few lines at the top of the first page had been written in pencil, obviously added after the main section.

To whom it may concern:

> *In the event of my death, I want you to understand why I did what I did.*

The writing in blue pen followed.

> *She died quickly and with a modicum of suffering.*
>
> *This came as no surprise. Unlike so-called crimes of passion which are invariably messy, drawn out, and painful, I'd been planning her death for more than a week.*
>
> *She had to be eliminated because she'd learned something that I preferred she not know, which raised the possibility that she would pass that newfound knowledge along to others. I couldn't allow that.*
>
> *Had knowing the victim made it easier or more difficult for me? Of course, having known her cast me as a suspect, along with dozens of others. Murderers who are strangers to their victims invariably stand a better chance of getting away with it. There was a brief temptation to enlist the aid of another person, someone*

outside our circle of acquaintances, but I quickly ruled that out. The fewer people who know about a murder, the better.

That the murder took place onstage at the Kennedy Center Opera House would lead one to believe that I have a flair for the dramatic. But that was not the reason the area was chosen as the place to ensure her silence. I'd considered a number of settings— her apartment, on the street, or in a secluded room in the Opera company's rehearsal space at Takoma Park. She provided the answer by insisting that we meet on the stage that night, actually in the early morning hours, long after everyone was gone for the evening except perhaps for a couple of Kennedy Center security guards, who wouldn't come into the theater unless given reason to, which I certainly didn't intend to provide.

It should also be pointed out that my choice of a weapon had nothing—absolutely nothing—to do with the fact that the encounter took place on the Opera House's main stage, where the Washington National Opera would soon present the latest production of Puccini's warhorse, Tosca. Moments before dealing the fatal blow, I thought of the justified murder of the cruel, lecherous Scarpia in Tosca's Act II. The major difference was that this slaying was committed in shadows and without onlookers, while Tosca's stabbing of the cruel chief of the secret police would take place before thousands bearing witness to her defensible action. Of course, Tosca's dramatic killing of Scarpia is make-believe. This one was very real; I did not break into the aria "Vissi d'arte" before completing the act, as Madame Tosca has done thousands of nights on grand stages around the globe.

The victim was eventually found, of course, although it took almost a full day. I'd placed the body in such a location where few would have reason to go under ordinary circumstances. When her body was discovered, there was a flurry of media and law enforcement activity, and much was made of the fact that the homicide took place inside the revered Kennedy Center, and in that institution's Opera House, where betrayal, passion, intrigue, and murder take place on a regular basis—but only during performances on *the main stage. The press had a field day with opera analogies, the weapon used, the setting, and the connection of the deceased with the Washington National Opera.*

In the meantime, Tosca, and the larger comic opera that is Washington, D.C., itself—but that too often turns deadly— must, and did, go on.

And so must I.

> *Sincerely,*
> *Philip Melincamp*

Morris handed the papers to Berry. "Thanks," he said to Browning. "We know Melincamp killed the singer, but it's nice to have this. Dramatic, wasn't he?"

"And screwed up," Browning said. "A shame that he screwed up the young woman, too."

Morris and Berry left the room and the building. Once outside, Morris said, "Warren's in for a long, tough road once Homeland Security and Justice get hold of him."

"The kid was scared," said Berry as they walked to their car.

"It'll be out of our hands soon, Carl." Morris laughed. "You watch. They'll take credit for this whole thing, use the kid as a feather in their cap, another terrorist plot foiled. All we did at MPD was—everything."

As they drove back to headquarters, Berry said, "I have a request, Cole. A little favor."

"Shoot."

"Ray Pawkins got a couple of tickets to the opera last night for Sylvia Johnson and Willie Portelain. I had to pull the two of them out of the Kennedy Center early when the fax came in from New York. I'd like to buy them a couple of tickets so they can enjoy the whole show."

"Willie Portelain at the opera?" Morris said with a chuckle.

"He said he liked it. I owe them."

"Sure, go ahead. I'll hide it under—under continuing education."

FORTY

"Too many Americans have a misconception that German cuisine is brown, heavy, and blah. But Germany is actually the birthplace of organic farming. Modern German cuisine is fresh and flavorful."

So stated Marcel Biró, one of Germany's most celebrated chefs, cookbook author, and star of the Emmy-winning PBS reality-cooking series *The Kitchens of Biró*. He'd been brought to the German Embassy in Washington by the ambassador as a special treat for the fourteen guests dining there prior to attending the Opera Ball's gala at the Brazilian Embassy. The menu had been created by him especially for the occasion, and he was on hand to explain and extol each course.

"Your entrée is a special favorite of mine," he announced, "medallions of pork in a black cherry pepper sauce, with spatzle and braised fennel. The sweet tartness of the black cherries offsets the pork's flavor, and the black pepper adds just the perfect bite to the dish."

The evening had begun with tomato aspic with tiny shrimp,

which Biró said was a typical northern German dish. The salad was asparagus tips with tiny slices of sweetbreads, a southern German dish. The wines he'd chosen for the evening were a white from the Rhine, and a red Bordeaux imported from the house of Tesdorpff, wine merchants since the 15th century. A parfait of Williams pear with beetroot sabayon, Malvasier, from the island of Madeira, was dessert.

"He's absolutely charming," Annabel remarked to Mac as they savored the pork entrée.

"That he is," Mac agreed. He lowered his voice. "But I have to admit, my pedestrian palate is more attuned to sauerbraten, sauerkraut, and dumplings that sink immediately to the lower stomach."

She giggled and put a finger to her lips. "Loose lips sink ships, and dumplings," she said.

Everyone at the table agreed that the evening, at least the first portion of it, was a smashing success. The ambassador and his wife were a charming couple, and having the celebrity chef there only added to the sizzle.

They left the German Embassy and went to the evening's main event, the party at the Brazilian Embassy. As they approached, pulsating samba and bossa nova rhythms could be heard, and felt, a block away. An overwhelming contingent of security people, uniformed and in plainclothes, made their presence abundantly evident. The Smiths' invitations, accompanying photo IDs, and names from a computer printout were carefully checked, and they were allowed to enter the grounds on which the huge tent was the scene of a lavish, loud gala. Couples danced to the spirited music beneath rotating colored lights that painted an impressionistic swirl over everything, and everyone. Mac and Annabel made their way to a long table where uniformed staff poured cups of Brazilian coffee; they avoided the artfully arranged desserts. Costumed supers wearing elaborate masks were stationed at various spots around the dance floor to add color, and to chat with guests.

"When's the president due?" Mac asked his wife.

"A half hour," Annabel said.

A member of the ball committee approached. "Annabel," she said, "I hate to tear you away from your handsome husband, but we could use your help for twenty minutes."

"Mac?"

"Go ahead. I'll wander a bit, catch up with you for a dance in a half hour—provided it's a slow one."

He watched her move through the crowd, her decidedly female form lovely to look at from any direction. He walked without purpose across the dance floor to an area surrounded by high bushes, the band's volume buffeted somewhat by the foliage and distance. As with everywhere else on the embassy grounds, security was thick and tight. Two obvious Secret Service agents, their little earpieces a give-away, stood with two uniformed MPD patrolmen and a heavyset black man, whom Mac assumed was another cop. He was right.

"Excuse me," the black man said, "but aren't you a lawyer?"

"I was," Mac replied. "I teach law now. Mackensie Smith."

"I knew I recognized you," Willie Portelain said. "I testified in a couple of cases where you were representing the perps."

Mac laughed. "I preferred to call them defendants," he said. "I recognize you, too, Officer."

"You were tough in that courtroom, man," Willie said. "Made me sweat on the stand. Name's Portelain. Willie Portelain, detective over at the First."

They shook hands. "Looks like every police officer in the city is here tonight," Mac said, looking back into the crowd.

"All I know is, I'm here."

They were joined by Sylvia Johnson. Willie made the introductions.

"My wife's on the committee for this affair," Mac said. "I lost her for a while. Duty called."

"Are you an opera buff, Mr. Smith?" Sylvia asked.

"Afraid not," Mac said. "They roped me into being an extra—a super—in *Tosca*."

"You were in the opera last night?" Willie said. "We were there, only—"

"Duty called us away, too," Sylvia said.

"You didn't get to stay for the whole performance?"

"We had to leave after the second act," Sylvia said.

"Right after she stabbed that guy Scarpia," Willie said.

"Dramatic scene," Mac said. "So, what's new at MPD?"

"Always something new," Sylvia replied. "Or the old becomes new. Were you involved in the Musinski case?"

"No," Mac said. "I'd given up criminal law by that time. They never did find the killer."

Willie's laugh rumbled from deep inside. "Case closed, Counselor," he said.

" 'Case closed'? You've made progress?"

Willie looked at Sylvia before answering Smith's question. They'd been sworn to secrecy about the Charise Lee case. An announcement would be made the following day, most likely by a spokesman for the Department of Homeland Security. But no one had said they couldn't discuss the Musinski murder.

"Yeah," Willie said. "That guy Grimes, who worked for Musinski at the school, confessed."

"Oh?" Mac said, processing what Portelain had just said.

"We knew it was him from the git-go," Willie said, "but nobody could ever put together a case against him, at least not enough to prosecute. Till now anyway."

"That's interesting," said Smith. "Wasn't there talk of missing manuscripts, musical scores?"

"That's right," Johnson agreed.

"The fellow who confessed, did he admit taking those, too?"

Willie shook his head.

"He swears he didn't even know anything like that was in Musinski's house," Sylvia said. "It'll probably be in the papers tomorrow."

"I see. Well, I'm glad you've cracked that case," Mac said. "Speaking of cases, anything new on the murder of the young opera singer?"

"No," Willie said.

"No," said Sylvia.

Mac looked at his watch. "Enjoyed the chat," he said, "and the update. Good work. I hope you get to see the third act of the opera. It's as good as the first two."

He left them, hoping to see Annabel and share what he'd just learned.

Annabel, too, was attempting to find her spouse. She was on the other side of the security divide. Next to her stood a tall man dressed in a costume and mask from Wagner's *Das Rheingold*. He moved slightly so that their sides touched.

"Excuse me," she said.

"Enjoying the evening, Mrs. Smith?"

The voice was familiar.

Ray Pawkins lifted the mask and smiled.

"Oh, hello," Annabel said.

"You look surprised," Pawkins said. "Even a little afraid."

"Afraid? I— Excuse me," Annabel said, taking a step away.

Pawkins grabbed her arm. "I think we need to talk."

Annabel looked down at her arm and angrily yanked it free.

Another smile, more a smirk, crossed Pawkins' face.

"I know that that weasel, Josephson, told you and Mac about me," Pawkins said.

Just then she saw Mac circumvent a knot of dancers and head in their direction.

"Yes, Ray, I think we do need to have a talk," she said as Mac joined them.

"Good evening, Counselor," Pawkins said pleasantly, raising his voice just loud enough for Mac and Annabel to hear him over the amplified music and the noise of the crowd.

"That's quite a costume, Ray," Mac said.

"Thank you. It's from *Das Rheingold*, Wagner's *Ring Cycle*. Of all opera composers, Wagner stands tallest. Of course, he's not to everyone's taste, especially those with limited patience to sit through the entire *Ring*, but—"

"Ray knows that Marc Josephson spoke with us about Dr. Musinski and the Mozart-Haydn scores, Mac."

"Really? Care to explain, Ray?"

"To you?" Pawkins said snidely. "I don't owe you or anyone else an explanation. But since you got suckered into it, I'll be happy to answer your questions. But this is hardly the place."

"I agree with that," Mac said. "You name the time and place."

"My house. Tomorrow. Noon. I'll even make you lunch. I'm not a bad cook when I put my mind to it." He rattled off the address. "Oh," he said, "I see Genevieve over there waiting for me. I promised her the next dance. Do you samba? Probably not. See you tomorrow. *Ciao!*"

Mac and Annabel watched him go to where Genevieve stood, grab her in his arms, and sweep her onto the dance floor.

"So arrogant," Annabel said.

"He is that. He also didn't kill Musinski."

Her eyes opened wider. "How do you know that?"

"Straight from the MPD. One of Musinski's acolytes at the university has confessed, the same one they've been focusing on since day one. Whether Ray stole those scores is another question. Should be an interesting conversation tomorrow, and if he's as good a cook as he claims, we'll get a decent lunch out of it, too. Dance, Mrs. Smith?"

As they snaked their way to the dance floor, they were stopped by a wall of security forces that parted the dancers like the Red Sea, creating a secure passageway for the president of the United States, Arthur Montgomery, and the nation's first lady, Pamela Montgomery. Surrounded by Secret Service agents, the evening's honored guests stepped up onto the bandstand, to a cacophony of applause, cheers, and whistles. They were joined on the stage by a half-dozen members of the Domingo-Cafritz Young Artist Program.

"Good evening," the president said into a microphone, that simple greeting in a voice familiar to millions of Americans generating another outburst of unbridled approval. Mac and Annabel stood in a tight knot of people and listened. The president spoke of the importance of the Washington National Opera to the cultural life of the nation's capital, and to the nation itself. "They say that politics is sometimes like opera, full of intrigue and maneuvering, backbiting and betrayal. I wouldn't know about that." He paused, eliciting the expected laughter. "I can only say that attending the superb performances at the Kennedy Center, with the vision, creativity, and immense talent of Maestro Domingo always in evidence, causes politics to take a backseat for those few hours, the magnificent voices and spectacular settings lifting the spirits."

The applause was loud and long, and not at all surprising.

"And I'm privileged to be standing here next to the next generation of opera stars, who will sing their arias on stages all over the world, ambassadors of peace and understanding between people."

More hands came together.

"I know that these superbly talented young men and women will entertain you a little later in the evening," the president said. "Now I believe the *real* opera lover in the Montgomery family has something to say."

The First Lady replaced her husband at the microphone and started to speak. She'd gotten out only a few words when the sound of a weapon being discharged crackled through the heavy, moisture-laden air. There were shrieks and cries of confusion. Secret Service agents surrounded the first couple, wrapping them in the protection of their own bodies, guns drawn, eyes everywhere. Guests closest to the bandstand saw two agents leap on a man dressed in the white uniform of a kitchen worker and smother him against the floor. A weapon flew from the man's hand and skidded through dozens of pairs of patent-leather and high-heel shoes, until coming to rest against a woman's foot, causing her to wrap her arms around the neck of her tuxedoed husband and climb up his torso as though he were a tree.

The first couple was virtually carried from the scene, across the dance floor, past hundreds of partygoers with horrified expressions on their faces, beneath sharpshooters stationed on rooftops, and to the waiting bulletproof limo. Chaos reigned. Some guests, convinced that they would all be slaughtered, made for the exits. Others sought answers. The shooter, his arms wrenched behind his back, was transported away by four Secret Service agents. "You bastard!" a man yelled.

"Who is he?"

"He's a terrorist," others answered.

"How did he get a gun in here?"

Bill Frazier, the Opera's chairman, grabbed the microphone and called for calm.

Mac and Annabel turned to the couple next to them, a U.S. senator and his wife. Mac had served on a committee chaired by the politician. The senator was ending a cell phone conversation.

"A terrorist attack?" Mac said.

"Right," the senator replied. "They've gunned down Congressman Chapman. Christ, he was out walking his dog. The mayor of Denver survived an attack against him."

Two security men whisked the senator and his wife away.

Frazier's continuous call for order had some effect. The Brazilian band began to play again, and a couple took to the dance floor in a show of confidence.

"Please," Frazier said, "let's continue with the evening despite the dreadful attack that's just happened. Everything will be fine."

Mac wanted to leave, but Annabel said it wouldn't look right if she left. He agreed, and they stayed to the scheduled end of the festivities. There was little dancing; most of the time was taken up with conversations about the event everyone had just witnessed.

Mac and Annabel returned to their apartment and watched the news on TV. The anchors and reporters stumbled through their reports, basing them on the sketchiest of facts. Some guests at the ball were interviewed, but offered nothing of substance: "What were you feeling at the time?" was the most frequently asked question, and elicited little. Chairman Frazier spoke of how shocking the attempt on the life of the president and first lady had been for everyone who was there to enjoy a festive evening celebrating the Washington National Opera. "Thank God," he said, "that the assassin's shot went astray and no one was injured."

Homeland Security Chief Wilbur Murtaugh was rousted out of bed, briefed, and held a hastily convened press conference: "This was obviously an orchestrated terrorist attack on leading public officials," he said. "Our hearts go out to Congressman Chapman's family. He was a dedicated public servant, gunned down in the prime of his life. Fortunately, the President and Mrs. Montgomery were saved through the actions of the heroic men and women charged with protecting them. The gunman is in custody and being questioned as we speak. I can offer no further information about him at this time. The two men whose attempt on the life of Denver's mayor was thwarted by authorities are also in custody. Congressman Chapman's killer remains at large. The threat meter has been elevated to Red-Two, and will remain at that level for the foreseeable future. Thank you. I'm not taking any questions at this time."

The president's press secretary's statement from the White House said only that the president and first lady were fine, and expressed their heartfelt condolences to Congressman Chapman's family.

Mac and Annabel sat quietly in front of the television and allowed the journalists' words from its speakers to come and go. Finally, at two, they turned off the set and went to bed, as stunned and angry as the rest of America.

෨

The phone in their apartment rang incessantly the following morning, the calls a combination of questions and theories about the thwarted assassination attempt on the president and first lady, and the one against the congressman that had succeeded, others rehashing the ball's success. It had raised more money for the Washington National Opera than any previous Opera Ball. Bad news with good news, the bitter with the sweet.

At eleven, Mac and Annabel took their car from the underground garage — the parking spot had added $35,000 to the condo's sale price — and drove to Great Falls, where they found Pawkins' home. He was in front hauling bulging green leaf bags to the garage. An odd sight.

"Welcome," he announced grandly. "Come on in. Onion soup, a salad, and the best French bread in D.C. is on the menu."

They entered the house. "Get over last night?" he asked.

"It's not something you get over," Annabel said, "at least not this soon."

"We live in perilous times," Pawkins said. "Might as well get used to it. Nothing new on the news. Just confusion. Come, take a tour of the old homestead."

They ended in his elaborate study, where the strains of an opera— *Death in Venice* by Benjamin Britten, he explained—poured out of speakers. "Britten wrote it for his lover of many years, Peter Pears. That's Pears singing the title role."

They gravitated to the kitchen, where Pawkins had set a long table of antique French pine. A vase of freshly cut flowers dominated the middle.

"A drink to celebrate?" he asked. "Bloody Marys are mixed and ready to go."

"I don't think a celebration is in order, Ray," Mac said.

"I disagree, Mac. *Tosca* is a smashing success. Last night's Opera Ball raised a ton of money and is still D.C.'s social highlight. We lost a congressman, but the president emerges unscathed. And I am about to embark on a new phase of life."

Pawkins poured drinks whether they wanted them or not, and joined them at the table. He raised his glass in a toast. "To all things good, Mr. and Mrs. Smith." One of the cats jumped up on the table, and Pawkins shooed him down. "All right," he said, smacking his hands together as though cueing someone, in this case himself. "One, I did not murder Aaron Musinski."

"We know that," Mac said.

"Oh? How?"

"It doesn't matter."

"I knew it was Grimes from the beginning. So, my friends, your assumption that I did in the crotchety old bastard was wrong, terribly wrong. Frankly, I'm hurt that you would even think me capable of such a thing."

"It wasn't an unreasonable possibility," Mac said, "considering what Josephson told us. Now we know differently."

"I would certainly hope you do, and an apology is in order."

Annabel ignored his call for them to apologize. "What about the Mozart-Haydn scores? Did you take them? Josephson claims you did. He had an impressive array of evidence to back up his accusation."

"Of course I took them. Everything he told you about that is true."

His easy admission of guilt silenced Mac and Annabel.

"You look shocked," Pawkins said. "I can't imagine why, a pair of worldly people like you. I spent twenty years with MPD, watching my fellow officers steal whenever it was convenient. They'd do a drug bust where a hundred packets of crack were found. How many were reported? Eighty? Ninety? The rest were sold to the same drug dealers who were busted and who walked, thanks to our screwed-up legal system."

"Are you justifying what you did because of what others have done?" Annabel asked.

"You bet I am," Pawkins said without hesitation. "I never did any of that. Steal drugs to put a few bucks in my pocket? Disgusting. I was a straight arrow, a complicit one maybe, looking the other way when my colleagues crossed the line. And do you know what? I never really blamed them. Cops don't make a lot of money for putting their lives on the line every day to keep fat cats like you and the rest of official Washington safe from the bad guys. How much did you rake in, Mac, when you were defending the scum of the earth?"

"That misses the point," Mac said. "And don't broad brush your fellow cops, Ray. Most of them are honest, and you know it."

Pawkins sat back and slowly shook his head. "How could you ever have thought I'd killed Musinski? Why would I have? I didn't know he had those manuscripts. He'd come back from Europe with them only a few days before. No, I just happened upon them while I was spending time in the house trying to figure out who'd killed him. There they were, in his briefcase. They looked valuable, but I couldn't be sure. I took them and had them authenticated by a source in Paris. He put me on to a collector named Saibrón, who gladly coughed up a half mil for them, which I graciously accepted. Everybody was happy, including yours truly. Nobody got hurt. I got paid enough to live decently. I took care of that whining little creep, Josephson. He'll have enough to live happily ever after in some British old folks' home. Saibrón made a profit, and the guy he sold the scores to can sit every night and drool over them. Everybody's a winner."

"A lot of people got hurt," Annabel said, "and nobody won. Dr. Musinski's heirs got hurt. So did the public that might have enjoyed those scores at some credible arts institution. You're the biggest loser, Ray. You're as bad as any cop who stole drugs from a dealer and sold them for a profit. Interesting that you've never once used the word 'stole.' "

"Want me to?" Pawkins said. "I *stole* them. Feel better?"

"I'd like to go, Mac," Annabel said.

"And miss lunch? I make a dynamite onion soup."

"In a minute, Annie," Mac said. To Pawkins: "Doesn't it concern you, Ray, that you're sitting here and openly confessing to us that you committed a major felony?"

"Why should it? What are you going to do, run to Carl Berry at MPD and tell him what I just told you? You don't have any proof, unless you have a tape recorder going, which I seriously doubt. They'll laugh you out of the place, Mac. I'm a retired Homicide detective. I left the force with honors, enough citations to cover a wall. Besides, defense lawyers like you aren't the most popular people with cops."

Pawkins stood. "Ready for lunch?" he asked.

"We'll be leaving," Smith said. "We've lost our appetite."

"Suit yourself," Pawkins said, following them from the house to where their car waited in front. "Last chance for Raymond Pawkins' gourmet onion soup. I won't be around here much longer to make it again. I'm selling this house back to the guy who originally owned it. He lives over there in that mansion. He wants it for his daughter and her family. Make a nice family compound, everybody close to the old man so he can rule the roost. I'm heading for Florida, Fort Lauderdale. The Florida Grand Opera's pretty good, not up to WNO's standards, but not bad. They've been around for more than sixty years. Plenty of work as a super. I'll get my PI license and—"

Mac started the engine, put the car into gear, and drove away, seeing in the rearview mirror a smiling Pawkins waving good-bye.

Annabel's anger turned to tears. "Damn him," she said. "Every-thing's been so wonderful lately, so perfect, the opening, the ball, everything."

"Life's like opera, Annie," Mac said as he pulled onto the G.W. Memorial Parkway. "You have to have a villain to put things into perspective. There wouldn't be a *Tosca* without a Scarpia. By the way, do you think I should cheat a little more to the right while I'm on the stairs in the last act? It's my good side."

EPILOGUE

At five o'clock, Milton Crowley did what he did every evening at that time since returning to his cottage in Wareham, Dorset, southwest of London, the home of T. E. Lawrence, and the site of his fatal motorcycle crash in 1935. An effigy in St. Martin's Church of Lawrence of Arabia, in Arab dress, was a popular tourist attraction.

He pulled down a wicker tray with handles from where it perched on a hook in his kitchen, and placed it on the table. Each item he positioned on it was in precisely the spot where he always placed it—a small, cut-glass decanter into which he'd poured enough single-malt Scotch for two drinks; two Venetian crystal goblets that he and Cora had purchased during a holiday in Venice; four white-bread tea sandwiches, two with egg, two with salmon; a compact Grundig shortwave radio; two napkins; and a photograph of Cora in an oval, gold filigree frame with a stand.

He carefully opened the screen door of the cottage with his foot and walked down a short, grassy slope to where a white wrought-iron bench and table sat next to the gently flowing stream that had been the main reason for him having purchased the cottage, which was stoutly made of ashlar blocks of local Purbeck stone.

He set the tray on the table, brushed off the bench with one of the napkins, sat, and drew a deep, contented breath. It was a fair day, the sun warm, the sky all blue and white. The chirping of reed warblers from a patch of wild celery on the opposite bank caught his attention, and he returned their message with a bird sound of his own. Bluebells, rhododendrons, and azaleas grew along the stream's bank; he imagined painting a still life of them, had he that talent.

He removed the glass stopper from the decanter and poured the Scotch into both glasses. He stared at the photograph for a moment before raising his glass to it: "To us, Cora. To many beautiful days in this lovely spot on God's earth."

He drank from his goblet and ate two of the sandwiches. His eyes became moist. He turned on the radio, which was already set on the BBC, lit a cigarette, and listened to that day's news. British news items came first. Then the announcer turned to news of international interest.

"The simultaneous terrorist attacks on American political leaders, which resulted in the death of a United States congressman, and includes an attempt on the lives of the mayor of a major American city and the president of the United States, were part of a much wider terrorist plan, according to an American spokesman, Wilbur Murtaugh, Secretary of the Department of Homeland Security."

An excerpt from Murtaugh's statement played:

"This diabolical scheme to simultaneously attack our government leaders has been thwarted in all but one case, which resulted in the death of a revered member of the United States Congress. It was through the diligent and unyielding efforts of this department, and related federal intelligence and law enforcement agencies, that the plan was uprooted, the potential perpetrators identified and apprehended. For those who have doubted the efficacy of our efforts to protect American citizens through such initiatives as the Patriot Act and the National Security Agency's Subversive's Surveillance Act, our success in this, the latest terrorist assault on our government leaders, should lay those concerns to rest."

The newscast ended with a review of Covent Garden's production of Mozart's comic opera, *Le nozze di Figaro*, which the reviewer found wanting.

Crowley turned off the radio, leaned back, closed his eyes, and listened to the faint sound of the flowing water, and of the birds. He opened his eyes, leaned forward, and again held up his glass to the photograph. "To another day in this insane world, Cora. How fortunate we are to be here."

He finished what was in his goblet, poured the contents of the second one back into the decanter, stood, stretched, picked up the tray, and carried it to the cottage.

MARGARET TRUMAN has won faithful readers with her works of biography and fiction, particularly her on-going series of Capital Crimes mysteries. Her novels let us into the corridors of power and privilege, poverty and pageantry in the nation's capital. She is the author of many nonfiction books, most recently *The President's House,* in which she shares some of the secrets and history of the White House, where she once resided. She lives in Manhattan.

ABOUT THE TYPE

This book was set in Electra, a typeface designed for Linotype by W. A. Dwiggins, the renowned type designer (1880–1956). Electra is a fluid typeface, avoiding the contrasts of thick and thin strokes that are prevalent in most modern typefaces.

11/06